WILDERNESS OF THE HEART

SEVEN GATES

6/15/2007

Maureen. you were very much a part
of shaping this book. I hope
you like it.

Mary Stafton

Also by Mary Staton, *From the Legend of Biel*, 1976, Ace Science
Fiction Special Number One, series two, re-issued by
iMaginalFictionPress, fall, 2007.

WILDERNESS OF THE HEART

SEVEN GATES

Mary Staton

iMaginalFictionPress
eRealm

Wilderness of the Heart – Seven Gates

All Rights Reserved © 2007 by Mary Staton

iMaginalFictionPress

iMaginalFiction.com

ISBN: 978-1-4243-3754-5
Printed in the United States of America

To the Source of all creation
To those who just want to live
To Katrina Eastlake and Gregory Rainoff

Wilderness within and wilderness without
are one and the same
for in truth there is no within no without
only imagination.

Dear Inhabitants of the Four Realms:

As you know, recently an acolyte on pilgrimage beneath the surface of the earth happened upon an unexplored cave complex that contained, among other finds, an earthen burial urn protected by a canopy of spider web. The urn is approximately 2,000 years old and contained three items – a petrified human placenta that is now under examination, a bracelet with no beginning or end woven of red human hair with black human hair braided to form a runic inscription, We act and we are acted upon. *The last item in the urn is a thumb-size cylinder containing text written by an unidentified scribe, an inhabitant of Shadow-Time, that unknown period between the ancients and our own era.*

The text is written in a series of codes that are taking longer than anticipated to decipher. Thus, in response to your urgent requests we have agreed to release the first completed section. Also at your request, fingers to lips, we retreat leaving all editorial intrusions for a future volume when the whole has been assembled.

Respectfully,
Eo, Master Scribe of the Four Realms

First Gate – Birth

After the great collapse reduced earth to ash and cold silence a single structure emerged from the ruins and has stood alone on the surface for two millennia. Covering vast acres, Great City is shaped like the dome of a mushroom and populated for the most part by citizen-units who cooperate without question because there are no more questions. Just as there is no more outside. But that is elsewhere for the moment.

Here, beneath the surface of the earth and independent of Great City, darkness fills the veins and hollows of raw stone like blood but is unable to extinguish the light of a single wick on the ground in front of an old man who is seated on a cushion with his ankles crossed and his hands resting in his lap. His eyes are closed and his face is peaceful beneath the hood of a plain brown robe as he intones a call because that is his purpose whether the call is answered or not.

The sound is from his chest and throat, a low reedy monotone, a sustained "O" filling and spilling out of this small alcove that is only part of the cave complex he inhabits. The call goes on and on, broken only by occasional sips of breath. Then it fades and the silence is complete.

After a moment the old man opens pale green eyes and returns from where he was. He stands effortlessly, takes off his robe, folds it and drops it on the foot of a sleeping mat. He pulls a long undershirt off over his head, folds it and drops it on top of the robe. Naked but for a loincloth, long white hair and beard flowing to his waist, he begins a series of stretches, his body lean and supple, belying his age as he moves slowly from one position to another. Finished, leaving the wick lit, he lies down on the sleeping mat, adjusts a pillow beneath his neck and pulls the cover up to his chin.

"Source willing," he whispers and is asleep.

***

Great City's population numbers eighty thousand. Most are citizen-units who inhabit the lane – a long meandering tunnel that fills the bottom two-thirds of the structure, ascending and descending, curving over, under and around on itself like intestines with no beginning, middle or end. Airless and dim, the lane is wide enough for

3

rows of citizen-units to walk the same direction on paths that don't cross.

Evenly spaced doors on either side of the lane occasionally whoosh open or closed as citizens-units drift into or out of identical workdays, sleeping pods and Medical or MED stations. At any given time one third of them are in workbays, one third are in sleeping pods and one third are wandering the lane evenly spaced and identical but for different colored monitor suits that indicate their different functions and specializations. Engineered for life without attachment, citizen-units have no possessions, no desires, no place like home, and no plans of their own.

Such total control is made possible by the monitor suit, a form-fitting technology no thicker than a microfilm of skin covering the entire body, even eyeballs, and attached with deeply anchored filaments. The suit provides sustenance, recycles waste, protects against anti-dogma and murmurs gentle neuro-commands.

Sleep now. It's time to wander. Check-in, please. Workbay just ahead.

Identifiable by her light blue monitor suit, a Prime Researcher steps off the lane, whoosh/whoosh, into a smooth black glass environment. Like all others, this workbay contains only an elaborate harness suspended from the ceiling.

The Prime researcher turns and backs into the harness. Coming to life it embraces, lifts, and supports her as she is interfaced with the archives of the ancients, a tech-location her neuro-awareness interprets as a vast digital chaos with no center, no floor and no ceiling.

Floating facedown and weightless, she filters out the roar of exploding data and replaces it with Bach, a slow second movement. Then she dives down into the chaos in slow motion, scanning this way and that, seeking and not finding until something snags her attention.

Faint flickering, over there.

Standing on nothing now, she walks carefully in slow motion toward a small cloud sparking faintly, almost eclipsed by nonsense spiraling around it. Leaning, she peers at coherence. Words.

Ikhnaton.

Moses.

The Pre-Socratics.

A find.

Pure anti-dogma.

Maneuvering carefully lest she jar the coherence, disturbing it

4

beyond recognition until it settles again, if it does, the Prime Researcher moves jangled bits aside to uncover a big, deeply rooted nugget of legible data. Surgeon-like, fingers barely touching her controls, she extracts the nugget from its nest of babble, brackets it in a file, enlarges the file to the size of a boulder and turns it inside out, like a cave. Then slowly, as though diving into long-sunken treasure, she enters the contents of what must have been someone's private library, now a delicate swirl of data-bits forming titles, sentences, volumes.

Socrates and Plato.

Jesus.

Mohammed.

Freedom and Orthodoxy.

Purges, Crusades, and Inquisitions.

Wilderness Ways.

A sentence floats by.

If you make me an altar of stone, do not build it of dressed stones; for if you use a chisel on it, you will profane it.

She captures the sentence and reads it again.

Suddenly that string of words is an arrow shooting through her chest from back to front and she is arrested as though in a beam of light that calls her to follow the path of that arrow because a clock has started ticking somewhere and it's time.

Now.

The moment has come. It's time to leave Great City.

Now or not at all.

She files the data, turns off the Bach then returns to her launching platform and signs out. The harness releases her. The monitor suit inquires why she is leaving the workbay so soon. She shrugs then shakes her head as though confused. Accustomed to her eccentricities, the suit clears her to proceed. She steps to the door, whoosh/whoosh, and out onto the lane, taking her place in the slow stream of citizen-units.

Wandering as usual, unaware of the lane as anything but indefinite glare, registering others only as warm spots to avoid, she does nothing she hasn't done before except that this time her movements are infused with the faintest hint of purpose because a clock has started ticking somewhere and she *will* find it this time, a way out. The moment has come and she has only to follow.

Citizen, your levels are breaking standard for mood. I'm going

5

to administer a wee antidote. The next MED station is just ahead on the right. Please turn in.

She nods agreeably and keeps going. The antidote kicks in. She jellies and walks on, going past the MED station. The neuro-commands intensify.

Citizen, you are to check in now.

Moving faster, she bumps into someone. Startled, they stand frozen for a moment, not knowing what to do. Then she bolts away.

You are to stop and check in immediately! The Next MED station is coming up on your left!

Irresistibly drawn by what leads, she passes the MED station. Without the aid of a station or a sleeping pod the monitor suit can only do so much to stop her. Nonetheless, it tries. She jellies again and again, each time shaking it off.

You will stop now! YOU WILL STOP AT ONCE!

She's never been yelled at before. Neuro-commands fill her head with white light and pain as she rushes through a blur of reflections.

Then her scanners read something different, perhaps a shadow on the indefinite surface of the lane. She lurches into the shadow, careens around a corner and stops in her tracks because suddenly everything is infrared and unfamiliar.

ALARM! ALARM! THIS IS A HOSTILE ENVIRONMENT! ALARM! ALARM! ALARM!

The neuro-screaming is unbearable. Head in hands she turns around scanning, unable to read the red glare. No matter. She stumbles on.

STOP NOW! SECURITY! EeeEEEEK!!! EeeEEEE!!! EeeEEEEEK!!! ASSISTANCE NEEDED NOW!!! EeeeEEEEEEEEEEK!!!

***

A dozen Security Primes are on shift in separate workbays scattered through Great City, plugged into and floating through the sea of normally placid data concerning activities of citizen-units. Suddenly there's an explosion of input and the data-stream goes turbulent.

ATTENTION! ATTENTION! WE HAVE A POTENTIAL

ESCAPE! A citizen-unit has entered a forbidden environment through a bolthole in northeast quadrant of level C. That resource is now somewhere between the outer skins of Great City, northeast side. More precise location is unknown at this time.

Independent of each other though in perfect sync, the security primes scan that sector and find the breach – a flaring red wound in the data pouring out of the location in question. Silver monitor suits agleam they zero in and hang on for the bumpy ride to that location. At the same time they send an alert to Great City's head of Security of whom they know nothing.

***

Monitor suit yelling incoherently, the Prime Researcher bolts out of a forest of technology, lunges across a high catwalk and collides with a wall. When the static clears she gropes her way along the wall and comes to the threshold of a small maintenance station. Head spinning, she enters and scans.

One side of the room twinkles with lights on a big panel. Monitor suit clicking and whining, she touches, finds buttons and starts pushing. Nothing happens. She jabs faster and harder. Nothing happens. She runs her fingers over the twinkling lights, finds a bank of toggle switches and starts flipping.

Suddenly an explosion of steam is followed by a jolt that nearly knocks her off her feet. Stunned, blinking, she reads star-patterns and wriggling worms of purple neuro-current. Then a large pale gray oval comes into focus and she understands this oval to be a hole, perhaps a way out.

***

Beneath the surface north and east of Great City, the old man is lying on his back snoring softly. The single wick near his head licks his serene profile to the color of honey. Suddenly, still asleep, he twitches ever so slightly as though alerted to a faraway sound.

The calling-dream.

After such a long wait it has returned – strong and insistent this time.

Someone has entered the field. Someone is up on the surface, calling, and he hears the call as a bubble rising from an ocean crevasse, a perfect pearl exploding in a cry for help.

"…Si…" he murmurs, waking. "I come."

***

All things having changed in an instant, the Security Primes are now bombarded by flurries of incoming data from the site of the incident with the Prime Researcher. It's a turbulent ride as they direct citizen-units out of that area, seal the bolthole, and try to keep track of the resource. At the same time they've gotten through to Great City's head of Security who for all the Primes know is floating in a workbay, too. But that is not the case.

George Biggs Boltin is not down with the citizen-units. He is, rather, just leaving his office up in The Heights where those in charge live very different lives. And he's not happy about being stopped like this.

Early 50s, crisply tailored in a navy blue tunic and matching trousers, Boltin is always aware of how boyishly good-looking he still is, and trim though he has to work at it. His skin is pampered and pink. Light brown hair is graying at the temples and coifed to frame sparkling periwinkle eyes. He's standing frozen in the doorway, staring into his darkened office, trying to comprehend that what isn't ever supposed to happen just occurred on his watch.

"Are you telling me, wait a minute, are you telling me that a citizen-unit found a bolthole and went through it?"

"Affirmative." Data from the Security Primes is delivered by an uninflected genderless voice that comes from the room's only illumination at the moment, a large blinking control panel behind his desk.

"Where's the resource now?"

"Outside, moving down a maintenance ladder toward the surface."

"WHAT?! You let the unit get outside?!" Boltin throws his arms up in the air then squeezes his temples between a thumb and forefinger. "Why wasn't the resource stopped?!"

"The unit would not obey commands. The monitor suit injected all of its control-meds. A Security team arrived just as the unit climbed through the hatch but was unable to follow because guards are not programmed for the exterior."

Boltin rushes into the dark office and around the desk. He knees his executive chair out of the way then turns to the control panel and adjusts the room's lighting to mid-level, illumining behind him a plain round carpeted space with a flat low ceiling, all the color of whiskey. He activates his desktop screen and turns to it, looking down as it flares to life.

"Take charge of the unit's monitor suit and direct it back inside the next hatch down."

"Warning: given the unit's current position on the dome any attempt at control could result in a fall."

"NO! There's to be no damage to a resource!"

Boltin unfastens his collar and taps different areas on the desktop screen, pulling up a hurricane of data from the Security Primes. He locates the citizen-unit's identity-marker and touches it, opening the file.

"A Prime Researcher!" more alarmed now, Boltin leans over and reads. "Female, age thirty. Condition excellent. Ovaries left intact for possible harvesting. Difficult to handle. Requires close monitoring." He pulls up her stats and gasps. "Productivity, top .05 percent," he whispers, looking sick. "Tech-secretary!"

"Yes, sir," the voice is female and deferential.

"I need to see the Presider immediately."

"One moment, sir."

"As soon as that unit touches down," Boltin turns to his control panel, "I want you to take control of the monitor suit and bring it back inside through the nearest deployment bay. That resource is not to leave the base of Great City. This is highest priority. Understood?!"

"Yes, sir.."

"Also, get surface technology up and running as soon as possible."

"We are on that now."

He's turning back to his desk when the tech-secretary relays a response to his request.

"The Presider is on his way up to the port of Great City and being briefed to greet the arriving Space State ambassadors. He is not

9

available until after the ceremony except for an emergency. Is your matter of sufficient gravity to interrupt him?"

George Biggs Boltin is stopped in his tracks by a sudden bolt of clarity.

"No, wait!"

"Yes, sir."

Boltin strides across his office and presses a button on the wall. A wetbar emerges. He pours a tumbler of high-grade Mello, his drink, and stands slugging it down, assessing the situation, trying to figure out his next move on a gameboard that has suddenly become complicated because George Biggs Boltin has plans to replace the current Presider with himself when the moment comes and losing a resource, especially one of this value, would put an immediate stop to that.

He sets the empty tumbler on the wet-bar then walks back and checks the time indicator in the corner of his desktop screen. He stands looking down, quickly thinking it through, remembering his history – how he's never failed before, never even broken a sweat, how everything has always happened on schedule and according to plan. Increasingly certain he can pull it off, that his Primes will have the resource back and functioning long before tomorrow morning's council meeting, Boltin dismisses the precipice at his feet as a minor annoyance.

"Tech-secretary!"

"Do you wish to be put through to the Presider?"

"No, no. It was just something I wanted to inform him about. Put me first on the agenda for tomorrow morning's council meeting instead."

"What reason do you want given for this request?"

"Um, to report on a recently closed bolthole. There was an incident. Everything's under control."

"Yes, sir."

Almost late for the ceremony up top and figuring out who to blame for the unit's escape, Boltin fastens his collar as he rushes from the office through his stark and masculine quarters out to a long wide hallway called Council Row with five doors on either side and at the far end big double doors leading out to the bright public square reminiscent of an ancient indoor mall complete with an atrium, fountains, escalators, artificial foliage, vending stands, shops, cafes, bars, and stewards male and female, all in their plain dark tunics and trousers, rushing to and fro or standing at small tables for hurried meals or moving aside for Boltin who trots to a bank of elevators.

As a council member he has priority and likes to use it. He orders half a dozen stewards out of a lift and rides alone up to the port of Great City to greet the four Space State ambassadors who are just now arriving from the transfer station.

***

Miniscule on the face of Great City and unaware that far above a big shuttle from the transfer station is easing butt-down through the open sky-dome, the Prime Researcher works her way slowly rung by rung down the rust colored structure toward the surface, stopping only when forced by cramps but not for long. Then, clinging again, dangling, blinded by static, she gropes downward for the next purchase.

Finally one foot touches something soft then the other foot is down. Trembling violently, she hangs onto the last rung as the monitor suit whines trying to restore homeostasis. Then she releases the rung, turns around and stands wobbling.

Not programmed to interpret anything but Great City, she registers vast nothing. Featureless gray and flares of static. Not light, not dark.

Suddenly a blinding arc of neuro-current brings her to her knees as the Security Primes take control of her monitor sit. Then, just as suddenly, an explosion disconnects her from the Primes and she is flung on her back dumb and senseless.

All is quiet for a moment. Then the monitor suit hisses and sparks, whines with feedback as more attempts are made to connect and take control. Then the attempts stop.

After a long moment, the Prime Researcher raises her head and looks around. She sees gray static. She hears a silent call that must be followed. Twitching with occasional bursts of current as the Security Primes try to establish control, she struggles to her feet and stands wobbly for a moment then takes her first steps away from Great City.

***

11

Beneath the surface, the old man is in the main chamber of the cave complex illumined by a single wick. Hurrying, wearing only a loincloth and moccasins, he retrieves a thick bedroll from a niche and carries it onto a large elaborately patterned rug. He unrolls and positions the bedroll then turns to clicking sounds as a sizable creature enters the chamber. A mutant arachnid.

"Si, Solaris, I'm on my way."

Pale pink, translucent and covered with fine gold hairs, the big spider approaches and stands looking at him peer-like, her downy back easily reaching to his knees. Her legs are long and angular. The largest segment of her body is more than twice the size of a human head. She grinds her jaws, as though speaking.

"Si, Solaris, I'll be careful," he nods. "Stay with Source."

She clicks once in response and watches him pick up the wick and stride across the chamber to a tunnel that leads to the grotto where, surrounded by water sounds, he quickly twists and fastens his waist-length silvery hair into a tight topknot then winds the equally long beard into a neat roll beneath his chin.

Leaving the wick behind, the old man takes off his moccasins, splashes out into a large pool, and swims across to a wide veil of waterfalls at the far side. Behind the falls he hoists himself up into a long, tight, steeply ascending tunnel and climbs monkey-like toward the surface.

***

Laboring with each step, the Prime Researcher staggers a serpentine path away from Great City. She's finding it increasingly difficult to go on because of a new obstacle. Darkness. For which she is not programmed.

No longer able to form neuro-commands, the monitor suit squeaks and whines, hisses and sparks as it continues to function at the most basic level to keep her alive. She jellies, staggers then stops. She tries to take the next step and can't. She stands wavering, scanning her surrounds and reading only darkness streaked with static.

Forcing another step she trips and falls across something hard. Sprawled, she tries to get up and can't. So she rolls onto her side and curls up into a tight ball. Then she's asleep. And her sleep is fitful.

12

***

"What happened?!"

"The unit stopped moving."

"Why?!"

"That is unknown at this time."

"IS IT DEAD?!"

"We continue to read basic functioning from the monitor suit."

Tunic off, perspiring, George Biggs Boltin is standing and staring down bug-eyed at the infrared glow on his desktop screen – a real-time satellite image of the Prime Researcher curled up on a piece of rubble not all that far from the base of Great City, still within easy reach except for the fact that the Security Primes are unable to take control of the monitor suit and the surface technology can't be deployed yet because it's jammed up in spec-check. In addition, there's no way to determine her status from here.

"How long can a citizen-unit survive out there?"

"As long as the monitor suit is functional or for twenty-four hours after the suit was last serviced."

"How much time do we have?"

"Fifteen hours but it's impossible to be precise because each suit is different as is the unit wearing it."

Boltin stops pacing and stands perfectly still, mouth open, blinking furiously, unwilling to surrender his destiny.

"I want a squad of Security guards programmed for the surface and deployed immediately, accelerate spec-checks. I want that unit back *now*."

"Copy. Spec-check cannot be accelerated…"

"WHAT'S THE PROBLEM?!"

Boltin stands trying to organize his thoughts and finds his head full of white noise. He plops into his desk chair then stands back up, strides across the room and opens the wetbar. Hands shaking, he reaches for the decanter of Mello then changes his mind, fills a tumbler with Focus and drains it. Then he strides to the control panel and stands hands on hips wrestling with a decision that could expose him but there's no option.

13

He needs more power, more speed and efficiency. This necessitates the use of additional juice off of the main grid for which authorization is required. Plunging ahead, Boltin punches in code that calls the rest of his Security Primes off of the lane or out of sleeping pods and into workbays, thus tripling the size of his front-line workforce. The maneuver siphons unauthorized energy from the main grid but if anyone notices, Boltin will do what he always does: blame someone else.

***

Coughing and shivering, the old man lights a wick to reveal a stone chamber on one side of which is a rack of metal shelving stacked with equipment, gear and neatly folded garments. He whisks off the loincloth and steps into a silvery skintight garment with an attached hood that leaves only his face exposed. He pulls on boots that lace to the knee then slides his arms through the harness that secures the breather's filtration system between his shoulder blades.

The old man brings the attached facemask up over a shoulder, activates the technology imbedded in the glass and immediately feels the silvery suit contract, warm him, start to collect and recycle his body fluids. He puts the sustenance tube into his mouth then straps on the facemask behind which everything is bright green and clear.

Inhaling and exhaling long mechanical hisses, the old man extinguishes the now superfluous wick. He swings a long gray cloak across his shoulders, raises the hood and fastens it around the facemask. He closes the cloak all the way down. Being longer in back, it trails behind him as he finishes his preparations by stuffing an identical cloak into a bag and slinging the strap over his head so it rides on one haunch. After pulling on gauntlets that reach to his elbows the old man tucks two short fat skis and two poles under one arm. He tosses the long backend of his cloak over the other arm and strides into one of several natural offshoot tunnels.

Ascending, he keeps a steady pace and after several turns arrives at a polished metal door. He touches one side of the door and it spirals open to reveal a small, brightly lit chamber made by human hands and filled with sparkling technology. He puts on the stubby skis then plucks up a small hand-device and presses it with a thumb to

14

darken the chamber as a door in the far wall spirals open onto the surface and deepest night.

The old man steps outside and is momentarily arrested by emptiness. Then he turns to close the portal with the hand-device, which is pocketed. He drops the long backend of the cloak and tech-shielded by surface gear he moves out with long, graceful cross-country strides, heading south and west through the dunes, erasing his trail as he goes. And soon he's swallowed by darkness that is complete but for the faintest disk of haze-obscured full moon rising halfway up toward zenith.

***

"Any change?"

"Negative."

Boltin's office is illumined only by reddish glow from his desktop screen. He paces back and forth, back and forth, face blanched and drawn, chewing his lower lip, doing his best to stay calm while the Security Primes try to get surface technology functioning and take control of the unit's monitor suit. Meanwhile it's almost tomorrow.

"Is there any way we can extend the life of the monitor suit?"

"Not without recharging it."

"If we can get the Security guards down there in time can they recharge the unit's suit?"

"Affirmative."

"What's the status on the guards?"

"They are in a MED station near the deployment bay being prepped and programmed to tolerate and interpret the exterior."

"Deployment time?"

"As soon as possible."

Boltin grimaces. "And the surface technology?"

"Ditto."

George Biggs Boltin spins around, throws his arms into the air, strides to the wetbar and pours yet another tumbler of Focus. He drains the glass, returns to his desk and squints down at the Prime Researcher as viewed by satellite from far above curled up on a piece of rubble out on the flats that surround Great City. Jiggling with adrenalin and not accustomed to uncertain outcomes, George Biggs Boltin starts pacing again because that's the only thing he knows to do.

***

When the moon is at zenith, the cloaked and hooded figure glides to a stop in a valley, removes the stubby skis and sticks them in the ash then scrambles up the steep face of a dune. Even though the old man is tech-shielded and camouflaged and even though it's the deepest part of night, there's enough ghostly moonlight to make him visible to the naked eye of a trained hunter. Near the top he drops to his belly and slithers the rest of the way to the ridge. Behind him is a maze of dunes. In front of him are the flats on the northeast side of Great City, wide and littered with rubble.

Hunkered down, he touches one side of the breather's facemask to ignite technology that illumines, clarifies, zooms in, measures distance, evaluates terrain, and plots a route. He raises his head above the ridge to scan a wide arc back and forth from the base of Great City outward, seeking the one who came to him in the calling-dream.

There.

In faintest moonshadow.

Not far from the base of the enormous structure. On the ground. Still radiating heat.

He locks in on his objective and rolls over the ridge. Staying low he scrambles down the face of the dune to the flats where, sprinting with the agility and endurance of a much younger man, he heads for the one who sang the calling-dream.

***

The Prime Researcher is curled up in the shadow of Great City sleeping fitfully because the monitor suit is trying to function on its own. It belches and emits soft, dissonant arpeggios. Then the Security Primes attempt to take control again.

16

Screeching and whining like a badly tuned radio, the suit wakes her. She twitches and jerks. She rolls onto her back with difficulty, unable to do anything else until the unsuccessful intrusion stops.

She raises her head. Disoriented, she scans static, trying to understand where she is and why. Then, blinking, she knows it's time to keep moving. After struggling to her feet she stands wavering for a moment as though drunk. Then she lurches on away from Great City.

***

"ALERT TO CHANGE IN STATUS! The unit is moving again."

"What direction?!"

"North and east."

"Where are the drones?!" Boltin screams.

"The gaggle is deploying now."

"And get those Security guards down there!"

"The guards are in final spec-check…"

"I said NOW!" Boltin leans down close to his desktop screen, tracing the Prime Researcher's slow trajectory with a rigid finger as though able to squash her like a bug.

***

The hatch she used to exit Great City is still open. Inside, the maintenance station is glaring with lights focused on a console of technology that is the launching platform for six identical drones. Programmed and ready to go, gleaming needle-like and smooth in their cradles, the drones measure the length of a hand and are made of dull gray metal. Thick at the rear where the power system is, they taper down to wicked and very dangerous points.

In response to a prompt from the Security Primes, six silvery needles hum with life and rise in unison to hover above their cradles. They assume formation, close as fingers, and exit the hatch. Barely illumined by the moon, now at zenith during what would have been the

17

old spring equinox, the drones follow her digital scent all the way down to the base of Great City where they find a distinct trail and set off following it.

***

Her neuro-awareness abruptly goes fuzzy then goes quiet. Arrested by eerie nothingness she stands wavering and confused. Then the approaching gaggle of drones takes control, infusing her with a power surge causing the monitor suit to snap and spark. Staggering, she forces another step, loses her balance and sink to her knees.

The drones round a chunk of twisted rubble and lock in on her. Chirping and buzzing, they approach and circle her shoulders just out of reach. One darts in from the rear, injects her in the haunch and is returning to its place in the circle when out of nowhere and moving fast, an inexplicable shadow flashes by as she tumbles forward like a dumb beast, face in the ash. Bewildered by the sudden arrival of the unexpected, the drones aren't quick enough to avoid being snatched out of the air one, two, three, four, five.

Drone six, however, is elusive. It manages to stay just out of reach, clicking and whining, moving erratically, relaying garbled data back to Great City as the cloaked and masked figure fires a little hand-device finally bringing the thing down.

The six drones are quickly disabled and flung to one side. The spare cloak is pulled out of the bag at his hip as the old man rushes to the collapsed Prime researcher. He stoops down and wraps her up in the second cloak, careful that she is completely covered. Then he hefts her over a shoulder, stands, adjusts the weight and is trotting back toward the dunes at a pace he can keep up indefinitely.

***

"WHERE'D SHE GO?!" Boltin shrieks. "WHAT HAPPENED?!"

"Our technology is unable to answer either question."

"What do you *read*?!" he pulls his hair.

18

"Everything is normal."

"What do you mean everything is normal?!"

"Readings indicate a normal surface. There are no bio-forms anywhere within range."

"THE UNIT WAS RIGHT *THERE*!" he points at a spot on his screen. "What's going on with our technology?!"

"Systems are functioning perfectly."

Mouth open, eyes bulging in disbelief, Boltin clenches and un-clenches his hair as though trying to pull coherence out of his head with both hands. He finally manages to exhale, turning around one way then the other. He stops, facing the control panel behind his desk.

"What do we have from just before this happened?"

"That data is currently being analyzed."

Boltin turns back to his desk and pulls up the live analysis. Staring down, his face goes slack as he scans, understanding that the game has shifted radically and he will have to scramble to survive.

"Tech-Secretary!"

"Yes, sir," the female voice is calm.

"I have to see the Presider immediately!"

"Are you aware of the hour?"

"WAKE HIM UP!"

"Your request is on the way."

In the ensuing silence Boltin stands staring down at his desktop screen scanning data on what happened as the preliminary analysis emerges. He looks sickened by what he sees. Then the tech-secretary has a response.

"The Presider will meet you in his office now."

"I'm on my way." Snatching his tunic, Boltin runs out of his office and through his quarters, down the long common hall of Council Row then out through the big double doors into the public square, footsteps echoing in a place that is empty and dimly lit at this time of night.

***

The presider's private office is a dim inner sanctum of sufficient size to indicate his status without diminishing his stature. Evenly illumined by artificial twilight and filled with the faint scent of cleansing fluids, the space is circular, defined by a smooth metal wall, a plain low ceiling and deep carpet, all the color of pewter. An impressive metal desk with accompanying prestige chair occupies one side of a room that is otherwise empty. Access is from two doors, opposite each other and both now hissing open then closed as two men rush in.

"You said it was urgent." The Presider strides to his desk and sits, his face a granite question mark under the cold beam of light that comes on to shine down on a full head of brushcut steel gray hair. In contrast to Boltin, Paul Prescot Reed is small, wiry and without charm because, having the mind of a viper, he doesn't need it. Inscrutable and ascetic, Reed sleeps very little and even at this hour is crisp and fresh in his usual impeccably tailored slate gray tunic and trousers.

A second beam shines directly on the center of the floor in front of the desk. George Biggs Boltin rushes into the light and stops, his face a mask of righteous indignation, his delivery soft and rapid-fire, his voice barely under control.

"Yesterday afternoon a citizen-unit found a bolthole that was left open by Maintenance. The unit went through the bolthole and was momentarily lost between the dome-skins. The unit was subsequently located again in an exterior maintenance station, which was also left open. This unit was flagged for intensive monitoring yet her monitor suit lacked sufficient control-MEDs. So I sent a team of Security guards but the unit opened the hatch and climbed out before they could get there and the guards couldn't pursue because they're not programmed for the surface though I and former heads of Security have repeatedly petitioned the council for that capacity in order to be able to react quickly to an event such as this. That not being the case, this particular citizen-unit was able to climb down a maintenance ladder to the surface and start walking across the flats. She was finally stopped by darkness."

Paul Prescot Reed sits taut as a bowstring, expressionless and silent. Boltin goes on.

"The problem is compounded because Great City's exterior surveillance technology was designed for military purposes. Since there's been no need for it, the technology hasn't been used since its initial testing. It was supposed to have been upgraded by Maintenance on a regular schedule. That hasn't happened. I know it's bad form to discuss other members of the council but shouldn't we be able to assume that someone who's gotten this far knows something about their function? I checked. It turns out that Maint-enance hasn't been following the schedule of upgrades for my surface technology – none of it – and that has to be done before I can deploy. And Medicine," Boltin throws his hands in the air as though astonished by the incompetence of others, "leaving that unit without sufficient control-MEDs is beyond irresponsible."

"What's the current disposition of the resource?" Reed's voice is raspy and barely audible.

"Oh, it gets worse," Boltin shakes his head. "Just before midnight a gaggle of drones was dispatched to disable the resource and stand by until Security guards could be deployed for retrieval – all the while I'm having trouble getting anything up and running because it hasn't been maintained. The gaggle found the unit, approached and injected a massive dose of disabler. Then suddenly one by one everything went blank for five of the drones. The sixth drone went inactive seconds later."

"More technical problems?"

"No," Boltin shakes his head in disbelief. "Indications are that the drones might have been captured, de-activated somehow."

"What?!" the Presider is out of his chair leaning over the desk. "De-activated by *what*? Where's the resource?!"

The two men stare at each other, equally shocked. Boltin blurts it out.

"We don't know."

"You don't know?! What do you mean you don't know?!"

"The unit was there. Then suddenly everything went blank and the unit wasn't here anymore. Surface readings were normal again, absent any signs of…"

"Captured and de-activated by WHAT?!"

"We can't be certain yet. The data is still being analyzed but it appears to be a bio-form of some kind."

"A bio-form!"

"We'll know conclusively when…"

"What kind of bio-form, Boltin?"

"Preliminary indications are that it's possibly…human."

"There are no more humans on the surface! That was taken care of in the beginning! The surface is regularly scanned, dead as a bone. There are no humans anywhere but in Great City and the Space States!"

"I *know* that, sir!"

For a moment the only sound is faint hissing from the ventilation system as the two men stare at each other. Then Reed leans over the desk and glares at his head of Security.

"Let me get this straight, Boltin. Are you telling me that our drones found the escaped citizen-unit, disabled it then lost it to a bio-form that might be human when there are no more humans out there but somehow one managed to appear, take out six drones then vanish with our resource?"

"Yes. Lapses in Medicine and Maintenance made it impossible for me to stop the unit. The monitor suit was insufficiently supplied with MEDs and in addition, a bolthole and a maintenance station were left wide open and vulnerable. On top of all that, none of my technology has been updated and should have been, according to schedule, causing our response time to be…"

The Presider raises a hand for silence than stands leaning over his desk, thinking. After a moment, he straightens up, steps away from the desk and the light shining down to stand in shadow half turned away, military-erect and stone-faced, looking into the distance.

"When did this happen?"

"Just now. I insisted on seeing you immediately."

"What are the specs on the citizen-unit?"

"You want to see this yourself, sir." Boltin has begun to perspire. "If I may…" He gestures to the Presider's formidable desk.

Reed nods curtly. Auxiliary control in hand, Boltin ignites the Presider's desktop screen, pulls up the appropriate file then retreats to his place under the cold light. Reed steps to the desk and stands looking down, his face expressionless as he reads.

"When will the unit's monitor suit expire?" he asks, eyebrows raised because of her stats.

"Fifteen hours from now."

"So we have two problems," still scanning, Reed holds up fingers. "First, in a few hours an invaluable resource whose file has red flags all over it and whose location is currently unknown will cease to function. Second, a bio-form is involved, possibly human."

Reed stands gazing down at the file then up at the plain low ceiling. Finally he looks at his head of Security. Again, his raspy voice is barely audible.

"Bio-forms don't exist in a vacuum, Boltin. If there's one there has to be more."

Great City's head of Security shudders as though hit by a

shockwave. That part of the bad news hadn't occurred to him yet. He swallows a sudden gusher of bile.

"What are you going to do, Boltin?" Reed's face is murderous. "How are you going to find that unit in time?"

"Security guards are scheduled for deployment at dawn. Satellites have been re-tracked. I'm doing everything I can to get the technology up and running in time. They can't get very far between now and…"

The Presider slams a hand down on his desk. "Why haven't we known about this before?! After all these generations why is Great City's head of Security just now discovering we're not alone here?!"

"Sir, scanner and satellite readings have never picked up any indication that…"

"Well evidently they've missed something!" Reed sinks down in his chair, leans back, squints into the distance and twirls a ball of nothing between his thumb and forefinger. "No one steals from Great City. Not on my watch." He turns a predator's gaze onto his head of Security and whispers. "I want that unit back and functioning. And I want whoever took it. Tech-secretary!"

"Yes, sir." The voice is flat and genderless.

"Call a council meeting for one hour from now."

"Yes, sir."

Reed moves around his chair to the door and stops.

"I'm not going to waste energy on you now, Boltin. Or on how this happened. You have two objectives. Take care of them with all dispatch and maybe save your hide."

The hiss of the door closing startles George Biggs Boltin back to life. He rushes out of the Presider's private office and through the stark waiting room. Footsteps echoing, he jogs through the grand hallway, across the big vestibule and out into the public square, still dimly lit and empty because most people in The Heights are asleep at this hour.

T aking decades to run its course, the great collapse was a product of greed, clashing dogmas, and the convulsions of an expiring planet. Had these three factors not converged on such a massive scale, some of those who just wanted to live might have had a chance. But that was not to be. Instead, the great collapse marked the conclusion of a world.

Those who founded Great City made their move just before the tipping point, the time when it became apparent that there was no going back, no slowing it down and no stopping it. Originally negotiators for C.E.O.s, Presidents and Divine Patriarchs, the Founders were the ones who actually wielded power. They were the pragmatic realists who met face to face in private and spoke the same language and made the deals. And as the great collapse shifted into high gear they concluded that without drastic action they were trapped in a game of total devastation with no escape and no winner.

A plan evolved. A timetable was established. Wheels were set in motion. On a particular day, the Founders vanished down into an unknown very large, very bright, very safe place to join previously assembled staff plus carefully culled officers and troops. There were also teams of engineers, technologists and, of course, those who keep things clean and pleasant.

All assembled were evenly divided by sex, genetically pure, and passionate about survival. When the underground location was sealed there were enough problem solvers, workers and resources down there to make a new future, and the Founders understood that there would be plenty of time to plan a world more to their liking. Thus in secret was Great City conceived.

***

One chamber in the cave complex is brightly illumined but not by wicklight. Glaring tech-lamps on tripods are strategically positioned at different heights around a glass tank filled with a transparent substance that is neither liquid nor solid and smells like vinegar. The tank is round, not quite chest-high, and easily large enough to contain the light blue Prime Researcher who is drifting weightless, immersed but for her head, which is secured to the padded rim of the tank by a chinstrap. The skin-tight monitor suit renders her featureless, devoid of particulars, revealing only that she's gaunt and vaguely female.

White hair and beard rolled up tight, the old man is standing at the tank near her head. He's wearing a loincloth and what looks like a welder's hood with the facemask up. He's arranging instruments on a cart next to which is a wide-mouth glass jar that reaches to his knee. His body is pink from scrubbing at the sink behind him. Finished arranging the instruments, he lowers the facemask, activates its magnifying technology and leans against the rim of the tank.

"Source willing," he whispers taking forceps and a laser scalpel from the tray.

With the focus of one building a ship in a bottle he lifts the tight fabric away from her chin and slices it open with the laser scalpel. He peels back the filmy fabric and zaps a filament that connects her to the suit. He slices and peels and zaps his way from her chin down to her pubis then starts a cut on the inside of her arms and across her chest from wrist to wrist. He disconnects more and more filaments and drops more and more pieces of monitor suit into the jar at his knee. All the while, the Prime Researcher remains limp and inert, her exposed flesh grayish-white in color, like the belly of a fish.

When the fabric of the suit has been removed the old man rinses his hands with a little hose attached to the tank then opens her jaw with a clamp. He takes a long thin speculum from the tray and activates nano-instruments in its tip then lubricates it. After adjusting the controls on his facemask he threads the speculum down her throat, moving quickly, watching his descent on a screen inside the facemask.

Working his way from deep in her throat up toward her mouth with swift sure movements lest he block her airway, he lifts, slices and zaps, freeing the long tracheal sleeve and dropping it in the jar by his knee. He re-positions her, changes instruments and disconnects the fabric of the suit from the filaments in her anus and vagina.

The Prime Researcher is naked now, anchored by the chinstrap and drifting in the jell. Her body glistens with fine gold filament-ends, like whiskers. Touching them the wrong way can activate their terminus points with the force of lightening.

He begins with the shortest ones, easing them out and dropping them in the jar. Still unconscious, she twitches reflexively. After that it's slower going. The remaining filaments penetrate deep and the slightest mistake can cause death or incapacity.

Since heading off in different directions roughly two thousand years ago, the Space States have grown in size and evolved to post-capitalist societies linked by technology and the conviction that vibrant communities thrive on openness, fairness, freshness, and an equitable balance between labor needed for the common good and leisure for the pursuit of personal purpose.

As they moved out into the universe they discovered that spacetime could not distance them from their place of origin. On the contrary, Space Staters remain deeply attached to a ruined planet and its past as their anchor in directionless void.

Earth.

Home.

That to which everything is oriented. The womb of all that is good and true. Or at least familiar.

Space Staters crave story from earth to tell them who they are and why on a mission with no end to find suitable new homes yet to be located because every hoped for option has turned out to be untenable – but then again in terms of the size of the whole they're only an inch or two from where they started. So when Great City made contact and put the offer on the table with a few samples, the Space States quickly agreed to supply energy, water, food, raw materials, finished goods and technology in exchange for virtual content from the past.

Hence, the value of the archives of the ancients.

***

Not having been opened since it was initially sealed, a deployment bay on the northeast side of Great City is almost ready for use. Reminiscent of a loading dock and lit by bright neon, the space is wide and low, supported by columns of thick I-beams. The front wall is composed of the door and its mechanisms. The other three walls are lined with drums of fuel, high-tech equipment, ordnance, tools and workbenches. Tanks, troop carriers, bull-dozers, cranes and large weapons are parked in rows facing the door. The bay has been hosed

26

down and smells of wet concrete and carbon-fuel exhaust.

Teams of Maintenance technicians in bright orange monitor suits are just now noisily finishing what took longer than anticipated because these tasks are new and there has been confusion getting them done. One group is rearranging vehicles to clear an area in front of the closed door. Another group is at a workbench readying half a dozen small arms for use. A third group is coiling hoses. And a fourth group is at the door, getting it ready to be opened. When they're finished, the technicians depart through an inconspicuous side door.

A freight elevator descends and settles with a rattling of metal at the rear of the bay. The grate clangs open. Six big Security guards in glistening black monitor suits step out of the lift. Muscular and aggressive, they stride to a workbench, pick up and check their firearms then move to and spread out in front of the door where they activate their weapons and stand ready to spring.

The lights go dim so as to direct most of the current in northeast quadrant to the critical task of raising the door. A sustained burst of steam is accompanied by the hiss and crackle of electricity and the clang of retracting bolts then the deafening screech of metal grinding on metal as the heavy door rises with agonizing slowness then, malfunctioning, stops halfway up.

Standing in dusty glare that angles into the bay, four of the six guards show signs of agitation. Adjustments are made by remote SecurityPrimes. The guards settle down. Following instructions they move out through the door – open just enough to clear their heads – and stop at the top of a long gradual ramp.

Suddenly, one of the guards short-circuits, goes rigid with spasm, falls backward under the plummeting door and is crushed. Another guard starts to wobble. Adjustments are made.

The wobbly guard settles down and stays with the others as, weapons cocked and aimed, scanning left and right and straight ahead they advance slowly down the long ramp. When they reach the surface the Security guards take off, sprinting with unnatural cheetah-speed across the littered flats toward their objective, all but the wobbly guard who is running just as fast as the others but off on his own, jerky tangent.

***

A loose thread must be tied because the escaped Prime Researcher would not have left that spectacular find back in the workbay without compelling reason.

Great City prides itself on efficiency. Citizen-units are gestated one at a time to fill specific needs. Egg and sperm are selected and joined then put in a birthing-vault. Nine months later, but for the absence of a natural mother, a normal human child is born. After examination, if all is well and the unit is up to standard, filaments are inserted and the infant is swaddled in a pre-monitor suit. Thus begins orientation to life in Great City.

The problem is that before, during and immediately after birth, humans are aware of be-ing. For most, this be-ing is extinguished as they are squeezed into the only life they will ever know. But a few units consistently chafe under Great City's perfect solution. From all different functions and specializations, no matter what measures are taken, these citizen-units continually push at the margins.

Such a one is the recently escaped Prime Researcher whose long history of deviation began when once as a wee potential she was directed to a workbay for a study session. She backed into the harness and the technology embraced her, whooshed her neuro-awareness into the learning-zone. A light blue Prime Researcher was there – she'd learned her colors and shades by then. The Prime Researcher was holding a rectangular object and she heard words in her head.

This is a book.

Then a sky blue hand opened the book randomly near the beginning and turned the pages toward her. A finger was tapping the page and someone was talking but she didn't hear because she wasn't listening because she could read by then and was, right where the finger was tapping.

"If you make me an altar of stone, do not build it of dressed stones; for if you use a chisel on it, you will profane it."

Then it was the end of the lesson and she was told they no longer exist, books or any other remnants of the ancients.

Such things are anti-dogma, no longer pertinent. All items that did not further the purpose of Great City were destroyed during The Purification. Content remains, however. In the archives of the ancients. The archives hold what is needed to sustain Great City.

Archives.

She'd encountered the word before but this was the first time it connected to anything – to a sentence that had taken root in her for some reason and was already producing a plant that had to grow. It was then she knew she was going to be a Prime Researcher and explore the archives discovering altars and stones, looking for that sentence again to find out what it means.

After years of training in Mentals, on becoming a Prime she immediately justified their investment with a stream of high-value finds – chunks and sometimes whole pieces of art, literature, music, history, philosophy, scripture, that sort of thing. Prolonged exposure to anti-dogma is not without risk, however, especially when a unit is pushed hard. And she was pushed very hard.

So she began to dream. Her fluctuations were noted. Her doses were adjusted. Dream persisted, bizarre scenarios of running from danger and crawling through holes.

Then something happened. Dream turned into a dot of negative space far out in front of her and she was drawn to approach that dot. Gradually, dream after dream, she drew closer to the dot until she could finally recognize it as a hole, a window, a way from darkness to light.

Dreaming, she began to hear a faint sound from the other side of that hole, like a voice. Not words, just sound. And the more she heard that voice the more she was attracted to it and wanted to find its source and finally one day in the workbay when this tale began, she saw the sentence again and seeing it startled her to silence and through that instant of utter silence she heard the calling-dream clearly and understood that there's a difference between a library about freedom and freedom itself. And the first step on the path to actual freedom involved getting out of Great City. So she did.

***

By noon an overwhelmed George Biggs Boltin is fighting off panic. Jittery from too much Focus, he's standing at the wetbar in his brightly illumined office, wearing rumpled undershorts and a gaping paisley silk robe, stunned by yet another failure. The Security guards have been counterproductive on all counts, siphoning time and energy away from the missing resource and whoever took it while destroying the site where every-thing happened and life went bad. In addition, the unit's monitor suit is due to expire in a few hours and he doesn't have a clue what to do without a trail of some kind and a trail is not forthcoming.

Soft, pink and glistening with perspiration, Boltin hastily refills the tumbler, takes it to his desk and stands squinting down at a gray real-time satellite image of the area labeled point A, where the unit was snatched, not far from the base of Great City and clearly disturbed by the Security guards who are now lying inert and useless on the ground, six more resources lost and point A is now the end of the line.

"Where's point B?!" he screams, heaving the tumbler at the wall.

"That cannot be determined…"

"Shut up!" he slams a fist down on the screen.

Suddenly everything in Boltin's office goes dark and he's in shadow cast by ambient light from the hall. He spins around to his control panel and sees it dark. He jabs at it then pounds on it. Nothing happens.

"TECH-SECRETARY!"

There's no response. He runs down the hall to his front door and finds it locked, unresponsive to his hand on the identity-pad.

"No, no, no." He pounds, "TECH-SECRETARY!" He kicks the door then runs back to his office bellowing, "TECH-SECRETARY!"

Frantic, Boltin runs into his bedroom and flicks on the light. It works. He rushes into the bathroom and flicks on the light. It works. Same with the living room and kitchen. He runs back to his office again and nothing works.

"Shut DOWN?! HAVE YOU SHUT ME *DOWN*?!"

Boltin spins around holding his head then rushes to the open wetbar. Hand shaking, he fills a tumbler with Mello, gulps it down in one swallow and pours another. Then he stops, mouth open, body almost rigid.

It's as though a candle has appeared in the dark of his desperation and he can't move for staring at it. Tumbler poised halfway to his mouth, face drained of illusion, George Biggs Boltin stands unshielded from what has become the central fact of his life. The two carefully cultivated assets that made his ascent effortless are of no use in this situation and they're the only tools he has. But charm and ruthlessness can't find him a trail.

***

30

The Prime Researcher lunges back and forth, bucking and heaving with seizure so violent her head slips out of the chinstrap. The old man reaches for her and can't get a good hold. Flailing, she sinks under the jell, slippery as a fish. He finally gets a purchase and hauls her close to the side of the tank, doing his best to keep her head up. Then the seizure abruptly stops and she goes flaccid.

Moving quickly he checks her breathing and fastens her head back in the strap. He lowers his facemask, plucks up tweezers and pulls the last filament the rest of the way out of her nose. She lurches as though filled with current and gasps like someone surfacing from too long under water. Then she calms.

He drops the filament into the glass jar and checks her breathing. He washes his hands and pops the light blue lenses out of her eyes, causing her to blink reflexively though she see nothing. He rinses her eyes out with water then takes off his magnifying headpiece and sets it aside, watching her closely all the while, not awake yet, not aware, just alive.

The old man turns to the sink and counter behind him. He picks up a sizeable hourglass that hasn't been used recently and turns it over, starting the sand. He selects a small stone from a bowl full of stones and sets it on the counter.

After studying the stone for a moment the old man picks up a stylus. He dips it in ink and draws a glyph on the stone – a graceful black line arcing up from lower left to upper right and a shorter, frowning line in the center.

He sets the stone on the counter next to the hourglass and the dish of small stones. He stoops for the big jar with the remains of the monitor suit and carries it past a steaming thermal pond to the back of the chamber and a narrow passage that leads to the acid well.

Using a rope and pulley system, the old man raises a stone lid off of a large hole in the ground. He leans over the hole and without ceremony drops the jar down the long shaft, waiting to hear it hit the acid below. Then, satisfied that not one molecule of the suit can be traced here, he lowers the lid and returns to the former Prime Researcher to check her vitals.

Satisfied with her condition so far, he frees her head from the chinstrap, lifts her out of the tank and carries her like a baby out into the steaming pond, not stopping until warm water is almost up to his chest. Supporting her head, he washes jell off of her then himself.

When she is bathed clean the old man takes her back to the tank area for a blanket to wrap her in. Then he carries her out of the delivery chamber through a faintly lit tunnel back to the sleeping alcove and out into the main chamber where the big spider is a bizarre angel hanging on a thread halfway down from the ceiling directly over the rug and the sleeping mat.

He lowers the former Prime Researcher to the mat, positions her on her back, aligns her carefully then covers her with a blanket. Overhead, Solaris grinds her jaws. The old man looks up.

I was spotted on the surface. We must assume they will try to find us. Check the high veins and chambers for untoward signs.

Solaris clicks once in response then ascends her thread, skitters across the ceiling, down the wall and out through the tunnel that leads to the grotto. Attending the former Prime Researcher, the old man checks her pulse and her breath then lifts her waxy eyelids. Finding her stable for now, he goes back to clean up the delivery chamber.

***

For a sense of the whole of the archives imagine everything ever generated and preserved during the time of the ancients, every object, thought, sound or sign that somehow left its mark, produced corporately or privately in any medium – the contents of all museums, libraries and databases, all conclusions and the trails that led to them made by science, philosophy, art, and religion, all traces left by politics and business, research and education, high and low culture world-wide from beginning to end, collected, transposed then poured into a huge new mode that was supposed to function efficiently except that everything exploded into a chaotic sea of churned data with no bottom, no surface and no shore, a vastness of bits and fragments whirling around and stormed up because technology doesn't always do what humans intend it to do.

The archives were the only way stewards could have the privilege they desired, which would never be generated by their closed system. Such value could not be allowed to remain inaccessible. Under intense pressure and after continued failures, engineers and technicians of Great City decided to approach the problem from a different angle.

A new function was created. It was to be performed by citizen-units, an elite group composed of Mentals, Researchers, and Prime Researchers who were programmed to work the archives by hand, go in, retrieve and assemble product, which would cost more than anticipated and there would be less of it. But at least the stewards would have something to sell.

***

A second gaggle of drones floats out of the hatch into thick afternoon haze. Chirping to each other and the Security Primes, they drift toward the surface, reading data off of the maintenance rungs. Halfway down, two of the drones suddenly dart away from the other four. After a moment's hesitation the errant drones begin to spin erratically. Then they plummet to the surface where they remain lodged and unresponsive.

Lacking their full compliment, the remaining four drones are con-fused. They have difficulty obeying a simple command to ascend and go back through the hatch to their cradles. The Security Primes reprogram and re-patch. Finally, the quartet of drones ascends in sloppy formation. After a moment's stubbornness at the hatch, they enter the control station and nestle down in their cradles for adjustment. The two drones down on the surface take longer to rouse. Eventually, however, they are coaxed up to join the others.

***

Great City' Presider is standing in his private office taking a moment alone before the final appointment of a long day that started last night and is about to go into tomorrow. When he hasn't been in council meetings he's been in trade negotiations with the ambassadors from the Space States. Things aren't going well there, either.

Paul Prescot Reed drains a snifter of vintage Calm and returns the empty glass to a wetbar that closes so there's not even a seam in the wall. He moves to his desk and sits leaning back in the cold spotlight, staring straight ahead. Sallow flesh is drawn tight across the bones of his hawk-like face. He presses a concealed button to admit his head of Human Resources, last because her task is second in importance only to finding out who took the resource.

The door to his waiting room hisses open then closed behind a middle-aged woman who is shaped like a potato with skinny limbs and a round, spongy torso. She wears ill-fitting brown and wafts a distinct female odor. Tall and slightly stooped, she shuffles quickly into the spotlight that shines down on the center of the floor and peers at Reed. Her hair is dyed the color of nutmeg and sticks out around her head as though ravaged by static electricity. Her rubbery mouth is crusted as usual in each corner with milky spittle. In spite of these defects, Virginia Kahn Baker has served on this Presider's council longer than anyone else because she is deliberate and dogged and does not make mistakes. As such, she is one of two or three who occasionally serve as confidant or perform some task best left in the dark.

Skipping formalities, Reed gets to the point.

"How soon can you replace the Prime Researcher?"

"There's a twelve year old male potential coming up through Mentals," Baker's voice is high and thin, her articulation precise. "Assuming he, too, possesses the X factor and functions optimally, he might fit the bill. I've forwarded his file."

"When can he be ready?"

"Four years."

"Four years?!"

"Soonest," she nods glumly. "He can't go into the archives without a permanent monitor suit, which means bone growth must be complete. Technology has been working on a way around that for almost as long as there have been monitor suits. According to Medicine we can't speed up the unit's growth. I've got people working on it. But as of right now, four years."

Reed sits stone-faced and rigid for a moment, absorbing the devastating news. Then he blinks and looks at his head of Human Resources.

"And your second task?"

"I've identified four high-level stewards who meet your specs. Their files are in your confidential queue, ranked by score."

"All right," he swivels away from her, leans back in the chair and gazes at nothing. "I'll take a look and get back to you. Meantime keep this quiet. You may go."

Baker nods and moves toward the door that hisses open. Then she stops and turns back.

"What about Boltin?"

"What about him?" Reed shrugs.

"Council members are not happy about his attacks on Medicine and Maintenance. They've had enough of his arrogance."

"It's taken care of. Leave me."

Baker blinks at him then exits the office. The door hisses closed behind her. The spotlight on the middle of the floor fades to nothing, as does the light shining down on Paul Prescot Reed who sits in artificial twilight not moving – the first Presider in Great City's long history to be faced with anything other than the well-executed order of things.

"Who are you?" he hisses at an elusive enemy.

Reed stands, adjusts his tunic and activates the desktop screen. He pulls up the files from Human Resources and arranges them side-by-side for a quick comparison. As usual, Baker gave him a good short-list.

After studying the files for a moment he extinguishes one. Then another. He reads the two remaining files closely then straightens up and extinguishes the desktop screen.

"Tech-secretary."

"Yes, sir."

"Inform HR that I want the first ranked replacement candidate brought to a conference room in Founders' Hall immediately and discreetly for an interview with me. Candidate is to be told nothing and will wait until I'm ready to see her. No explanation."

"Understood, sir."

With that, Paul Prescot Reed exits his private office for a quick shower then a very late dinner alone, as is his custom.

***

The single wick lighting the main chamber of the cave complex was placed out of flailing range hours ago when, assisted by herbal concoctions from the old man, she began to purge Great City's toxins. Now naked and limp, the former Prime Researcher is lying face-up on a clean towel, one of many eased under her to protect the sleeping mat.

35

He's kneeling beside her, gently sponging her with astringent.

Though she has yet to wake, the purging process has not been a quiet one. Intermittent seizures have been bracketed by racking cramps, shivers, sweats, spasms, diarrhea, vomiting and lots of stench. Sometimes her eyes are open and she stares at nothing, senseless in all ways. Between these bouts he has coaxed her to suck down mixtures taken from bottles and vials neatly arranged in a metal box with foldout trays, placed off to one side within easy reach.

***

The bathroom in Boltin's quarters is filled with billowing steam because the shower has been running full-blast for some time now. As can be seen through the heavily fogged glass door, he's in there, leaning back against the white tile wall under pelting water, still wearing his undershorts and dressing gown. Having come face to face with his limitations and been defeated by them, he gathered a supply of Mello, retreated to the shower and hasn't moved since except to raise a bottle and suck or drop the empty and stoop for a full one.

Stunned by this surprise ending, Boltin came here because there was nowhere else to go – certainly no point remaining in his office after the technology was extinguished without warning or comment and it was impossible to leave his private quarters, send out a distress call or demand an explanation. So he gathered bottles of Mello from his ample store and took them into the shower.

Now, lost in white noise, George Biggs Boltin doesn't hear the front door of his quarters open or the six big Security guards in glistening black monitor suits troop down the hall two-by-two. He doesn't notice the intrusion into his bathroom. It even takes him a moment to register that the shower door has been yanked open and two guards are standing in steam with the other four visible out in the hall. Boltin smirks, drains his bottle, drops it to the floor and is stooping for another when one of the guards reaches in to turn off the water.

"Come. Now." The voice is oddly disembodied and distorted.

Fear flickers momentarily in Boltin's eyes but is quickly replaced by arrogance. Dripping wet, he shrugs and exits the shower with some awkwardness.

"Take your hanz off me," he jerks an elbow away from their assis-tance and wobbles out to the hall where guards move into position, in front, behind, and beside, indifferent to his condition or his former status.

The guards escort him through his quarters to the front door they left open. There, Boltin is suddenly flooded with sobriety and refuses to continue. After a struggle that is embarrassingly feeble, Great City's former head of Security is dragged out into the wide hallway called Council Row on either side of which nine other doors are open, each threshold occupied by a council member who is staring at him, pleased he has fallen so far and so fast.

Boltin sneers at them as he is supported and escorted the long rubbery way to the end of the hall and out into the bright public square crowded with stewards of all levels going about their business though momentarily all stopped in their tracks, staring at him, blaming him. Head down he mumbles obscenities as the guards take him diagonally across the square to a commandeered lift. Then the door closes and it's just him and the guards going down until the lift finally stops and opens onto an unfinished corridor with a few dull bulbs hanging from the ceiling.

The guards open one of several identical doors on the corridor and take him inside. They return almost immediately without him, lock the door and depart.

Inside, the cell is small and dingy, illumined by a single dim bulb over the door. Boltin is sitting on the floor leaning back against the dirty white wall even though there's a cot. Across from the cot is a hole in the floor that exhales a foul stench. On the wall above the hole is a dripping faucet.

Boltin tries to stand and can't. The exertion starts everything spinning so he crawls to the hole and vomits repeatedly, long strings of yellow Mello. When he's finally able to lean slumped again, George Biggs Boltin sits wide-eyed, panting softly, utterly sober and devoured by fear.

***

The former Prime Researcher is inert on the sleeping mat. The old man is seated behind her, ankles crossed, hands in his lap. His eyes are closed. His white hair is down, beard flowing. He's wearing the brown robe again, hood up.

Without disturbing the stillness, as the last grains trickle out of the top globe he reaches down and turns the hourglass over to start the sand falling again. He plucks yet another stone out of the bowl and places it in a neat row with other stones for a total of fifteen. Then he resumes his silent vigil.

This is the most difficult part of leaving Great City. Through the centuries only a few have managed to escape. Some wandered until their monitor suits expired. Others were found through the calling-dream. Of those who made it this far several could not complete the journey and died unable to tolerate experience of a radically different awareness.

***

Dawn happens slowly. Haze that is constant turns from rusty black to rusty gray. Nothing stirs. There is no other indication.

The second gaggle of drones floats out of the hatch again as a blurry sun clears the horizon. Six silvery needles hover for a moment in formation, gleaming in the dirty light. They descend to the base of Great City. They find the spot where the Prime Researcher first stepped down.

Functioning perfectly, the drones relay data that confirms the data relayed by the first, destroyed gaggle of drones. They easily locate the trail taken by the Prime Researcher and follow it to point A where the unit disappeared. Once there, they seek evidence of what happened.

***

Her eyes flutter open and as though stepping out of a mirror the former Prime Researcher shifts from oblivion to awareness.

Her be-ing, here/now.

For an instant she understands herself to be a portion of matter in a mattered realm, both distinct from and one with, a vibrant

38

coalescence of bones and cells, blood, synapse and sinew whirling through spacetime with all the rest of what is. These are her facts and she wakes to live them. Then she's overwhelmed by a blizzard of immediacy and everything is unfamiliar as lying on her back she starts, gasps and sits abruptly, blanket falling to her waist.

Stunned, she looks down and sees her naked chest and stomach, her arms and hands then her legs uncovered by the blanket whisked aside. Trembling, tentative, she wriggles her fingers. She makes a fist then stretches out her arm. She brings her hands to her face and touches then rubs her bald head, strokes her shoulders, breasts, ribs, thighs, knees, calves, ankles, feet, toes all soft and smooth and amazing.

Light and dark confuse her. She looks around, unable to distinguish figure from ground. Drawn to the glow of light, she turns and sees the wick on the ground behind her. Squinting, she raises a hand to shield her eyes and studies glare as the bright teardrop of flame becomes distinct. Then she tries to get up.

Movement starts everything spinning. At each stage she waits it out. Then she's on her feet, standing naked and wobbly as a newborn four-legged and overwhelmed by the fact of her being.

Focused on remaining upright she's not aware that someone is seated behind her, lowering his hood. As the last grains of sand fall, the old man picks up the hourglass and turns it over. He takes the first of seventeen stones, the one marked with the glyph, and drops it in a pocket of his robe. Then he scoops up several of the remaining stones and lets them trickle softly into the bowl.

Startled by the sound, she freezes, stares through the glare of wicklight without seeing. He slowly drops the rest of the stones into the bowl to make a cascade of melodic sounds. Then he stands.

She cocks her head. Uncertain, she steps back as shadow rises from the ground in front of her.

"Welcome to the Refuge." His words are soft and clear.

She gasps and stands dumbstruck by the power of the sound of a human voice heard for the first time in the air.

Light from the wick on the rug between them defines the planes and angles of a face that is framed with billowy white. She's riveted by pale green eyes as he speaks again, softly, to reassure a wild thing.

"I am One-Who-Waits, also known as Isham. We met through

the calling-dream."

Trying to understand, she stares at him with enormous dark eyes. She waves a hand in front of her face as though to stir an illusion.

"...Where?" she croaks, startled by what it feels like to voice a word.

"This is the Refuge, a cave complex beneath the surface some distance north and east of Great City."

She blinks, frowning at a wisp of memory-smoke that suddenly forms then vanishes before she can grasp it. Inching forward she studies him.

"You...helped...me..." she whispers, not knowing how she understands this.

"That is the purpose of One-Who-Waits at the Refuge."

Smiling, he draws something from his pocket. He holds it up and out between thumb and forefinger so she can see it.

"This is your name-stone. It marks your birth and is painted with a glyph because we must all be named." He holds it out for her to take.

She reaches and he drops the stone into her hand. Drawing it close, she studies two intersecting lines. One arcs up gracefully from bottom corner to opposite upper corner. The other line is shorter and droops across the center of the rising line. She looks at him, puzzled.

"It's the insignia of an air sign, the mark of One-Who-Wanders seeking what does not exist until it is found."

She searches his eyes. Then she looks back at the stone and studies the insignia. Concentrating thus, she begins to shiver.

Movements slow and careful, Isham picks up the blanket and drapes it around her shoulders. He steps back, giving her plenty of room while she gazes around the dimly lit main chamber washed with gold and shadows. She looks back at him and nods slowly, stunned.

"It is good," she whispers as a tear escapes and rolls down for her first taste of salt.

Holding the blanket in place she steps closer and touches his face with a fingertip than draws it back, shocked by the force of his vitality. She reaches out again, touches with a fingertip then her palm to explore warm ins and outs of weathered flesh. She strokes the sleeve of his robe and examines strands of his beard. Then she yawns and leans against him, snuggling, in-haling his fragrance.

"It is good," she murmurs sinking as he catches her and eases her down on the mat because she's fallen asleep.

Second Gate – Orientation

SpaceTime is not a void. That it seems to be so is an illusion. In fact spacetime is a continuum from infinitely small to infinitely large, neither empty nor still but crackling with energy that is majestic in all its magnitudes and manifestations.

Then there are products of human doing.

Brightly illumined, Space State Hope drifts through endless night momentarily eclipsing vastness. The ship is a long thick titanium cylinder ringed with arc lights, technology and portholes. Constant plumes of billowing steam exhaled by stacks and spigots create an almost cloudlike atmosphere around a structure built to sustain forty thousand people with plenty of elbowroom. The inner surface of the cylinder is laced with crisscrossing enclosed bridges through which pedestrians and carts loaded with goods cross from one side to the other while dwarfed shuttles float around and through the mother ship like bees tending their queen in slow motion as they ferry crews and passengers to and from vessels in the surrounding convoy that consists of, among other things, agri-barns, silos, processing plants, laboratories, vacation spots, and huge blobs of water.

Half a dozen high-velocity cruisers are clustered around a maintenance hub above S.S. Hope though one is now at her stern, a shadow on the bright enormity of the mother ship being prepped for a trip to earth. Built for distance and speed the cruiser is triangular in shape and reminiscent of a manta ray with flexible delta wings and a long tail that houses the velocity-gatherer.

It didn't take long for Space State geniuses to figure out that wormholes are open windows, thresholds through which it's possible to shift from one location to another without traversing spacetime. This process is called threading, and velocity is the key to threading a wormhole. Now a journey that once took lifetimes can be completed in a few nautical weeks or days. The lengthy part involves getting to and from a wormhole. The trip through is instantaneous.

Spewing steam, the H-V cruiser disconnects from the mother ship and drifts back to a safe distance behind and below the convoy. After a moment's trembling hesitation, flares of neon light erupt around the smaller ship as it generates the shield needed for the journey to the wormhole. Then the cruiser disappears like a pebble dropped in black water and S.S. Hope moves on, eventually swallowed by darkness.

***

It being imperative to get the former Prime Researcher up and grounded as quickly as possible, when next she woke the old man helped her into a long undershirt, a robe and moccasins like his then dropped her name-stone in a little cloth bag that hangs from a cord around her neck. He led her slowly through some of the more easily accessible parts of the cave complex. She was awkward at first as she learned to keep her balance climbing up and stepping down while dealing with the robe. He stayed back from her difficulty and her wonder, helping or explaining only when asked. On returning to the main chamber they rolled up her mat and took it to the opalescent chamber where she will sleep while here. Then in the kitchen alcove she watched and sniffed as, sleeves rolled up, long hair and beard tucked into an apron, Isham ground herbs and spices and sliced river-vegetables for a simple stew that will take a while to cook and be her first sustenance other than a cup of broth and lots of water he showed her where and how to void.

Now in the main chamber, wrapped in their robes, hoods up, they're seated across from each other with a wick on the rug between them and one on each corner. Savory fragrances wafting out of the kitchen alcove set her stomach growling and the noisy sensation puzzles her. She sips from her mug, still amazed by water and what it feels like to swallow. Then her attention is snagged by One-Who-Waits who reaches for the figure-eight object near his knee and turns it over again.

"What's that?" she points, hungry for what he knows.

Isham holds the hourglass up and out to catch light from the wick so she can see two graceful globes attached by a thin waist, the one on top full of tiny white grains trickling down into the almost empty chamber below.

"This is time moving through space," he points to the narrow waist that joins the globes. "You are here/now."

"...Here/now..." she murmurs, leaning closer.

"It's an hourglass," he holds it out for her to take.

"...Hour...glass..." she whispers, hefting then bringing it close to study the trickling grains. "Hourglass," she ponders sound and

43

meaning and their connection around the object in her hands.

"It's used to help newcomers locate themselves in spacetime."

"Have others come to you in the calling-dream?" she blinks at him, surprised.

"Only a few manage to escape. But from the beginning of Great City there has been a One-Who-Waits at the Refuge. I myself have delivered three, including you." The slightest hesitation precedes his next words. "This time is different, however."

"Different?" his tone unsettles her.

"Normally you would have a more prolonged recovery period. But I was spotted up on the surface. In the flurry, data was most certainly sent back to Great City and they now know that someone else exists."

"What does that mean?"

"You were a valuable resource. I am a threatening mystery. We must assume they will try to find us."

"NO!" she whispers fiercely, coiled like a spring and ready to flee. "I can't go back."

"Correct. The path is irreversible," Isham's voice is calm and reassuring. "You must simply be ready sooner than one would desire. For the moment, however, there's no cause to be alarmed."

"Can they find the Refuge?"

"I don't know. They've never had reason to try. Now they do," the old man smiles wryly as he strokes his mustache with a thumb and forefinger. "We are not without ways of protecting ourselves, however. The keeper is in the upper chambers and veins checking for signs of penetration. So far there's time to get ready but not to waste."

"Keeper? Aren't you the keeper of the Refuge?"

"No. I'm the current One-Who-Waits. The keeper is a different matter entirely."

"How do I get ready?" She regards him with the determination that got her here.

"Move. Explore – anywhere but through the tunnel at the back of the sleeping alcove," he points. "That part of the Refuge is only for the keeper and One-Who-Waits. Eat and drink as much as you can without discomfort. Sit and ponder. Sleep and dream. Ask questions."

Dazed by the flood of instructions she takes a sip of water then gazes at the smooth reddish dome of the main chamber. It feels comfortable around her, like a roomy second skin protecting her from whatever is beyond this moment and this location.

"Have you always been here at the Refuge?"

"No," Isham looks off into the distance. "I was a Medical technician in Great City until fifty years ago."

"Great City…?"

"Yes."

Her attention flits then comes to rest on a mystery that turns her eyes to pools of India ink.

"Is fifty years a long time?"

"Time is relative. For most humans fifty years is a long time but it seems like an instant because we live here/now while what was and what will be are only shadows that follow and precede."

Puzzled, she looks down at the hourglass in her lap. She picks it up and brings it to eye-level, squinting as white grains of sand fall from the upper chamber.

"How much time does this measure?"

"One hour."

She nods, trying to get a sense of how long an hour lasts. Is it fast? Is it slow? Is it elastic?

"The ancients spoke of twenty-four hours as a day and seven days as a week and fifty-two weeks as a year," she looks a bit startled by the sudden infusion of information from the archives.

"Si," he smiles.

"You've been here fifty years."

"No. I left Great City fifty years ago. I've been here at the Refuge for forty years."

She ponders this, trying to figure out how many turns of the glass are needed to mark that much time. How many turns of the glass was she in Great City? How many turns ago did the moment arrive and she follow it, staggering through gray static, desperate to be somewhere else?

"How did you find the Refuge?"

"The same way you did," he strokes his beard. "My need became a calling-dream."

"Why did you leave?"

"There was a One-Who-Waits here already."

"Where did you go?"

"That is not to be revealed. For now all you need to know is that the Refuge is an outpost, a way station. Ah," he sniffs then stands, "the stew has matured." He rolls up his sleeves, gestures for her to stay and disappears into the kitchen alcove.

Alone, One-Who-Wanders sits examining the elements of this new realm and is drawn to understand how the whole is so much greater than the sum of its parts. Then Isham returns carrying a tray on which are two steaming bowls of stew and two mugs of tea. He sets a bowl and mug in front of her and a bowl and mug in front of his cushion then puts the tray to one side and sits, feet crossed, hands in his lap, studying her.

"We inhabit a vastness not made by human hands," he speaks softly. "How did all of this come to be? What sustains it?"

She looks at him wide-eyed, without an answer. He continues.

"Some say one thing, others say another and millions have died for the difference – or, in my view, for no reason at all. What matters is to be thankful for what is provided through means beyond our own power. I address my gratitude thusly."

Isham raises his face and closes his eyes. She studies him carefully as he grows very quiet. Then something mysterious seems to arrive, settle in and resonate through him.

"Source of all creation you are holy. Thank you for life as well as awareness of life. Thank you that One-Who-Wanders has found the beginning of her path. Thank you for the sustenance we are about to share and the beauty that is constant around us. Inhabit our awareness that we might not profane these gifts. Stay with those who love you and find those who seek you. Let this be done as it has always been done and will always be done."

The old man opens his eyes, picks up his bowl and nods for her to do the same. As though returning from elsewhere, she blinks and watches him bring the bowl to his face, close his eyes, inhale appreciatively and sip.

"Eat," he whispers.

One-Who-Wanders reaches for her bowl and lifts it, pleased by the heft and warmth. She brings the bowl to her face and inhales then sips hot savory broth and is amazed by temperature and the play of flavors in her mouth. Wide-eyed she sips again, drawing in a slice of mushroom, fascinated by the texture in her mouth as she chews.

***

Urgencies related to the missing Prime Researcher have delayed Paul Prescot Reed's interview with the possible new head of Security. It's late morning when he finally enters the conference room to stand by the door in silence, assessing, giving her plenty of time to be uncomfortable in his presence. But she remains unnerved.

Karin Lassiter Kohl didn't flick an eyelash when, after waiting in here since last night with no explanation, the door abruptly opened and the Presider himself entered the room with a gust of power. She merely turned from a thought-experiment to face him and hasn't moved or spoken yet, either, though it's only been about twenty seconds.

Tall, lean and martini-cool, Lassiter has a dancer's body and grace. Prematurely white hair falls straight to the shoulders of a beautifully tailored dove-gray tunic. Matching trousers fit like water, flattering long legs. But it's the eyes that dominate, intense eyes the color of smoke – predator's eyes like his own.

"They call you the Assassin," Reed's voice is barely audible. "Why?"

The faintest smile flits across her lips.

"I have on occasion been an instrument of exposure, calling attention to those faking competence." Her words are soft as rain.

Reed raises an eyebrow, changes tack.

"You were assigned to George Biggs Boltin in Security several years ago," his tone is challenging, "an assignment you'd repeatedly applied for and clearly wanted. Yet you left almost immediately. Why?"

"Security was a joke under Boltin. There were two major lapses the first month I was there. I filed a report and copied him because that's how I function: up front and personal. He froze me out. I don't stay where I'm not useful so I asked for a transfer and got one."

Reed studies her for a long moment then clears his throat and steps forward to the edge of the light.

"All right. To the point. Boltin is gone. I need a new head of Security. You're on probation. If you're not up to the job you're out immediately. So use his place on Council Row but don't settle in yet. Clear?"

"Crystal," she betrays no other response.

"You have one objective and no holds barred. I want whoever took our Prime Researcher. Alive. Technology and Engineering are covering Boltin's area until a replacement arrives. They'll bring you up to speed then you're on your own. Questions?"

"No."

"Fine, get started."

The Presider turns, opens the door and leaves the conference room as abruptly as he arrived. Karin Lassiter Kohl pauses only a moment to close her eyes, raise her face to the low ceiling and exhale. Then Great City's new head of Security strides off to Boltin's quarters as the door hisses closed behind her.

***

After that first meal the former Prime Researcher helped One-Who-Waits clean the kitchen alcove. Then, sleepy with a full tummy, wick in one hand, hourglass in the other, she found her way to the opalescent chamber where she took off her robe, got into the bedroll and fell asleep.

When she woke some time later the top chamber of the hourglass was empty. She understood that at least an hour had passed. Maybe more. But how long is an hour?

She still didn't know and felt she'd lost track of something important. So hurrying, wearing only moccasins and her undershirt she snatched up the wick and the hourglass and rushed back to the kitchen alcove expecting him to be there but he wasn't.

"Halloooo?"

"Yes, here!"

She whirled at the sound of his voice and he emerged from the tunnel at the back of his sleeping alcove, robe off, wiping his hands on a soft cloth, hair and beard rolled up, clearly having been engaged in some kind of labor. He washed his hands, filled mugs with water from the cistern and broke off chunks of bread while she explained what had happened with the hourglass, how she'd fallen asleep and lost track of time. He chuckled, taking the glass from her and setting it up out of the way.

"This tool has served its purpose.

"What?"

"You are now anchored in your own here/now."

Her eyes were large and dark with questions as she munched her chunk of bread. He smiled broadly.

"There is much to learn. What would you like to do first?"

48

"Explore."

"Very well. We go together this time. After that you're on your own because I must tend other matters." He took two thick woven belts from a basket and handed her one. "Take one of these anytime you go beyond the boundaries of the main chamber. Fix it like so."

One-Who-Wanders imitated clumsily as Isham threaded two pouches onto his belt then filled them, one with wicks and a firestarter, the other with roasted pods. Done, he fastened the belt around his hips, helped her with hers then led her into the grotto and a more detailed tour, slow this time because, all distractions being equal, her attention flitted here and there without rhyme or reason and she stopped continually to examine reflections on water or to stand transfixed by the movement of light and shadow on stone.

She needed words, craved them. When she pointed, asking, "What?" with huge black eyes, he gave her the word and she murmured it back to him, reveling in the sensation of making sense with sound, forming and pushing it out through her lips into the air.

"Rivulet...Minnow...Lichen...Waterfall...Perspiration...Slither...Dragonfly...Stalagmite...Echo...Salamander...Moss...Follicle ...Albino... Striation..."

She picked up a big rock igniting a fierce blue glow from underneath.

"Fire-worms," he whispered. "Activated when weight or pressure is taken off of their bodies."

Each word brought a deep and satisfying relief. Often, she was overjoyed when word and thing together referred back to something in the archives.

Once they stopped by a pool of still water and stood looking down, each holding a wick high and she could see two forms on the surface of the water, one tall and thin the other not so tall. She turned and looked at him, eyebrows raised.

"Reflection," he said. "That is you and I, mirrored."

She leaned over and stirred the water with a finger then waited for it to still and when it did she saw him standing beside her, wick high, and a squatting form that had to be her, One-Who-Wanders. They stayed there a long time while she moved her wick up and down and back and forth and stirred the image then let it settle again so she could see Isham standing and her squatting, fascinated. And all the while he was teaching her to function, how to know when water is safe to drink, how to light a wick in total darkness, what flora and fauna to avoid.

And she was tireless.

When they returned to the grotto she was drawn to the big pool with the falls on the far side. Mesmerized, she removed her moccasins and walked out into crisp clear water up to her chest, turned to look for him and found him floating on his back not far behind, unobtrusively watchful. He taught her how to float then how to dogpaddle then how to swim, which she did with determination if not grace out to the wide veil of falls while he stayed in the middle watching her climb onto a boulder directly beneath the thin cascade and, wavering at first, stand for a long time arms out in an ecstasy of awareness.

***

The four Space State ships were originally intended as tourist destin-ations for people who could afford a week or two of weightless experience in accommodations similar to those aboard merchant and military vessels. Five-star hotel/casinos were on the drawing board and decades away from realization but the more primitive SpaceXperience vessels were under construction when everything began seriously falling apart and the vicinity between earth and moon became dangerous.

Those working on the four vessels maneuvered themselves and their ships around to the dark side of the moon and were alone there long enough to engage in passionate discussion about what to do. They voted and set off in craft that were unfinished but deployable and self-sufficient, heading in different directions on a common mission to find interim housing and perhaps intelligent life while waiting for things to settle down back home. A fraction of their current size, each ship contained no more than a hundred people.

Under continuous construction the ships gradually grew in size and beautifully engineered complexity. Growth was stopped when each community reached a size large enough to provide diversity and small enough to retain a sense of the whole. Included in the design was enough personal and common elbowroom to allow for a sense of standing firm on a huge ocean liner. Of late there has been talk of expansion through starter-states.

S.S. Columbus, S.S. Ulysses, S.S. Friendship, and S.S. Hope were still well within their own solar system and in the early stages of expansion when signals from earth suddenly stopped. This had always been a possibility but the abruptness of it, the silence, produced an immediate, profound and unanticipated shift. Adrift and stunned, those aboard the Space States sank into a deep despair because it had actually happened.

Earth was no more.

It had been destroyed by its own stewards.

Humans. People. Just like us.

Is this a tendency?

Those aboard the Space States began to spend countless off-duty hours combing through what they had brought of the past, which wasn't all that much because no one had anticipated that they wouldn't be going back to the surface. So they had mostly personal items and memorabilia, images of lovers, friends and family, lots of then-contemporary music, games, films, fiction, plus a few classics. They gathered all of it together in a database that was scanned and studied in prolonged reverie on all four Space States because only there, pouring over bits of home could they find relief from the melancholy that was otherwise constant.

During this time the Space States made a difficult collective decision not to rendezvous and hover in the dark together but instead to stay on course and keep looking for a new home because they hadn't gone all that far yet. A necessary by-product of this decision, however, was the development of a way to traverse the increasing distances between them.

Concurrently, the Space States continued to monitor the silent earth and were startled when within only a few generations and out of the blue they picked up faint signals from something called Great City. After improving the quality of transmission and after the requisite introductions, an offer was put on the table: content from the archives of the ancients in exchange for goods and resources.

On one end the technology was almost ready. On the other end Great City had begun to generate product. It didn't take long for the first shipments to arrive and payment to be made. Since then the flow of trade has continued without interruption until of late when Great City started trying to pass off pigs as princesses.

***

51

One-Who-Wanders and Isham returned from exploring and went to the kitchen alcove to be warmed and dried by heat from the oven. Gnawing on a piece of bread she watched him season a kettle of soaking grains and vegetables then hang it over the fire to cook. He made fragrant tea and led her back to the main chamber where they are now, robed and hooded again, seated across from each other with a lit wick between them and one on each corner of the elaborately patterned and perfectly positioned rug that seems to anchor the domed space to a geometry which extends in all directions far beyond this time and place. Content and relaxed, mug in both hands up near her face, she studies One-Who-Waits who is sitting with his eyes closed, sniffing his tea.

"What's beyond Great City and the Refuge?"

"Beneath the surface there is stone, some of it naturally carved out by antediluvian rivers and seas. Some of it was blasted open by humans and is inhabited. Great City is the only thing I know of on the surface. The rest is dunes and dead air, not habitable without life support of some kind. There's also a transfer station between earth and the moon, where product from the Space States is delivered."

"Space States?"

"Great City's trading partners. I know no more than that they exist," he shrugs regretfully then takes a sip of tea and looks at her again. "There is also a place best never spoken of. But you asked and I will answer. That place is called SubTurra. For now I will say no more about it. If there are other locations than those I do not know of them."

Mulling his response, One-Who-Wanders holds her mug near her nose, inhales the tangy tea, and wants to know more. Thus preoccupied, she's startled by clicking sounds from behind, from the tunnel that leads into the grotto. Turning around she gasps as a large bewildering creature emerges from the tunnel and, lots of legs moving very fast, skitters past her across the rug to One-Who-Waits all the while making staccato sounds that could be language or music to one who understood. He listens, nodding "good" then gestures to the former Prime Researcher.

"Begging pardon for our lack of manners. This is Solaris, keeper of the Refuge. Solaris, meet One-Who-Wanders."

Covered with a thin layer of fine gold hairs that catch the light, Solaris turns to study the new arrival. Eight long legs support her body, which is reminiscent of an oversized human brain outside its cranium.

Two short arms covered with silky brown fur are folded up by the keeper's little head, which is hard, mahogany brown, and burnished to a fine shine. But it's the eyes that compel – huge eyes composed of hundreds of hexagonal facets, iridescent red, staring at her intently.

Taking delicate steps the keeper advances until she's less than an arm's length away. Because One-Who-Wanders is seated on a cushion, the two of them are face to face. Thousands of multifaceted red lenses that vibrate with intelligence study her for what seems like a long time during which neither moves. Then slowly leaning forward until they are almost nose to nose the keeper begins to grind her jaws, generating a deep hollow sound that grows louder and more intense until it is resonating through and filling the chamber with layers of delicate harmonics composed of chitterings, tinklings, clickings and bell-like tones high and low and in between that hold meaning, sense she does not understand but, hypnotized, wants to.

The sound gradually fades. The keeper leans back. One-Who-Wanders sits wide-eyed and open mouthed for a long moment before blinking and returning from where she was – a most pleasant non-place.

After retreating several steps the keeper stops and stands softly grinding her jaws, aiming the sound at Isham, still seated on his cushion. This time the hollow rasps and tones are slower, as though the big spider is considering a matter of some importance. Eyes closed, One-Who-Waits listens intently until she's finished. Then he strokes his beard with one hand and, nodding, regards the new arrival.

"Solaris says you are a child of the Refuge," his nod is one of agreement. "She understands that you have only recently come to awareness of this realm. Nonetheless, she asks permission to initiate you before we leave – should you agree, of course."

"Initiate?"

"Yes."

"What does that mean?"

"The keeper wishes to give you her milk."

One-Who-Wanders can't take her eyes off of the big spider who is staring back, red eyes flaring spectral colors in the wicklight.

"Her milk?"

"Yes."

"How?"

"Through a bite."

He pulls his beard aside with one hand and leans forward. She

53

glances away from the keeper long enough to see two crescent-shaped little scars facing each other just above the bowl of his throat.

"It has something to do with a fluid she emits," he releases his beard and leans back. "Beyond that I don't know how it works nor can I express what it's like to share a certain level of awareness with a creature so utterly other."

"Is that what will happen? I'll be able to understand Solaris?"

"One does not understand the keeper. One listens and one learns."

She sits quietly for a moment, confused. Then she looks at Isham.

"What should I do?"

"That is not for another to say. And how can you know? It's too soon. But when you do know, Solaris will, too, and take care of the rest. Should you refuse, the matter is dropped without prejudice as far as the Refuge is concerned." He gets to his feet and stretches elaborately. "Now if you don't mind, I'd like to sleep while there's a moment to do so."

She nods. He blows out all but two of the wicks, takes one into his alcove and leaves the other for her. One-Who-Wanders remains on her cushion watching the keeper, sensing benevolence toward friends and primal fierceness toward all others. After a moment, dromedary-like, Solaris lumbers to her feet. With a little bow the big spider turns, skitters up the wall and across the ceiling to its center where she stops, almost invisible.

One-Who-Wanders stands and looks up, trying to distinguish spider from stone. Unable to do so she finally leans down for the remaining wick and ducks into a tunnel that leads to the small chamber with a high ceiling, called the opalescent chamber because of its many-colored iridescent streaks that bleed pearls, lace and crystallized flowers.

She pulls the robe off over her head. Long undershirt hanging to mid-thigh, she stretches, imitating One-Who-Waits. Then she lies down, pulls the cover up to her chin, turns over onto her side and is asleep.

For this last meeting of a long day the Presider is seated at the head of the table near the door of a conference room off of Founders' Hall. With him are his heads of Technology and Engineering. Karin Lassiter Kohl, the interim head of Security, is standing cool as a moonbeam at the foot of the table delivering her first report to peers on the council. The tabletop screen glows with a gray satellite image of the northeast side of Great City then the flats then dunes.

"As you know, the Prime Researcher was snatched from Point A near the base of Great City," Lassiter taps the clearly marked spot near her thigh. "The location was badly disturbed by Boltin's ill-advised Security guards and as yet yields no usable information. As of this morning when I took charge, the second gaggle of drones was still stuck in the same search-pattern that yielded nothing. I reprogrammed the gaggle and by mid-afternoon it had sniffed out faint threads of a digital trail heading north and east into the dunes. Now it gets interesting."

Wearing a fresh putty-colored tunic and trousers and betraying no fatigue whatsoever, Lassiter leans out over the table and traces a loopy line across the screen toward the Presider. She nails him with smoky gray eyes then looks at the heads of Technology and Engineering.

"It took the gaggle twelve hours to follow a path that should normally have taken thirty minutes, tops. It seems that the resource and whoever took her were tech-shielded, hence, very difficult to follow, forcing the drones to stop repeatedly and circle back to find the trail again. By dusk they finally arrived at point B, twelve miles into the dunes," she taps the clearly labeled spot out in the center of the table. "This is the end of the trail as far as we know. It's now surrounded by the gaggle. Satellites have also been reprogrammed to scrutinize the entire area. So far there's been no activity of any kind."

"Query?" Malcolm Pierce Whitaker, head of Engineering and one of the older council members, raises a finger and looks at Lassiter.

"Yes," she takes the interruption in stride.

"Do you assume that point B is in fact the end of the trail?" tall and patrician in his uncomfortable chair, Whitaker regards the new head of Security with polite skepticism, hoping for more from her than they got from Boltin.

"Point B may just be where we stopped for the night." Lassiter smiles without defensiveness. I instructed the gaggle to do a pre-liminary scour of the surrounding area and nothing more was found. I decided not to waste energy on a wild chase in the dark but instead to treat point B as the end of the trail pending more information. Other drone-gaggles are being upgraded for deployment. The first one ready will be sent to reconnoiter point B and determine if it is indeed the end of the trail. Regardless, in my opinion, point B has to be penetrated. We need to know what, if anything, is under it."

Whitaker of Engineering nods, satisfied for now. Magrit Abram Shen, head of Technology seated across from Engineering, is not convinced Lassiter is a good choice for that position and she's far too careful to let that show.

"And the bio-form that stole our resource, anything new there?" Shen's voice is whispery, almost child-like.

"Readings are badly scrambled but analysis of what we've got indicates that the bio-form is human, probably male."

"With technology capable of eluding our own," Shen muses to the delicate hands folded in her lap.

"Yes," Lassiter is agreeable. "That means we have to find out who they are, i.e., penetrate point B as soon as possible. Which is not Security's purview."

The two women lock eyes.

"Exactly," Shen smiles without showing teeth.

Reed levels a piercing gaze at Technology and Engineering then at his interim head of Security.

"Why would someone steal a citizen-unit?"

"One soon to die," Shen reminds the other three.

"They want our technology," Whitaker is certain of this.

"The question is," Shen muses, "did he know the unit would terminate so soon?"

Reed looks at his new head of Security and raises a finger for silence. Lassiter is standing at the foot of the table, head tilted to one side as though trying to hear something faint in the distance. Then she blinks, looks quite surprised and whispers.

"What if she's not dead? What if the monitor suit was recharged by whoever helped her? Or what if the suit was removed?"

The question is followed by a moment's dumb silence. Then, amused, Shen tilts her head to one side and smiles patiently as to a moron.

"According to Medicine it's impossible to remove a monitor

suit from an adult citizen-unit. That much disturbance of the filaments would leave you with a blob of incoherent bio-mass."

"Have they tried?" Lassiter smiles.

"What does it matter? The Prime Researcher is no longer in play. Let it go. We need to focus on penetrating point B."

"Agreed. We also have to know if she's alive," Lassiter holds firm. "Whoever took our resource has technology sophisticated enough to allude us. We must assume they have other capabilities as well, perhaps even a way to remove a monitor suit without damage to its wearer."

Shen looks away and clucks her tongue, exasperated that a newcomer is being allowed to monopolize an important discussion with idle speculation. But Reed doesn't stop her so Lassiter rushes on.

"Let's find out. Have Medicine experiment with a few low-value units to try and remove their monitor suits without loss of functionality."

"That's a second-tier consideration, Lassiter, not important right now," Shen's voice is soft and childlike even when the woman is furious.

"Let's assume," not giving the Presider time to intervene, Lassiter leans into the conference table, her words a steady stream and one stiff finger raised to prevent interruption. "Let's assume it's somehow possible to remove a monitor suit and end up with a functional package, someone who wakes up and remembers where she came from. This is a Prime Researcher we're talking about here. How much does she know? What might she have taken away from Great City that could harm us?" Lassiter turns to the Presider. "How long can we afford not to examine such a possibility while whoever took her gathers more information on us in addition to what he already has? Can't we risk half a dozen non-essential units…"

Reed raises a finger for silence and looks at Whitaker.

"Does Engineering have questions for Security?"

"Yes," the older man clears his throat. "What's beneath the surface at point B?"

"According to ancient maps," Lassiter is ready, "point B is located at the south end of a string of what were called National Parks and monuments – land left largely pristine until near the end. Famous for canyons and stone formations. The parks were strung together along a river that was a critical water supply at the time, meandering down hundreds of miles from the north."

"Now buried under tons of toxic ash and debris," Whitaker mutters to himself while activating his tech-pad for some rapid calculations. "Ash and debris are no problem. A thick layer of stone, on the other hand, could present a challenge."

The Presider raises a hand to stop the talk and looks at the three of them then points a finger at Technology and Engineering.

"You two come up with something to penetrate point B. Whatever it is, get it out there as soon as possible. Whoever stole that resource also destroyed six of our drones. He has the ability to render himself invisible to us while he goes wherever he wants on the surface. Based on those two things alone it's not beyond reason that he can keep a citizen-unit alive or remove a monitor suit and end up with a functional unit, someone full to the brim with information about Great City. Tech-secretary!"

"Yes, sir," an uninflected, genderless voice fills the conference room.

"Contact Medicine. Have him work with Human Resources to select half a dozen low-value citizen-units. I want their monitor suits removed one at a time in such a way that the units survive with functionality. Highest Priority."

"Yes, sir."

Reed turns to Lassiter who is smiling ever so slightly.

"While Technology and Engineering figure out how to penetrate point B and Medicine gets busy I want you to take the lead with Human Resources on a history of escapes from Great City. I also want an updated surveillance report on the trade ambassadors. Boltin seems to have forgotten all about them and we've got to find a weakness, some way to force them to shift their position." Then the Presider is out the door on his way to a strategy session with his trade negotiators.

"Tech-lab." Shen and Whitaker rush out of the conference room. Lassiter heads back to her new office to start the history of escapes from Great City.

***

The deepest location in the Refuge is called the pit. Accessed through a sizeable hole in one side of its low ceiling, the pit is now illumined by a wick and almost completely filled with stacked aluminum boxes containing data meticulously recorded through the centuries, plus folded equipment and big hemp duffels filled with various goods and stores.

Isham One-Who-Waits is at the hole in the ceiling, covered with stone-dust and perspiration. Hair and beard rolled up and out of the way, he's wearing a loincloth, undershirt, moccasins, and a headlamp with a bright beam. He tosses a bedroll and two big soft bags down then hops into the pit. Stooping, he arranges the new items neatly in whatever little space is left. Then standing wedged in under the low ceiling he covers everything with a heavy tarp – not easy because the space is so packed.

Solaris scuttles to the hole in the ceiling and peers through. She chitters to him. Isham nods.

"Seal it up," he smiles ruefully.

Taking the wick, Isham climbs out of the pit to be replaced immediately by the keeper who, with great speed, starts laying down a thick fuzzy web like white cotton candy laced with dewdrops. Soon the tarp is covered then obscured and the big spider is working her way up toward the hole and out to where One-Who-Waits is on his haunches a short way farther on up the steep tunnel, wick extinguished, miner's lamp sending down a bright beam. She clicks her jaws once.

Finished.

"Go ahead," the old man nods.

Solaris straddles the entrance to the pit, now white with fuzzy web and dewdrops. She raises her rear section and contracts it, squeezing out a clear droplet that falls to be replaced by another then another and another as she rotates slowly, forcing out a thin stream, a chemical tripwire which can only be crossed or disarmed by the keeper of the Refuge.

Done, she rests throbbing for a moment before following One-Who-Waits on up the steep tunnel to a junction where they separate. She heads for the surface veins and crannies to look for signs of intrusion. He takes a tunnel to another deep chamber that must be similarly prepared.

***

Somewhere in Great City, a male Maintenance-unit wearing a bright orange monitor suit and nearing the end of his usefulness is instructed to enter a MED station and lie down on the gurney. Under close supervision by the head of Medicine, the Medical Primes command their technology to anesthetize the unit. That done, accompanied by sustained whirring and clicking sounds, half a dozen complicated mechanical arms unfold from the ceiling, gravitate to the gurney and hover poised above the Maintenance-unit.

Surgical blades and tweezers flick pinging into position at the end of each arm and point like rigid fingers at the body beneath them. Because the Medical Primes have never done this before, their movements are slow and jerky. The blades and tweezers are guided to slice and peel the fabric of the suit from the front of the unit. When that is done – with no little blood – the long arms retract their blades with high pinging sounds of steel on steel.

The unit is lifted and turned over, repositioned for removal of the suit from his backside. Lifting, turning and setting the unit back down on the gurney puts pressure on the now-exposed filament-ends, activating each one of them, especially those around his navel, throat, and nose.

Face down the Maintenance-unit bucks and heaves with such force that the gurney's technology is damaged and several of the mechanical arms dangle broken as he implodes with spasm that will not let go until whatever remaining life is wrung, flung, gone and the man is limp, brain-fried, dead, having broken most of his own bones. One down and five to go.

***

Wick high, One-Who-Wanders moves through a long, meandering tunnel, uncertain where she is, trying to find the grotto and increasingly confused because nothing looks familiar. In addition, she's tired from exploring for hours, thirsty because there's been no drinkable water since the last few sips, and hungry because her pouch of seeds has been empty for a long time now.

It seems ages ago that she woke fresh and determined to be ready to leave the Refuge at a word from Isham. Setting out to explore in her undershirt and moccasins, she went into the kitchen alcove and was startled by Solaris who looked at her then skittered out across the main chamber and through the back of the sleeping alcove as though on an urgent mission. She found something thick and sweet in a pot on the hearth and ate a bowl of it while pondering the keeper's invitation.

After rinsing and stacking her bowl so as to leave the kitchen alcove the way One-Who-Waits likes it, she took one of the cloth belts and two pouches from their storage basket. She threaded the pouches onto the belt then filled the smaller one with wicks and a firestarter and the larger one with roasted seeds. Then she headed off to the grotto to explore.

Now she's lost.

The tunnel turns sharply and in a few steps she's at the end of it, standing in a small rounded chamber with a low offshoot on one side and no other way out. One-Who-Wanders stands studying her options. She can go back the way she came and be just as lost there as she is here or she can keep going and probe the offshoot.

About to go out, her wick sputters. Moving quickly she lights a fresh one and stows the used one in the pouch with the remaining fresh wicks and lots of stubs. Then stooping, wick aloft she enters the low tunnel that shrinks around her almost immediately so she has to crawl.

Descending headfirst, the tunnel becomes smaller and closer around her until there's barely room to move. She tries to go back and can't because gravity and her steep downward pitch prevent that. So she inches forward, coughing and blinking tears out of her eyes.

The tunnel abruptly levels off and opens up a bit. The air smells different, cooler. Wick out front and inching forward, scraping elbows and knees, she sees a splotch of darkness up ahead. A hole. An opening. Ignoring considerable discomfort, One-Who-Wanders advances toward the hole then works her way through and out.

Wick high in one hand she stands looking up at an enormous rose of space that blooms around her all smooth and the color of sunset, the color of flesh. Stunned by the size and beauty of the place she turns around looking for something familiar but everything is new. She uses time and wicks to comb the big chamber high and low peering into shadow, seeking a way out and not finding one.

Her wick begins to sputter. She gropes in her pouch for another and can't find one, only stubs, lots and lots of useless stubs.

She stares at the flame, willing it to keep burning as it reaches the little clay holder and goes out. Gasping, she paws desperately at the pouch, seeking a usable wick and there are no more. Then she stops, stands very still in utter silence, blinking at rings of afterglow that are almost immediately swallowed by darkness, and there is no greater dark than that embraced by stone.

Blindsided by panic she turns around then stops, unable to breathe. She is at one and the same time trembling violently and completely frozen, utterly disoriented, craving light as she craves air but everything and nothing are spinning faster and faster and she needs to get out of here, back to the main chamber and One-Who-Waits and light and air but there's only panic and she wants to scream but can't, can't go spiraling out of control.

She sinks to her knees then rolls up in a tight ball on the ground, rocking back and forth, trying to breathe, wanting to scream. Then she's aware of something else, something seeping through the panic to her awareness.

Sound.

Deep and resonant, steady, throbbing rhythmically, growing louder and louder until the rapid clickings and grindings and reverberating harmonics are a counterpoint to the bottomless terror that makes it impossible for her to breathe. Suddenly a deafening explosion only she can hear causes her to gasp and then something is put into her hands.

A pouch.

Frantic, she sits up and jerks the pouch open, spilling wicks. Groping, she finds a wick, lights it with shaking hands and holds it up.

Solaris is standing on the ground in front of her, making the sound. Red eyes ignited. The keeper's jaws are moving so rapidly that her mouth is only a blur.

"Help me."

Solaris is abruptly silent.

"Help me get ready. Give me your milk. Please!"

The keeper tilts her burnished head. Then abruptly, quick as can be seen, the big spider has straddled One-Who-Wanders and is making a loud grinding sound with her jaws, grinding more and more rapidly, making chittering chirping clicking ticking sounds that grow faster and higher in pitch, weaving a tapestry of synchronized pulses that lull both of them down to a place otherwise inaccessible.

When the sound reaches an unbearable intensity it suddenly stops. A long thin tongue unrolls out of the keeper's open jaws and stiffens then the big spider dips forward, touching her tongue to the soft spot at the base of One-Who-Wanders' throat, puncturing two little crescent-shaped holes.

The injection begins. She's on her back, straddled, mouth and eyes wide open as the keeper's milk is pumped and pumped and both of them are pulsing with it.

Then it's over. The tongue is retracted and One-Who-Wanders is catching her breath. A drop of blood swells out of each wound, hangs heavy then rolls down to stain the stone beneath her.

Solaris is making sound again. But the sound is different now, filled with sense. Looking up through roiling color One-Who-Wanders recognizes the keeper standing over her, straddling, gazing down, her jaws a blur creating sound that is now language.

Discomfort and disorientation from my milk will not last long. Tu Comprehende?

One-Who-Wanders is covered with perspiration, panting, lying on her back looking up at the keeper who is going in and out of focus. She nods.

...Si...

What my milk means to you will only become clear through time and as you remain true to your purpose. We are irrevocably bonded now, however, autonomous equals of different species who observe the boundaries and courtesies one creature owes another. Tu comprehende?

Looking up, the former Prime Researcher is finally able to focus on the keeper's face and million eyes.

...Si...

I must go tend other matters. You should have no trouble finding your way back to the grotto and the main chamber. If we do not meet before you go I wish you fullness of life, fidelity of purpose, love, and profound gratitude for every heartbeat. Walk your path well, child of the Refuge.

And the keeper is gone.

After a moment lying on her back blinking up, the former Prime Researcher touches the wounds at her throat and finds them numb. She checks her fingertips and sees blood. Then that hand falls away and she drifts down, down because it seems that nothing, not even her own blood, not even threat from Great City, can disturb the deep tranquility she feels.

***

Great City's tech-lab is a big round space defined by stainless steel and glass with a ceiling that is higher than most in The Heights. The lab looks even more spacious right now because it's been cleared of stewards for a demonstration attended only by the Presider, the heads of Technology and Engineering, and the interim head of Security, all gathered in front of a large glass cylinder that is standing on end. The cylinder contains a device recently acquired in a trade deal.

"Space State technology," Shen whispers reverently, tapping commands on her tech-pad so that what appears to be a lead brick floating in the center of the cylinder morphs into a cloud of white steam. "It's called a shape-changer. Space State first responders have been using these things for decades to probe unfriendly environments. We requested one as a curiosity and it came in just before they stopped delivering product."

Shen glances at the Presider, standing with his arms crossed, peering at the contents of the cylinder, waiting to be convinced. She taps keys and the white steam comes to life. What seems to have no form or substance of its own morphs into a glutinous worm then into to a drill-bit then into droplets of water and on and on and on while Whitaker waxes rhapsodic.

"There's no end to the forms the shape-changer can assume. Options can be continually added as situations demand. It can be liquid, viscous, vapor, solid, whatever is required. The device is electro-magnetically hinged and composed of millions of tiny cells, called nits."

Intrigued, the Presider steps closer. Lassiter moves with him, her pale gray eyes narrowed in admiration while a large part of her awareness is focused on the dynamics of the group. Whitaker joins them, leaning down.

"The beautiful thing is that unlike our drones, segments of a shape-changer function independently. As long as two nits, a positive and a neg-ative, are able to connect, they can, should the need arise, reproduce and fully reconstruct a new shape-changer in about 24 hours, depending on the conditions."

"What about transport?" Lassiter inquires. "How does the shape-changer get to point B?"

"On its own steam, as quickly as a drone." Shen smiles delicately.

"When can you deploy?" Reed looks back and forth from Technology to Engineering.

"As soon as we run a few more tests…"

"No more tests!" the Presider rarely raises his voice. "We don't have time for tests. Keep half of the shape-changer here so it can reproduce. Get the other half out there and make adjustments as you go. Again, how soon can you deploy?"

Technology and Engineering look at each other and blink.

"We'll have it out in half an hour," they both say.

"Good. Get busy." Paul Prescot Reed turns and, heels clicking on the hard floor, heads for his private office to meet with Efficiency concerning how to keep Great City functioning until the Space States come to their senses and start delivering product again.

***

"Solaris has discovered a colony of drones camped out directly overhead. We have to go. The Refuge is ready, are you?"

One-Who-Wanders wakes sitting up on her sleeping mat in the opalescent chamber, blinking at Isham who is standing in flickering wicklight at her feet wearing a loincloth and moccasins. His hair and beard are rolled up tight.

"We go now?" she touches the two fresh wounds at the base of her throat then gets to her feet.

"Yes. Gather all things human in here and bundle them in the robe. Bring the bundle and the sleeping mat to the main chamber as soon as possible," he turns to leave as she's pulling on her moccasins.

"Solaris gave me her milk."

"I know," his smile is quick then he's gone.

Hurrying, One-Who-Wanders spreads the robe out on the sleeping mat then gathers the jar of fresh wicks, the firestarter, the belt and pouches and puts them on the robe. She chugs down the rest of the water in a mug, plucks up a drying cloth and an almost empty pouch of roasted seeds and lays everything out on the robe then makes a tight bundle and sets it aside. She rolls up the sleeping mat, fastens it with the attached straps then gets to her feet, picks up bundle and bedroll and heads for the main chamber.

65

***

A length of wriggling wire emerges into mid-afternoon haze from the hatch that has remained open since the Prime Researcher left Great City. Gleaming, the string follows the maintenance rungs down, down and stops just above the soft surface where it hovers for a moment, throbbing with instructions.

Out at point B the gaggle of drones activates a stealth beacon. Even though the shape-changer has the coordinates, they're not taking any chances. The string explodes into a vaporous cloud. Then just as suddenly, it collapses down to something that resembles a dart and heads out with the speed of a bird returning to its nest.

***

Wearing headlamps, having left everything but their undershirts and moccasins behind for Solaris to conceal, Isham One-Who-Waits and One-Who-Wanders climb the steep tunnel behind the falls and finally emerge coughing and shivering in the chamber with the surface gear. The old man lights a wick and heads toward the rack of metal shelving. He extinguishes his headlamp, takes it off and gestures for hers.

"Remove your clothes."

Isham stows the headlamps then quickly disrobes. He tosses her a limp silvery garment then takes one for himself. Standing with his back to her, he steps into the garment and pulls it up with impressive facility until only his face is exposed. Behind him, One-Who-Wanders is having difficulty with the slippery fabric but after help from him they both look like fish with human faces.

He holds up a cylinder the size of a forearm with straps dangling from it and moves behind her. "This is a breather," he threads her arms through the straps. "A necessity on the surface." He adjusts the cylinder between her shoulder blades and fastens the harness across her chest then brings the attached facemask up and fastens it in place, making certain the seal is secure.

"Breathe."

She does. The mechanical hissing sound is disconcerting. But everything is bright and clear. No need for the wick. And she's stopped coughing.

Isham is standing in front of her again wearing his own breather. Hands on either side of her face, he's adjusting the technology imbedded in her mask, causing colored blips and lines and graphs to pulse unobtrusively down one side of the plate of smartglass that covers without obstructing her view. He steps closer and peers at her, his face ghosted behind his own mask.

"There's a sustenance tube near your mouth," his voice is quite clear on the tiny speakers in the facemask. "Sip judiciously so the suit can keep up with your need."

He adjusts the controls around her face. A faint red line appears, vertically bisecting the mask, drifting left and right as she turns her head.

"The red line is your compass. Keep it directly in front of you as much as possible. Avoid ridges. Hug valleys. The cloak is your main shield. Do not remove it for any reason."

Isham drops a substantial garment across her shoulders and fastens it all the way down then carefully closes the hood around her facemask. He helps her with gauntlets that reach almost to her elbows and she's completely covered, shielded and pleasantly warm.

"Come."

He gathers and drops the long backend of her cloak over her arm. Then, without putting on a cloak of his own, he heads toward a different tunnel than the one he used before. It takes several strides for him to realize she hasn't followed. He turns to see her rooted to the ground, standing in front of the shelves of gear.

"We're not going together," she whispers.

"That's correct," he nods. "I'd hoped to part properly but Solaris and I agreed there may not be time. Source willing, I'll head after you soon. First, Great City must be lured away from the Refuge."

"And Solaris?"

"This is her home. She chooses to stay and protect it as long as possible."

That said, One-Who-Waits turns and heads on into the tunnel at a brisk pace. Unhappy, she follows. After a few turns they arrive at a metal door in the stone. He touches one side of the door and it spirals open to reveal a small brightly lit chamber full of shiny technology –

not the same chamber he used before.

One-Who-Wanders follows him in and stops. Isham kneels in front of her with a pair of stubby skis that fasten onto her boots. "You may find these awkward at first but without them your progress will be slow." Isham stands and clasps her shoulders.

"There are no words..." She feels an urge to speak but doesn't know what to say.

"Or time for them," he interrupts. "Stay with Source."

Before she can say anything One-Who-Waits picks up a control-wand. Everything goes dark. A door spirals open directly in front of her.

Startled by afternoon glare until the facemask adjusts, she has no time to form a thought before the gentle pressure of his hand on the small of her back propels her forward. She steps onto the surface awkwardly because of the skis. The door spirals closed behind her.

One-Who-Wanders is outside and the portal is gone – she heard it close through her technology. There's no going back no matter how much she craves the familiar. The path is irreversible.

Through her facemask she sees on either side two dunes rising high, their ridges softened by haze. She finds the faint red line and steadies it in front of her nose. Then, breathing loud mechanical hisses, unaccustomed to the bulk of the gear and the feel of the skis, she starts out, following the red line along the valley heading north and east. In a few steps she rounds a shoulder of dune and disappears while inside the portal Isham is standing very still, face raised, eyes closed.

My love?

***

Beneath the surface some distance north and east of the Refuge an old woman stirs in her sleep. Lying on her side with a child pressed against the small of her back, she opens eyes that are milky white and sightless thought it's immediately clear that the woman sees everything.

Isham?

She blinks, wide-awake in a dim chamber that is a resting place on the way elsewhere. Half a dozen others in this group are curled up here and there, snoring softly while their companions are scattered standing watch. Two widely spaced wicks provide the only illumination while people are asleep. The old woman sits up, careful not to disturb the child.

Isham?

Something has happened, beloved. I must close the Refuge. A new-born from Great City is on the way alone. Female. I'm heading south to cause confusion. Source willing I'll come around the eastern way and we'll be together soon.

Aye, comprehende. Source willing in all things, heartmate.

Then he's gone from her awareness.

The old woman rubs her broad, nut-brown face and gets to her feet. Short and sturdy, she puts on plain brown breeches, heavy knee socks and ankle boots. Her hair is white and kinky haloing her head.

At the back of the chamber a tall man wearing a loincloth stirs then stands and stretches. He lights a wick and dresses quietly, pulling on a silvery undersuit, leaving the headpiece back and his waist-length red hair free. He laces boots up over his ankles, slings on a heavily loaded pack and adjusts the straps. Then he goes to the old woman and blessings are exchanged without sound.

Source be with you.

And also with you.

He leans down for an exchange of kisses then moves quickly, silently to the mouth of the cave and is gone. Four adolescents are now up and dressed, slinging on packs. They go to the old woman for blessing then head out single file after the man, displaying the same quiet quickness.

***

One-Who-Wanders is on the surface moving undetected farther north and east away from Great City and starting to get the hang of the skis as the smudge of sun lowers beneath the high horizon, turning the sky lavender for a second.

Miles behind her the shape-changer crests the ridge of a dune and dips down into the valley where point B is surrounded by a perfect circle of six drones, all planted butt-first in the ash, attentive for something to transmit back to the Security Primes in Great City. The shape-changer slowly descends to the center of the circle of drones and hovers several feet above the ground for a moment, lightly stirring the ash. Then it morphs into a drill-bit, descends the last few feet and disappears.

Everything is the same again. The drones, for all their stealth vigilance, have missed the one thing sought.

***

The announcement was made early this afternoon. Karin Lassiter Kohl, known by some as the Assassin, is officially Great City's new head of Security. She has moved into the quarters on Council Row that once belonged to George Biggs Boltin. It seems the Presider took note when low-value citizen-unit number 4 of 6 survived the removal of her monitor suit. It doesn't matter that she's inert and on a respirator. Technically, she's alive.

Lassiter didn't take long to get a team of citizen-maids and Maint-enance workers scouring and hauling and transforming her new quarters. Stripped of all signs of its former occupant, the head of Security's rooms have been transformed by more than just a coat of cool gray paint. The living room is now a gym complete with mirrors, floor space for aerobics, racks of free weights plus various machines positioned to face a wallscreen that is fed from the office so she can work while working out.

The kitchen has been stocked to her specifications with blenders and mixers and special ingredients because she rarely eats solid food, preferring concoctions made by her personal citizen-unit. The bathroom now includes a dry sauna and a steam cabinet. The bedroom is the treatment room where massage and other non-surgical techniques including sex are employed to keep her young and supple.

The office has also been transformed. The big desk and prestige-chair have been removed and replaced by the zero-gravity chaise she uses for sleep. A small table and chair for meals are near the control panel. Most important, the circular floor-to-ceiling wallscreen is finally arranged the way she wants it: ablaze 360 degrees with surveillance files, each a real-time window into one of the many worlds within the world that is Great City.

One section of wallscreen contains live feed of the interior of the structure – all locations from all angles. Through this section of

70

screens Lassiter has access to citizen-units and stewards, excluding only council members and the Presider. Another section contains live feed of the exterior of the structure, top to bottom. Still another contains satellite feed of the entire globe. Fate not yet decided, George Biggs Boltin has his own screen, its prominence serving to remind Lassiter what happens to the unprepared. Then there are four special screens, one for each of the Space State ambassadors.

Lassiter likes to work standing in the center of the room, where she is now, hands on hips, crisp and cool in her dove gray tunic and trousers, studying a real-time animated graphic of the shape-changer huffing its way down through ash toward stone. So far nothing of interest has been found but then again the device has just started its journey. The feed is direct from Technology. If something happens, she'll be in informed. That gives her a bit of time to explore what Boltin was ignoring.

Using her tech-wand, Lassiter dims the shape-changer then turns to and opens surveillance files on the ambassadors from the Space States, neglected singly and as a group since they got here. An official portrait masks each window, indicating that the ambassadors are in closed session with the Presider and his team consisting of Trade and Archives. She can eavesdrop or not but again knows she'll be flagged if needed and decides to tend to something else.

"Jerrod?" she turns to him.

"Here, mam."

Lassiter's personal citizen-unit is standing in the threshold that leads to the rest of her new quarters. A top-of-the-line nearly perfect human specimen, he serves as her assistant, masseur, trainer and maid. He cost more than she could afford at the time but has made her highly focused life easier by tending to what she doesn't care about but can't let slide. His monitor suit is a special fabric called TruFit and a special hue called Brazilian Tan. His maleness is unmistakable and impressive, always slightly tumescent. Jerrod's one flaw is his voice, minimally distorted and rendered hollow by filters that cause him to sometimes purr, sometimes slur.

"Transfer the feed on the ambassadors into the gym so I can study their files," she unzips her dove gray tunic, removes it and hands it to him. "I want a cardio workout on the floor followed by a massage, shower and half a protein shake."

"Yes, mam." Jerrod moves to the control panel to switch the feed on the ambassadors into the gym. Then he heads down the hall followed by Lassiter who has kicked off her shoes, unzipped her trousers and is wearing a skintight tanktop and briefs the color of water to another of her extraordinarily disciplined workouts because more than anything she must never look older than thirty-five.

***

Isham One-Who-Waits returned to the main chamber of the Refuge and has just now finished restoring it to its natural state. Ready to head south, the old man is wearing the silvery skinsuit, soft boots, a big backpack and, around his neck, the little red bag containing One-Who-Wanders' name-stone, which must not fall into the wrong hands.

On her way to seal the kitchen alcove, Solaris skitters into the main chamber from the grotto and stops abruptly. She's thinner now, depleted from spinning so much toxic web and still not done. Chittering softly, she lumbers up onto a boulder and looks Isham directly in the eye.

It's time to say goodbye. They've done it before on sensing a prolonged spell of silence from the calling-dream. But this is different.

Isham takes the bag from around his neck and gives it to Solaris who receives it in furry paws, brings it to her mouth and runs her long tongue around it as though tasting.

"Keep it safe with the other records."

The big spider nods then turns multifaceted red eyes on her friend of so many years. Grinding her jaws she generates a humming sound that grows louder and louder. Then a soft explosion heard only by One-Who-Waits is followed by what sounds like tropical rain and, eyes closed, Isham rides the rhythms of what is not farewell but more like warnings and instructions each to the other concerning the Refuge and how to protect it. Then the sound stops.

One-Who-Waits opens his eyes and strokes the keeper's back. He adjusts the straps on his pack to balance the load for a long journey south beneath the surface. Then without looking back he exits the main chamber through the tunnel in the sleeping alcove and heads toward the southern boundary of the Refuge, moving as fast as he can.

72

***

After all these centuries of trade the Space States have learned very little about Great City. It's a closed society. In all this time Space Staters have not been able to determine even such a basic thing as Great City's population.

Through the years, Space State ambassadors have consistently estimated that there are 4,000 or so stewards in The Heights and several dozen up on the transfer station. But that doesn't jibe with centuries of purchase orders indicating that the population of Great City has to be at least 20,000, maybe more.

Inquiries about this discrepancy have been met with claims of sovereignty, as have all requests by ambassadors to see the infrastructure or meet the workers of Great City. Indeed, the council will not even grant permission for the Space States to land anywhere on earth for archeological purposes, stating that such an infringement would be considered an act of war.

So closed is Great City that, amazingly, in all this time there has been no intermingling of the two populations. Where one would expect curiosity there has been none on the part of the stewards. In generations of face-to-face trade negotiations there has not been one tryst or act of treachery. Repeated invitations for stewards to visit one of the mother ships have been turned down. No steward has ever defected or been beyond the transfer station.

And as far as is known, in all this time no one from the Space States has been below The Heights of Great City. No Space Stater has ever seen or even heard of a citizen-unit.

***

Not willing to stop though her legs and lungs were on fire, One-Who-Wanders kept moving undetected north and east away from Great City until midnight when her facemask suddenly went dark and she could no longer see the ghosted-green dunes or the vertical red line that is her polestar or the fuzzy blur of moon hanging high in the haze. The facemask warned her several times, flashing bright red letters.

73

TIME TO STOP!

She ignored the warnings because the thought of stopping, being alone in all that desolation whipped her on. She needed to stay awake, keep moving, hear the labored hisses of her own breathing because the farther away she got from the Refuge and Isham One-Who-Waits and the keeper, Solaris, the more she found herself haunted by what was destroyed so long ago, gone now because the ancients were smart but not wise.

So the facemask went dark and she was forced to rest. Unable to do anything else, she sank to her knees and toppled to one side curled up in the cloak, her sleep twitchy because of muscle cramps.

Third Gate – Connection

Dull black and triangular in shape, H-V cruiser Mohawk from S.S. Hope bursts out of darkness on a parabolic approach to what resembles a furious pinwheel in the night. The crew and elite first responders on board are in the shielding vault, encased in tons of super-lead and locked in chem.sleep because the threading process is for technology alone. Similar cruisers, one each from S.S. Columbus, S.S. Ulysses and S.S. Friendship are standing by their respective wormholes but will not thread until the first responders on Mohawk have completed their reconnaissance mission.

The cruiser's position is sent to Command Ship Phoenix, stationed four wormholes away, and Mohawk is cleared to proceed with dispatch. The bulbous velocity-gatherer is reeled in and clamped to the stern. The delta wings are furled to embrace the hull and serve as armor. Then counter-thrusters in the nose are ignited and, straining against gravitational pull that would crush the ship to nothing but for human cleverness, the cruiser moves into position at the window-of-commitment to face what is now a blinding funnel of distorted light, a raging rapids of light, light spun, churned, compressed and sucked into the dot of hyper-void that is a wormhole.

The ship is at the outer edge of sustainability and vibrating fiercely when the velocity-gatherer ignites and is instantly roiling with a contained thermo-nuclear reaction that dwarfs anything possible before the great collapse. The counter-thrusters are extinguished as all that energy is released in a focused blast lasting no longer than a fraction of an instant. And H-V cruiser Mohawk is elsewhere.

***

Solaris is racing back and forth across the opening of a big vertical fissure that now contains items from the main chamber: the cushions, the rolled up rug, wicks and their globes, all those things. When the fissure is sealed the big spider climbs down to the ground, heads off for her next task and suddenly stops, alerted by something indefinite.

Head raised tilting this way and that, she turns around listening. She chitters softly. She skitters forward half a dozen steps then stops. Listening, she extends her tongue, waves it around and finally catches the scent again. She charges through the tunnel into the grotto – way down and directly beneath point B.

The keeper stops and listens, bobbing her head up and down. She rubs her two paws together miser-like then holds them up and out, sensing a chemical scent not native to the Refuge. Alarmed, she looks around with multifaceted red eyes, sees a multifaceted world devoid of human signs, scrubbed clean and none too soon because something wicked has indeed arrived.

What?

Where?

Sound.

From overhead, coming closer.

Grinding.

Solaris backs into the darkest of the dark. She filters out the grotto's water sounds and hears it again.

What?

Overhead.

Whirring.

Tongue out tasting the air, Solaris presses herself against the stone and looks up, frozen as something long and thin that smells like metal pierces the ceiling then withdraws back through the tiny hole whence it came.

Silence.

Nothing happens for a moment. Then a spritz of neon-blue vapor pours out of the hole and drifts down almost to the floor of the chamber. Hovering like a thin little cloud, the vapor begins to explore, roaming slowly around the chamber, sniffing, curious.

Drawn to heat, it eventually locates Solaris and approaches slowly to touch tentatively then withdraw and analyze. Puzzled, the vapor returns and winds hissing around the big spider from toes to nose before withdrawing again to analyze more data. Finally, confused and curious, the vapor floats up and – snap! – is suddenly no longer mist but now solid, a scalpel reaching in for a slice of tissue and that's when the keeper strikes.

Whip-quick, Solaris throws a blanket of deadly web around the device, spins it round and round into an ever-tighter ball then injects it with poison from her tongue. Clutching her trophy she rushes down, down through tunnels and chambers to the acid well where she tosses the intruder into the long shaft, waits to hear the splash then freezes, head up, listening again, flicking her tongue, knowing this is just the beginning but unable to discern anything else, most certainly not the few male and female nits hiding in plain sight back up in the grotto.

***

"WHAT WAS THAT?!" Engineering jumps as alarms go off in the tech-lab. "I thought the bio-form was supposed to be human!"

"IT IS!" Wide-eyed, Shen looks helplessly at her mentor then they both lean into the big monitor on the desk in her glass-enclosed office beyond which both of their crews are suddenly running back and forth, trying to figure out what happened to the shape-changer with no way to do so because the feed has gone dark.

"What happened, Magrit?"

Great City's head of Technology looks at Whitaker, sees fear in his eyes and makes a decision. Moving quickly she pulls out her keyboard and types furious commands to her technology, patching a long section of the shape-changer's boring descent into a loop and getting ready to feed it to the Presider and the head of Security to cover its sudden disappearance.

"What are you doing?!" Whitaker hisses.

"Giving us time to try and figure out what happened to the shape-changer without Lassiter crawling all over us claiming that we're the cause of this particular failure."

"Are you insane?" but for the crews working outside of her glass office Whitaker would physically restrain her. "What if one of them is monitoring the shape-changer right now?! It's a capital crime too tamper with data critical to the well-being of Great City!"

"It's been a long, boring descent, Malcolm. Unless one of them was actually paying attention when the shape-changer went dark they'll see the loop and assume the little guy is still grinding his way through stone, trying to find something interesting. Or they'll call and ask what happened." Ignoring him and moving fast, Shen overrides live-feed for the Presider and the head of Security and patches the loop on through.

"Magrit!" Whitaker hisses, shielding the monitor, glancing around at the stewards outside the office, here for hours, too, intently focused on the task of deploying the shape-changer and unaware that the head of Technology has just placed them all in jeopardy. "You are committing a crime," his voice is barely audible.

She swivels around and looks up at him, brings joined hands to her face, gathers her thoughts then blinks little girl eyes and speaks barely moving her mouth.

"I'm taking the time to explain because you were my mentor. But we're going to do this my way."

"Do what?"

"Survive. I am not going to let the Lassiter bring us down, Malcolm. She's a blamer. I intend to survive what seems to get worse the more we try to fix or understand it. You know very well that her finger of blame is going to be pointed at someone every step of the way. But it's not going to be pointed at me. And if you're careful, it won't be pointed at you, either."

Whitaker's eyes are small and blue and tired. As an engineer he knows the importance of inflexible rules and principles and is uncomfortable straying beyond them. But she's right about Lassiter. Nodding ever so slightly, the oldest member of the council sinks back down in his chair.

"Five minutes, no more."

She nods, already focused.

"I'm going to collate what we have from when the shape-changer broke through the ceiling and started to explore the cavern," she furiously taps at her controls. "I want to know what that thing was," she leans into her screen. "See if you can find any traces of nits, male and female, to reconstitute the shape-changer."

Thus the two of them take a few bracketed moments to try and get a sense of what's real, what they've got to work with. But there's nothing in the databanks with which to compare whatever it was that destroyed the shape-changer. And their technology is crude in comparison to the Space States. Whatever little heartbeats may or may not be out there in the dark remain inaudible.

***

Karin Lassiter Kohl is standing in the middle of her office surrounded by illumined screens, studying one in particular as she's been doing off and on all night. Now barefoot, platinum-colored hair freshly brushed and gleaming, wearing a satiny pearl-gray nightshirt and ready for an hour's sleep, she's taking a final look at the ambassador from S.S. Hope, unaware that a screen behind her just went dark for an instant then flared back to life with Shen's loop of the shape-changer's descent.

Curious, Lassiter enlarges the screen of interest so it eclipses all the others, leaving her in semi-darkness and surrounded by life-sized real-time feed from ambassador Davenport Baxter's bedroom. He's on the bed, naked, tangled in the sheets, damp with perspiration and sleeping fitfully after a long night's restlessness. Her interest in him does not register to her as anything extraordinary – even when she steps closer and studies the image of a hip she'd like to touch – because stewards early on learn the disadvantages of feeling and Lassiter is a master at not doing so.

Groaning softly, Dav Baxter wakes, turns over and works his way to the edge of the bed. He sits. Of a sudden, his life-size image and Lassiter are blinking face-to-face causing her to stumble back, surprised by his ocean-blue eyes and hair the color of autumn.

He leans over, head in hands, wide awake and exhausted because he's not supposed to be here but on his way back to S.S. Hope because his three year tour of service to the common is complete. But everything has gone wrong. Now he's stuck here indefinitely.

Baxter yanks the blanket off the bed, wraps it around his shoulders and pads into the front room where he collapses on the couch, stunned by the turn of events. He pulls a chip out of his memory-book, loads it in the play-dock and turns it on. As long as he's feeling miserable he might as well go all the way.

Music flares and continues throughout, his favorite ancient slow jazz, brushed drums, cool bass, a few melodic tones on synthesizer, very simple. He lowers the volume. The word, "PILAR", spirals around the room in different neon colors then fades and disappears. The projector throws the first hologram image onto the space in front of him and directly behind Lassiter who turns and follows his gaze to see a young woman the color of amber standing almost real and life-size in Baxter's bedroom and Lassiter's office.

Who?

Sooty and sweaty yet sexy enough for a boiler room calendar. Head shaved, bandage across one eyebrow, she's wearing work boots, cargo pants and a tight tank top with SGT. MEZON in orange letters across her chest. A belt heavy with gear hangs from a cocked hip. The grin is infectious and as the image rotates Pilar Mezon moves her helmet to the other hand and re-cocks her hip. That image fades to be replaced by more as Dav Baxter sinks down to the floor and leans back against the couch, exhausted.

"Expect the unexpected," she told him laughing when they first met in the TinderBox Bar. He knew of her from news flashes and spotted her wearing civilian clothes, sitting alone at a table when she was coming off of a short medical leave. He wanted to thank her for her service so he approached and looked down as she looked up and Dav knew something was happening to him and it had to do with her though it was commonly understood she had no interest in men, at least not romantically though she *was* chemically juiced up that night and sending out pheromones to attract one such as himself.

Now thirteen years later wrapped in a blanket and unable to sleep, stuck in Great City's Heights indefinitely because there seems to be no compromise on the issue of trade and who sets prices, Dav Baxter is watching a different image of Pilar in summer tans, showing off the blue-black shadow of a new brushcut, her skin the color of sunlit honey, her eyes startling sea-green and almond shaped flashing on either side of an oft broken nose.

"I never promise more than I can deliver," she told him that night after they'd stared at each other for a while him standing her sitting. She gestured for him to join her and he could only stand there staring down unable to respond and her looking up full of sizzling mischief with a gold ring hugging the top of one ear and he couldn't sit or walk away but stood there knowing she was nitro for a regular fellow like him. So being sensible and scientific he finally found his voice and thanked her for her service again and tried to walk away. She laughed and downed her tall glass of HeavyWater and him standing there on fire from her green eyes talking to himself: run, fool.

She stood – shorter than Dav by half a head but heavier and more densely muscled. She pulled her card from her pocket and stuck it in the slot to pay for her drink. Then she playfully bumped his thigh with her ass.

"I have a proposition." She explained it before they were out the door.

And it being so simple he acquiesced.

How could he not?

They went to her place, high up on the outer rim of S.S. Hope with a view of eternity. "One night only," she whispered, pulling off his shirt, appreciating his pale runner's body. And of course it wasn't that simple. Nothing is simple when humans go belly-to-belly.

Her place was neat and clean, muted colors, metal and glass, sharp corners and sudden vistas. She led him by the hand, wasting no time, him glad of that, seeing no images on the walls other than a few spectacular holos anyone can buy, of explosions, abysses, meteor-storms, crashes, all made famous by elite first responders who go in and come back with whatever needs retrieving. Nor did Dav Baxter see signs that someone else might also live here or visit frequently. Then there was no more looking around because they were busy, with her being surprised by his energy and pleased by his stamina and him being transformed by the refiner's fire of her heat.

"I like you," she whispered once during a pause. "If this takes and you don't ever try to change me not even a little bit maybe we can figure out how to share some of our equal time with the kid. You know. Both parents." She raised her head from his chest and looked at him with almost neon green eyes. "You in?"

How could he not be?

So Dav Baxter took the night Pilar Mezon offered and hasn't touched her since except in friendship – or mooned or brooded about it. That was the deal. Still, he's been unable to want much of anything else ever since. Other women, and a few men, have been sincere, helpful, witty and attractive, all good things but not compelling. They haven't rendered him helpless with hope, tears or loneliness. They haven't been able to keep him coming back
over and over for thirteen years when he could easily have done his half of the parenting without ever seeing her again.

Early in the morning Pilar took a quick shower and, gear clanking over her shoulder, pecked him on the cheek and left to report for duty only to be furloughed and shuttled back to S.S. Hope as soon as she showed. Five months later Ero was born.

Lassiter studies an image of Pilar standing naked in profile, compact and athletic, head back, laughing, one muscular arm supporting her very advanced pregnancy, the other covering full breasts. Then there's Pilar demurely nursing the child, looking up uncharacteristically shy. Pilar in hospital a year later, lots of bandages, one leg and her neck in traction, pins sticking out of an elbow, grinning like a boy. Then she's in dress whites using a cane and he's off to one side with little Ero in his arms and they're pretending to be a family as the Admiral at that time draped her neck with the Medal of Valor and now the boy has turned out to be just like the mother who craves risk.

The alarm goes off in the bedroom, several measures of Bach, a slow second movement to wake him gently. Dav Baxter pops the chip out of the play-dock and puts it back where it belongs in his memory-book. Then he gets to his feet, pads into the bedroom, turns off the alarm and tosses the blanket on the bed.

Naked, pale and wiry, covered with freckles and golden hairs, he pulls on a pair of pale blue shorts and a matching singlet that fit like water. "S.S. HOPE" is in white flash-script on his chest. He straps on white running shoes that are little more than soles then exits his guest suite, passing doors to the other ambassadors' suites on his way through the big double doors at the end of the hall and out into the public square, empty because of the early hour.

Baxter trots loosey-goosey across the square to an archway announcing an entrance to Liberty Park where he intends to run ten miles every morning before breakfast. He stops to stretch at the park's entrance then heads out alone on the half-illuminated trail through dusty imitations of the ancient natural world.

That leaves Lassiter standing in the middle of her office watching Dav Baxter run circles around her like a stallion on a lead. His breathing is soft and even. His steps are light and sure. She has forgotten the need for an hour's sleep.

***

"...ZZZZZZZZZZZZZZZZZZZZZZZZZZZZZZZZZZZZZZ..."

The sound is annoying. One-Who-Wanders opens her eyes, yanked from sleep to awareness. Everything is green. The alarm stops and she can hear the agitated hiss of her breathing. She lifts her head, knows where she is and why.

Moving ignites soreness and she sits with difficulty. She sucks on her sustenance tube and looks around, blinking at dunes. Overhead, the haze is turning wooly green and a ghost of sun begins its upward climb. She gets to her feet and stands leaning over, hands on knees, already exhausted.

It's time to go on.

She straightens up to find the vertical red line and heads out as the sky lightens, moving with a kind of shuffle that is both walking and skiing, her legs and lungs already on fire. Nothing matters but the next step, think only of that, she tells herself, somehow knowing not to dwell on the fact that she is traversing a realm where life is no longer welcome and if she stops the ash will rise up and permanently embrace her, too.

***

Stewards of Great City are bred from Founders' genes, gestated in special citizen-units and birthed in a nursery located between The Heights and the lane. Every steward is a composite of two of the several dozen Founders and carries two surnames of equal weight (Prescot Reed, Lassiter Kohl, Abram Shen) indicating the particular lines from which that person is derived – given names being randomly assigned from a list of those available. From birth on, the only point of being is stewardship of Great City through advancement and eventual membership on the council with the supreme perk of admittance to Founders' Hall.

Constant attention from citizen maintenance-units cannot erase the effects of age on Founders' Hall or rub luster into what is now dingy. That said, the council chambers are large and round with a low ceiling and big double entry doors at the rear then a wide expanse of carpeted floor in the center of which is a large arc of dais with ten equally spaced impressive desks and ten flags of office and ten prestige chairs facing the Presider's dais with its even more impressive desk, chair and flag of office.

The chambers are dimly lit by individual brassy beams that shine down through the false ceiling – a suspended and gilded seal of state – onto each of the ten desks belonging to those responsible for the functions of Great City. Trade, Engineering, Technology, Archives, Medicine, Human Resources, Security, Services, Maintenance, and Efficiency are all present, working at their tech-pads or standing and talking quietly.

They wear plain tailored tunics and trousers in solid colors that range from black and gray to dark greens and blues or browns. Lassiter, attending her first council meeting, is wearing pale gray and sitting alone at what used to be Boltin's desk, studying data on her tech-pad, trying to eavesdrop on Shen and Whitaker who are conferring just out

84

of ear-shot.

With no fanfare, the Presider enters the hall from an inconspicuous door behind his desk. The chamber is immediately quiet as council members stow tech-pads and return to their seats. Wearing his usual slate gray and looking grim, Reed steps up onto his dais and sits ramrod straight, not hiding his unhappiness that a regularly scheduled morning council meeting was delayed two hours to give Shen and Whitaker time to figure out what happened to the shape-changer and they still don't know because they're having trouble accepting data which indicates that the attacking bio-form is non-mammalian, probably an invertebrate and quite large.

"To begin," Reed wastes no time, "let me reiterate that Great City's position on the manner in which prices are set for product has not and will not change. The council has repeatedly endorsed me on this and I'm confident that all stewards stand behind us on an issue that has been decided and will not be un-decided or re-decided," he looks at them stony-faced and raises his hand as though swearing an oath. "So affirmed."

The council members repeat, "so affirmed," a few without conviction, Reed notes.

"By stopping deliveries, the Space States have in effect declared war on Great City. In response, as of this morning all product from the archives of the ancients has been taken off the market, even catalogs. Nothing is available. Nothing will be available until after shipments resume from all four Space States. In that regard I've made several decisions without consultation that I'm confident you will affirm." Reed nails each of them with a hawk's glare.

"First, I would like to thank the heads of Trade and Archives for trying but as they have failed they are being re-assigned effective immediately to work on the lane in non-managerial positions." Reed looks at the two men, the thinnest smile on his lips. "This is not a permanent termination. You may try for advancement in good time but now you must leave Founders' Hall."

Heads turn as the two men stand and step down off of the back of the dais. Eyes down, former Trade and Archives exit through the tall double doors. Reed doesn't wait for the air to settle before going on.

"For the time being, I'll handle negotiations myself and will entertain no lobbying for their replacements. Which brings us to a matter of gravest importance that Efficiency is going to walk you through while I'm with the ambassadors for the morning session." Reed looks at the remaining eight council members. "As of now, Great City is on Half Measures."

First there's shocked silence, faces frozen stupid looking at the Presider. Then it breaks and murmured consternation disturbs the usual decorum on the council-dais. Tech-pads are brought forth, fearful glances exchanged. Reed, of course, misses nothing.

"Benit will walk you through specific measures each of you will need to put into effect immediately – exceptions being Technology, Engineering and Security, given special dispensation for the defense of Great City. What this means is that there are now limits where previously there were none. For the indefinite future all we have is what's on stock here and what we have been feverishly bringing down from the transfer station and, of course, what we're able to generate ourselves.

"By noon I want a report from each of you on Benit's desk detailing how you're going to suck every ounce of dead air out of your function. And before tomorrow morning's council meeting I'll want to know what further cuts you can make – and rest assured there will be further cuts. Benit will collate those reports for a full-picture that will be in your queues as soon as I sign off on it. Expect to be scheduled for a meeting with him sometime today. In addition, I am making a formal request of the council for an advisory memo concerning the disposition of the former head of Security whose name shall be purged from Great City and will not again cross my lips. For the sake of morale I'd like to act on that as soon as possible. I suggest something terminal."

Heads nod as Reed steps down and exits the council chambers through the door behind his dais. A moment's stunned silence follows his departure. Then Great City's head of Efficiency stands, looks down at his tech-pad and clears his throat.

"I've forwarded Great City's updated inventory to each of you." Not yet middle age, Jonathan Hale Benit is refined and precise, a tall crane of a fellow whose voice is high and thin. "The Presider wants it checked against what each of you actually has in store."

It's going to be a long meeting.

***

86

Beneath the surface a mile directly east of Great City, Isham One-Who-Waits slings off his pack, removes the headlamp and stands, eyes closed, face raised, listening because Solaris has been tapping at his awareness for some time now. He's not surprised the Refuge has been penetrated, the intruder caught and disposed of. They agree that this is probably not the end of it but since the best thing he can do is what he's planning to do, Isham blesses his old friend and breaks the connection.

One-Who-Waits puts on surface gear, opens the portal, exits and closes it behind. He scrambles up the steep shoulder of a dune into high sun and haze. At the ridge, he opens and lifts up his cloak to stand like a warrior against the ruined sky with the rusty mass of Great City directly in front of him.

Radiating signals, he counts under his breath. When he's been exposed long enough Isham drops and fastens the cloak then scrambles down the dune to the portal. Inside, he removes most of the surface gear and takes off through a maze of narrow cavities that resemble the laciness of bone marrow.

***

"…So I'll be bringing crates of fresh summer vegetables from crops here in agri-barn Shenandoah where I work with a really great team of mad scientists. Just kidding." A hologram Dav Baxter touches the hologram waist-high crops as he walks down the rows. "Corn, red peppers, cucumbers, beans, zucchini, different kinds of lettuce. Not enough to last three years, of course. That's a long time. I'll miss it here…"

Something about his voice, the accent and reedy timbre of his voice causes generalized heat and anxiety that have nothing to do with the strenuous cardio workout Great City's head of Security just finished. Wearing a white sleeveless leotard and nothing else, Lassiter's chalky skin is slightly flushed. Her platinum hair is fastened atop her head while stray wisps cling to her neck and face. She's standing in the middle of her ice blue kitchen, sipping a concoction whipped up by Jerrod and studying the hologram floating in the middle of the larger room that is now the gym.

This particular file is a sort of holographic calling card each ambas-sador brings by way of personal introduction to the stewards of Great City who couldn't care less. Dav Baxter chose to speak from where he works, out in agri-barn Shenandoah, wearing baggy pants and a flowing shirt, breeze ruffling his hair, insects buzzing around him as he strolls beneath an artificial sun through rows of bright harvest-ready vegetables.

"...But three years isn't forever. Hopefully one day I'll be back, coordinating the barn again, planting and growing and harvesting more food for Space Staters and the people of Great City. I'm looking forward to seeing earth and meeting all of you. And getting back here."

The holo-image fades. Lassiter takes the card out of the projector and is turning to Baxter's real-time live-feed screen and him running again when the Security Primes interrupt.

"BIO-FORM! BIO-FORM!" the sound fills her private quarters.

"What?!" Lassiter spins out of the kitchen, down the hall to her office and the appropriate section of screens. "Talk to me, what happened?!"

"Satellites picked up a heat-reading that lasted nine seconds then stopped. Originating 1 mile directly east of Great City."

"Only one signature?"

"Affirmative."

"That's it?" Lassiter glances up at George Biggs Boltin's screen, sees him vomiting.

"Plus the bio-form was human and male."

"Where is he now?" Utterly focused on the critical event unfolding in front of her, Lassiter misses something of critical importance on a different screen right behind her.

***

Running is easier on S.S. Hope than in Great City. Gravity is the same, earth Gs, but there, on the perimeter-paths, Dav Baxter can see stars, sometimes comets, planet-rise, gaseous clouds, blinding borealis-flares plus shuttles drifting back and forth outside and maintenance crews cleaning or repairing. And if he's on one of the inner rims there are views into libraries, museums, stadiums, parks, classrooms, conference rooms, engine rooms, meeting halls, transport hubs, the command center and, best of all, real flora almost everywhere, cleansing and sweetening the air.

By way of contrast, Liberty Park is a dreary place, usually empty but for the occasional tired looking older steward on the occasional bench, taking a break from what seems to be an extraordinary amount of pressure on all of them lately. No matter. Liberty Park is the only place to run in Great City and that's what marathoners do. They run.

Dr. Davenport Baxter is a marathoner. So he runs. Every day. It's a need, especially when he's cooped up indefinitely like now.

Strides long and strong, breathing easy, he settles into the groove of an indefinitely sustainable six minute mile. As is his habit here in The Heights, he scans discretely, always looking for a peek behind Great City's veil. He's entering dusty imitation aspen grove when the park's illumination lurches noisily down to half its normal level. Dav slows to a trot then stops, alone on the path. He looks around, puzzled.

"Attention stewards and guests of Great City," the tech-voice is female and seductive. "Liberty Park is being closed for repairs and will remain closed until further notice. Please leave the area now. Exits will remain clearly marked until all sections are clear."

Hands on hips, Dav Baxter is walking in a tight circle as the illumination dims gradually, giving whoever might be here time to dash out of the park. He's about to obey the order when he notices a faint red glow just above eye-level off the path to his right through moldy diorama, where the outer wall of The Heights ought to be.

Moving fast, hands out in the dark Baxter approaches red glow that becomes the word MAINTENANCE. His fingers touch a wall. He gropes, feels a doorframe and handle, turns the handle, eases the door open a sliver, peers out then opens it wider and stands gawking at the enormity of dimly lit space that separates the two dome skins and is laced with catwalks, platforms, metal stairways and ladders, banks of technology and bundles of pipe, all stretching from side to side and up and down and around until obscured by the curve.

Dav's attention is drawn to a platform on a lower level across the chasm and he's even more astonished by half a dozen bright orange people, even their hands and faces. They seem to be working, turning knobs and pulling levers, hauling things. Then Dav Baxter jerks back and stays hidden in shadow because someone has come silently along the catwalk on the other side of the wall and is standing in the open

89

doorway.

An orange person. Close enough to touch. Checking the door. Trying to understand why it's open when it should be closed. Not attending anything else because not programmed to discern someone pressed against the wall just inside within easy reach.

Frozen, wide-eyed, Baxter studies the featureless orange person who reaches in for the handle and draws the door closed. He counts to three then rushes back to the path immediately across which is an exit from the park and he's out. It being hopeless for a Space Stater to go unnoticed by stewards in The Heights, Baxter explores his forehead with tentative fingertips, feigning slight injury. No one pays attention but everyone notices.

"Got disoriented when the lights went out," he says to everyone and no one. "Thought I saw an exit sign," he shrugs, working his way across the square to the other side and his guest quarters, wondering how he's going to tell the other ambassadors what he saw without endangering them or himself.

What are his options? Does he *have* options in a realm where surveillance is constant and foolproof, vulnerable only to human folly?

What remains of the sky flares lilac for an instant then fades and shadows lose contour. Were she not wearing the facemask with its red line to follow she would have to stop because without the smudge of sun there's no way to differentiate one direction from another. Without the surface gear she would long ago have suffocated or collapsed from thirst or died of hypothermia and been detected. Instead, legs leaden, she shuffles and glides unnoticed through one meandering dune valley after another and is now miles farther north and east of Great City, alone but for the mechanical hiss of her own breathing, concentrating on each step, knowing that if she stumbles or falls and sinks down into all that softness she will be tempted to curl up and stay where stopping is not an option.

Everything glows green because of the facemask and dead but for her cloaked presence. As night deepens so does the sense of desolation, of being lost and forgotten in a realm to which life is no longer welcome. The effect is despair for which she is unprepared and without remedy but to try and go faster but her legs won't cooperate.

Then One-Who-Wanders rounds the shoulder of yet another dune and gasps. Everything is instantly in focus again and she's pulled up short by someone tall, cloaked, hooded, wearing a breather and walking briskly toward her from a medium distance having come many miles mostly underground to emerge at this moment from a portal into deepest twilight. He stops. They regard one another for a moment, both in heavy surface gear. Then he speaks.

"Isham said you were on your way." The voice is male, distorted by the breather's facemask. "Quick."

Without warning her knees buckle and she's sinking. He reaches her in time, catches, lifts, then turns, goes back and vanishes into the portal, which also disappears and she's standing inside, supported from behind with several others and their headlamps a blur around her. The cloak and breather are removed but not her skinsuit. That's all she sees before a cloth is put over her eyes and tied behind her head and there's total darkness. But she can feel her surface boots and gauntlets being removed replaced by soft gloves and ankle-boots. She hears words for others spoken by someone behind her who is supporting her by the arms.

"Seal it up."

His voice is deep and resonant. He's standing behind her,

close, touching. He passes something around and taps it against her stomach.

"Drink. All of it."

One-Who-Wanders brings a flask to her mouth, tips and squirts thick winebroth. She gulps hungrily, stopping only to breathe. When the flask is empty she passes it back. The flurry of movement stops. They gather around.

"It takes a moment," his whisper is deep and husky and his breath smells of spices, of what she just drank.

She can feel intense focus aimed at her by people who are extraordinarily quiet. She sniffs, smells him, smells them, smells stone, smells moisture. And they're all very still, as though waiting for something to happen.

Then it hits her. Energy and sudden clarity. Even though blindfolded, she has a sense of where she is and that there are four of them plus him close behind, that they are male and female and young but for him and he is the one responsible for an important outcome. Another jolt hits her and her stance changes.

"Hut," he whispers moving to her side.

He takes her upper arm as if to guide. Two move out in front. Two guard the rear. They move off into a tunnel.

The descent is gradual. He stays beside her, clasping her elbow, guiding as she gets the feel of the stone and the bright clarity brought by the drug. Nothing is said, however. She hears only the sounds of their steps and their breathing.

Then she's hit with another wave of energy. Her strength is more than fully recharged. Attributing this to the winebroth she picks up the pace.

He relaxes his hold on her arm to a gentle touch, guiding with the slightest pressure. And she is instantly responsive.

***

Isham One-Who-Waits has traversed a difficult and complicated network of ravines beneath the surface to finally arrive at a portal 1 mile directly south of Great City. Technology in the portal informs him that the first portal he used to attract Great City's attention has been located by drones but not penetrated. Satisfied, he straps on a pair of surface skis, picks up a hand-device and thumbs the control to open the portal onto a valley between two long tapering dunes at the end of which is the flats then Great City, a brown smudge in the dawn.

Staying low, Isham shuffles up the long gradual shoulder of a dune to the ridge. There, high and silhouetted against the dull sky, he once again raises the cloak to break his shield thus calling Great City's attention. Finished, he skis down the dune to the portal, facemask warning him that he has been spotted.

Once inside again, Isham seals the portal, takes off the bulky surface gear and stows it in his pack. Then he heads west, into an elaborate system of ancient drains and sewers that don't even smell anymore.

***

Paul Prescot Reed is alone in a most unusual room known only to Presiders of Great City and the Maintenance-units that keep it clean. It's called the Crow's Nest and was designed as a motivator and a test of courage – a motivator because nothing inspires aggressive people like the face of failure, and a test of courage because nothing terrifies stewards more than open space, endless dunes beneath dead sky, the ruin of what was. Indeed, assignment to the transfer station is a torture endured by those who need incentive to try harder, focus more on the interests of Great City than their own. This terror of space is the reason Reed insisted that negotiations with the ambassadors be held on the surface, in The Heights.

Located in the outer dome-skin about halfway down the northeast side and smelling of bleach, the Crow's Nest is an 8 x 20 foot slice of raw concrete one long side of which is the only window in the entire structure. The ceiling is low. A single recessed bulb shines down on a bright blue plastic portable toilet. An old prestige chair is positioned in front of the window. On the back wall, a big storage cabinet rises almost to the ceiling and both doors are open.

Uncomfortable as he is here, Reed came to the Crow's Nest to be alone, try to come up with a different perspective on the situation. Then he got an urgent page from Doug Smythe Hews of Medicine requesting his immediate presence at a meeting with Security about the

93

removal of monitor suits. Not yet ready to leave the Crow's Nest, Reed is attending the meeting virtually, watching on the monitor that is located in the storage cabinet but saying little.

Lassiter and Hews are in a Medical recovery room standing on either side of a naked citizen-unit who is lying on a gurney. The unit's monitor suit has been removed and he's breathing quietly on his own. Smythe is on the far side and Lassiter is on the near side of the gurney. She's bending over, looking down, eyes narrowed, nodding ever so slightly. Smythe is talking into the camera.

"...Don't get me wrong, sir," still in scrubs with his surgical mask dangling, the compact and precise head of Medicine is delighted with his accomplishment. "The unit is a long way from volitional functionality but brain-waves are approaching normal and autonomic systems are operational. Give me enough citizens to learn on and I'll be able to remove a monitor suit easy enough." He chuckles, amazed. "Everything changed when I took charge and did the procedure myself instead of entrusting it to the Medical Primes. It needed softer hands."

The citizen-unit was ready for recycling anyway and is no loss to Great City. His moist and wrinkled gray flesh is repulsive somehow, like a fetus, like someone old who was never born.

Reed turns away. He walks to the tinted window and looks out at toxic haze and dunes. Behind him on the screen, Lassiter lifts one of the unit's eyelids and peers close.

"So the escaped Prime Researcher could in fact be alive," she murmurs, looking down at the gray face.

"Yes," Smythe is proud.

"And functional."

"We're a long way from making it actually happen, Lassiter. But yes this unit proves it's possible..."

The Presider isn't listening but looking out at the flats then dunes as far as he can see. From the Founders on, every steward has been certain that beyond Great City is a dead world, not even ghosts. Now the possibility that the former Prime Researcher might be alive and functioning, that she might have been helped by others, that advanced technology is involved, plays with Reed's imagination as he looks out from halfway down the outer skin of the dome and imagines an army stretched from one side of the horizon to the other, come to destroy Great City, riding strange invertebrate beasts like the one that captured the shape-changer.

Paul Prescot Reed takes a gulp of Calm and dismisses the

image of the approaching army. Such play of mind is unproductive. He straightens his tunic, extinguishes the screen then dims the overhead light and heads back to Founders' Hall to prepare for the morning council meeting.

***

Whether humans are there or not, the Refuge teems with life that wafts and drifts and flits, streaking the dark with faint patches of incandescent flora or thin clouds of neon insects or rivulets of glowing water. Movement is constant here as elsewhere beneath the surface. Small creatures can be heard scurrying or scuttling, noisily rubbing their hands or knees together, generating simple tunes that are accompanied by the occasional drop of water falling from a considerable height.

The keeper's lair is a deep hole in the ceiling of the main chamber. She's curled up in it now, depleted and asleep. Finally finished with her many tasks the big spider is dull and shriveled to such a degree that she has entered a form of hibernation in order to recover as quickly as possible.

Meanwhile far back in the nooks and crannies of an offshoot from the grotto, shape-changer nits that weren't captured have located each other. Producing their own thin blue glow they have finally generated enough critical nit-mass to begin the slow and silent process of reconstituting the shape-changer, making adjustments on the way because much was learned during the first encounter.

***

The Presider has temporarily replaced his previous heads of Trade and Archives with two people meant to serve as nothing more than placeholders. Instructed to remain silent, especially in his absence, which is currently the case, Walter Wilson Evans of Trade and Sharon Reed Baker of Archives have once again pulled up the original contract and are having it read aloud by a tech-voice clause by clause, including notes and footnotes on its interpretation for the last 2,000 years.

95

Needless to say, it's a numbing exercise for the ambassadors who are in effect being held hostage in a dimly lit room that is too warm because of half-measures of which they know nothing. In short, the ambassadors are having trouble staying awake while their hosts are juiced up on Kafi and won't come down without an antidote.

"...see the aforementioned reference to clause 3.2.7a..." the tech-voice is flat, genderless, and distorts most of the consonants.

Dav Baxter is present. To say he has had a difficult time of it since he saw the citizen-units is to minimize the task of holding an important secret because to share it would expose the ambassadors and their mission to unknown consequences. Unable to figure out how to circumvent Great City's Security surveillance and inform the others of what he has discovered, Baxter has not slept or eaten since he opened the door on the orange people working between the dome skins, since one of them appeared on the catwalk outside, close enough to touch, featureless and robotic. In addition, his way of working things out, running, is no longer available because Liberty Park is closed, leaving Dav Baxter crawling out of his own skin.

"...to insure that when incoming product is unloaded a steward shall be present to inspect the manifest..."

Everyone in the room noticed the sudden dramatic change in Dav Baxter and came to the same utterly logical conclusion as to its cause: having served his three years Baxter should be heading back to S.S. Hope right now and he's not and no one knows how long the ambassadors are going to be stuck down here or how ugly this is going to get. It's a very simple explanation for how all four Space Staters feel, stuck as they are with a long recitation of the original contract and all its clauses and adjustments and notes on those clauses through centuries of countless meetings. In spite of his not having slept since he saw what he saw, Dav Baxter is the only ambassador who is wide awake and he has had no chemicals, nothing but water.

To his far left, recently arrived for her three years and yet to bond with anyone is ensign Ria Siloam from S.S. Columbus. Built like a middleweight wrestler, Siloam is military, an apprentice first responder who hasn't even been on her first mission yet. Her hair is regulation buzzcut and light brown. Her dress whites are crisp and worn with pride. When not negotiating she studies old files on Great City or works out in the gym to stay mission-ready.

Tran McKenzy from S.S. Ulysses is a man of diminutive stature with no body fat. In a different world he might possibly be a juggler or an acrobat. Wearing his hair in a long golden pigtail, Tran is in fact an M.D. who is miserable with allergies and claustrophobia when down in The Heights. Given that his current stay here is open-ended he's having a particularly difficult time and self-prescribing Space State medication to lower the anxiety and needless to say, all meds have side effects.

Last is Raf Kyrry from S.S. Friendship, now lead negotiator. A master welder, Kyrry is in the fullness of manhood, brown and muscular with long dark hair and velvety brown eyes. Even he hasn't had any luck wooing a steward of either sex. Given Tran's condition and Siloam's newness on the team, Kyrry hoped to lean heavily on Baxter but let go of that notion this morning.

"...For further examples of this precedent see footnotes *a* through *h* in appendix A..."

"That's enough," Dav Baxter stands, trembling, blinking rapidly. "I've had enough. Whatever you people are up to..." He stutters to a stop, unable to go on or to move. Then suddenly he bolts out of the conference room leaving everyone certain about the cause of his behavior.

***

They stopped once to rest. One-Who-Wanders slept without stirring and had no sense how many turns of the hourglass might have passed before she was wakened. The blindfold was adjusted and the same man who tended her before gave her more of the sweet winebroth. The others were already up and in formation when the drug kicked in and everything was clear again.

The trail was long and difficult this time. Mostly descending. They had to use ropes to get down into a sizeable empty chamber with a high ceiling and several offshoots. The man in charge brought her down on his back.

"Scatter but not far. Rest on alert," he whispered from close behind and she could smell his spiced breath, feel his heat.

The youngsters vanished silently. He stepped in front of her.

"Take my belt."

She groped, felt warm fabric between his shoulder blades. He reached around behind, took hold of her wrist and lowered it to the thick belt around his hips.

"Come."

She felt the tug and followed him through a long meandering tunnel until they arrived at a place where he is pressing gently down on the top of her head.

"Low."

They stoop through a deep threshold and emerge into what feels like a comfortable stone chamber, warm and fragrant, of modest size. He's at her side, one hand resting lightly on her shoulder, telling her to stay. He removes his hand and steps back.

Only then does she realize that someone else is here.

In front of her, standing across from her, several body-lengths away. She's being examined. Then something snaps and ripples through her as the other opens – just a bit because should Curanda open fully the one examined would lose awareness.

The suddenness and magnitude of the sensation cause One-Who-Wanders to see even though she's blindfolded. Light. It's as though she's filled with someone else's light. The sensation deepens. She sees and hears and smells and tastes and is saturated by a being ablaze, arrested by brightness that scrutinizes.

Gasping, she attempts to scrutinize in return but distinguishes only light. Then, willing it, she reaches out and discerns overwhelming energy from which she would not voluntarily return.

Then it's over.

The illumination is gone.

Here/Now is ordinary again and someone is speaking.

"Aye," the sound is a low whisper directed to the man behind her. "And she's curanda."

He inhales sharply.

"Please remove her blindfold and leave us."

Her eyes are uncovered and she pulls back the hood of the silvery skinsuit, blinking against sudden light. The man who brought her here is gone before she can see him and she's regarding the blur in front of her as it slowly comes into focus.

An old woman. Small and plain. Smiling. Standing a body-length away and wearing a dark robe with the hood up but not so far as to shade her nut-brown face and milky eyes that are aware of everything though the woman is obviously blind.

"Isham dreamed us to be alert for you," the old woman's voice is deep, soft and welcoming.

One-Who-Wanders blinks, returns the smile.

"Who are you?"

"We are creatures adrift in eternity and sustained by Source. Some call us stone-people, others wilderness or remnant-people."

The old woman steps forward.

"You've come a long way and we'll get to more questions later. Meantime, welcome to TrezArches and our yearly ceremony of wicks. And please forgive the blindfold. We make no exception to a precaution upon which our survival depends. Now. There's food, bathing and sleep. In which order would you prefer them?"

"Sleep. Please." It's no contest.

Nodding, considerate of her guest, Curanda reaches for a wick and leads the new arrival through a labyrinth of stone pillars to a smooth chamber of modest size. The old woman puts down the wick and points things out.

"Waterflask. Bedroll. Bathing water. A drying cloth. Rubbing oils. There's a sinkhole. We're nearby, preparing for the ceremony. Should you have a need there's only to call," Curanda murmurs gently peeling the silvery skinsuit down and off of a very tired traveler. Then she helps One-Who-Wanders into the bedroll.

"Sleep 'til you wake." And the old woman is gone.

***

Space State vehicles are normally brightly colored and lit, blazing through the universe to attract attention from one spectrum or another. But H-V cruiser Mohawk out of S.S. Hope is in stealth-mode and emits no light of her own at this time nor does she reflect light from other sources. Barely visible and seemingly stationary, the graphite smudge is being pushed for all she's got and has already covered half the distance from the wormhole to the outer edge of earth's solar system.

Inside, the ship is gravitized to slightly more than earth-Gs. Crew and guest quarters are brightly lit and comfortably functional, rather like an ancient nuclear submarine but roomy and with lots of large portholes because Space Staters crave openness and the expansive beauty of their meta-environment.

Mohawk's control cabin is in her nose, a bubble of one-way

nu-glass currently occupied by all four crewmembers, each harnessed into a comfortable chaise, looking up at overhead screens. The women are wearing bright jumpsuits and turtlenecks. Their boots are soft ankle-tops, like athletic shoes. All four have brushcuts, a requirement in the military regardless of sex.

Navigator and oldest member of the crew is Second Lieutenant Ethel Marin, a skinny little woman the color of yeast. Marin is a reader who rarely speaks but when she does people listen. The engineer is Ensign Wanda Mu, referred to by all as Big Wanda, a florid woman with pendulous breasts, an enormous behind, light brown hair and dandruff, who is constantly at or over the weight limit for cruiser duty but manages to pass the physicals anyway and go on taking care of her beloved Mohawk. The technician is a pint-sized creature named Cha Hua from S.S. Friendship. Latest addition to the team, Cha Hua is tattooed all over with a work in progress, an image of her totem animal, the salamander. The little technician grins constantly and says little that is actually comprehensible but she's worth her lead-weight in oxygen because she can get into and out of impossible spaces to make repairs.

In charge of it all is Commander Ingrid Steele. The Viking. A blond and willowy clock-stopper who owns a Medal of Valor and is lusted after by those of all genders. But Ingrid is not available. She long ago committed her love to one who loves back but not exclusively. She's held the ship together through a decade of impossible odds. Perhaps even more difficult, she's kept the team together through the vicissitudes of being human in a world that is never perfect.

Ingrid finishes, re-reads and sends her daily report to the bridge on Command Ship Phoenix. Then she turns her attention to an overhead screen showing Mohawk's passengers.

Team Falcon.

Six elite first responders back in the training tower. Five Falcons are spotting Corporal Sh'rai McCloud who has been chosen to pilot the windrider for the reconnaissance mission. McCloud is now high up in the gravitized tower, completing yet another arduous work-out to prepare for the mission.

Worn like clothing rather than entered like a vehicle, windriders require strength and endurance to pilot, which is the reason to train in gravity. Hence, the tower – a shaft that when extended rides Mohawk's back rather like an ancient elevator shaft the equivalent of five stories high. The walls are transparent from inside and beyond them is perpetual night and star-froth. Retracted, the tower is flush to the back of the cruiser.

McCloud is up as high as she can go in the tower, barely visible on Ingrid's screen. The five spotters, stationed around the floor looking up, are crisp and clear in the foreground. Normally a first responder is dressed in bright color to contrast with the environment but McCloud is wearing a skintight black training suit with only an oval of face exposed. She's also wearing black electro-magnetic belt, boots and gloves that connect her to a powerful grid, allowing her to simulate in gravity the movements needed to pilot a windrider in weightlessness thus strengthening muscles and flexing joints as she swims in space, maneuvers up, down and around the tower, takes heart-stopping leaps from top to bottom, bounces from wall to wall, swings like a pendulum – all moves that must be fluid, automatic, and sustainable once she's actually out in space.

"Here we go, last run," McCloud rasps into her throat mike. Then, six feet tall, 180 pounds of stone-hard muscle, she leaps out into a beautiful swan dive with the grace of a dainty ballerina. Halfway down she lowers her feet and skids to a stop in midair then skips through space to the wall and starts running horizontally around the wall first one way then the other. Increasing her speed, she runs up and down the wall, faster and faster. Then she begins maneuvering between walls, bouncing and angling her way up and down as though repelling – each move requiring enormous core-muscle strength, lightening reflexes and the daring of a ten year old.

Two thirds of the way up the one of the walls, McCloud gets cocky and crosses her electro-mag lines. She pops away from the wall and starts spinning in space. Attempting to regain control, she gets confused like a caterpillar trying to figure out which foot to move next. Then she's plummeting. The spotters manage to get under her and break the fall but not completely as is evidenced by a loud and sickening pop.

"Oops," big Wanda hears it and turns to look at her screen. "That wasn't supposed to happen."

"Nope." Commander Steele releases her harness and is out of the chaise. "Marin, take command." Holding onto overhead support struts Ingrid works her way back toward the control cabin's exit hatch.

"Got it," Ethel taps away at her thigh-pad, splitting her screens in half, one side for each job.

Wrinkle of concern bisecting her one eyebrow, big Wanda watches Steele leave the control cabin while Cha Hua intones a long word from her own private language. Then the hatch is closed and Ingrid is hurrying back through the gleaming spine of the ship to the changing room, which is located at the base of the training tower.

Steele slides the glass door open and steps just inside, staying back out of the way. McCloud is gasping in pain as teammates ease her down on a gurney, shoulder and elbow terribly askew. Sgt. Quester Bates, Falcon 2, the team's big paramedic, quickly injects McCloud with something powerful then moves around to the arm.

"Hold her down."

Two take McCloud's legs and a third takes the other arm and shoulder. Lt. Mezon wedges a mouthguard between McCloud's teeth then holds onto her head. Bates grabs the arm and yanks with a twist and a loud pop followed by a groan from McCloud.

Shoulder and elbow are realigned and being bound. But that doesn't begin to address the fallout from this accident. Such injuries are part of being a first responder. But Corporal McCloud will not be going anywhere in a windrider very soon. That means someone has to take her place.

Back by the sliding glass door, Commander Steele studies Pilar Mezon, Falcon 1, who isn't supposed to be on this or any other mission right now but on leave recovering from a recent surgery to replace a knee joint that has yet to be calibrated and covered with synth-skin. Thirteen years older now but no less agile, wearing shorts and a gray T-shirt like her teammates, Pilar whispers something to McCloud, causing the corporal to laugh. Then she straightens up and looks at her crew, pointedly ignoring Ingrid who is tall and slender and lovely and hasn't moved since she got here. The crew looks alternately concerned and guilty.

"It was nobody's fault," Pilar's voice is a husky rasp. "Every windrider pilot has made that mistake with the same result because if you're going to get tripped up it'll happen when you're as deep in the zone as you can go. I'll have a report ready for Command in two hours." Pilar releases a long sigh and rubs her face with both hands. "Read it if you want to before I send it on. Feel free to edit or add your own comments. Meantime I'm not to be disturbed."

"Question?" Quester Bates pulls a blanket up to McCloud's chin and readies the gurney to be moved.

"Go ahead."

"Now what?"

"Far as I know, team Falcon is still the one chosen to go in and

102

find out what's what so decisions can be made and that's what we're going to do."

"Who's going pilot the windrider?"

"I'll tell you when I know."

With that Lt. Pilar Mezon strides toward then past Ingrid Steele without acknowledging her and on out into the main corridor or spine of Mohawk, heading back to her cabin and a difficult decision because it was no call when McCloud was still in the game. She was undoubtedly the best person for the job.

***

By the beginning of the great collapse a surprising amount of blasted-out and finished-off space already existed beneath the surface of the earth – much of it big, deep and sophisticated, some of it occupied, some of it old and abandoned, some of it contingent on surface events. There were military installations and research facilities. There were government offices. There were corporate and religious headquarters. Some of the underground cities were connected by hundreds of miles of underground four and six-lane highway.

In addition there were countless mines of all sizes and networks of tunnels, some with ways in and out of dark wilderness. Independent groups occupied some of these spaces, individuals related by blood or bonded by common interest but lacking formal organizational structure.

The history of incorporated peoples who went under-ground is well documented. In contrast, there are only shadowy tales of how those now variously referred to as stone-people or wilderness-people or remnant-people came to be. What is agreed on is that small groups went down into raw space, learned to survive, evolved their own ways and remained hidden from the worlds emerging above and below.

***

Lassiter deployed several gaggles of drones to scour the area

103

of the first sighting, one mile into the dunes directly east of Great City. So far, nothing. She sent additional drones to scour the area around the second sighting one mile into the dunes directly south of Great City with the same results. In anticipation of his next move and following his pattern she's sent two gaggles directly west and stationed them one mile into the dunes on that side of the structure. There's nothing now but to keep probing the two original hot spots south and east and wait for the next sighting.

Great City's head of Security turns her attention to an issue of almost equal importance. Dav Baxter. Who walked out of trade talks this morning, effectively giving the Space States the initiative and putting everything in freefall. The Presider wants to know what's going on and how to get the upper hand again.

In palest gray trousers and unzipped tunic, Lassiter uses her tech-wand to open Baxter's file and scroll back in fast-motion through several days to him waking then pulling out the card from his memory-book. Something about the contents of the card calls her to look there for clues. She stops at the first holographic image of the dark haired woman of whom she knows nothing but who seems to have some kind of hold on Dav Baxter, a woman whose vitality is almost overwhelming.

Lassiter expands the image to life-size. Fascinated, she moves closer, staring at Pilar's wild and broken Aztec beauty from thirteen years ago.

A shadow of black hair on a gleaming skull. Golden skin. Green eyes startle with their frankness. Lassiter highlights the image.

"Primes?" she whispers.

"Yes."

"Do a search of the Space States' daily news and briefings to the ambassadors. Pull up every mention of Dav Baxter and trace each reference back to its source. In addition, I've bracketed an image from Baxter's memory-book. I want to know who this woman is and the nature of her relation to Dav Baxter."

"Level of importance?"

"Bump it to the top of my queue, to be superceded only by matters on or below the surface."

"Copy."

The Screen loses its highlight, indicating that the Primes have absorbed the command. Lassiter resumes her study of the two of them together – Dav waking up, looking at the revolving holograms of the woman. Great City's head of Security turns from Baxter to the woman, trying to understand with no experience of attachment except to her own ascension. She moves closer to the screen and stares at both Space Staters.

Stewards are taught that Space Staters are inferior due to a shared contagion called feeling, which Lassiter has never seen or been interested in trying to fathom. She sees it now in Dav Baxter, in the raw hunger of a man for a woman.

"Jerrod!"

Her citizen-unit steps forward from the doorway into the office. She doesn't notice his arrival for being distracted by the two images. "Jerrod!"

"Here, mam."

"Oh," she whirls around, startled, stares at him, doesn't want. "Never mind, go away."

"Yes, mam," he steps back.

"Go to your sleeping pod."

He disappears down the hall, into the treatment room and she's alone again, staring at Dav Baxter while he looks at the dark woman, his face split open by love that is contagious and ignites in Lassiter the need to be in his physical presence, to measure his actuality against the image. Just once. Somehow.

***

All dawns are the same where there is nothing to distinguish one day from the next, not even a breeze to stir the ash, only cold silence made a bit more visible. This did not have to happen.

A mile directly West of Great City, another portal opens and closes. In surface gear again, One-Who-Waits sidesteps up a dune to its ridge. He stops at the top, raises his cloak and stands there for a moment, radiating data to the gaggle of drones not more than two dunes away. Then he drops the cloak and glides back down the ash to the portal that closes just in time to bewilder the drones that almost caught up with him.

Inside, he listens at the portal until he's satisfied the drones can't find it. He exits the portal back into a stone tunnel that leads to a small cave. There, he removes the surface gear for now and sits to rest and eat and drink water. Then, finished creating diversions, he slings on the heavy pack and heads directly north.

***

The Presider is with his heads of Security and Human Resources in one of the conference rooms off of Founders' Hall. Because Great City is now on half-measures the room is close and dim, its occupants perspiring and uncomfortable, paying the price of sovereignty.

Reed is at the head of the table. Virginia Kahn Baker is on his right, bursting the seams of her chocolate brown tunic. Karin Lassiter Kohl is on his left, in pearl gray, uncharacteristically flushed for some reason. Baker is rattling off data concerning escapes and attempted escapes.

"Since the beginning of Great City there have been 422 attempted escapes. Only 72 have been successful."

"Only!" Reed snorts. "*One* is too many! Seventy-two is enough to start a civilization with! Go on."

"In terms of Function and specialization, desertion cannot be predicted by assignment or position. They cover the board. Except for stewards. There have been no desertions by stewards."

"What does that tell us?" the Presider turns to Lassiter who is staring at nothing, mouth slightly open. "Lassiter!"

"Oh, sorry, sir."

"I'm asking you what that tell us."

Karin Lassiter Kohl looks at the Presider blankly for a moment then snapping out of it comes back into focus. "Apologies, sir. I was thinking about…about the last three sightings of the bio-form."

"We'll get to that later. Right now I want to know how, given the nature of our control over them, how it's possible that even one citizen-unit could conceive of trying to escape. What's wrong with the monitor suits? Why don't they work with everyone?"

"I'll talk to Medicine and Technology and get back to you soonest," Lassiter makes a note on her tech-pad.

"Yes, see to it. Go on, Virginia."

"In terms of escape route and direction, again, that seems to be universal, too. There's not one direction preferred over others. And if

106

there were, how would citizen-units find it?" making a note, Baker mutters, "Something else to consider..."

"It's the cumulative effect that concerns me." Reed stands to pace. "Through the years, one piece at a time, the deserters could have assembled chunks of critical information about Great City. What else have you got?"

"Any of the four deserters prior to our current loss could still be alive and functional." Baker wipes her glistening face with the back of her sleeve. "Three males, one female."

"Classifications?"

"An Engineering Prime, a Medical technician, a Maintenance unit, an Efficiency calculator and, of course, our Prime Researcher. One would be quite old if alive, but possibly functional. They range in age from 40 to 93, with our Prime being 30." Baker, tunic immodestly open at the neck because of the heat, sucks from her bottle and holds it in her mouth, sloshing it around, because water is now rationed.

Reed stops pacing. He studies the close ceiling for a long moment, as though trying to solve a chess problem.

"Our sudden vulnerability comes from an unexpected direction. We've always felt the need for defense against possible attack from space. We took precautions in case the Space States decided to return and claim what isn't theirs anymore. But from below?" he looks at the two women. "Impossible. The Founders eliminated that possibility before the doors of Great City were sealed."

"Well, they must have missed a few," Baker shakes her head, "and now we have to deal with it."

"What of ours did the defectors take with them? What kind of world could they have made for themselves?"

"Classifications of the deserters indicate that if in fact their knowledge was to be pooled someone would have a great deal of critical information about us and how we operate."

"I want heavy surface equipment readied for deployment. If I have to I'll blast open the entire continent to find and destroy this threat to Great City," Reed turns to his head of Human Resources. "Comb the files of the escapees who could still be alive. I want to know exactly what they could have taken from here."

"Yes, sir."

"Now back to your duties," and Paul Prescot Reed stalks out of the room.

***

Just as there is no utter and complete silence anywhere in the universe so also there is no perfect darkness, not even in the deeps of blindness or stone, there are only different ways of reading what is manifest. So it is at the Refuge, not dark and silent but aglow with a faint blue pulse of life, rather like what one might have encountered fathoms beneath an ancient sea filled with layered sounds of being.

And so it is that through this faint blue glow and throb a recharged Solaris is restlessly prowling the Refuge. Remaining as inevident as possible – though when she descends, the silk thread unraveling from her posterior makes what to her is a fierce rasping sound and the clatter of her claws on the stone sometimes eclipses everything else and she must stop, hold her breath, stick out her tongue and sniff, try to locate what is almost here again but so faint, so weak.

Meanwhile, at the back of a remote tunnel leading away from the grotto, a thin wad of mist the color of dirty gauze is hovering above the floor, slowly stretching itself thin then compressing back to something about the size of a child's fist. The shape-changer has replicated to half-strength and is attempting to re-establish contact with Great City.

***

Stewards of Great City are born and raised in a sort of hybrid isolation because bonding is taboo in The Heights. Bad for efficiency.

Assigned to individual quarters as soon as possible, pre-stewards are privately tutored by technology. They are kept clean and organized by citizen-units and are in the actual presence of others only a few hours a day for one of three purposes – occasional hands-on highly competitive problem solving exercises called games, the required one-on-one competitive sport, and simulated job interviews designed to test a pre-steward's knowledge and diligence.

For stewards there is no childhood or leisure. Privileged as they are, stewards have no more story of their own than do citizen-units down below. Stewards do not share intimacy or touch. Sex is with a citizen-unit. Except for meetings, a steward's life is spent alone in, for the most part, one-room private quarters, with the wisdom of the Founders remaining unchallenged because, well, what's the option?

***

Dav Baxter has been compulsively walking around the big public square for a long time now, going faster and faster, driven by a bad case of toxic energy that's been gathering since he saw the orange people between the dome skins. With Liberty Park being closed and nowhere to run, he has to do something to expel what's making him sick while he figures out how to tell the other ambassadors what he saw without endangering them.

Stewards make way for him, stop and watch the crazy Space Stater who seems on the verge of spinning out of control, something most unseemly in The Heights. Perspiration stains his T-shirt and sweatpants, which are inappropriate attire for the public square.

"Dr. Davenport Baxter?"

Suddenly a bulky young man in deepest wine-colored tunic and trousers is standing in front of him, blocking his way. Dav tries to go around. The young man moves to block him.

Dav stops. He dabs at the perspiration on his upper lip and feels bristle because he hasn't shaved since he saw what he saw, has been too distracted with remembering, with apprehension that the stewards know what he did, what he learned and are just playing him along.

"Dr. Baxter?" the young man asks without warmth.

"Yyes," Dav stammers, about to jump out of his skin from jitters that could be soothed by running.

"Come with me, please."

The young man turns and starts to walk away, expecting to be followed, not looking back to check. It's only then that Baxter notices several other bulky young men standing nearby, paying close attention, ready to do what's necessary to make him comply. Outmatched and with no options, Dav turns and does what he was told to do, which amounts to no more than following the young man back to his suite in the guest quarters where, on Lassiter's instructions he is medicated and put to bed while she tries to figure out what to do about what's happening to her.

On the surface again because his next destination could not be reached any other way, Isham One-Who-Waits is hugging the dune valleys, making good time skiing directly east, away from Great City and the setting sun. About four miles into the dunes he stops, opens a portal, quickly enters and closes the portal behind him.

Leaving the breather's facemask in place Isham pulls off his gauntlets and the hood of his cloak. After checking that the portal is secure, he leaves it for a long descent down a natural shaft to the bottom where he hauls his pack through a close crawlspace to emerge in a sizeable chamber with many offshoots, like a starburst.

The catacombs.

Almost three hundred women and men rest here, returned to stone. They are his predecessors, his teachers, those who served the Refuge as One-Who-Waits before him. Each now occupies a little stone alcove somewhere in the catacombs. He has come here to rest before heading out on the long trek east.

Isham finds a smooth spot on the ground near one of the walls. He lights a wick and removes the surface gear. He pulls the bedroll out of the pack and opens it.

Weary, the old man strips all the way down to skin. He carefully lays the surface gear out to dry. Then, not bothering with food or drink, Isham quickly thanks Source for his arrival here, gets into his bedroll, curls up on his side like his predecessors and is asleep.

***

It being imperative to maintain circadian rhythms even in space, H.V. cruiser Mohawk is on automatic, battened down for "night" as it were. In the relative silence one can hear the low pulsing drone of the gravitizer and the harmonics of the power systems beneath a choir of different sleep sounds made by eight of the ten women on board, in their bunks adrift and dreaming.

Unknown to each other, however, in separate parts of the ship, two are awake, carrying enormous responsibility and feeling the weight. First, illumined only by the soft red glow of safety lights, Lt. Pilar Mezon is alone in her cabin on the top bunk looking out of the big porthole directly overhead. Second, commander Ingrid Steele is alone in the bubble of Mohawk's control cabin, leaning back in her chaise, keeping watch though there's no need because the ship takes care of itself. Nonetheless, wearing downtime sweats, she's leaning back in her chaise an alert sentinel, a dark silhouette against stars and the faint green glow of the cabin's technology.

Wearing gray workout shorts and tank top, Pilar is unable to sleep. She checks her wristwatch and reads 03:06. She swings her legs over the top bunk and hops down to the floor. As she lands there's a mechanical pop in her new knee, the one yet to be calibrated and covered with SynthSkin. She catches her breath from the zap of electric heat and flexes the knee, relieved to find no discomfort. Then she pulls on athletic shoes and quietly exits her cabin to find out if she can do the dance one last time. It's just something she needs to know before she makes her decision. And she wants to find out minus input from others.

From deep nothingness One-Who-Wanders is first vaguely aware of a sense of well-being that accompanies the very air itself, a soft buzz of life pouring in from beyond the small chamber she's been sleeping in though she can't be sure because she's never heard these sounds before – voices and laughter, bells and windchimes riding on odors of incense and food. Her stomach growls. From nearby she hears giggling and rolls onto her back.

"Shhhhh…"

One-Who-Wanders open her eyes. She's in the small chamber, dimly illumined by a single wick, and remembers being brought here by the old woman who sees though she's blind. Curanda.

She hears more giggling from nearby, behind her head. Two or three sweet little voices. She turns to look, sees shadow, hears scampering. Then it's quiet again.

One-Who-Wanders blinks up at the low sandstone ceiling and stretches beneath the blanket, feeling stiff and sore everywhere. Naked, she gets to her feet slowly, blinks, yawns, relieves herself in the sinkhole and looks for something to wear against the chill. She finds a long slip folded on the foot of her bedding and pulls it on. Then she heads for the waterflask and is draining it when startled by a sudden awareness of someone else in the chamber.

Whirling around, One-Who-Wanders squints and sees only shadow. Then a second entrance to the chamber is made evident by someone standing there, someone small who steps forward into amber wicklight.

"They said you woke up."

A child. With a husky voice. A little girl with huge dark eyes that sizzle beneath a cap of straight blue-black hair. Her face is round and golden brown, glowing with excitement. Her clothes are simple – a soft shirt, a quilted doublet and trousers with felt boots that come almost to the knee, all of different brown hues and laced with bright ribbons as though for a festive occasion. The girl is holding neatly folded clothes in her arms and bluntly scrutinizing the new arrival. Then a big grin reveals gaps from missing front teeth.

"I'm Esa. Curanda sent me to help because she's busy with the women and I'm old enough to help now."

The two regard each other for a long moment, like wild and

curious creatures in an ancient clearing. Then an electric charge pleasantly impales them both, passing between them with great force, joining them. The charge deepens until the two are flooded with each other, suspended in each other, exploring, assessing, enjoying.

The moment passes. They blink wide-eyed, surprised to be snapped back into ordinary here/now.

"Curanda did not indicate that you are already so strong or beautiful. She sent these for you to wear. Then we're to go up to the pools and help prepare the women to conceive. You're called One-Who-Wanders?"

"Yes."

"Tsk, those pesky Refuge names are always a mouthful. The little ones call you something else. Not so clumsy. Skye. They call you Skye."

"...Skye..."

"Yes. They're old enough to understand that you come from Source and also from beyond stone. They know that beyond stone there is something called sky, something they imagine to be very beautiful."

"Skye One-Who-Wanders. My name?"

"If that pleases you," Esa grins.

"Yes," hands to her chest, eyes closed she beams.

"Good. I'll tell da since he'll be introducing you to the assembly."

The girl hands Skye a plain gown of dusty blue and shows her how put it on and tie it at at her throat. She points at the fresh but healing wounds.

"The big spider bit you?"

"Yes."

"What does that mean?"

"I don't know."

Esa adjusts the mandarine-like collar, ties the gown at one shoulder then down the side to her thigh. The skirt is full, its hem dusting the tops of her feet.

"Who's da?"

"My father. R'io. He brought you down from the surface."

Skye blinks, suddenly pensive as the child helps her with comfortable felt boots and winds a dark red sash around her waist. Then Esa holds out a plain robe of forest green. The sleeves are elbow-length and deeply cut, with secret pockets to be explored. Last, the girl offers a soft pale yellow cap with earflaps and ribbon ties.

"Curanda said this is to keep your head warm. Until you get hair."

Skye One-Who-Wanders puts the cap on her head. Esa ties the ribbons then steps back beaming to admire. "Come," she takes the newcomer by the hand, grabs the lone wick and heads for the hidden entrance.

They emerge almost immediately onto the floor of an enormous cavern in which people of all ages male and female are setting up campsites and walling off private spaces by hanging gauzy white cloths to create open air enclaves connected by walkways that are broad enough for several abreast. The energy is electric and the din builds as more arrive from different points of entry.

Everyone has a job of some kind except for those too young to help who are gathered in one place and cared for by rotating shifts of adolescents. Musicians and performers gather in small groups, quietly warming up. More people straggle in, find places and establish their camps.

Halfway across the cavern they encounter a group of men who are standing together talking quietly and seriously. Like Esa, the men are wearing soft shirts, quilted doublets and trousers with felt boots, all in muted colors, tied together with bright laces.

"There's da now. Wait here," Esa murmurs, leaving the newcomer behind because she's to have no interaction with others until properly introduced to the whole.

Esa approaches one of the men in the group. He's tall and sinewy with bright red hair tied at the nape of his neck, hanging down between his shoulder blades. Esa tugs his hand and points back at Skye One-Who-Wanders. He stares.

The girl stands on her tiptoes trying to tell him something but it's no use. He's not listening. He's fixed on the newcomer whose face he has not seen because it was covered by the breather's mask or obscured by the blindfold. She's standing back where Esa left her, equally transfixed because she hasn't seen him until now, either, and suddenly she can't breathe for the sight of him not three body-lengths away, his eyes the blue of bluest flame.

Startled, the man finally looks at Esa then leans down and listens. He answers her question and straightens up but does not turn back to the group. Instead, he continues to stare at Skye as Esa comes back to her side and takes her hand again then leads her on through the gauzy maze and din toward the other side of the cavern, passing on the

114

way musicians finding different grooves, jugglers warming up, cooks brewing magic, acrobats, storytellers and, finally, on the other side, a switchback trail that goes all the way up.

They start climbing. It takes a while but near the top they stop to look down at the scene below – a blur because she can't forget the man with red hair staring back at her.

R'io.

He is most real.

In this new fullness, this thick whirl of distraction, of everything new, of sound and fragrance, rhythm and melody, laughter and celebration, he is most vivid. The memory of his proximity on the journey here blots out everything as Esa takes her hand and leads her into the women's chamber where those who drew lots allowing them to conceive are being prepared for two days and three nights of trying.

The chamber is wide and deep with a low ceiling, sandstone arches, wicks scattered high and low and many small thermal pools in which those who drew the lots are soaking while others tend them with teas, wines, oils, spices and incense, preparing them to receive seed. Music from a lone singer crooning softly of desire for the seed and the child is meant to arouse and does as Esa leads Skye past several occupied pools surrounded by women wielding fragrances, potions, herbs taken from little glass jars more beautiful than precious jewels. They stop at a pool off to one side near the back of the chamber where the ceiling lowers gracefully. Wicks are floating on the pool in little porcelain cups filled with fragrant oils.

Three women are at the edge of the pool. Curanda is seated on a cushion to one side, grinding herbs and blending ingredients. A large bear of a woman with her trousers rolled up over her knees is seated on a cushion at the edge of the pool, supporting the head of the third woman who is naked and immersed in the water, here to conceive. The big woman at the edge of the pool looks up and smiles warmly.

"Welcome, One-Who-Wanders. I am elder Moss, child of Curanda and Red Tail, half-sister of R'io and aunt of Esa. This is my beloved, Luz. You are welcome to affirm our endeavor."

"I'm honored," Skye One-Who-Wanders touches her heart with her right hand.

Curanda, mixing herbs in the background chuckles then waves to the new arrivals and pats nearby cushions.

"Come. Sit. Learn."

***

Commander Ingrid Steele was still in Mohawk's control cabin, drifting through thoughts of Pilar when she noticed on her technology that the windrider training tower was being extended. She checked her first responder itinerary, found no session scheduled and was turning on the monitor to check as Pilar entered the tower wearing gray shorts and T-shirt plus electro-mag belt, boots and gloves.

Ingrid sat quietly loving and hating, enraged that Pilar would endanger the mission and go into the tower alone on an untested knee. She watched stunned then amazed then drawn in. After half an hour watching the faultless performance on her screen, Ingrid released her harness, left Mohawk in the dependable hands of Space State technology and layers of backup systems to move through the spine of the ship lit for "night" and laced with sweet sounds of others sleeping.

She entered the tower and is now standing in darkness at the bottom, pressed against the wall, watching Pilar complete a long and vigorous workout that was really a test, an audition passed with flying colors as the victor backflips down from the ceiling the equivalent of five stories and nails a perfect landing in the center of the padded floor with just a quick, electrifying click in the new knee but her expression remains defiant as, buff and sweating, she strides past Ingrid trailing the scent of wintergreen and on out to the showers, leaving the one person who can haunt her dalliances standing in starlight, shielded by nu-glass walls that are evident only as a slight shimmering on the darkness.

A shower is turned on. Ingrid moves out of the tower and closes the door. She punches code into the control box and hears the tower retracting overhead. She walks thoughtfully back through a short corridor still lit for "night" toward the shower sound into a bright metal room with stalls on one side and sinks and mirrors on the other and drains in the floor because all water is recycled.

One metal stall is occupied by Pilar who is privately paying the price for her determination. She finally turns off the water, leans against the wall for a moment then opens the door and steps out, ignoring Ingrid. The buzzcut is salt and pepper now. One eyebrow is vertically cut in half. But her cheeks are still broad and honey-colored,

116

her lips full and suckable, her green eyes penetrating – this woman of opposing desires that had to be satisfied, who wanted a baby the old-fashioned way as well as freedom to jump off of every cliff in sight.

Naked, she steps onto the drier and activates it. With a loud whine the donut-shaped drying element moves slowly down her body and back up to its starting position, leaving her dry and moisturized. Refusing to show discomfort or fatigue but unable to hide all of it, Pilar moves to a locker and is about to open it when Ingrid breaks the silence that has been winter between them since Mohawk left S.S. Hope.

"Do you know what's wrong with the knee and how to fix it?"

Ingrid's speaks softly. Her words are matter-of-fact, without condem-nation. She knows what must be done and how to do it. But that doesn't make it any easier.

Pilar's head dips then comes right back up. It's the sound. The texture of Ingrid's voice can do that to her. And only Ingrid could have seen it when she landed. Pilar blinks, opens the locker door and reaches for a fresh gray T-shirt then shorts.

"Do you think Cha Hua could help?" same manner and tone, no judgment, just an impersonal offer of assistance.

Pilar turns to Ingrid who is still standing in the threshold, leaning against the jamb, hands in pockets, looking straight ahead. No judgment, just offering to help.

"I have to do this, Ingrid."

"Yes."

"For Ero. For Dav."

"Yes."

"You approve."

"No. But I can't stop you and won't try," Ingrid looks up at the ceiling. "You're responsible for team Falcon and this mission. You call the shots." Ingrid looks at Pilar. "How's that for a graceful surrender?"

"What?" Pilar shrugs, "You all of a sudden trying to make up for trying to keep me off this mission," she steps into flipflops.

"You were too soon out of hospital and, yes, I went to Command and tried to block you. However, now that we're here, for the sake of the mission I have no intention of trying to interfere with your duties. But don't expect me to cheer you on. At least not yet."

Ingrid turns to go. Pilar reaches out, touches, brings back, embraces tenderly against the wall as though comforting a child.

"I need you with me on this, babe. I need you to believe I can do it. I'm not being suicidal here. I thought a lot about it. No one else on the team has the experience for this. I need you with me. I want you to be my dresser."

Ingrid blanches and pulls back then goes blank, trying desperately not to feel anything. Censoring her response she turns away. Pilar leans back an inch or two, regards. Smiles. Then, a bit sad, she steps back.

"Well at least we can talk to each other again now there's a slight thaw at the poles." Then, impish, Pilar steps forward, leans in. Kiss. Lips. Soft. Then she pulls away to leave as though nothing has happened. "Now let me get an hour's sleep before reveille."

Ingrid looks at Pilar with disbelief.

"It never ceases to amaze me how everything is okay as soon as you get your way."

"Only you can send me off right, babe," Pilar grins.

"Do what you have to do, Pilar," Ingrid turns to go. "But don't ask for my help. Not right now, okay?"

Ingrid strides back to her quarters and a few hours of agitated sleep. That leaves Pilar Mezon with aches and pains from many sources that are eclipsed by the importance of her new job on this mission.

***

Wilderness-people have developed capacities that are inexplicable and mysterious to those not adapted to darkness and stone, capacities evolved for a realm where sound is of primary importance. Most of them travel in spread-out bands of a dozen or so, staying away from each other so as not to overgraze the wilderness, careful to leave no footprint, no evidence of their existence – not for fear of discovery, though that is a constant and driving force in their lives, but because they are dependent on the delicate inter-locking systems that sustain them.

Bonded by a common belief that nothing from Source can be owned and everything from Source belongs equally to all, stone-people migrate slowly, foraging, planting, harvesting and tending with a sense of time, place and season. Somehow, the scattered groups know where others are and when to come together, as they have now, almost three hundred of them.

The ceremony of wicks at TrezArches is one of the largest stone-people gatherings. It marks the one time in the year for conceiving new life by those who drew the lots. This is not to imply that during the rest of the year there isn't abundant coupling. But by common agreement those unions do not result in pregnancy because the environment is finite and the population must be controlled.

A dozen couples will try, some bonded pairs, some near-strangers. By custom, the female chooses and the male is free to decline without prejudice. If past records are predictors, there might be six pregnancies resulting in maybe three or four live births of which perhaps two will live.

Others here at the ceremony of wicks are from different clans and traveling groups. They bring with them all things human and, for the most part, honor the long tradition of putting differences and difficulties aside for three nights and two days of music, storytelling, athleticism, bargaining, special food, and falling in love.

The ceremony begins with song. A dozen singers are stationed around the otherwise empty chamber of rituals. They hold wicks aloft, the only light in the big flesh-colored oval of arched space, and share a breath of silence having just completed the song-ribbon prayer for those who drew the lots, who are on their ways elsewhere to mate for the purpose of seeding a child.

Then the singers leave, all but one, a girl just into her menses, from R'io's band. She steps forward to stand poised on an airy perch. She raises her virginal face and her wick. In a voice that is sharp and piercing the girl intones a plainsong hymn that ricochets off of the stone.

"Source of all creation – supreme, sublime, beyond compare or comprehension – you are reality! You fill us with sustenance and beauty! Come everyone from near and far, celebrate creation!"

The girl sings to all directions, sending the call far beyond the sentries at different entrances to the TrezArches cave complex.

From a distance, another singer joins her and another and another stationed around the chamber of rituals, announcing the presence of Source, calling the people to come celebrate what sustains them. The call builds and builds to a crescendo then stops abruptly for a moment before drummers start the beat and lead the different groups into the chamber of rituals with their offerings of light and life and song and dance and food.

When all the groups are in, the babes are presented – three this year, a most excellent crop. Held high, their names are chanted with great rejoicing. And finally, most unusual, a new arrival is introduced by the person who brought her to stone-people.

So it is that Skye is alone in one of the tunnels, waiting for R'io to take her into the chamber after the last babe is celebrated. She hasn't seen him since that one encounter with Esa and is distracted by his absence. Then, somehow, he's standing right next to her just as the drums go quiet, their cue to enter.

Taller than her by at least a head, he's dressed as before, only now his long red hair is loose and his doublet is closed with crimson laces and he won't look at her and the deep wrinkle of concern between his eyebrows puzzles her. He takes her hand and Skye wonders what it is about his proximity that makes her tremble so. Then he steps forward, leading her out into the big sandstone cavern that is occupied by almost three hundred people dressed in their celebration colors, most standing to dance, all looking at her with intense interest.

She can hear her heart slamming as he places his hand in the small of her back and gently nudges her forward. He steps back. She turns, not wanting him to be so far away. His eyes of purest blue flame are looking at her again, that way again, sipping the breath out of her. Then his words are strong enough to fill the cavern.

"This is Skye One-Who-Wanders, curanda! Escaped from Great City! Birthed at the Refuge by Isham One-Who-Waits! Now of wilderness-people and L'escola!"

And she, too, has a story.

R'io motions for her to stay then he steps back even farther. The singers take up the threads of her tale and spin them around the cavern as drummers join in and the sound gets loud again, an explosion of welcome. And in the middle of it all he is most real and looking at her that way then turning to disappear back into the tunnel.

Esa comes forward, takes her hand and leads her to where Curanda and elder Moss are waiting to go eat. Then the drums are loud again and people welcome her then dance or go for food or move toward the bargaining stalls while she, Skye One-Who-Wanders, can't breathe or stop trembling for the vividness of him.

***

120

After the fact, Great City's head of Security informed the Presider that she had instructed assistants to quietly remove ambassador Baxter from the public square because of his increasing agitation. He was escorted back to his quarters and is now sedated and under guard. Such behavior is not tolerated in The Heights even though it's understandable because Baxter has completed his duties here and should be on his way back to S.S. Hope. Nonetheless, bla, bla, bla. The Presider cleared her to inform the other three ambassadors that Baxter is ill and under quarantine.

No one was surprised. So far questions have been easy to field.

While dealing with Baxter she was also busy monitoring the surface for signs of the bio-form and continually checking in on the shape-changer now prowling empty tunnels and caverns finding no signs of bio-forms, no indication humans were ever there, no hint of the creature that attacked. After brief consultation with Reed she instructed her Primes to activate all machinery and earth-moving equipment in the deployment bay on the northeast side of Great City. She also had a workout with Jerrod and attended two meetings, all the while wrestling with herself about seeing Dav Baxter in the flesh.

Yes/No?

The call of his actuality is compelling. Each new discovery deepens her curiosity. The Primes have informed her that Dav has a thirteen-year-old son, Ero Mezon, who recently completed his first level cadet training with highest marks and is currently serving as the cadet-aide to the captain of central command. The boy's mother is what they call an elite first responder off on a mission somewhere and unmistakably the women in the images from Baxter's memory-book though they do not seem to be what Space Staters call a couple. No more can be learned because the rest is classified Personal Information and not available but through court petition.

As with all addiction, eating feeds the appetite. Lassiter is now edging toward the conviction that it is in the best interests of all for her to pay Dav Baxter an official visit and thus, with a bucket of reality douse this firestorm called feeling. She has first, however, to figure out how to justify breaking the old and strictly enforced taboo against unauthorized contact with Space Staters, who are considered inferior.

Lassiter turns from the shape-changer to check George Biggs Boltin who is a shade of his former self, pale and almost transparent with the start of a scruffy beard and a lot of fear in his fevered eyes. As though deliberately withholding the pleasure, she studies her other screens, checking that all is as it should be, not wanting to get caught like Boltin looking the wrong way. Finally, she turns to Dav Baxter who is in the bedroom of his suite, sleeping the sleep of the drugged, a bit of drool trailing out of his slack mouth. Then her tech-secretary breaks the silence.

"The Presider wants you in conference room number six immediately. Your destination is not to be revealed to anyone."

"Yesyes," zipping her tunic, Great City's head of Security rushes out of her office, away from the slightly tumescent citizen-unit whose purpose is to meet her every need but Jerrod can't find the missing resource or the bio-form that stole her. Jerrod can't blur her constant awareness of Dav Baxter. So, what good is he other than to keep her exercised, massaged and fed.

***

Cha-Hua's workroom is a pigsty in the belly of H-V cruiser Mohawk. It's lined with old metal lockers and boxes spewing their guts of wires and adapters and cables and rags and headsets and tools and parts for technologies that no longer exist. Tacked up all over the place are hologram duplications from ancient nature magazines and calendars, most of them images of salamanders, Cha-Hua's totem of adaptability.

Lt. Pilar Mezon is sitting on the big cluttered workbench, one leg up and straightened out under a very bright neon lamp. Cha Hua is standing on a stepstool leaning over the knee, peering through magnifying glasses. The little technician is wearing a stethoscope, its other end pressed to the underside of Pilar's knee. Head down, listening intently, Cha Hua is wearing khaki shorts, a tanktop and flipflops. Her tattoo is visible as a full-body work in progress with parts complete and parts barely sketched in – bright pink and lime green, a design intended eventually to cover everything but an oval of yeasty flesh around her eyes, nose and mouth.

Delicate tools in her other hand, Cha-Hua is probing, squinting, listening, occasionally murmuring gibberish to herself as she tries to calibrate the knee, looking for what might be causing the little nip of electricity that flashes through the replacement part when Pilar lands a certain way. The innards of the new implant resemble a wad of

122

writing worms that are in fact hybrid creatures, virtually a new life-form invented by one of the Space State scientists before he was out of 8th grade.

The little technologist is humming syllables of her private language as she makes a micro-adjustment and tickles the joint with the softest touch of current. Then she puts the tools down, removes the glasses, pats Pilar on the ankle and babbles something incomprehensible.

Nodding, Pilar flexes the knee, hops off of the table. She throws a sidekick then sinks into and rises from a few squats. She walks around one way then the other, nodding, satisfied.

"Oh yeah. Thanks, Cha."

And Pilar is out the door, heading back to the training tower to try the knee again with the rest of the team spotting her and not happy about her decision to be the one to pilot the windrider even though they understand she has to do it because of Dav and Ero.

***

At TrezArches, the drumming and singing and dancing and feasting and trading and intimacy went on for a long time before the last person sank to the ground and all were asleep but sentries out on the perimeters. The chamber of rituals is now dark but for a few scattered wicks and quiet but for soft snoring.

Skye and Esa, among others, are in the big chamber, curled up like puppies on warm stone, having exhausted themselves with food and dancing and the noisy bazaar. During that time, the other members of R'io's group were on their own, finding old friends, swapping tales, falling in love. That left Esa to serve as a very proud guide for Skye One-Who-Wanders.

R'io did not reappear. Curanda was nowhere to be found. So the two returned to the big chamber and fell asleep. They are thus curled up together when a blind young man from L'escola approaches.

His name is Wim. He shakes their shoulders. Esa is instantly awake. Skye has to struggle and looks up at the boy.

"Come," he whispers, beckoning.

They follow him out of the chamber of rituals through a long tunnel to a smallish chamber that is occupied by members of L'escola

123

and several other, older, very serious people. Now that all are here R'io addresses the group.

"A runner from the western nethers arrived just before the ceremony began. It is confirmed. SubTurran miners are approach-ing that area, close to the chamber of records. They must be lured away. L'escola drew the lot. We leave in half an hour. Change to traveling clothes with full packs."

R'io looks at Skye impersonally. Hard. Unfriendly.

"My preference is to leave you here until we can swing back around and reconnect. Curanda and elder Moss disagree, saying one learns best when there's no option. Elder Martin and Jabaz are neutral. But you are one of us now, not to be told what to do. It's your decision. However, I must inform you the journey is arduous even for those born to the stone and it may be long."

"I am L'escola now and belong with you," her resolve is visceral.

Unhappy with her response but unable to do anything about it, R'io turns to leave the chamber. "Esa, please help her change into proper traveling clothes and get her equipped."

"Si."

With that, R'io is gone. The others are leaving. Esa is tugging Skye back through the tunnel to their encampment and stone-people traveling clothes – brown breeches, red knee socks, ankle boots, soft blue shirt, green doublet, the yellow cap with earflaps, and a headband with a light attached so she can see without using her hands. The pack she wears is big and full and she and Esa are joining the group that is ready to head out.

As the holder of several ancient song-forms and responsible for passing them on to the next generation, R'io's group is called L'escola. Skye brings their number to twelve and all are now in traveling clothes with headlamps and heavy packs, heading out on a westward trail to the nethers, which serve as a buffer between the wilderness and SubTurran territory.

Jabaz, very tall and thin and dark, is out in front with two students – Schiara, the young girl who earlier called the people from her airy perch, and Wim, the boy with milky white eyes and equally white skin and kinky blond hair tied at the nape of his neck with the first signs of gold fuzz on his chin.

Next out is portly elder Martin, philosopher and escapee from SubTurra. He's with Esa and her older half-brother, Axl, starting on a logic lesson. Axl is a more compact version of his father, R'io. A strong handsome adolescent, the boy radiates confidence that sometimes borders on arrogance and is sweet on Schiara. Some distance back but keeping up, Curanda is with Skye One-Who-Wanders, teaching survival skills as they go. R'io and elder Moss bring up the rear with Jak and Juarez, the two oldest students – Jak, the girl, being ready to move on and train with a different group while Juarez just got here. They're sweeping up, watching for errant tracks and finding none because their colleagues up ahead are being careful.

***

Great City's Presider and head of Security are walking quickly across the public square to the tech-lab because Shen and Whitaker suddenly started receiving live feed from the now sufficiently reconstituted shape-changer, showing them what's beneath point B. On the way, using the time, Paul Prescot Reed issues instructions.

"The bio-form is trying to lure us away from point B. I want that surface equipment down and digging, blasting. Whatever it takes to get us down into point B soonest."

"Yes, sir. As per instructions equipment is being prepped now."

"Good, get it done."

Illumination in the square has been dim since Great City was put on half-measures. But the problem isn't dimness, it's the heat. Lower-level stewards with their tunics open at the throat watch the Presider and Karin Lassiter Kohl cross the square, hoping for something good but seeing only grim faces. As more and more details have trickled down concerning Great City's current situation, as more and more is being asked from each of them they begin to resemble a herd growing restless because of a certain terrifying smell in the air.

"Sir, I'd like to propose something regarding ambassador Davenport Baxter," she doesn't break her stride or look anywhere but straight ahead as is her habit.

"I want his guts in a jar. What about him?"

"A face-to-face meeting. I want one."

Reed stops in his tracks, causing her to stop and turn back and them to stand face-to-face half a body-length apart with him squinting at her for a long moment.

"Why?"

"Something is going on," her smoky glare is penetrating. "I don't put much weight on the explanation given for his behavior."

"Which is?"

"He's cranky because his tour finished and he should be on his way back to S.S. Hope."

"You don't buy an explanation that makes sense?"

"No. I think something happened. I've been checking old Security logs and something about his behavior doesn't jibe. I need to be with him, ask questions, look into his eyes."

Stuck between a rock and a hard place and with no other immediate hope of changing the dynamic, Paul Prescot Reed looks long and hard at his head of Security, acknowledging in an academic fashion that she could be aesthetically pleasing were she not so intense with ambition. Blinking, pondering her request, he looks around at the sluggish activity on the square.

"I'll consider it."

"There's not a lot of time, sir. Clearly…"

"I said I'll consider it!"

"Yes, sir. Of course."

Reed turns and, followed by Lassiter, enters the foyer of the Tech-lab, striding on back to the lab proper where Shen and Whitaker are standing bent over the big monitor. They make way for Reed and Lassiter who lean down and squint.

"What are we looking at?"

"Our shape-changer. Back from the dead," Shen whispers, amazed. "It reconstituted itself and is exploring a very big empty cavern directly under point B."

"Find anything?"

"Not so far, sir. No signs of life."

The shape-changer slithers through the tunnel that connects the grotto to the main chamber of the Refuge. Having learned from the first encounter, the device has split several times and is now four diffuse and gaseous gray smudges drifting in loose formation, each lighting its own way and sniffing independently, on the prowl for clues, inhabitants, bio-forms, the creature that attacked, anything at all, and continually transmitting shadowy emptiness back to Great City.

Rounding a corner, the shape-changer drifts into a deep pocket and stops in front of a floor to ceiling patch of white fluffy stuff like opaque cloud that seems to be pouring out of the stone, eclipsing the contents of a vertical crevice, the one loaded with items from the main chamber – cushions, wicks, the rolled-up rug.

The shape-changers approach and sniffs without touching. Unable to determine the nature of the white stuff that has so far been found nowhere else, one of the shape-changers suddenly morphs into a long thin pipette. The pipette tentatively approaches the cottony white stuff and sucks in a goodly amount that is then released into another shape-changer that is now a high-tech beaker/evaluating device.

Tipping this way and that, the beaker is carefully examining the whitish substance when all of a sudden it explodes, the beaker, and is no more, not in any form. Then the pipette shatters, falls to frozen pieces on the stone ground. The two remaining sections of shape-changer immediately split so there are four again, though thinner now and slower.

Solaris suddenly appears, striking out of nowhere slinging thread and spitting toxic droplets, on the attack. The big spider is also making the most horrible noise, a deafening explosion of staccato rage. Cornered, the shape-changer manages for the most part, to evade the keeper's wild thrashing, all the while continuing to transmit back to Great City where Shen is screaming.

"I WANT CLARITY ON THAT IMAGE!"

Inside her glass-walled office, Great City's Presider and heads of Technology, Engineering and Security are bent over the darkish big screen on her desk, trying to see though it's impossible to determine what's going on. Outside the glass office, technicians and engineers can be seen running back and forth as Shen bellows.

"GET ME SOME CLARITY!"

The shrieking is enough to drive one mad – deafening, rhythmic, staccato, dissonant pounding away at one's awareness.

"AND GET THAT SOUND DOWN!"

This last command bounces around a lab that is suddenly quiet as all screens go dark and silent but for a worrisome dripping sound that is clearly not of Great City. Then an image appears on all screens – Solaris, cornered, panting, frantic, one front leg cut off at the shoulder, pouring blood.

"Sweet hell's teeth, what is that thing?" Whitaker whispers. "Kill it."

"We don't have the juice," Shen shakes her head, frustrated.

The keeper staggers to one side. Another leg goes wobbly

beneath her. She sinks to her knees, tipping sideways.

"What is it?" Reed whispers.

"I don't know," Whitaker whispers. "But it's destroying our shape-changer. We have to pull back, give it another chance to reconstitute."

"The shape-changer can't reconstitute itself indefinitely," Shen straightens up and looks at the others. "We must use what remains of this one carefully."

"Pull the shape-changer back," Reed takes charge. "Let it do what it has to do to come back up to speed. Have it split and multiply several times. Meantime Lassiter is prepping equipment to go to point B and blast the place open, find out what we're up against. Lassiter, come."

With that, Paul Prescot Reed and Karin Lassiter Kohl are heading out of the Tech-lab and only when they get out do they realize that the lab is the only place left in Great City where the temperature is still normal and cool.

***

After a break for sleep and food, L'escola tackles the difficult task of an almost vertical ascent from the wilderness up several thousand feet to the edge of the nethers – miles of low, flat space carved out of stone by ancient miners, level on level of it, supported by massive squat pillars. Schiara and Wim have shimmied up the sheer cliff with coils of rope over their shoulders and are now at the top, hauling up packs and gear while the others easily scale the wall – all but elder Martin who is a bit portly for this kind of thing and, so, is helped by his beloved Jabaz.

Esa shows Skye how to loop a rope under her arms to serve as a harness. Skye insists on trying to climb without it. They compromise with Skye agreeing to loop the rope over one shoulder. She starts up and doesn't get far before she needs the rope and slips.

R'io's hand is suddenly there, catching then holding her up. He is not amused.

"If you are injured we must leave someone behind with you because you do not know the stone and the stone does not know you. Follow instructions exactly, even from Esa. When you get to the top

128

turn off your headlight. We go on from here for a while in common-awareness. Sip the winebroth."

When she finally drags herself over the ledge onto a deep shelf all the packs and gear are gone, except for hers, and so are the people. She gets to her feet, reaches down for her pack, slings it on, sips winebroth then turns off her headlight.

The sudden darkness is disorienting. She doesn't know where she is. But he told her to turn off her lamp and she must do as told even though fear is welling up fast. Then Curanda is with her somehow, not touching, not within reach, but with her, guiding.

Breathe. Listen.

She does as she is told. Gradually she becomes aware of something like the sound of approaching bees. Then it hits her like a shock wave, common-awareness. The force of it takes her breath away, hurling her into vertigo.

Everything is a jumbled blur. Static. Then she's aware of Curanda again.

Steady. Listen. Hear. Know.

The old woman is oddly illumined in Skye's awareness, as are they all through clearing static. And suddenly she's with them in a kind of glowing clarity. She sees by hearing.

They are at the edge of the nethers. In front of them is a slice of perfectly horizontal space 6.5 feet high by 16 miles wide and stretching out easily 20 miles in front of them. An ancient mine. The open space is supported by even rows of squat pillars carved out of the stone every 20 feet or so.

Skye is aware of the others, especially Curanda and Esa on either side, lined up to her left and right, hyper-alert and ready to advance. She feels a sort of faint thumping in her throat and understands it as the signal for all of them to start out across the nethers to the other side where they must search for the miners and lure them away from this particular path into wilderness.

Suddenly, with an almost sickening lurch, common-awareness deepens. She understands instructions not intended for her but for Schiara, Wim and Jabaz.

Stone-whisperers out front. Sweep. We are now in the way of quiet.

And they head out, inevident in all ways, not disturbing even so much as the molecules.

Dav Baxter is sprawled on his bed asleep. The lights are dim. One of Lassiter's beefy male assistants is sitting in a chair near the door, bored with work on his tech-pad.

A small cart is next to the bed. It's loaded with syringes, little bottles of medicine, atomizers, sterile pads – everything needed to control someone's mood indefinitely.

Now that Great City is on half-measures the heat is oppressive, more so than anyone anticipated. Lassiter's assistant is perspiring heavily. Floating at the bottom of a stupor, however, his metabolism lowered with medication, Dav Baxter is as dry as talcum powder.

The door opens. Another assistant enters, also male, also large, also perspiring. He goes to the table, picks up an inhaler, turns to Baxter and sticks the business end of the inhaler up Baxter's nose, activating the spray. Yanked from nowhere to bleary and wretched consciousness Dav groans and turns over. The recently arrived assistant turns to the other chap and nods at the cart with medicines.

"Get that stuff outta here cause it wasn't ever here, see. This never happened. Mr. ambassador here is, shall we say, sick and getting better. Musta been something he ate."

The lower-level assistant does as told, removing the cart from the room. Meanwhile Dav has rolled to the edge of the bed and is sitting, head in hands, woozy and hung over.

"Dr. Baxter, you're late for a meeting! We thought something was wrong!"

Dav looks up, confused.

"Frankly, sir, you need a shower first. Up you go."

Dav is helped to his feet. Weak, stooped and nauseated, he shuffles toward the bathroom then stops and turns back to the assistant.

"Where are the other ambassadors?"

"Waiting for you. Come on, shower-up!"

Dav shuffles into the bathroom, into the shower where he wants to stay a long time but is not allowed.

***

A windrider is used by Space State first responders to access places too small and dangerous for regular craft. The vehicle consists of three parts: the suit, the support system, and the power system. Other equipment is worn as needed.

For most pilots, putting on a windrider is a ritualized process, similar to the ancient traditions of dressing a priest for high mass or a matador for the arena. This is especially true for Pilar Mezon. Even though she's done it hundreds of times, each time is a sacred event because it's quite possible she won't come back however determined she might be to do so.

Phase One of her preparations is now complete. It began with music and desperate lovemaking of a fierceness shared only with Ingrid. The two then proceeded on in utter silence through the internal and external cleansing.

Now, naked and gladiator strong with scars to prove it, Pilar steps out of the shower into the dryer. The heat element drops down around her body then floats back up and rests in its OFF position, leaving her bone dry. She reprograms the machine and covers her face with an oval mask. The circular heating element drops down around her body again and floats back up leaving her covered and white with talc but for her face. She steps off of the footpads and moves to Ingrid who is holding what resembles a simple pair of silky long johns, holding them down and open for Pilar to step into.

Ingrid pulls the skintight suit up over Pilar's body, matching little sensors in the fabric of the suit to Pilar's implanted terminals. Each sensor is snapped into place and finally but for an oval of face, Pilar is completely covered in thin, creamy white and almost transparent fabric – the first layer of the windrider. The second, slightly more substantial layer of the windrider is put on in a similar manner.

Through the entire process Pilar and Ingrid share a deepening silence. Nothing needs to be said. They are in sync, having done this before and understanding the importance of it being done properly.

The twelve members of L'escola have crossed the nethers and are currently stopped for the night at a place called the Listening Post. Uncharted and untouched by SubTurran tools, the Listening Post is a large meandering cavern with a low ceiling. Below through several hundred feet of granite is the beginning of SubTurran territory, miles of it stretching out in all directions on many levels. Above them through several hundred feet of stone is a toxified aquifer.

Half of those from L'escola have headed up, out or down to stand watch. The other six are scattered through this chamber, using their free time for rest and solitude because they will stand watch or move in a group soon enough. All are in the way of quiet but not of silence and darkness. Hence, wicklight glows faintly here and there and whispered speech is allowed.

Needing to be alone, Skye One-Who-Wanders found a place some-what removed from the others though still within hearing and sight. She's standing over her opened bedroll, exhausted and about to lie down. Then she notices wicklight approaching, carried by someone small and square.

Curanda. A large pouch hangs from one shoulder. She sets down the wick – it's not for her, after all – and whispers.

"The time you would ordinarily spend on watch is better spent on continuing to learn. Others will take your shift. I've asked Esa to teach you handtalk."

Curanda reaches into her pouch and pulls out a flask about the size of a fist. The flask has a strap attached so it can be worn around the neck and tucked into one's shirt.

"This is for tomorrow. It's similar to winebroth but much stronger. Just a touch to the tongue. Comprehende?"

"Si," she sniffs the bottle then drops the strap over her head and the bag down between small breasts.

"You're doing well," Curanda reaches up to pat a weary shoulder. "I must tend the others."

Savoring the compliment, Skye watches the apparently indefatigable old woman turn and move toward another faintly glowing wick then she sinks down onto the bedroll, reaches for her flask and a slug of water and is popping seeds into her mouth, aware of R'io's presence though as far as she knows he's nowhere near. Then she notices the soft amber glow of wicklight bobbing toward her again. She stands, hoping. When she sees it's Esa, she smiles anyway.

The little girl stops near the foot of the bedroll and touches a finger to her forehead. She raises her eyebrows, asking permission to sit. Receiving it, she steps onto the bedroll and plops down facing Skye who is now seated, too.

Bracketed by their wicks they regard one another, smiling. Then not smiling, just regarding. Connection happens suddenly and deeply and Skye One-Who-Wanders is filled with unspoken words.

Wilderness-people use different talk-modes. There's drum-talk, rune-talk, mouth-talk or speech, mind-to-mind like we're doing now, common-awareness when a group of people goes mind-to-mind like when we were crossing the nethers. There's also handtalk. I'm supposed to teach you. Tu comprehende?

Si.

Let's start. I show. You repeat.

Esa lifts dimpled hands from her lap and manipulates them slowly, showing the simplest and most obvious signs. Skye imitates, clumsily at first, clinging to their common-awareness for a sense of things as Esa's hands dance increasingly fluid and subtle signs.

Good. No more common-awareness. Only handtalk.

Esa starts putting chains of signs together, slowly at first. Then the little girl's hands and fingers dance elegant combinations. Skye tries to imitate. Rolling around on the bedding, they laugh soundlessly at mistakes and share food and water from Skye's supply, talking with their hands all the while because there are many questions.

~ What's a curanda? ~

~ Anyone capable of common-awareness. ~ Esa signs carefully so Skye can follow.

~ Can't everyone do it? ~

~ No. Common-awareness is a capacity not shared by all. Like sighted-blindness in those among us who have no way to see, yet they do. ~

Skye ponders this.

~ Are curandas special? ~

~ Special? ~

~ ...Of higher rank...better somehow...~

~ Oh, no. ~ Esa looks confused. ~ All creatures are from Source. All are special, none more than another. At least that's the ideal. Curandas just have an unusual ability like, say, perfect pitch. ~

~ So there are people who are not curanda. And there are

133

curandas, plural. Then there's Curanda. Is that her name? Why aren't you also named Curanda? ~

~ Curanda was so-named at birth by the curanda of the group who recognized extraordinary abilities in the newborn. Too, every group has at least one curanda. We have more than is typical because of the kind of music we teach. Our curanda is Curanda, my grandam. Isham is my grand da. ~

~ Curanda and One-Who-Waits are coupled? ~ Skye is surprised.

~ Coupled? ~

~ Together. A pair. ~

~ In the way of intimacy? ~

~ I guess. ~

~ Story has it they got together right after he arrived. ~

~ But they don't live together. ~

~ It's not necessary for two to live together to be in the way of intimacy. Anyhow, they did. Live together. Raised my da. Grand da stayed quite a while before he was called back to be One-Who-Waits at the Refuge. Grandam is busy with her own work of passing the heritage down to those of the next generation. Doesn't matter. They are bonded by Source. ~

~ R'io is their son, your da? ~

~ Yes. And Axl is my half-brother because R'io was chosen to seed another woman before he and my dam were bonded. ~

~ Who is your mother? Where? ~ Skye shivers from sudden coldness that has nothing to do with temperature.

Esa looks down.

~ My dam is with Source. ~

Skye nods solemnly.

~ Was she from Great City? ~

~ No, from a different band of remnant-people. Curanda says R'io and my dam loved each other in a way that forbids all others. After she returned to Source, da went deep into the wilderness alone for a long time. When he came back he said he would never love again. ~

Skye nods as something sinks beneath her. Her hands fall to her lap. She gazes around. Throughout the low space she can see a few wicks burning, see silhouettes of people returning from watch while others stir to take their places. Tearing, she tries to swallow a sudden inexplicable sadness that somehow relates to R'io.

Esa stands then stretches and yawns. She bows and touches fingers to her forehead then signs.

~ You learn fast. ~

~ You teach well. ~

They regard one another, one wistful the other grinning. Then the girl turns and moves off through the squat pillars to her nesting place with Curanda. After a moment Skye removes her clothes, takes a last slug of water from her flask and slides between the warmed layers of her bedding. She blinks up at shadow then blows out the wick. Much of her sleep-time is flooded with something new: disappointment.

***

Flushed and edgy, Great City's head of Security is with the two big assistants. She's wearing pearl gray and walking down the hall between them to where Dav Baxter was brought for a face-to-face she seems unable to cancel even now on the way when it's still not too late. Intimidated by Lassiter and uncomfortable in the heat, the assistants stay back a bit then stop on either side of a door with an F in its center.

"Wait here."

The door hisses open. Lassiter enters the conference room. The door closes behind her. Her eyes adjust.

Because of half-measures the room is dimly lit and empty but for Dav Baxter who is at the far corner, arrested in the process of turning around to start pacing back the other direction. He's staring at her bug-eyed, wearing slacks and a turtleneck sweater, both navy blue. Dark rings anchor his eyes and he looks exhausted, desperate with worry though not because she kept him waiting for over an hour, kept herself waiting to think it through one last time, calculate the risk of this somehow being used against her to deflect her final push to the top of all things Great City. Then watching him on the monitor she didn't care anymore.

Dav Baxter stands looking back at her and she's arrested by the power of his actuality. Half a head taller and quite thin now that he hasn't eaten in a while, his hair is reddish gold, his eyes cobalt blue and

135

deeply shadowed. Even though he's been drugged for a while there's more vitality in him than in any steward she's ever met.

Standing there alone with him, frozen, she understands the taboo against contact with Space Staters. She understands because when Dav Baxter's curious gaze is turned on her she can't speak but only stare at him as at an on-rushing force she would pursue should it be deflected.

Nervous, blinking, he rubs his hands together. He paces back and forth then returns to stand in front of her. His words make no sense to her because she does not dream that he might have secrets of his own.

"All right. Okay. So you know. Now what?"

He waits for her to say something. She doesn't, can't. He blinks and, having played the opening gambit, is forced to go on.

"I'm, uh, Dav Baxter, ambassador, S.S. Hope, coordinator of agri-barn Shenandoah. And you are…?"

Her lips move slightly but nothing comes out. It's as though she's walled-off from coherence. Then she clears her throat.

"Karin Lassiter Kohl. Great City's head of Security."

"Yes. Yes."

They stare at each other.

"Now what?" Baxter can't swallow because his mouth is too dry.

"I'm not sure…" She has no idea what he's talking about.

"I was right," eyes closed, he nods again, seeking options.

"Right about what?"

It's a mid-size room. She didn't want a small room for this meeting. She wanted plenty of space, room to stay away. But standing here now, in his presence, she finds herself unable to remember that he is the enemy and she's here with the Presider's permission not to turn all gooey in her clothes but to find a chink in Baxter, get him back on track so they can go on with negotiations. But the heat and the force of his reality make the room close.

Dav Baxter shrinks it more by stepping closer. He looks drawn, exhausted from artificial sleep.

"How many are there?" he whispers.

"How many what?"

"How many of *them*?" he points at nothing, the wall.

She looks blank then manages to speak.

"I called this meeting…"

Then something clicks. She gets it.

"What do you mean, how many are there?"

She needs to care about the answer. But as she steps closer she's distracted by wanting to touch him, smell him, burrow.

Until recently not much frightened Dav Baxter, commoner of S.S. Hope, coordinator of agri-barn Shenandoah. His main concerns were for Ero, Pilar, his work, and running times. But what he saw beyond the door marked MAINTENANCE frightens him more and more though not nearly as much as the woman standing in front of him with smoked gray eyes who has suddenly and unexpectedly begun to waver slowly and hypnotically like a cobra about to strike and he hasn't a clue what this conversation is about and all he wants is get out of here, to the other ambassadors, inform them, try to get through to the shuttle up at the transfer station. But he can't do anything for being locked in here with a woman who has entered an altered state. He blurts out the first thing that comes to mind, says it too loud, breaks the spell.

"Why did you want to see me?"

Lassiter says nothing, only rivets him with her eyes. As though magnetized she steps closer, leans, inhales his scent and steps back, regarding him soberly all of a sudden.

"What have you seen?" she whispers, looking into his eyes.

Dav Baxter doesn't respond because it is dawning on him that she doesn't know what he saw. She's here for another reason. What?

He stands numb and dumb, wondering how to let the others know what he saw, how to get back to the transfer station and S.S. Hope and Ero and maybe Pilar, how to prepare for what's to come whatever that might be, how to endure indefinite confinement in Great City wondering if the occasional ambassador who did not come back, who was lost in service to the whole, saw what he saw and was taken out of commission which seems to be happening to him now but then again he can't be certain because she doesn't know that he saw anything and wouldn't be asking her questions if he hadn't given her reason.

Then why was she here?

Dav Baxter steps back. He blinks and collects himself. Then hoping she'll tip her hand, he gestures to indicate that she's in charge.

The room is suddenly too small for Karin Lassiter Kohl. He's too close and she can't breathe. For the first time in her life she is deflected from her purpose.

It's so much better not to feel, not to be drawn to another with such inevitability.

Great City's head of Security turns abruptly on her heel and exits the conference room, leaving Dav Baxter unsure what had just happened. Then the two assistants enter the room, move to the ambassador and escort him back to his hospitality suite for more drugs.

***

Down in the catacombs, Isham One-Who-Waits is yanked from sleep to awareness by a brief and horrible dream of Solaris flailing and screaming and spouting blood then nothing, silence, darkness. He lights a wick and tries to slow his breathing so he can contact her. But he's too agitated by the dream.

Isham rises and gets dressed in the silvery skinsuit. He puts on a headlamp and moves off into the catacombs to renew his purpose. Passing alcove after alcove occupied by a mummified predecessor he finally arrives at the one he has come to see, the newest shrine. He arranged it for Awa, his predecessor the woman who birthed him.

She is curled up like a fetus on her side. A small earthen urn shaped like a bird is cradled in her arms. The urn contains a cylinder in which are copies of her favorite poetry and scripture, studied constantly during her long tenure.

Still not calm enough to try and contact Solaris, he pauses for a moment, concern etched on his face. He sighs. He closes his eyes. He tries to smile.

Beloved, I fear for the Refuge and Solaris. Something has happened. I dreamed…

Miles to the north, having stopped with L'escola and now standing watch, Curanda opens to him, receives, and tries from a distance to soothe.

***

"I need bait."

The Presider is sitting at his desk in his private office, which

138

is dimly lit with four faint spotlights shining down, one on him. Virginia Kahn Baker of Human Resources, Doug Smythe Hews of Medicine and Karin Lassiter Kohl of Security are standing in front of the impressive desk. Paul Prescot Reed is seated in his power chair, whispering barely audible instructions, determined to assert control.

"I need bait. Use the orange monitor suit you just successfully removed, Smythe. Recycle it for Boltin."

"Sir?" the head of Medicine gulps, perspiring heavily because of half-measures. "Do you mean…"

"I want that monitor suit put on George Biggs Boltin. He's going to be put on the surface to serve as bait. Do whatever you have to do to fix the suit to keep him alive and moving indefinitely."

"Ah, yes. Sort of reverse the experiment."

"Whatever," Reed turns to his head of Human Resources, potato-like on her stick legs, perspiring heavily. "That way it doesn't count as an additional loss on your ledger, Virginia."

"For which I am grateful," a little white ball of spit dances between her lips.

"This goes public as it happens," Reed lowers his gaze to his hands on his desk. "I want Baker and Smythe to make the announcement prepared by Virginia and okayed by me. I want unanimous support from the council. I want you to use this to fire people up, get them irritated and focused, energized. This is top priority, Smythe."

"Yes, sir."

Reed turns to his head of Security.

"Get surface vehicles up and ready to take him to point B. When the enemy comes out to get him, we pounce. If they don't take the bait we'll blast the whole area to pieces. Whatever it takes. Now get out and make it happen."

***

Skye One-Who-Wanders wakes to others stirring off in the distance and wicks beginning to dance. She sits, ignoring sore muscles. She crawls out of the bedding.

Sensing no hurry from the others, she stretches and twists, rolling out kinks. She goes into deep shadow and relieves herself. Returning to her things she lights the wick Curanda brought, stoops for

139

the waterflask, washes her hands, rinses her mouth and pops in a few seeds.

The shirt slides down soft and dry to her hips. She pulls on her knee-high heavy stockings then her pants and is reaching for the doublet when she notices a wick moving toward her. She squints. She recognizes.

R'io's steps are strong and sure. He halts a few body lengths away. She can't catch her breath and is no longer puzzled by that but enormously pleased somehow as they regard one another through the glow of wicklight. The connection is powerful and immediate. And she can't breathe.

"May I approach?" he says softly.

"Si."

He steps closer. Wicklight bounces off a face that's long and pale and roughly chiseled. His hair is blood red in this light, tied back for travel. His belt is low on his hips, heavy with tools.

For a moment he merely regards as though drinking, as though assessing not her but himself. Then he opens to her and she to him and they sink through each other both startled by what knits together so suddenly and with such force. He moves closer, holding the wick up and forward to see her, thus illumining himself, too. His eyes are the blue of hottest flame. She sees nothing else and is engulfed by what she sees.

"…Skye One-Who-Wanders…"

It's a deep salt whisper. And she's grateful because she needs to hear his voice.

"I've not been in the way of intimacy with another since Esa's mother was lost in birthing her. When she returned to Source, something in me died and I vowed not to love again in that way. Since then there has only been learning and purpose for me. Others have called. I felt no response. Tu comprehende?"

His voice is a resonance to bathe in. Nothing else matters.

"…R'io," she whispers. The word is heat in her mouth. She says it again. "R'io."

"Tu comprehende?"

"Si."

His presence is heat. Or is it the wick? He nods slowly as though gathering his thoughts and finding that difficult.

"Since your arrival I've spent my sleep-time with Source, asking to be released from my vow. And Source has answered. Tu comprehende?"

"Si," she whispers and as though by itself, her hand floats up to his cheek to hover without touching.

He stops for a moment, leveled by the closeness of her hand. Then he goes on.

"I speak now because what's next can't be anticipated. We will be on the edge of SubTurran territory. There could be great danger and I must focus only on how to get us all through it intact. However, should Source allow the way of quiet again my hope is that we can share time and decide if the way of intimacy is right for us."

She looks at him, unable to speak for a moment. Then she whispers.

"I long for that."

He closes his eyes and takes a deep breath. Her hand is still raised to his cheek but not touching. He leans his face into it then turns his head and kisses her palm gently. After a moment of surrender to her hand he raises his head and steps back. He switches from speech to common-awareness.

Until the way of quiet you must be to me as one of the others, all equally precious. I cannot be distracted. This means that for now what longs to be explored and expressed must wait its time. Tu comprehende?

Si.

He steps back and holds the wick out.

"How beautiful you are."

"Until the way of quiet."

He touches his forehead with a finger then turns and strides quickly back toward the others who are beginning to sling on their gear.

***

George Biggs Boltin, Great City's former head of Security, is still in the dirty white cell somewhere beneath The Heights, still wearing his stained dressing gown over undershorts because nothing else has been provided. He's lying on his side curled up in a ball, rocking back and forth, staring at the blank wall across from the cot, unable to determine if he's alive or dead, awake or asleep, not caring enough to try and find out.

Time has become a blur of sameness. Boltin stays mostly on the cot, getting up to drink water from the faucet or evacuate into the hole in the floor or suck at food shoved through a slot in the door then drop the empty pouches down the hole in the floor. It's all the same. Awake, asleep, alive or dead, it makes no difference. He isn't even aware of how much he's perspiring because of the heat or of the fact that the dirty white room is dimly lit because of half-measures.

Then something happens to the wall. Boltin raises his head, confused because the wall across from the cot has flickered to life. It's now a screen filled with someone's life-size face.

A woman. Very pale. Almost white hair.

She's peering at him. Her eyes are intense. Someone he knows from long ago. From before. From work. Lassiter, who tried to stab him in the back. She speaks.

"As Great City's head of Security I've been charged with informing you that a decision has been made regarding your disposition," her tone is impersonal.

Boltin is suddenly shivering like a chick in the rain because the cramps and the sweats that come and go are here again, personally ushered in by Karin Lassiter Kohl who has taken over his quarters, his function, his destiny.

"You will be taken to the public square," she continues. "Charges will be read. Punishment will be announced. This will happen soon."

The screen goes dark. The cell is just a dingy blur on his awareness.

"Soon?" he croons.

Then he vomits into the hole.

***

Once Pilar was dressed in the layered windrider skins, the circuits had to be activated, which took a while, allowing the little pilot to catch several hours sleep while all systems were checked. That done, the two women went to the windrider tack room, where they are now with the rest of team Falcon.

Much longer than it is wide, the tack room is a sterile metal space adjacent to the airlock through which she will deploy from H-V cruiser Mohawk. Pilar is standing in the center of the room wearing the suit that covers everything but an oval of face with a plain rubbery non-reflective fabric that is gray in color for now. The rest of the windrider is in pieces on the walls – the outer skin, helmet, boots, gloves, her physical support system, the power system, the harness, lots of nuts and bolts and straps and struts and, spanning all, the wings, furled on their long, flexible extension rods.

Working quietly and efficiently Ingrid and the rest of the team, even McCloud who is useful with her good hand and arm, methodically dress Pilar in boots, soft hood, gloves and life support. Ingrid and the others remove the substantial and complicated harness from the wall and gently drop it down over Pilar's head, buckling the shoulder straps down then fastening the ends around the pilot's chest and between her legs.

Only once do Ingrid and Pilar make eye contact and what passes between them is the memory of shared moments strung out through time and place. Ecstasies. Pains. Worries. Hopes. Declarations of independence. Then they go on, one nut and bolt at a time, taking the parts off of the wall and putting them on Pilar, about 100 pounds of gear plus bandoliers full of shape-changers and other Space State gadgets the elite first responder has chosen to take with her on this mission. Deployed, of course, the whole weighs nothing.

***

Even though the climb was steep and Skye One-Who-Wanders had to use ropes to keep up, L'escola has made good time. Some distance from their destination they've stopped to rest, half of them asleep, half on watch.

Scattered throughout the jagged cave they're suddenly alerted by sound. Faint at first. From above and off to one side, growing steadily louder until the sound is a deafening and profane screech of metal on raw stone and the sentries are running coming back, fear in their faces.

"DRILLING!"

The sound intensifies until it's an unbearable scream. The younger ones hold their ears. The sound goes on and on, louder and louder. And they're frozen, flooded with the wail of tool on stone, unable to follow R'io's handsign instructions. Then through what she knows is the combined strength of R'io, Curanda, elders Moss and Martin plus Jabaz, a fierce ripple of power snaps them all into common-awareness and the shrieking of the stone is dulled somewhat.

They're breaking through, into Little Bitter Hollow.

Flood the tunnel.

NO!

It's the only way!

Curanda is right.

Aye.

We go up around behind them.

R'io signs to everyone. When he's finished, she does what the others do. Hurrying, she takes off her pack and tosses it up to a ledge where someone catches and stows. Then she heads out with the others, moving quickly through an offshoot, following Curanda and the youngest ones with R'io and Jabaz bringing up the rear.

They climb up a dry water-smoothed tunnel. Moving through, they hold their ears because the sound is coming from very close.

Then it happens. With a horrible cracking sound a drill bit breaks through. The hole widens rapidly. Then a triangle of spinning drill-bits breaks all the way through, kicking up crushed stone, shrieking unbearably.

Rushing now, Curanda leads them all to an offshoot tunnel that ascends sharply then blossoms into a big lopsided chamber with a concave floor that is really more of a basin with a large hole at its bottom. The rest of the camber is composed of vaulted and jagged walls that converge at a high ceiling. Halfway up one side is a wide shelf with a big boulder leaning against the wall.

Scrambling to keep up with the others Skye glances down through the big hole at the bottom of the basin and can see more and more drill bits breaking through with glaring light and steam as a growing wound is opened in the stone. And the stench caused by the friction is sickening.

Moving quickly, the group heads up the walls of the chamber like spiders, Skye, too, functioning mostly on adrenalin and abandon. Halfway up, the group splits in two – youngsters staying with Curanda and elder Martin, the others going with R'io who is heading for the ledge with the boulder leaning against the wall. Skye starts toward R'io's group.

NO!

Ignoring him she scrambles on up to help and finally gets to the others who are on one side of the boulder, using a lever and pushing hard. At first, water seeps. Then it gushes. Then a great wall of toxic water is crashing into the cavern filling it because not enough can escape down the hole and they're all scrambling up the walls trying to get out of the way.

As in slow motion, like a gleaming fish, she leaps sideways out of frothed water seeking a handhold to pull herself out of the irresistible downdraft. She gets a hold but not a good purchase. She loses a boot to the churning water. Then she's being sucked down, pulled down and her hand can't hold against the force.

He gets fingertips on her wrist as she's sucked under then torn away and dragged into the chaos caused by too much water avalanching into a space not big enough to hold it. The other boot is ripped off. And she knows he's right behind her, thrashing underwater for her, getting fingertips on her heel.

BELT!

She's got it.

Then she's smashed against the floor of the basin spiraling down, thrashing. Impossible churning, around and around, over and under. Still, she holds onto the belt as she's flushed through the drain-hole into the raging river below. She slams into stone. Her head snaps back and everything is blue-white pain for a moment. Then there's nothing, not even darkness.

Fourth Gate – Forgetfulness

The underbelly of H-V cruiser Mohawk is stealth-graphite, smooth and featureless. A hatch opens in the center, dark on dark. Something like a seed or a pod or a larva emerges, also dark, and shiny as though moist. Then, curled up, furled around herself, Falcon One is sucked yawing and spinning away from the cruiser into starless dark that becomes recognizable as the pitted backside of the moon. The ship arcs away, on around its stealth orbit, rapidly shrinking to invisibility as she plummets (an optical illusion).

Snap!

The windrider's wings unfurl with a satisfying thud across her shoulders and between her legs. Lt. Pilar Mezon comes out of her slow spin and stands in space, stabilizing – wings extending easily twice the span of her arms, legs straight, feet together, arms and chest out, a diaphanous T visible only because she is slightly lighter than the background dark-of-the-moon, this particular craft having been programmed to blend into its context.

Dragonfly-like in texture, the wings are wired with tiny veins of technology that pick up light from however distant or indirect a source and turn it into usable energy – if nothing else is available a simple flashlight will do and one is dangling weightlessly from her belt. The outer skin of the windrider suit plus the boots, gloves and helmet are made of a fabric that is less than an eighth of an inch thick, flesh-like in texture, comfortable, formfitting, non-restrictive so that even with all she has on, Pilar Mezon is still clearly female.

The facemask is a film of transparent nu-glass that bubbles slightly and serves as her information center, with readable data all around the edges of what is, for her, both window and screen. Optional equipment is strapped or holstered to her arms and legs, including a tool belt, serious-looking sheath knife, a sleek sidearm and crisscrossed bandoliers that contain among other things a goodly number of shape-changer cartridges because she never deploys without them.

Stealth missions are by nature silent. This one is no exception. That means there is no communication between the windrider and H-V cruiser Mohawk or Command Ship Phoenix while Falcon One is out here. But there is sound and for that she's grateful – having once been on a mission where her helmet malfunctioned and she was in a decibel-void for over 72 hours, a form of torture not to be forgotten. This helmet is working perfectly and she hears her usual cocktail of soft white noise: the hiss of her own breathing, her heartbeat, her digestive system and the murmur of the technology talking to itself and to her in rhythms and tones and textures all familiar, immediate and comforting.

Using the keypad on the back of a glove, Pilar programs the wings then opens her arms wide. In response to the adjustment, windrider and pilot lazily drift off toward the halo of brilliant dawn that defines the edge of the moon, exponentially picking up velocity so it doesn't take long to clear the dark and swing out into blinding light, exploding with speed as her wings are hit with the full force of the sun's energy.

She half-furls the wings and tilts them for more control as the gust nearly sucks the breath out of her (optical illusions in space can do that, even to seasoned pros). Then she's stopped, stabilizing, mouth open, hanging in space, looking at earth for the first time.

Blinking, Pilar finally remembers to breathe. She's seen countless holos of what it's like now, earth. But nothing could have prepared her for the actual death of it.

The lady-jewel of all creation, now a tarnished coin. Flat gray with traces of faintly rippled landmasses separated by deserts and dead seas. Behind her the waning moon glows overwhelmingly crisp and bright. And somewhere between here and earth but not yet visible is the transfer station with H-V shuttle/barge Emerson and maybe some answers.

Lt. Pilar Mezon, disciplined elite first responder, seasoned been-there/done-that kinda gal, brackets her feelings and turns away from earth, back to the job at hand. With no way of knowing how long she'll be out here (the current windrider endurance record is 21 nautical days while her personal best is 18) she sets the little craft on course then activates her alarm with a hair trigger to wake her at the first hint of anything untoward. Arms wide, legs together, she relaxes into a few hours of diffuse consciousness and, neither asleep nor awake, sets out to close the distance between her and the unknown without being detected by anything that might be there waiting.

***

Incorporated groups that went below to escape the great collapse often numbered in the thousands. Typically, after going down life was not so different from before – most true believers of whatever scheme aren't connected to any realm but their own anyway. The rules didn't change, just the location of their enforcement.

With long histories of mutual hatred and competition, these groups, for the most part, were not in contact with each other once they went below, particularly the large religious groups with their mutually exclusive rigidities. Whatever their differences, however, they all shared the same fantasy of return to the surface and a world reborn. It sustained them for a thousand years. Then one day the fantasy collapsed.

In the end, only the Founders of Great City had sufficient resources to return to the surface. Only they had planned to do so from the beginning. Only they understood that the surface would not be reborn and something else would have to take its place.

***

Gasping.

Held upside down vomiting water.

Others. Running. Lots of them. Noise and glare.

Rubber suits, bubble-heads. Humans? Rushing. Screaming snatches of words in a language she can't remember, hard words, barked commands, loud slurred static. Glare rushing around her.

Then it all slows down goes dim goes dark.

Everything and nothing.

Noise again. Glare. Searing pain as they ease her down into some-thing then wrap, strap, close lid. Click. Cold hissing.

They've locked her in a transparent capsule of some kind. Four of them run the capsule to a sled, fasten it down and get on with her.

Ignition. Loud.

The sled is rolling on tracks. Everything is speed and screech-ing. Then darkness.

A spasm of awareness ripples through her and explodes. Suddenly she's lurching against restraints and pain, gasping to get out. She frees a hand, reaches up and pounds unyielding transparency. She tries to get her other arm free but when she moves it, pain threatens to suck her away and that can't happen because she has to get out now and go back while still this close. Nothing else matters. She has to get back.

Where?

Pounding with her good hand, she frees a foot and kicks. The pain is an explosion of purple fury. Mouth agape, she fights it off. She tries to scream but nothing comes out. She tries to shake her head, no, no, no, no, no but it will not move and she can no longer try because pain will not allow it.

Sinking back, she gasps as the sled clicks along rails too fast blur bump squeal around glaring curves whiplashing, slamming back and forth. Then darkness is merciful.

***

Dusk.

Gray gauze.

Out on the surface Isham One-Who-Waits is fresh and rested for a journey of several hundred miles, all of them out in the open. The sun is setting behind him. Ahead, everything is tinted ghostly green by his facemask.

Moving rhythmically, he glides like an ancient cross-country skier through countless dune valleys, leaving no trace of his presence. The back end of the cloak erases his trail as he goes. He decided to be safe and take the long way around to enter the wilderness from the east. It doubles the length of time he's on the surface but he's weighed the risks and is taking them.

***

Completely shaved, naked and moist, George Biggs Boltin is lying uncovered on a gurney in a vault-like room filled with gas that is icy cold and smells of spearmint. He's paralyzed by the gas, unable to resist, but still conscious, eyes wide open, unblinking.

Robin Smythe Hews, Great City's head of Medicine, wants Boltin to feel what's going to happen, told him what was going to happen, whispered it viciously then left the room to stand looking in the round window. It's Smythe's way of saying thanks for not paying attention. Thanks for letting a Prime Researcher escape so the situation with the Space States could spiral out of control. Thanks for being oblivious to the enemy down below.

Skin pink and polished, officious in his white lab coat, Smythe looks into the room as, with much whirring of mechanisms, George Biggs Boltin is lifted off of the gurney by spiny mechanical arms and turned this way and that. Hiss/pop, hiss/pop. All but the deepest and most deadly of the fine gold filaments are being inserted so the monitor suit can be connected and control him.

Great City's former head of Security screams as nerves are hit and co-opted. The procedure has to be stopped several times while Boltin lurches. When he is still again, more filaments are added then tested, which is a long painful process on a normal adult.

***

Jolted by noise and movement, she opens her eyes as the capsule is lifted off the sled and rolled into a different, larger machine. Slam! Dizzying speed again. An urgent pulsing wail from outside accompanies this smoother ride.

Inside the conveyance, four of them stand over the capsule, their hands reached in through gloves. First, hurrying, they slice back her clothes, remove a hastily applied pressure bandage and stop a geyser of blood that spurts out of her left thigh. Then they swab her other cuts and bruises, hook her up to a drip and splint her right foot. They try to take the belt wrapped around her right fist to check for breaks in that hand. She won't let go.

"Leave it," one murmurs. "This is the boss's treasure. Let him decide what to do with it."

Another reaches in a glove and touches the two relatively fresh crescent-shaped wounds at the base of her throat.

"These aren't consistent with the rest of her wounds."

"Do they need attention?"

"No. Healing nicely. May get infected from the toxicity she just took a bath in but our antibiotics should take care of that."

"Make a note of them for the boss."

Then hissing fills the capsule, dusting it with sweet steam. She

151

sinks down through gray gauze. The pain comes and goes in waves but from a distance now.

When she surfaces all she knows is that she is adrift on a sea of pain between continents of darkness and this isn't where she wants to be. What was before is gone – indeed, there's not even a sense that perhaps there was a before and a place not here. It's as though she's passed through a barrier that cannot be re-crossed.

And she's alone here.

That much she knows. It's part of the pain.

Then gauze and glare. She understands not to move because even though the pain is far away it would be very bad if she were to move. She blinks, rolls her eyes seeking the source of hissing.

Beeping.

Pinging.

Blink.

Someone is peering in at her. Someone with a normal human head. Perhaps a man. They stare at each other through the hard transparency of the capsule that contains her.

She hears a pleasant two-toned chime. Others arrive and lean and peer. They're masked and wearing identical gowns. They are deferential to the man with the normal human head and no mask, whose hair is long and dark and oily and whose beard is heavy shadow and whose eyes are dark and hungry. She does not avert her gaze though the glare is almost blinding. Then he steps back and the others take over, one of them leaning down. She hears a click then static.

"WHO ARE YOU?"

The voice is too loud. Piercing. She winces and is flooded with pain.

"WHERE ARE YOU FROM?"

The questions arrest her. She has no way to respond. What was is gone. And this causes different pain. Pain that can't be touched by what they are doing to her, whether for good or ill.

***

Great City's head of Security is not what one would call gauzy but Karin Lassiter Kohl has definitely softened since she discovered the mother of all feelings. And the more she scans back through Dav

152

Baxter's surveillance record the softer she becomes even though she's looking for something particular because she knows she's missed something but not what. Now she's going back through yet another day, speeding it up, slowing down occasionally not because of something suspicious but because of the angle or the light on his face – she can't help it.

Shen and Whitaker are handling the shape-changer in the big cavern complex beneath point B. Several dozen drones now surround Great City at different distances into the dunes and are waiting for another sighting of the bio-form that circled the place. Earthmoving equipment and technology are being readied for deployment. Overhead, satellites are zoomed in, scanning every gram of ash below. Citizen-units on the lane and stewards in The Heights are all functioning within norms, which is remarkable given the circumstances.

She zooms in on Dav Baxter pulling up short in Liberty Park back when it was shut down for conservation purposes. Fascinated by the way he stands listening, she crawls the image forward, distorting the audio. The lights go dim. Dav Baxter turns to exit then changes his mind and goes the other way, into the diorama, toward a faint red glow on the dark background as the lights dim down to almost nothing.

Lassiter's eyes grow wide as she zooms in farther to see Dav Baxter open a Maintenance door, look through, see something and jerk back when a citizen Maintenance-unit appears, leans in, checks and closes the door. Baxter turns and starts back toward the path. She zooms in, examines his horrified face then returns the record to normal speed as he crosses the path, taking the nearest way out of the park and Lassiter is standing in her office with her mouth open because it happened on her watch and the Presider must be informed immediately.

***

Illumined by the faintest glow of moonlight, Isham One-Who-Waits sinks to his knees and digs a depression in the ash. He burrows into the depression, covering all traces of his presence and is asleep when Curanda's awareness pierces his.

ISHAM?!

Here, love. He sits up.

Oh, blessed Source! We've only now stopped for me to try and...

What is it?

SubTurran miners penetrated Mossy Vein, just below Stone Basin. To deflect them, we flooded the point of entry with toxic water. R'io and Skye One-Who-Wanders were sucked down in the flooding action and are lost to us – either dead or in SubTurra. They do not respond to our calls.

Where are you?

Heading for Mist Canyon, Cave of Waters. Are you near?

There's a portal directly north of here about a day's travel. I'll rest a few hours and head out.

Oh, Isham…

Is elder Martin with you?

No. He and Axl have gone close to SubTurran territory to try and learn more.

All we can do from here is trust Source to be with our son and new daughter wherever they are.

Aye.

Settling back down in his ashy bed, One-Who-Waits covers himself again. On his side, curled up around his pack, he's flooded with an almost paralyzing grief to which he is particularly vulnerable on the surface. She feels it from so far away.

It's night up there?

Yes. If you can call it that.

Cold?

Bitter but the gear keeps me comfortable. Rest now, love. We both need to recharge and conserve when we can.

…Aye…

***

SubTurra's new arrival opens her eyes to indefinite blur and glare, shadowy apparitions and questions. She blinks, understands she's still in the transparent capsule, prisoner in a sparkling unknown distorted world.

"Where are you from?"

"Who are you?"

"How did you get here?"

"What's your name?"

154

"Where are your people?"

She doesn't respond.

They modulate the sound, moving back and forth through different kinds of loud and soft until they arrive at what registers without distressing. They experiment with voices: young, old, male, female, sincere, seductive, demanding. They ask the same questions again and again. They try different languages and accents.

Snatches register. Her brain waves tell them so even though she doesn't respond. Finally they settle on a frequency and a timbre and a sex and a language and ask more questions, modulating further until frequency and timbre and voice and language sooth and lull her toward trust she understands to withhold.

They inquire about her clothes and the shat and vomited contents of her stomach, her earwax, her snot and saliva. They ask where she got that food those clothes and why cling to the belt.

Belt?

She doesn't know, either. So she sinks back down to oblivion.

***

Karin Lassiter Kohl is in her bathroom staring wide-eyed at a stranger in the mirror. She doesn't recognize that person. She sees in that woman someone who has caught the Space State contagion and is now stuck between conflicting desires.

The thought of going to the Presider is not acceptable. It's not that her own lapse would be exposed – someone else would take the fall. It's that for right now at least she can't put Dav Baxter in that kind of jeopardy.

"…What's wrong with me," she whispers, unable to take her eyes off of the frightened eyes in the mirror.

She wipes perspiration from her throat and forehead with the back of a hand. She knows the history. She checked to make sure. The few previous ambassadors who found out about citizen-units were all immediately disposed of in such a manner as to make the deaths look perfectly natural. Their ashes were returned to the transfer station with a cool note of sympathy.

Not wanting to call Pharmacy for a mood-leveler because she doesn't want a flag on her file even though it would be perfectly

155

understandable given the nature of her duties right now, Lassiter rinses out her mouth then washes her face with cold water and heads back to her office, knowing that the longer she takes to decide what to do about Baxter the more intricate the network of lies she will have to fabricate.

***

SubTurra's recently arrived female patient wakes again. In a different place. There's no loud hissing. It's warmer here.

Her vision adjusts. She's not in the capsule anymore but on a bed between crisp sheets. Alone.

The tubes are gone. She's no longer drugged. She hears only distant, hollow hissing.

This is a different place – same world, different place. She's got that figured out.

Not without significant discomfort, she turns her head to one side then the other, looking around as best she can. What she sees is nothing. Emptiness. Neither dark nor light.

Edgeless.

Shadowless.

Featureless but for distant hollow hissing. The ceiling and walls are blurry. They could be close or far.

She swallows. Her throat is sore. Her mouth tastes rancid.

After a moment's consideration, testing, she moves ever so slightly and finds more aching and weakness than pain. She frees her left arm from the cover and feels no pain though the limb is encased from knuckles to above her elbow in a heavy elastic brace. She wriggles her fingers, reaches up and feels a big painful lump on her cheekbone. She brings her other hand out from under the cover and finds it wrapped in something substantial and brown. She slowly unwraps a long felt strap with an iron buckle at one end.

Belt," she whispers, knowing only the word for the thing. She brings the belt to her face and inhales, smelling scents that suck her back down into the swirl of questions with no answers. But she doesn't drown because she knows two things now. She knows she has this belt for some reason. And she knows she will not relinquish it because, somehow, it's a point of connection.

Connection to what?

156

She drapes the belt around her neck then carefully and with effort moves the sheet aside and looks down at her body. A laced boot encases her right leg almost to the knee. Nasty scrapes and bruises are scattered here and there. She can't, of course, see the diagonal cut above her right ear, closed with many stitches.

She moves her arms and legs a bit. Turns her head. Pain levels are almost bearable.

Now what?

Silence.

Distant hollow hissing.

Nothing calls. Too tired to cover herself, she closes her eyes and retreats from consciousness. After a moment, an attendant in hospital greens enters from behind the bed, covers her and departs.

***

Deploying heavy equipment from Great City to point B proves to be considerably easier said than done. Some of the machines can be operated remotely by the Security Primes up in their workstations. But the big shovels and earthmovers must be manually operated on site. This means a sizeable number of citizen-units have to be radically reprogrammed to function on the surface.

Now, down near the bottom of the structure, several dozen citizen Maintenance-units are in MED stations, being prepped. Just below them, Maintenance technicians are working on the door of the deployment bay, it having malfunctioned the first time it was opened. Other crews of citizen-unit Engineers and Technicians are working on the machines, some of which are impresssively big and complex, all from the time of constructing Great City.

While Lassiter is coordinating all of this, thoughts and images of Dav Baxter create an irresistible warm breeze between her clothing and her flesh. She has yet to decide what to do about what he discovered because any such decision is clouded by the Space State contagion. What she has done is keep him knocked out, "ill" to anyone who asks.

"With what?" the other ambassadors inquire.

"Medicine is trying to determine that. Meantime, he's quarantined."

***

After generations of waiting, it suddenly became clear to incorporated groups down below that there would be no return to the surface. The surface no longer existed. It wasn't coming back.

Why this realization occurred everywhere at the same time is a mystery related perhaps to the fact that impossible fantasies are heavy and humans eventually collapse beneath their weight. When the different groups originally went down it was for the time being – however long that might last. Everything was fine, relatively speaking, until they realized that the fantasy of return was stillborn.

Entire populations instantly shifted into a void of meaning, a vacuum that was immediately filled, as one person described it, by "an overwhelming sense of being trapped in a coffin with too many other maggots." Paralyzed, these groups had to find another reason to go on, a new purpose. And they needed it fast because order was unraveling and there was nothing to keep the increasing panic at bay.

Again, in an odd kind of synchronicity, from disparate points beneath the surface and independent of each other, those in positions of power chose expansion as the antidote. If they could not return to a new life on the surface they would carve one out here below. The propaganda campaigns were vivid.

"Blast open the Life You Want!" "It's There For The Taking!" "Seize Your Opportunity!"

But it's hard to turn a nightmare into a dream.

So when propaganda didn't work because people were almost comatose with claustrophobia, force was employed. And the nature of life under-ground changed radically for all but a very few.

***

Sun high overhead, breathing long labored hisses, Isham One-Who-Waits is crawling on his belly up the shoulder of a steep dune. He stops at the ridge. SubTurran territory is directly beneath the surface here, spreading out all around him. SubTurrans don't come up but they

158

do constantly monitor the surface and before approaching this portal he always checks for surveillance.

Careful to stay low, he pulls a device out of a pocket in his cloak – called a Listener, a willowy silvery wand that telescopes out to almost twice his body length. He extends and activates the Listener. Then he raises it up above the ridge, turning it this way and that.

When he is satisfied no threat is near, Isham moves quickly. He de-activates and collapses the Listener then puts it back in his cloak. Hurrying, he skis down the dune's steep shoulder to its valley where he locates and opens a portal.

Inside, Isham quickly closes the portal then rushes through a complicated network of tunnels, twisting, turning, descending. Finally, heaving with relief and exhaustion, he removes his facemask, reaches for his almost empty water flask and drains it because he knows where more is from here. Taking a moment to breathe, the old man raises his face.

"Thank you Source, for the journey thus far and I ask your continued blessing on my awareness. Let this be."

Isham takes off the cloak, gauntlets and boots and stows them in his backpack with the breather. He puts a lamp around his forehead and turns it on. He slings on and settles into the pack. Then he heads out through a zigzaging tunnel of raw stone that is none too roomy on his way to meet up with L'escola.

Meanwhile, overhead where stars still shine in darkness, a small satellite has digested the stimulus that radiated so briefly from the surface directly below and then stopped. The stimulus is relayed back to Great City's Security Primes floating in their far-flung workbays. The chemically sus-tained and exhausted Primes ride the big swell in the data as the relay comes in. Because the information meets certain criteria it is immediately forwarded to the head of Security.

Karin Lassiter Kohl has just entered a medium size conference room in Founders Hall where Dav Baxter has been waiting for over an hour. She approaches in a professional manner, looking a bit hard as she nails him with smoky gray eyes that soften involuntarily when they meet his. Just then, a call from her Security Primes pings through her surgically implanted earpiece.

Dav Baxter, of course, knows nothing of the earpiece or the Primes and is startled when for no apparent reason Great City's head of Security snaps her head around then turns and is walking back out the door whispering, "bio-form?" He stares after her, puzzled, disoriented, groggy and needing a shave.

Like the first time, they woke him for this interview. They said something about another meeting, made him sower, brought him here. This time they provided a hard folding chair. He's sitting, as he was told – awake though diffused by drugs.

Meanwhile, just outside the door, the two assistants gaze after Lassiter who is running out the big double doors of Founders' Hall into the public square on the way back to her office. Since she left no further instructions the assistants stay where they are, bracketing the conference room door, looking competent.

**

Independent of and for the most part unaware of each other, incorporated groups beneath the surface began to carve out space. They blasted, bored, chipped and ripped their ways through stone to expand their territories, filling uninhabitable, toxified areas with the dust and rubble of their efforts.

Eventually different groups began to find each other going opposite directions in the same narrow tunnel. When desperate people find themselves on opposing sides of a zero-sum game they tend to recognize only two options: absorption or destruction.

For a while, co-option and destruction both roiled beneath the surface as populations fought then morphed together and went on to devour the next group. But eventually one group was larger than the few stragglers that remained. The dominant power had formed.

SubTurra is a force against which no other can stand.

**

Having changed from surface gear into stone-people traveling clothes with a headlamp on a band around his head, Isham One-Who-Waits is now sitting at the top of Mist Canyon, taking a moment to rest before what is always a risky descent. White hair and beard rolled up tight and out of the way, legs dangling, he studies the fog.

Deep and precipitous, Mist Canyon is shaped like a huge

mushroom standing on end with a dome at the top of a long jagged stem. At this partic-ular moment the dome is filled with weather. The light on his forehead barely dents the thick fog that drips down, causing the almost vertical walls to be slippery as soap. Tired from hurrying, he closes his eyes and opens to common-awareness with Curanda.

Beloved?
Si, Isham.
Where are you?
Nearing the Cave of Waters. You?
Lip of Mist Canyon, about to start down.
Conditions?
Never ideal.
Stay with Source.
Aye. Is there news?
Si, just now, from elder Martin. R'io and Skye were captured and are alive. Both are wounded though how badly is not known. That's it for now. Elder Martin and Axl have left SubTurran territory and are heading here with more information but traveling too fast to send. They should arrive soon, Source willing. We're on the move again, I must go.
Source willing, soon, love.

Isham shifts his awareness to the task at hand. Sitting, legs dangling, he takes a moment to center his awareness before the long descent during which there is no place to stop. Resting, turning his head this way and that, he studies the fog as it slowly swirls, billowing spirals around him. He sniffs. There's an iron smell to the wet air, a metallic coldness. He shivers.

When he feels settled and ready, Isham lowers his pack and gear over the side to hang from the belt around his waist, spinning slowly twenty feet down. He turns onto his belly and lowers himself over the lip onto the canyon's wall. Hugging moist stone, pack and gear dangling, he finds the path down, one finger and toehold at a time.

The windrider arcs into view. Its technology switches to a new program causing the wings to furl closed. The faintly glowing projectile stops, hangs poised and shimmering on the spacey background. Not asleep, not awake, eyes half open, face blank, Lt. Pilar Mezon is completely relaxed in a vertical position, standing, as it were, with her feet together, knees slightly bent, embracing herself and glistening almost white on one side from bright light bouncing off of the moon, which is not visible from here. Earth is on the other side. The transfer station is dark and tiny out in front of her, like a period at the end of a sentence.

"Zzzzzzz…"

Falcon One shifts instantly from a state of suspended awareness to one of focused attention and extinguishes the alarm by pressing a button on the back of her glove. She checks the readings on the inside of her facemask and finds herself on-target just inside visual-range of the transfer station for an edge-on approach.

After a few stretches and isometrics Pilar works the knee and is relieved to find it fine. Sucking down nutrients she checks her readings again. Then she programs the angle on her wings and is ready to make her approach.

Sliding the special telescopic lens down over her facemask Pilar zooms in until her visual field is almost filled with the transfer station. A flat disk. A thick coin ringed with shadowy delivery docks, all empty but one that holds S.S. Hope's shuttle/barge Ralph Waldo Emerson.

The shape-changers she sent out continue to read the entire area dark and dead. Zero-power. It should be ablaze, the transfer station, and it's not. It should be glaring with light. It should be a beacon for H-V ferries and shuttles come from unimaginable distances with goods in exchange for bits of the past. But it's not emitting a single erg.

***

She wakes again, uncertain where she is. The space is pale and in-definite. Then she remembers waking here before. She assesses.

The bed is firm. Her head and shoulders are slightly elevated. Her left arm is in a brace from fingertips to above her elbow. Her right foot is in an orthopedic boot.

She squints, peering around, sensing something beyond the vague-ness, having no idea what that might be. Stirring, she feels stiff and sore. She brings her right hand out from under the cover and studies the belt wrapped around her fist. She could get up but nothing calls, nothing stimulates, nothing attracts.

Pop!

A shaft of smoky light materializes and shines angled down off the foot of the bed. Someone wearing green clothes like hospital scrubs, wheels a comfortable dark green leather wingback chair into the shaft of light and locks it down then leaves.

The patient hears steps coming from behind the bed – hard heels on a hard surface. Someone is here. Next to the bed. Several feet away. She looks without moving her head.

A woman has arrived and is moving to the chair positioned several feet off the foot of the bed, her odor masked by an over-powering scent of spicy-sweetness. She sits.

The shaft of smoky light angles down across long dark hair that is silk on taut shoulders. Early middle age. Sitting in and framed by the chair. Her hands relaxed and folded in her lap. One chiseled knee crossed over the other. A tip of shiny shoe. Soft, dark, quiet. Warm smile.

"My name is Katya." The voice is perfectly tuned.

The woman clears her throat and sits poised, waiting for a response that doesn't come. Slender and tan, she's wearing a beautifully cut navy blue suit of soft fabric. Throat, hands and much leg are exposed. She sits leaning forward just a bit, head tilted expectantly, dark hair framing and shadowing the soft angles of her face. Two moss-green eyes are magnets.

"Do *you* have a name?"

After a moment the patient struggles, raises her head, lifts herself up and leans over, braced on one forearm, wincing. She blinks against spinning and pain. Peering, she regards the woman called Katya.

"What do you want from me?"

"We want to help you."

"Help?" She needs to trust and doesn't for some reason.

"Can you say my name?" The woman smiles kindly and tilts

her head. "Can you say, 'Katya'?"

"Who's 'we' and what's 'help'?"

"Well," Katya shrugs benignly and tilts her head the other way as though listening to a voice not her own. "For instance, maybe we could help by taking you back to your people."

Blink.

After a moment the patient eases back down, perspiration beading her upper lip. She closes her eyes then opens them, staring straight up at nothing. Then she turns her head and looks at Katya.

"My people?"

"Yes. Take you back. With your help, of course because we don't know who or where thy are."

The smile and the smell are both masks that prevents the patient from trusting. Katya goes on.

"We want to help you go home but we don't know where that is, you see. Now that you're awake you can help us."

"Who are you?"

"I'm Katya."

"No, who's 'we'?"

"I speak on behalf of the people of SubTurra," Katya smiles. "Who are you?"

The patient turns her head and looks away. "I don't know."

Neither speaks. Then Katya leans back in the chair and drapes her wrists over its arms. She tilts her head and whispers playful singsong.

"Yes you do."

Staring up at a ceiling she knows must be there, the patient moves her head slowly from side to side. No. She closes her eyes. A tear leaks out then rolls down.

"What was before is gone."

"Nope. It's in there somewhere. Head injuries sometimes result in short term memory loss. But I can help. We'll find it. Your past. The two of us. Work on it together. Shall we give it a try?"

SubTurra.

She finds the word chilling for some reason. She shivers. She wants the woman to leave and turns her head away pretending to fall asleep. After a moment, Katya stands.

"You're tired." The sympathy seems genuine enough. "I'll return after you've rested a bit and we can get started on our little project."

Footsteps retreat behind the bed. She hears an attendant come and take the chair away. Pop! The shaft of light is gone.

The patient opens her eyes and looks around. She can hear the faint hum of the ventilation system. She turns onto her back. The space is still scented with Katya's acrid perfume, now dissipating where there are no walls and no ceiling though she is without question enclosed.

What kind of world is this?

***

Members of L'escola straggle into the Cave of Waters at the bottom of Mist Canyon. Several put down their gear and immediately head back out to stand watch leaving Curanda, elder Moss, Wim and Esa to set up camp, light wicks, start a hot meal and maybe get some rest.

Now that they've stopped what happened to R'io and Skye hits them hard, Esa in particular. The little girl is standing near the spot Curanda chose for them to bed down. Her pack and bags are untouched on the ground at her feet.

A tall thin figure materializes through fog that veils the cave's entrance. He stops and speaks briefly to Schiara who is on watch just outside. Then he walks into the cave.

Esa looks up. Though the girl hasn't seen him since she was very young, they share frequent mind-to-mind exchanges and are deeply bonded. Plus they are all anticipating his arrival.

Isham One-Who-Waits has stopped inside the mouth of the cave to take off his pack and bags. Sobbing, Esa runs to him, holds on tight.

"Oh, grand da…"

He rocks and tries to sooth as she chokes on sobs. Then Curanda is with them. He opens an arm and draws her into the embrace. They stand like that for a long time, with the child sobbing, holding each other as everything hits hard, sinks in, annihilates.

Curanda draws Esa ever so slightly away and nods toward a place at the back of the cave.

"We're over there. Rest and get warm. We'll go calm down and join you soon." She leads the sobbing girl deeper into the cave where the waters are soothing and the sounds they make are sweet.

"What more do you know?" Isham turns to elder Moss.

"Only that they live and are both wounded. Elder Martin and Axl are moving too fast to send more and should be here soon, Source willing."

"We haven't met, lad," Isham looks at the boy.

"No, sir. My name is Wim."

"Soon as I rest, Source willing we can properly introduce ourselves."

"Oh, yes, sir. I'd be honored."

Isham turns to go for his pack and bags.

"I, I took the liberty, sir," the lad points. "I brought your things over here with Curanda and Esa."

Wim has already lugged Isham's pack and bags to the spot indicated. Everything is neatly set out and ready for use plus a flask of wine and a flask of water and a pouch of roasted seeds. The boy stands shyly off to one side, awed by someone he has long wanted to meet.

"Thank you Wim."

"Oh, yes, sir. My pleasure, sir."

Stocky and strong, the lad is a few years older than Esa. His broad cheeks are the color of summer fruit. Long kinky blond hair is tied at the nape of his neck.

Isham's sits wearily on his opened bedroll to take off his boots.

"I have another favor to ask."

"Yes, sir, anything."

"Were you there when R'io and Skye were sucked down by the water?" The old man releases his hair and beard and combs them out with his fingers.

"Yes, sir."

"When you have a moment, regardless of where I am, awake or asleep, please send me your memory of what happened. Can you do that, Wim?"

"I can give it my best, sir."

"Every detail. Thank you. Now if I might sleep."

"Yes, sir."

The boy is heading back to his own bedroll as Curanda and a calmer Esa approach their mats and lie down quietly. Curanda spoons into Isham, her back against his front. She reaches for his hand and brings it up to her lips. Near the entrance, elder Moss blows out her wick and lies down. Almost immediately there is the sound of soft snoring from the five of them. It's a skill stone-people have of knowing how to rest in any circumstances.

***

SubTurra's new arrival is sitting on the side of the bed, trembling from the exertion it took to get that far. Pale and gaunt, she's wearing a flimsy medical gown plus the brace on her ankle and the one on her arm. The belt is buckled and draped from shoulder to opposite hip. She dangles her toes on the floor for a while then stops, scoots forward and plants her feet. She closes her eyes. Determined to get up she braces her arms, pushes and stands wavering for a moment.

Everything aches. Sweat trickles. Her ankle is furious. Panting, exhausted, she sinks back down and, pop, the shaft of smoky light returns as before, angled and shining down just off of the foot of the bed. An attendant arrives with the comfortable wingchair, positions it in the shaft of light, locks it in place then departs.

Footsteps.

The powerful scent of something tangy-sweet.

With feline grace, Katya moves to and sits down in the chair. She crosses one chiseled knee over the other. Her fine silk jacket and skirt are the green of her arresting eyes. Long dark hair hangs straight, shadowing the angles of her face. A tip of shiny shoe. Professional compassion and intimacy with a stranger. There's nothing else to focus on.

"Hello. Do you remember my name?"

"I want to go home."

"Good," Katya smiles. "We'll help you."

"By myself. I want to go home by myself."

"Do you know how to get there from here?"

"No."

"Do you know where home is?"

"No."

Katya sighs.

"You're not strong enough."

"I will be soon."

"What is home called?"

"I don't know."

"Where is it?"

"Don't know."

"How are you going to get there from here?"

She looks away and squints, combing the fog in her head for clues, fragments of some kind, hints of what was before. There's nothing. She stares into space.

"I don't know. The path is irreversible."

"Oh?" Katya blinks and leans forward. "What do you mean the path is irreversible?"

The patient looks down at her knees, more chiseled than Katya's even. She moves her feet in little circles but it hurts her ankle so she stops and shakes her head and shrugs, bewildered.

"I don't know what it means."

"There's plenty of time."

"For what?"

"To remember."

"Nothing exists from before I got here."

Katya nods and changes tack.

"It would facilitate things if you told me your name. Perhaps we could talk more easily then, get to know each other."

"Name?"

"Yes. What's your name?"

She runs the fingers of one hand over her head, feels bristles, then the stitches on the cut over her ear. She blinks, shrugs.

"I told you and I told you I don't know."

"Who are you?"

"Don't know!"

Katya waits, full of professional concern. The patient sits on the edge of the bed rocking ever so slightly. Then she stops, looks at Katya and announces matter-of-factly.

"One-Who-Wanders."

A puzzled expression flits across Katya's face.

"One-Who-Wanders?"

"Call me that."

Head back, One-Who-Wanders looks straight up at what she can't determine – ceiling somewhere somehow because surely she's enclosed if this is SubTurra. A fat tear rolls down. She closes her eyes.

"One-Who-Wanders. I like that name." Katya is gentle. "How did you get it?"

She shrugs.

"What kind of name is One-Who-Wanders?"

After a moment, fighting the need to trust, she shrugs again. Katya taps her chin with a red fingernail.

"Did your people give you that name?"

"No."

"Who did, then? We're all named. How did you get your name?"

"People?"

"You came from somewhere."

"Evidently."

"Can you tell me?"

"No."

"Because you don't know or because you don't want to?"

She shrugs.

"Very well." Katya smiles and changes the subject. "How can we help you between now and when you start on your journey back home? What would make you feel better?"

After a moment, a word comes.

"Water," she whispers.

Katya signals. An attendant immediately emerges with a small rolling cart that fits comfortably over her knees. The cart holds a tray on which is a glass and a sweating beaker of water with crushed ice. The attendant pours and hands her a glass full of water then steps back. She takes the glass and sips then hands the glass back to the attendant and pushes the cart away. After a moment, at a signal from Katya, attendant and cart disappear behind the bed.

"That's dead water," One-Who-Wanders observes to no one in particular.

"What do you know about water?"

"It hasn't been alive for a long time, that water."

"What do you mean?"

"It's dead."

"It's our best."

"Doesn't matter. It's dead."

"Have you had other water? Water you liked?"

"Don't know," she shrugs.

"Where?"

"Don't know."

"Yes you do."

"Anyhow, I meant big water. A pool, a stream, a river. Water

169

I can get into."

"How do you know these things," Katya struggles to hide her astonishment. "Pool. Stream. River?"

One-Who-Wanders looks confused. Katya presses.

"Have you seen these things?"

"Don't know."

"We have big water here."

"Take me."

"When you're stronger."

"Now!"

"Very well," Katya nods after a moment then stands, steps closer and gazes down. "One-Who-Wanders. I like that name." She holds out a hand.

Wanting to trust, needing to trust and unable to, One-Who-Wanders takes the hand. Flesh to flesh. Palm to palm. Real. Soft. Warm. Human. Smelling too sweet.

Eyes lock.

Hands unclasp and Katya steps back.

"Water," she smiles, "coming up," and strides off to disappear behind the bed. The attendant emerges for the chair and takes it away. The shaft of light is extinguished. She's alone again in the pale indefinite space with the bed and nothing else.

***

The watch has been changed. Taking his turn, Isham found a perch half a mile into a meandering vein and is alert to anything coming from way up ahead.

Stone is comfortable once adaptation has occurred and the old man now leaning back in a smooth indentation, knees up, arms folded across his chest. A small wick is in a holder on a nearby ledge. His hair and beard are down. He's wrapped in a cloak and relieved to have finally gotten through to Solaris who stopped searching for the intruder long enough to respond.

No one has been able to get through to R'io or Skye One-Who-Wanders. But no one has stopped long enough and been sufficiently rested for a deep attempt. I propose we try together.

In tandem.

170

Si.

Back at the Refuge, Solaris is stationed in the main chamber. In the dim glow of nature's never-dark it's possible to see her severed leg regenerating and a certain fullness returned to her furry body. It's also possible to see that the big spider is profoundly concerned by what has happened.

Now.

Now.

They call.

R'io, R'io, R'io…

Over and over.

They call her.

Skye One-Who-Wanders…

They sing the names through realms and dimensions. They keep singing, blending their powers to try and connect with their targets until Wim comes to take the watch from Isham One-Who-Waits and Solaris returns to her silent prowling.

***

The corridor is easily wide enough for four attendants and her on a fast-moving gurney. She's aware of them trotting, stationed at each corner of her little rolling island. And she's aware of glare from overhead light captured in a tube that runs the curved length of this gleaming, spun-metal corridor through which she's being rushed.

After passing several intersections devoid of feature or occupant, the attendants slow the gurney enough to turn into another smaller corridor at the end of which they stop. She hears loud hiss/thup from near her feet and tries to raise her head but it's strapped down. The glare is intense. They roll her through another hiss/thup into a different space where everything is hard and gleaming. White tile. Sound here is echoey.

The attendants carefully position the gurney and lock it in place. They lower it almost to the floor. They remove her restraints, untuck the sheet and whisk it away. Then they spread out and leave her staring up at the underside of a huge white dome ringed with windows through which she can see brilliant blue sky.

When they came for her they took off her gown and gave her

a skimpy slinky suit of light blue skin-like fabric. She's wearing that plus the braces on her foot and arm and the belt draped from shoulder to hip.

She smells something sharp, raises her head, looks around and sees a great blue rectangle of swimming pool shimmering away from the right side of the gurney. The water is pale at her end, deepening to rich aqua as it stretches away from her. After a long moment studying the smelly water, she sits with effort.

The gurney is parked at the edge of the pool alongside a gradually descending L-shaped ramp. Two gleaming parallel rails follow the ramp from right next to the gurney almost halfway out into the pool.

She reaches for a rail and, using it for leverage, gets her feet over the side of the gurney and between the two rails. Taking a deep breath she pulls herself up. Wavering and weak, she steps forward and down.

There's that first cool kiss of water on her feet.

Familiar somehow.

She takes a step.

Then another.

The water is up to her calves. She stops.

Something wants to be clear and isn't. Something wants to wake in her and can't cross the threshold to awareness. And the pressure to know what she doesn't know deepens until it would devour her.

She stops, closes her eyes, reaches for it, grasps.

!

It's gone.

She wants it again, that feeling, that sensation of almost remembering. Gripping the rails she moves deeper into the pool, advancing one shaky step at a time and in so doing knows that though this is called water it's not what she somehow knows water to be. This is old and dead. It stinks of chemicals.

When the water is up to her shoulders she turns, looks around, sees bright blue water and sparkling white tile. She sees the attendants stationed at each corner of the pool. She looks straight up through high windows at brilliant sky. This isn't where she wants to be, lost in such an overwhelming sense of desolation.

Then something comes down on her like a hammer on an anvil.

Pain.

In her head.

Diffuse and sent from faraway.

She gasps. She grabs her head, grimacing and turns to go back, get out of the pool. All she knows is pain in her head, horrible pressure.

One of the attendants gets to her in the water and, cradling her, moves quickly toward the side of the pool. He passes her up to someone who eases her down onto the gurney. "Click!" the gurney is elevated and they try to roll her onto her back and take her hands away from her head. One finally manages to administer a calmative into her thigh and she goes limp. They strap her down and cover her up. Then, unconscious, she's on her way back to the place with no defining feature but a bed.

***

Great City's Presider and his head of Security are in Reed's private office. He 's seated behind his impressive desk. She's standing in the center of the floor. Both are glistening from the heat and bathed in cones of watery light. The rest of the room is shadow but for a section of the wall on one side where several screens are illuminated with live feed of a meeting currently taking place in one of the conference rooms in Founders' Hall. In attendance are the three Space State ambassadors plus Virginia Kahn Baker of Human Resources and Doug Smythe Hews of Medicine who have been instructed to obfuscate.

"You're refusing to comprehend my point," Smythe taps the table with a stiff forefinger.

"No. We aren't interested in your point. We demand to see Dr. Baxter in the flesh immediately. It's non-negotiable." Raf Kyrry is standing, leaning on braced arms.

"Sit. Down. I will explain once again…"

"No! We heard you the first time. We heard you days ago when you finally deigned to respond to our concerns. We're not here to negotiate. We're not here for explanations. We are here for Dr. Baxter and we want him now, in our possession."

"That is impossible and I have explained why," Smythe's condescension is meant to be withering. "Evidently you don't want to listen or can't understand."

Ria Siloam, her dress whites not so white and crisp as before,

173

leaps out of her chair and slams a hand down on the table before Kyrry can block further expression of fury. The third ambassador, Tran McKenzy is almost useless with anxiety on Siloam's other side.

Virginia Kahn Baker stands, her tunic and trousers straining to contain her bulk.

"As per a decision by the Presider and agreed-on unanimously by the council and ratified by every steward in Great City, there will be no further talk with the Space States or their representatives before a complete and formal apology for the current situation has been presented to and accepted by the people of Great City. This meeting is over."

Great City's head of Medicine stands and smiles sadly at the three ambassadors.

"I keep trying to tell you that Dr. Baxter is ill and contagious with something we are still trying to identify. He will not be allowed out of his sterile environment and no one is allowed in. I'm sure you can understand that, being similarly situated as you are in closed systems – a bug gets loose on one of the Space States and, boom, you may have to destroy a whole section to contain it, right? That's all we're trying to do." Superior in all ways, Smythe leaves the room.

Meantime, in the Presider's private office Paul Prescot Reed looks at his head of Security.

"Turn it off," he whispers. "What did you want to see me about?"

Lassiter raises her tech-wand and extinguishes the screens, leaving the room illuminated only by the two weak beams shining down. She turns to face him.

"As I reported, satellites picked up a brief signal from the surface east of Great City. The signal lasted a few seconds and has not been repeated. I programmed satellites to deep-scan that area and they've picked up what I believe are traces of tracks. 150 miles east of Great City. I think he was checking to see if we were following. He left a few tracks on the way, wisps, really. But I found them."

"Tracks?"

"Yes. They indicate that he's swinging a big arc around to the northeast. Then he disappears. Other than the tracks, there's nothing."

Reed leans back in his chair and studies his head of Security. Squinting, he taps his lower lip with a long forefinger.

"Our deserter has sophisticated technology."

"Yes, sir."

"Do you understand what that means, Lassiter?"

"Yes. It means that our worst fears might be true. It means that whoever's giving aid and comfort to our Prime Researcher may have the ability to detect us. And if they can detect us, they can monitor what we're doing. And if they can monitor what we're doing, they already know a lot more about us than we know about them. It would seem…"

"Seem, nothing!" the Presider slams a hand down on his desk. "Whoever stole our Prime Researcher is capable of sending out a scan to try and determine if we're following him. Then he disappears. She's gone. He's gone. They appear," Reed snaps his fingers, "they disappear. Where are they, Lassiter?! They have to be out there somewhere!"

"Sir, I am exhausting Security resources trying…"

"That's not what I want to hear! I want you to provide me with information I can take to the council, and I want it now!"

Karin Lassiter Kohl is about to explain when, disgusted, the Presider gets out of his chair and pours himself a jigger of Mello. Sipping, silent, he paces then stops and looks at her.

"When will the equipment be deployed?"

"It's in final-check now and…"

"I want point B dug up, blasted, bored into, hammered at until it tells us what we want to know!"

"Yes, sir."

Paul Prescot Reed stands glaring at his head of Security for a long moment.

"I need more performance from you, Lassiter."

"You shall have it, sir."

"So get back to work."

Nodding and tight-lipped she stands there for a moment wanting to bring up what she really came for and knowing perfectly well that now is not the time to mention what she has in mind concerning ambassador Dav Baxter. Instead, she turns and leaves the Presider's office for her own.

***

Down in their scattered workbays, the full crew of Security Primes has been dealing with many problems for days with no respite in the intensity of demands on them since the crisis began. Not one of them has been given a break. Some are beginning to show signs of stress.

Lassiter has driven them as hard as she has driven herself, forgetting in her zeal that even perfectly tuned and maintained citizen-units have limits. One hundred percent can be yielded for only so long. A few of the original crew, on duty since the Prime Researcher set off the alarm, are starting to show faint traces of static and sluggishness in their functioning.

***

The path is irreversible.

There's only to go on.

Those two sentences loop through her awareness like flies.

The path is irreversible. There's only to go on.

Then a command is added.

Walk.

Again and again.

Walk.

She has no choice but to obey the imperative. So she starts walking around the bed.

Wobbly and in pain, she stays close to her anchor at first then gradually widens her orbit. The pain in her ankle is nothing compared to the headache, a fierce forest fire raging at the back of her skull and down her spine. It stopped abruptly a few minutes ago. Now the path is irreversible and there's only to go on.

Wearing a flimsy medical gown with the belt draped from shoulder to hip and the braces on her leg and arm, she walks around and around the bed. And as her walking-circle widens she notices the absence of walls and ceiling and wonders what kind of space this is that seems to have no limits.

Lt. Pilar Mezon swings into position, furls the windrider wings and stops suspended in space for her final approach to the transfer station. Earth lurks over her left shoulder, haunting like a specter, like an apparition. Moon-glare bathes her from the right.

Camouflaged against a starry background, Falcon One studies the big lead-colored disk several nautical miles directly in front of her, revolving slowly on its axis. It should be blazing with light and it's not. She should long ago have been piloted in by a little tug but there has been nothing. The shape-changers she sent out earlier continue to report zero activity of any kind in the entire area. No life. No juice.

Pilar takes her stunner out of the holster on her thigh, activates it, checks the safety and puts it back, leaving the holster open. Then she flutters her wingtips ever so slightly and halves the distance to the transfer station in seconds. She stops again, scans and checks readings then halves the distance yet again.

From here, the transfer station is enormous. Battleship gray in the moonlight, the structure is easily three hundred yards across on the flat sides that are covered with dishes, mirrors, antennas, exhaust stacks, and spigots. The rim is ringed with big docking bays for Space State vehicles to back into butt-first and unload goods for Great City in exchange for virtual treasure from the past. Two long delicate extension arms reach out into space across from each other. Usually a litter of velocity-gatherers is tethered to each arm. Now there's one, belonging to H-V shuttle/barge Emerson.

That the transfer station isn't blazing with light bothers Pilar more than she wants to acknowledge – like seeing earth for the first time, the dead corpse a vivid reality, a presence (or rather an absence) she has been trying not to notice. She activates the optics in her helmet and programs the cameras located in her suit to automatically record everything from now on.

The transfer station turns on its axis and the front half of H-V shuttle/barge Ralph Waldo Emerson swings into view. The back half of the ship is locked in the docking bay, mated to the transfer station. The front half of the ship sticks out in space, a blunt appendage, dark and quiet.

Falcon One covers the remaining distance to the squarish under-nose of the Emerson slowly because she wants to look around on the way in. Once there, hugging Emerson's under-nose, she checks her readings again. No change. She follows reflected moonlight on up around the blunt snout of the ship to the insignia and name on the hull.

H-V Shuttle/Barge Ralph Waldo Emerson Out of Space State Hope from planet Earth.

The words circle the Space States insignia – a plain infinity sign in light blue, the color of ancient earth's daytime sky.

Pilar touches the words and the insignia with a gloved fingertip. The identity of the ship is not news, of course. But being here makes it real in a different way. She knows this crew. Good guys.

Trying to swallow her intuition, she turns to go on exploring and gasps, startled by someone floating feet first diagonally toward her around the hull from the opposite direction glaring in a bulky white suit with moonlight bouncing off the coppery facemask. The insignia on the left breast matches the one on the hull. It's a Space Stater, probably one of the crewmen.

His readings are dark, indicating that the astronaut is dead. He's toting a little sled loaded with torches, tanks of propane, crowbars, and pinpoint explosives among other items, leading Pilar to suspect that he might have been trying to enter the ship or the transfer station other than through a regular hatch. Why?

Falcon One pulls up close and toggles the body and the sled to the hull of the ship then reads the name on his right breast. R. LANIER. She clenches her teeth. Bobby Lanier wiped her out at poker too many times. He could be a jerk but he was a good engineer and she'd board his ship any time.

Why was he outside the vessel? Doing what? How Dead?

Pilar takes hold of his helmet, raises the visor and looks at Lanier's face behind the bubble of clear nu-glass. His eyes are open wide. He looks surprised. No. He looks angry.

Feel later, she commands herself, fogging her facemask for a moment from inside as she drifts on up and around the ship's hull, pausing to look through a porthole down into the empty galley then going on toward the crew and passenger hatch, which is wide open.

Before pulling herself through the open hatch Pilar touches buttons on her wrist. The windrider's wings retract and roll up into two long thin tubes that stretch from between the back of her neck to her waist. Then she floats on through the hatch and the open airlock into the ship.

No power. No gravity. No air. Only silence and wavery dark

178

awash with moonlight pouring in through the many portholes.

She flicks on the torch in her helmet for comfort more than anything because she can see perfectly well through her optics. Drifting, she looks around.

This forward section of the ship is for a crew of four and up to 25 passengers. To the left of the entry-hatch is the gym. She looks in. Empty. The big open relaxation area on her right is also empty.

Scanning high and low she finds no sign of anything untoward. Halfway down the ship's main corridor she locates the ladder that leads up to the control cabin and down to the power source. The corridor here is lined with doors to private quarters, all but one of them closed. She looks into the open one.

The young woman who was to have replaced Dav Baxter is floating back and forth slowly, gently bumping one wall, ricocheting off to another as though in slow-motion. Name: Dian Jaad, pre-school teacher, 27 years old and here to do her three years service to the common. Pretty girl. Innocent as those she tended. Her expression is one of surprised terror.

Pilar didn't know Dian Jaad. But that doesn't make it any easier to haul her into a hammock and strap her down then snap a blanket around her – all the burial the young woman gets for now. After checking the cabin for signs of what happened and finding nothing, Falcon One returns to the main corridor and pulls herself up the ladder into the control cabin, a bubble of nu-glass on top of the ship.

The other three crewmembers are harnessed into their chaises. Dead. They were apparently functioning, or trying to, when something happened. She checks them to verify that each is who he's supposed to be. She checks the ship's technology to find all of it dark, yielding nothing.

Swallowing nausea, Pilar exits the control cabin and follows the main corridor to its end – a closed hatch similar to those used to seal ancient bank vaults. The cargo hold is beyond this point. As is evident from the dead control panel next to the hatch, from here the rest of the ship is inaccessible. It's locked inside the transfer station behind a door that can't be opened because the power to do so is gone – which is why Bobby Lanier was outside.

But Falcon One has tools he didn't have. She takes a shape-changer cartridge from her bandolier, puts it butt-end into the port on the back of her glove and programs it to split four times, a process that will take a while.

Lt. Pilar Mezon exhales and closes her eyes as the sadness hits deep. For comfort, she dials up some ancient hard-driving blues then switches to a lone woman singing something plaintive and Appalachian. The elite first responder pulls herself through zero-Gs to the infirmary and the cabinet where bodybags are stored. She pulls out five of them, feeling guilty and grateful that one is not for Dav Baxter, the father of their son.

***

At ground level on the northeast side of Great City, the door that malfunctioned before, killing a Security guard, is open again, propped up with I-beams. Outside, the sun is just going down. Inside, citizen-units from Maintenance are attempting to start the machinery and get it headed on down to the surface.

The noise is deafening. Smoke from combustion engines billows, filling the bay. The stench is overwhelming – or would be for stewards who, of course, never actually touch what they make happen.

One by one, the ungainly machines head down the ramp to ash as fine as talcum powder. Backhoes, pile drivers, cranes, posthole diggers, supply vans, vans with explosives of all kinds, lumbering along. All heading for point B, which must be ravaged before they are satisfied.

Some of the equipment is operated remotely, by Main-tenance Primes located elsewhere throughout Great City. Other equipment is driven and operated by reprogrammed citizen-units from Maintenance and Technology. There is also a troop carrier with one driver and one occupant.

Sitting in the back by himself, buckled in and bouncing against the wall, George Biggs Boltin, Great City's former head of Security, is neither fish nor fowl. He's no longer suitable for stewardship and he doesn't quite qualify as a citizen-unit because he still has an independent streak that can only be broken with pain.

The orange monitor sit is a bit too small for him, especially around the waist. Also, having been cut away from its former occupant, the suit is extensively re-patched with whatever was available in the monitor suit scrap bin so he's a crazy quilt of colors.

180

Subjectively speaking, Boltin is locked in a new, askew consciousness – it being impossible to attach the suit deeply enough to shift him into proper neuro-awareness. He knows something is happening but not what. On some level he understands that what was is gone. He perceives fuzz, vague blurry light and shadow through the orange lenses. He hears voices not his own telling him what to do and most of the time obeys automatically or disobeys automatically – it no longer matters except when there's pain.

***

With the addition of Isham, elder Martin and Axl, L'escola's numbers have swelled. Hot food has been prepared, their first in days. Isham, Curanda, Axl, Esa, elder Moss and elder Martin are seated in a circle around a wick, breaking their fast with a steaming meal sipped and spooned from bowls. Taking their food with them, Jabaz, Wim, Schiara, Jak and Juarez have gone off to stand watch.

"When the SubTurran work crew realized they'd hit toxic water they sealed up the hole and started looking for other ways to get to where R'io and Skye might have come from," elder Martin pauses to sip his stew. "A new band of stone-people is shadowing them now, trying to lure them away. We skirted them and went into the hinterlands."

Axl is mute and sullen, focused on eating. It's clear that something is bothering the boy who eats with his head down, not listening.

"I found a small group of miners and eavesdropped," elder Martin continues. "They were talking about the two new arrivals."

Axl puts his empty bowl down, stands and stalks to the back of the cave where he sits on his sleeping mat with his head in his hands. The others look at one another. Elder Martin quietly explains.

"It was the boy's first exposure to things SubTurra. He took it hard. Knowing his da is captured in there. Alive and wounded – how badly we do not know – and perhaps sick from the toxic water. Even so, their sudden appearance has touched off a firestorm of interest with the SubTurrans. Headmon is making a fortune off of them."

"How?" Isham looks at elder Martin over his elevated bowl of stew.

"He's got them on Banding, a complicated semblance-technology. SubTurran's are addicted to it. It's their medicine for the panic. Headmon is always on the lookout for new content and now he's got it. That means they're in Central Control, somewhere near Headmon's residence."

"And where is that?" finished eating, Curanda puts her bowl down.

"Theoretically no one knows. I do only because I was assigned there and was able to escape before being recycled."

"How do we get inside the residence?" Isham tilts his bowl for the last of his stew and, chewing, places the bowl on the ground.

"It's easy enough to get into SubTurra. Getting in is not the problem. The problem is getting positioned once you're inside and then getting back out. There are ways to do both, however."

Everyone is finished eating. Esa unobtrusively clears the empty bowls and returns to her place in the circle. Isham takes a small glass pipe out of a pouch and fills it with green herb. He lights the pipe, puffs and passes it to Curanda who is sitting on his right. The old woman puffs thoughtfully several times and passes the pipe and the lighting wick across the space left by Axl (still on his sleeping mat with his head in his hands) to Esa who puffs and hands it on to elder Moss then elder Martin and finally back around to Isham who sets the pipe on the pouch by his knee.

"We must make important decisions now," he murmurs.

"Decisions that affect lives," elder Moss nods.

"Aye," Curanda agrees. "And as in all things, we ask Source for wisdom."

Axl stands and moves toward the group. He stops at the edge of the light and remains standing, long golden hair loose around his shoulders, beard wispy and white-blond. A thicker version of his da and just coming into his manhood, the lad's flame-blue eyes are hot with anger.

"Will you join us?" Curanda indicates his place in the circle with her hand then reaches for the pipe so he can share.

"We do not abandon those we love!" He scowls defiantly into the fire. "That is the stone-people way! R'io is my da…"

"Axl," Isham interrupts holding the pipe out to the boy, "please sit down."

As sometimes happens inexplicably between people, Isham and Axl have never been close, merely polite and formal. The boy wants to learn in his own way on his own schedule and has little patience for discipline not of his own devising. Isham, for whom every second of life is a profound mystery, does not understand the boy's lack of humility. The two stare at each other until Curanda speaks.

"Your feelings are understandable, Axl," the old woman nods to include everyone in the circle. "We all have feelings about what happened. Rage. Grief. Shame. Powerful feelings must be felt when they come. But they cannot be allowed to influence thinking that must be cool and clear if we are to be effective in what we decide to do."

Axl remains standing, glaring. Elder Moss clears her throat then speaks softly.

"Nephew, my brother would not hesitate to come after any of us." She looks at Axl and smiles. "And we're going to in for the two of them. Have a seat and help us figure out how."

Always responsive to his aunt's common sense, the boy sits, not looking at her or anyone else. Esa offers Axl the pipe and the wick. He waves them away. The silence is uncomfortable. Finally, Isham nods.

"Is there anyone who feels we should *not* go in and get them?"

No one speaks or moves.

"Those on watch must also be consulted. That seems to be the first thing to resolve."

"I think we should leave her there," Axl stands. "She caused it. Everything was fine before she came along. She arrives and all we got is trouble. I say we go in, get da and come out. Whatever happens to her is good riddance."

The others look at Axl in disbelief.

"That isn't going to happen and you know it," elder Moss murmurs softly. "Your da would only go back and get her – and not just because he loves her. He would go back because she is wilderness-people now. She is L'escola."

The others nod, agreeing. Axl snatches up a waterflask and strides out of the cave to go brood. Isham nods thoughtfully.

"Very well. Let's figure out how to do what must be done."

***

183

One-Who-Wanders is sitting on the edge of the bed wearing a medical gown. She's leaning over, face near her knees, rocking back and forth. The belt is unclasped, draped across her thighs ribbon-like.

Eyes closed, she runs her fingertips back and forth across the belt, back and forth barely touching, as though looking for tiny clues. She lifts the belt to her face and squints at it, sniffs it, runs the heavy fibers across her lips.

She stands and puts the belt around her waist again, buckles it again, trying all the holes. It doesn't fit. The belt isn't hers. It belongs to someone else. She's certain.

Who?

Blank.

Who wore the belt before?!

Unable to answer her own question, she takes the belt from her waist, fastens it then eases it over her head so it hangs like a bandolier. She's about to start off on another walk to test her ankle by going faster but is stopped by a thrumming pop of the atmosphere. The shaft of yellow light appears, shining down near the foot of the bed.

An attendant wheels in the big overstuffed leather chair, locks it in place and disappears. She hears footsteps, clickety-clack. She smells tart-sweetness.

Then Katya is sitting in the chair again, the shaft of light spilling across the lap of an moss-green suit. The skirt reveals plenty of leg. Moss-colored eyes invade with penetrating warmth and intimacy.

"One-who-wanders, your improvement is remarkable."

"My clothes." She blinks, surprised by what just came out of her mouth.

"We thought perhaps you might be ready to…"

"My clothes. I want them now."

Katya blinks.

"What brings this up?"

"I just remembered. They kept asking about clothes. Back in the capsule. That means I had some when I got here. I want them now."

Katya tilts her head slightly as though listening to something only she can hear. After a moment she smiles then nods.

"Very well."

Attendants appear. Garments are laid out on the bed. The attendants disappear.

She stares, not knowing what she expected when she made the

demand. Not knowing why she made the demand only that she made it and now these things are here and she must have had them on when she arrived.

What is the story of these clothes?

"We've cleaned and mended them for you."

Aware that Katya is watching, One-Who-Wanders moves to the bed and stands looking down at the garments. Then Katya fades from awareness and there are only the knee-pants and the shirt and the doublet and a sock and a boot – the latter two items having been picked up after she was captured. Those things plus the belt hanging from her shoulder are all she has of what was before and so much more than nothing.

The pants and doublet are mid-range browns, heavy for warmth, roughly woven and well sewn. She reaches out to touch the light blue shirt with both hands, as though caressing. So soft.

She takes off the belt and medical gown, drops them on the bed then reaches for the shirt, finds the front and raises it to let it fall down over her head and shoulders and hang loose at her wrists and hips. Facing away from Katya she pulls on the knee-pants and doublet then one sock and one shoe. Last, she lifts the belt over her head so it hangs the way she likes.

Everything fits. At one and the same time, the clothes feel completely strange and utterly familiar. These are her clothes. She's got that figured out. All but the belt.

What is their story?

Standing with her back to Katya, mouth open, eyes focused on something not here/now, One-Who-Wanders is exquisitely aware of the feel of the clothes on her body. She runs her hands over the garments like someone blind. They tell her only that she is from a realm not like this one. She turns to face Katya whose veil of composure has slipped out of place.

"…How beautiful you are."

"What does that mean?" she shrugs.

"See for yourself." Katya's composure is back in place.

Attendants roll a big mirror around from behind the bed and anchor it in place off to one side. Pop! Another light comes on and angles down softly on that spot.

One-Who-Wanders stands looking at a shiny rectangle that is taller and wider than she is. Liquid images are confusing, trapped in the silvery surface and it takes a moment to separate figure from ground and name the thing.

Mirror.

And in it is a person. The image of a person.

She approaches slowly, studying a slender creature with skin of palest golden brown and a shadow of dark bristles beginning to emerge on her scalp plus hints of lashes and brows. She steps closer and peers at solemn round eyes that are almost black right now. She sees a long, flattish nose, a wide mouth, full lips, a blunt chin, a swan's neck, straight shoulders. She sees One-Who-Wanders who is wary, who is an image in a pool of silvery water.

Then she notices two crescent-shaped scars, each about the size of a little fingernail, facing each other at the bowl of her throat. She reaches up, touches. The skin is shiny. Pink. Just healed. Tender.

"What is that?" Katya inquires from her chair. "What are those?"

One-Who-Wanders lowers her hand and stares in the mirror at the two little scars. Blank.

"Don't know."

Then the image of herself with all the unknowns opens up and threatens to swallow her. Desperate, she whirls around to Katya.

"Where am I? Who else is here? What do you want from me?"

Katya cocks her head as though listening. Then she nods and gestures to the bed.

"Sit down."

One-Who-Wanders moves to the bed and sits very straight on the edge for a moment. Then she leans forward, forearms on knees. Her gaze is penetrating, boring into Katya who, unable to tolerate the scrutiny, looks down at her hands and clears her throat.

"You are in SubTurra, the last great civilization…"

"Why are you keeping me here like this?"

"Like what?"

"Isolated."

"We're giving you time to heal. To adjust."

"I'm healed. Adjust to what?"

"Everything is different here."

"Different than what?"

"From what you knew before."

"How do you know that?"

Katya stands, takes a few steps away from the bed, hands clasped behind her back. Then she turns and smiles.

"You are not like us. It will take time for you to acclimate."

"What if I don't want to acclimate?"

"You're free to leave."

"Show me the exit."

"When you're ready.

"I'm ready."

Katya tilts her head as though listening. She nods.

"I have to go now."

Abruptly, the woman whose scent hides her true nature strides off behind the bed and disappears with the clack of heels on tile. Attendants come for the mirror and the chair. After a faint popping sound, the beam of light fades and everything is as it was.

The attendants arrive with food. She waves them away but they leave the tray on its cart. She shoves it aside, listens as it rolls on out into the misy void that surrounds the bed. Then she lies down on her back, arms out, looking straight up at nothing.

What kind of world is this?

***

Morning light illumines the flats and the trail toward the dunes made by Great City's earthmoving machines. It's not the ash so much as the rubble on the flats. It's the bits of bone and concrete and asphalt and rebar that give the recently deployed equipment so much trouble. Also, fuel needs were severely underestimated.

A few big pieces of equipment sank almost immediately into the ash as into quicksand. One of the big platform cranes leaned then toppled and is now lying down, being blanketed with stirred-up ash. Other machines are stalling, running out of gas or unable to get traction and so digging themselves in deeper.

The rest, a thinning line of vehicles, struggle on toward point B. The citizen-units on the scene, including George Biggs Boltin, have been ordered out of their conveyances to dig or lift or do whatever can be done to get the equipment to its destination.

Boltin is now staggering around with a few other citizen-units, trying to follow orders from the Maintenance Primes and get the vehicle moving again. He doesn't know where he is or what he's doing. He only knows to function as ordered or there will be pain.

***

Using a worklight to illumine the passenger cabin, Lt. Pilar Mezon closes the last white bodybag. She stops for a moment, facing a total of five bags, all tethered to the wall. Honor must be paid. Falcon One salutes then whispers the first thing that comes to mind.

"Rest in peace, commoners." The sound is hollow inside her helmet. "It won't be the same without you."

Then Pilar leaves the cabin and heads back down the ship's main corridor to the connecting hatch where the shape-changer is now multiplied and ready to help her open the hatch by taking a certain section of it apart – time consuming but it will do only minimal damage to the Emerson or the transfer station and her orders are to minimize harm.

***

Curanda, Isham, elder Moss and Esa are still seated around a wick sipping tea. Axl is restless, getting up, sitting down, occasionally moving to the back of the cave to practice throwing stones, making sounds that irritate Isham. Esa is lying with her head in Curanda's lap. Elder Martin is slowly pacing around the circle.

With wilderness-people since middle age, elder Martin is almost as old as Isham. He stumbled out of SubTurra into the hinterlands and, at the end of his strength, was discovered lost in a deep chasm by Jabaz. The two have been inseparable ever since. Beloveds. Of medium height and stocky, elder Martin's complexion is blotchy and dry with flaky gray patches because of a skin condition common among SubTurrans, a fungus of some sort. He's also completely bald, always has been, devoid even of brows and lashes.

"...Each canton is densely packed with several hundred thousand people and surrounded by satellite towns and hamlets that service the far-flung miners. Everything is monitored by Headmon from Central Control, which is where R'io and Skye have to be. You

188

best take only two or three in with you. Anything more is conspicuous and once Headmon targets you there's no escape."

"What's he like, Headmon?" Isham puffs on his little glass pipe and passes it to Curanda.

"Smart, vain, ruthless. Those around him never question. They obey. If they make a mistake or bore him, they are recycled, sometimes after being toyed with for his pleasure."

"And he's got R'io and Skye on what you call Banding," elder Moss takes the pipe from Curanda but doesn't puff.

"He floated them out on Banding to see if the public would bite and they did. He's making a fortune giving the workers little glimpses of them."

"How does Banding work?" Esa lifts her head from Curanda's lap. "What is it?"

"Banding is a descendant of the ancient holo-vision experience but much more immediate. The barrier between actor and observer has been removed and one is a participant in elaborate, utterly realistic fantasy. Very addictive."

"Poison," elder Moss gets up to refresh the wicks scattered here and there and when finished returns to her place and sits again.

"Like many things gone bad, Banding was originally developed to heal. Centuries later it's just a drug used to control people."

Esa shivers and snuggles closer to Curanda.

"In terms of R'io and Skye," elder Martin continues, "the miners I overheard found them on Banding. Headmon threw out a few little bits of bait to see what would happen and the fish all turned in the same direction at once. The selling point is good, exploiting the nature of their clothing and the fact that they came tumbling into SubTurra from nowhere. It had to have been immediately obvious that they weren't proper SubTurrans or miners or even hinterlanders but people from someplace else entirely."

Elder Martin stops. Head tilted to one side he stares at the group.

"That has to be a compelling mystery, one would think. A man and a woman fall into the world and they're from someplace else entirely." Elder Martin muses with his forefinger raised in the air as though to conduct a choir. "Genetically different just enough to send up a flag. Oh, yes. R'io and Skye are curiosities. Indeed, they seem to have ignited an almost mythic frenzy in the public if I can believe the miners. Which means Headmon profits from them now on the Banding

189

spectrum and that he intends to profit from them far into the future in many ways, including finding out where they came from and how to get here."

"Then we'd better go in for them now, not later!" Irritated by what seems like endless recitation of details he thinks he already knows, Axl stands again and moves to the back of the cave. He picks up his bag of throwing stones and starts to practice his accuracy.

"How does Banding work?" Isham tries to ignore sounds of the boy's pebbles glancing off of stone.

"You go into a Banding bar and get your economic clearance," elder Martin shudders, remembering. "Then you go to your assigned cot, put on your helmet, connect the electrodes and enter a technologically spun semblance that is for all intents and purposes real in terms of one's experience. You take your trip without ever moving a muscle. It's all fantasy. And keep in mind that there are Banding bars and there are Banding bars. The quality of your ride depends on how much you can pay."

Axl stops throwing stones and sits on his bedroll to brood.

"On Banding, the divide between action and observer is erased. The consumer has two choices. First, to be a passive witness of a scenario, say an unnoticed person at a medieval jousting tournament. Or one can choose to be an actor, one of the main characters or a supporting player, changing outcomes by one's presence."

"They do this to avoid panic?" Isham looks puzzled.

"Yes. SubTurran panic is to be avoided at all costs. There is, to my way of thinking, no greater torture. SubTurrans will literally do anything for more Banding time. Headmon can shut it off whenever, wherever he wants for any reason or for no reason. It's a constant threat and a frequent reality. He can institute a Banding blackout and throw masses of people or a single person into a panic from which recycling would be a mercy."

"SubTurrans know a horrid life," Esa muses.

Axl stands and returns to the group radiating anger.

"Yes," elder Martin agrees, reaching for the waterflask and taking a slug. "SubTurrans know work and they know death."

"What kind of work?"

"The vast majority are miners in the hinterlands. Many are in construction because there's always building and blasting going on for one reason or another. Further up the food chain people work in technology and medicine or the bureaucracies. The most privileged are

Banding content, usually athletes and entertainers. A very few serve as what are called specials to Headmon. I was a special. Headmon's philosopher. That's where you want to get placed. It's as close to the power as you can get."

"Specials?"

"The residence is fully staffed with servants of one kind or another plus carefully selected individuals Headmon keeps around for company or entertainment."

"How do we get in?" Isham sips from his waterflask. "How do we pass for SubTurrans? What skills do we need to become specials? How do we get into the residence? How do we make ourselves desirable to Headmon? Once in place then what? And, finally, how do we get out?"

Elder Martin nods and sits down on a small boulder. He runs a chubby hand over his bald head. Nodding, he stands back up again because of his sciatica.

"You go in with migrants."

"Migrants?"

"There are always streams of migrants moving from one place to another, seeking employment or space, something better than what they had. Most are sent back where they started from. But a few bring useful skills and are admitted. Those with extraordinary skills are reserved for Headmon."

"What extraordinary skills does Headmon find attractive?"

"Refinement. Headmon considers himself to be a very cultured fellow and does in fact have good taste though I found him a bit wanting in terms of personal hygene. He lives surrounded by the best – and some of the worst – of what remains from the ancient world. He seeks people who have something to offer by way of entertainment or pastime, people who know how to behave. And each of these people has a special skill."

"Such as?"

"In my case, philosophy. He has musicians, mystics, historians, conversationalists, gossips, scientists, and inventors. He always has a seer around to read cards and tealeaves and artificial clouds and ripples on the lake. He's attracted to beautiful women and gifted athletes."

"Where do we start?" Isham pulls on his long white beard.

"You need proper garments. Papers. Letters of recommend-ation. In-formation about SubTurran laws and ways. I can help you with all of that and connect you with guides."

Isham nods thoughtfully. Then he looks up and regards elder Martin who is no longer able to hide his exhaustion.

"Thank Source you were with the group when this happened, Martin. Go rest now. We have enough information for the moment."

"Yes. Yes, Rest," the former SubTurran turns and stumbles back toward the area he shares with Jabaz.

"We all need rest," Curanda sighs then stands. "Especially those who have stood watch for so long."

Elder Moss stands. "Axl, Esa, let's go relieve Jabaz and the others.

Axl is already heading out at his own pace muttering, "When are we going to get on with it?!"

***

Ankle throbbing, One-Who-Wanders limps back toward the bed from the wide circle she's been inscribing around it. Her face is covered with perspiration. Her shirt is stuck to her back. Her body is sore and her head is throbbing again from another headache. But she feels better for having pushed her limits and the only way she knows to do that here is to run.

She looks up to see Katya walking toward her from somewhere behind the bed, wearing black workout togs that fit like water from shoulders to ankles. A piece of gleaming technology is clasped to the inside of her left forearm, stretching from elbow to wrist. Smiling, Katya holds out her arm.

"I brought you something."

The device resembles a thin layer of shimmering mercury. Held in place by straps and clasps, it is smooth and featureless but for five little control keys – four arcing down the wrist and a larger one near her elbow. She can see the distorted reflection of a person on the gleaming surface.

"Come!" Katya barks instructions.

Two attendants emerge from behind the bed bringing with them a comfortable leather couch. They position the couch next to the bed then approach One-Who-Wanders with a shiny device for her left forearm. They put the device on then disappear behind the bed.

"You're now wearing a navigator identical to mine." Katya

holds her arm out for the other to see. "Top of the line Banding-access technology. With this device you can go anywhere you want, be anyone you want, do anything you want, effortlessly." Katya's smile is knowing and mysterious. "I'll take you out the first time then you're free to wander at will."

Katya taps the keys of her navigator with quick red fingertips. Finished, she holds out her arm again. The device is now a screen with a picture, a wide panorama of greens and blues. "For now, your navigator is linked to the one I'm wearing."

She looks, sees the same image stretching from her own left wrist to her elbow.

"Ready?" Katya strolls to the couch and sits. "Get on your bed." She looks at One-Who-Wanders with a mischievous grin then raises an eyebrow and presses a key on her navigator.

JOLT!

It's almost like being turned inside out. She's blinded by violent shimmering.

Then she's someplace else, blinking at a big field surrounded by tall, fragrant pines. Long emerald grasses are swirled by gusts of breeze and release their scents of green and loam. The sky is jewel-blue and high. It's warm, though the sun is not yet halfway to its apex. She sees erratic butterflies, hears the buzz and throb of insects, bird-chirp and squawk.

"This is one of my favorite places," Katya, transformed, inhales deeply. "We call it a meadow."

"I understand what it's supposed to be."

Katya turns and looks at her, astonished. "How do you know that?"

One-Who-Waits shakes her head, not knowing how she knows. Then she shrugs.

"Data."

"Data?" Katya mouth falls open. "Where have you come in contact with data?"

"Don't know. Don't even know what data is."

She regards Katya who seems to be listening to someone else though no one is here. Then One-Who-Wanders looks around at the meadow, not convinced – but of what she couldn't say.

"Why did you bring me here?"

"Isn't it beautiful." Katya holds out her arms and looks at the robin's egg blue sky.

"What's all this for?"

Katya lowers her arms.

"We thought you might like to get to know our world. We thought that since you enjoy walking and running so much you might like to do it in more interesting and challenging places. That's what Banding is for. The navigator can take you anywhere you want to go and you don't have to move a muscle. Think of it as entertainment while your body heals."

She wants to trust and can't. Katya waits for a response. When one doesn't come she smiles with false warmth.

"Where would you like to go?"

One-Who-Wanders shrugs.

"Then I'll choose for us," Katya presses the large key near her elbow.

JOLT.

They're on a cliff overlooking a veld that stretches as far as eye can see. The heat is suffocating. Scorched earth and grass are vast and dun-colored under blazing sky. Parched scrub and trees are scattered here and there. Way out in front, faraway herds meander toward a ribbon of glistening river. Flocks of birds whirl out of wind-flattened trees. Insects annoy. Breezes carry sounds of distant bellowing and cawing and smells of dust and animal dung. A great snowcapped peak crowned with roiling white clouds is majestic in the distance.

"Go on," Katya gestures at the scene around them. "Explore. When you come back I'll give you a few pointers then you can go wherever you want."

One-Who-Wanders turns around slowly, gazing mouth open at the panorama. Everything seems so familiar, even the heat. How could that be? Then something clicks into place and she's loping toward long grass beyond which is a gleam of reflected light and the smell of a river.

Startled birds explode out of shrubs as she runs through grass that stings her face and hands. She feels through her feet what she sees at her feet: dry earth and stones. Then she's scrambling down the riverbank, leaping out into rapid current. Swept along, head up, vigilant, she paddles hard scanning both banks of the river then the sky, for what she has no notion.

The riverbank on both sides is steep here, bordered with weeds and the occasional tree drooping out over water that is suddenly colder and faster and the banks steeper and farther away as one river joins another. Then, from up ahead, she hears a different sound. Growing louder and louder. Roaring. And she understands that she's heading toward a mighty falls.

Seeking options she kicks and paddles toward the shore on her right, edging toward it across the current. Up ahead is a tree with one long heavy branch hanging low over the water. She aims for that and starts swimming hard.

Sweeping by, she leaps up and grabs hold. Struggling, she pulls herself up onto the branch, dripping water, shirt and pants clinging, belt worn like a bandolier, braces on her leg and arm. Straddling and embracing the limb, she catches her breath then sits up dripping water, water rushing over her toes, roaring on downstream.

She hears insects buzzing around her head. She wipes her eyes and looks around.

It's perfect.

There are no seams. The semblance is convincing.

But there's a hollowness to the illusion, a thinness that causes her to remain skeptical. Clinging to the branch she scoots back to the trunk and hops down to the ground. Hugging the edge of the river and staying low she quickly rounds the bend and is stopped in her tracks by deafening roar and the sight of white thunder plunging over a high wide shelf to a lake far below. She stands staring.

What would happen if I went over the falls?

Would I die?

One-Who-Wanders turns and runs back along the river bank to the tree with its drooping branch. She climbs and goes out as far as she can, her weight bending the branch down toward the churned water. Then she leaps out into space.

The water is cold now, frothed and tumbling. Swimming as hard as she can she aims for the middle so there's no going back. Roaring becomes constant thunder as she nears the falls, no longer in control of anything because force and momentum have taken over. She's propelled. She's tumbled faster and faster. Everything is white froth and she's barreling toward the edge then plummeting over with such velocity that awareness is sucked right out of her. Then everything is stopped by a shockingly sudden explosion /implosion of elements.

THUD!

Panting hard One-Who-Wanders wakes sitting up on the bed in the middle of the pale indefinite space. Astonished to find herself dry and safe, she looks at Katya who is standing next to the bed, glaring down, not pleased.

"Do you think we'd let you die?"

Hard eyes lock.

"I wanted to find out." One-Who-Wanders looks around blinking, uncertain what just happened.

"For your information, this level of navigator is programmed with a built-in safety feature." Katya steps away from the bed. "The user is returned Home instantly should things get out of control, as they sometimes do."

"What kind of world is this?"

"The only one there is." Katya smiles, changing the subject. "When you press the large key you activate the navigator," she points. "That's the main control and accesses all locations. The other four buttons control different aspects of a location: illumination, climate, terrain and obstacles. Just follow the instructions on the screen." Katya walks toward the fog behind the bed and is gone.

And everything is whirling for One-Who-Wanders as she lies there looking up trying to figure out what just happened while attendants remove the couch and bring in a tray of food she doesn't want.

Fifth Gate - Story

Command Ship Phoenix is an old and noble vessel anchored wormholes away from earth. Sponsored by all four Space States, the ship is constructed almost entirely of nu-glass and built in levels to resemble a tall stack of transparent coins. From this perspective, the vessel is upright and wobbling a bit as it slowly revolves on its vertical axis, holding position near Anderson's Harp, a billowing cloud of pink star-froth almost a light-year deep.

Different kinds of vessels surround the Phoenix. Shimmering transparent spheres contain the academy, the hospital, the arena, the forest with hiking trails, and a beach complete with waves for surfing – size being irrelevant in space where boundaries don't exist. Traffic includes the ship's own shuttles, ferries drifting to and fro like lazy insects, H-V cruisers, tugs, troop carriers and barges, all arriving, queuing-up for service at the maintenance stations, unloading, loading, and preparing to go back out on their missions.

The Command Ship coordinates all Space State vehicular activity. Named after an early commoner, Thome Phoenix who designed the prototype velocity-gatherer, this ship keeps track of all others when they are a certain distance from a mother ship, in international space as it were.

A city unto itself, the Phoenix houses fourteen thousand sailors, first responders, cadets, scientists, technologists, mechanics, dock workers and visitors among others. Throughout, form follows function with simplicity and elegance. Surfaces gleam softly, their natural materials buffed to a fine shine with plants and flowers everywhere providing color. The ship's interior glows with light and activity though the dormitory levels are dimmed and quiet.

Elevators run from top to bottom making movement through the ship fast and easy. Wide paths, gravitized as is the entire vessel, spiral around the outer surface of the ship and provide a genuine workout for the several hundred who can be seen small as grains of rice in comparison to the whole.

Bright with light and efficiency the ship's bridge occupies the heart of the structure, is the coin between the two ends as it were. The circular space has a high ceiling and transparent walls for the openness Space Staters need. It's also a bit cold because the captain likes a crisp atmosphere.

Adjacent workstations ring the bridge facing outward. Each is oc-cupied by a specialist, male or female though it's difficult to tell as they all sport regulation brushcuts. A second, smaller ring of workstations is occupied by staff. The inner ring of workstations is for officers of the deck. Uniforms consist of soft boots, comfortable trousers, turtleneck and sweaters, (a few are wearing fleecy vests) variously colored and labeled to indicate name, rank, area of responsibility, and such.

In charge of Command Ship Phoenix is Captain Beryl Porter, 69, from S.S. Ulysses. Porter is an old pro who worked her way up from swabby. Leaning on one elbow in her captain's chair, hand in her silvery brushcut, she is a woman quiet and direct, known for her skill and her economy of words. At this time her brow is furrowed from waiting endlessly it seems for communication from Falcon One on recon to the transfer station.

Her long-term second in command is Captain Rol M'Gree out of of S.S. Friendship. Short and wiry with sallow skin and pale blue eyes, M'Gree is an engineer by training and rock-steady in a crisis. That's why she chose him for the spot and how he keeps it because crisis is only a punctured hull away in space or a fire that gets out of control or a meteor-mine that someone's injured in or any number of sudden emergencies that happen even when everything is perfect and all are on their toes.

A sturdy young man wearing cadet-blue is standing braced slightly behind Captain Porter. Of medium height and muscular, Cadet First Class Ero Mezon sports a light brown brushcut plus matching peach-fuzz on his chin and upper lip, which will need to be shaved soon. His eyes are dark in a face that is square with high cheekbones.

It was his good fortune to be first in his class and win the honor of being cadet-aide to Captain Porter while the academy is on term break. He moved here from his quarters out in the academy just before his mother was deployed. The last time he spoke with Pilar she was in hospital getting a new knee.

It hasn't been easy. Those around him have watched carefully if discreetly. It's getting more difficult, waiting for her to check-in. Then there's his father from whom no reliable word has come since a few days before the ambassadors went down to Great City and communications started arriving out-of-code.

Cadet Mezon looks straight ahead. It's not his job to observe or listen or speak or feel. His duty is to serve. And Captain Porter likes to make her own tea. So there isn't much to do but stand by and be conspicuous.

Restless, Beryl Porter rubs her face with both hands and stands to walk around.

"M'Gree take com please."

"Aye, capn." he nods and swivels the com-screen to face his chair.

Tired of waiting and unable to do anything about it, Beryl Porter walks slowly around the bridge followed by her cadet-aide who is doing too good a job hovering. She circles first one way then the other, sometimes looking over a shoulder, sometimes not. Near retirement, Porter is soon to deploy to a sweet little crib back on S.S. Ulysses where she wants to organize her journals and start that book about why it's important to maintain standards at the academies. She rounds the bridge a last time and returns to her seat.

M'Gree gives her a tight-lipped smile and turns the com-screen back toward her chair. Porter leans and taps a button. Then she speaks.

"All hands, all hands, all ships and passengers abroad. This is Captain Beryl Porter of Command Ship Phoenix." The announcement is public, going out to any Space Stater anywhere who wants to receive it. "Orders for H-V cruisers Galileo, Athena and Dervish. You are to thread your respective wormholes immediately and wait just on the other side for further orders. Blessings. Over and out." In the background, specialists and officers look at each other then back at their consoles – work doesn't stop because of a crisis.

A young man wearing a light green jumpsuit with a red triangle on his left breast approaches Beryl Porter and touches a sensor to her carotid artery while reading a gauge held in his other hand. He leans down and whispers something to her. She shakes her head no. He shakes his head yes and speaks to her in a way no one else on the ship may do. Frowning, she returns the com to M'Gree and stands, glaring at the doctor. Then waving off her cadet-aide she leaves the bridge to do as she was told

***

The man in charge of SubTurra has dimmed the indefinite place in which his new obsession is being kept because she's asleep on the bed, lying on her side, hands up near her face and clasped as though in prayer. The unused navigator is on the foot of the bed. She has refused to take off her clothes, even to bathe.

Her sleep is agitated. Sometimes she moves her hands and fingers in strange, inexplicable ways, as though talking to herself. Sometimes her movements are smooth and fluid, sometimes insistent with questions and demands. Then she grows still.

Headmon is fascinated. She is to him an island of interest in a boring world. Studying her from the shadows of his control room now lit only by the single illumined screen, he zooms in on her hands and leans forward, a silhouetted figure with long hair and a doughy profile, a man who regards illusion and fantasy as art forms and himself as a master manipulator. Such engagement is the only pleasure left to one who has everything including the entire legacy of the ancestors.

Suddenly, One-Who-Wanders gasps and wakes sitting bolt upright holding her head, clearly in pain that causes her to cry out. This makes sense, of course. She did, after all, suffer a concussion. Nothing for it but taking the time to heal. And mild drugs. But nothing to dampen her edge that he finds so fascinating.

***

Packed up and ready to go, having shared their last hot meal before leaving Mist Canyon and the Cave of Waters, the members of L'escola are seated around the now-cold fire, listening to Isham who is going over the plan that has emerged and been agreed on by everyone but Axl. The lad is standing off to the side, away from the others, furious about the place he has been assigned in the scheme of things.

"Source willing, Curanda and Esa and I will enter SubTurra while the two other groups…"

"Why Esa?" Voice raised, Axl steps forward. "Why not me?"

"Again, Axl. Esa is young enough to be regarded as an innocent assistant to Curanda. And you are destabilized by anger."

"I can get it under control!"

"We can't take the risk. It is decided."

He's my da! I have a right to go in for him!"

"Axl," Curanda's voice is soft and soothing, "you do not have the right to endanger fragile plans. You're too hot to be of help inside SubTurra."

Flushed with frustration, the lad groans, turns away from the group, throws a stone then moves to the back of the cave. He fiddles with his pack then kicks it.

"Axl," Isham patiently explains yet again, "elder Moss, you, Schiara and Will have perhaps the most important job of all…"

"What's more important than helping my da who's in even more danger now because you want to bring her out, too! Skye One-Who-Wanders ruined everything! She turned his head and he got stupid."

"What's more important is getting R'io and Skye and the rest of us back to the wilderness safely. And you are more helpful outside than in. Now hear me clearly, lad. The plan has been agreed upon by everyone but you. You can help and I hope you will. It's your choice. But continued complaints can no longer be allowed to prevent us from going forward."

"Why worry about her?!" The boy shouts. "She's the reason he's in there! She's not even one of us! She arrives and suddenly we're all in harm's way!"

"She is from Source, Axl, just like you." Isham looks at the boy steadily. "And a daughter to me. Taken captive against her will. Now make your decision and let that be the end of it."

The boy glares at his grand da then at the others. He goes back for his pack and leans down, hesitating for only a moment. Then he slings on his pack, grabs the straps of his food and water flasks and stalks toward the mouth of the cave as elder Moss calls out, stopping him momentarily.

"Should you wish to join us, remember Schiara, Wim and I will be camped at Little Bitter Falls waiting for the signal from elder Martin."

Axl strides out of the Cave of Waters without looking back and disappears into swirling mist. Schiara stands to go after him. A kind look from elder Moss stops her. The girl sits back down.

"Source-willing, he'll rejoin us and do his part," Curanda sighs.

"Axl has his father's fierce heart," elder Moss nods, "and his mother's gentleness. It must be difficult learning to balance those two apparent oppositions. But he's learning and I trust him."

"To continue," Isham clears his throat. "Source willing,

Curanda and Esa and I will enter canton Equa through different checkpoints."

He looks around at the group. Then he turns to Curanda and Esa, on either side. He takes hold of their hands.

"Because we have been unable to contact R'io or Skye through common-awareness, it remains uncertain whether or not we can be in contact with any of you from inside SubTurra. It's possible you will not know where we are or *if* we are. But the three of us have agreed not to come back without R'io and Skye. However long it takes. And, however long it takes, not one of you is to come in after us."

The others nod, understanding but not necessarily agreeing.

"The second group will go with elder Martin and Jabaz to our point of exit and wait there for us to emerge. The third group will go with elder Moss near the surface where they will wait for a signal from elder Martin or me. Questions?"

There are none.

"Comments?"

There are none.

"Let's go," Isham stands.

The remaining members of L'escola get up and sling on their packs and bags of food and water. They gather in a circle. Isham and Curanda bow their heads as do the others and Curanda raises her hands to bless them.

"Source be with R'io and Skye, with each of us and with Axl. In all cases whenever possible, let us do no harm. Remember, we seek only to retrieve what cannot be stolen."

"Aye."

"Abide with Source."

In silence, they form their groups and leave the Cave of Waters, following separate trails out of Mist Canyon to other trails that will take them to their different destinations.

***

The headaches are unpredictable. This one faded after several minutes of intense pressure behind her eyes. Now she's fine. There's no lingering grogginess or other symptom of having been sorely distracted by something unidentifiable.

203

One-Who-Wanders scoots to the edge of the bed, removes the brace from her foot and takes a few exploratory steps. The soreness is bearable. She removes the brace from her arm, makes a fist, flexes the arm and is satisfied. She turns to the bed, picks up the navigator and clasps it on her forearm. It feels smooth, silky, silvery and weighs almost nothing. When she presses down lightly with her thumb, the navigator lights up and words appear.

THIS IS LOCATION-CONTROL. THIS BUTTON (>) IS CALLED THE SEND KEY. PRESS LIGHTLY TO SCROLL. DOUBLE-CLICK TO MAKE A SELECTION.

She presses (>) lightly. Columns of options appear and she arbitrarily chooses two from the column labeled Beginner: "Glacier" and "Ocean Cliff." She's shown a picture of each option and asked to verify her selection. She does.

The screen changes and she's instructed to use the smaller keys near her wrist to adjust the locations for light/dark, climate, placement within the location, and obstacles. When finished, she's informed by more words on the screen.

YOUR SELECTIONS ARE PROGRAMMED. THEY CAN BE CHANGED AT ANY TIME, EITHER HERE OR FROM INSIDE THE LOCATION DURING PLAY. WOULD YOU LIKE TO MAKE ANOTHER SELECTION?

She taps No.

VERY WELL. WHEN READY, PROCEED TO YOUR FIRST LOCATION BY PRESSING THE SEND KEY. WHEN YOU WISH TO CHANGE LOCATIONS CLICK THE SEND KEY AGAIN. WHEN YOU WISH TO RETURN HOME DOUBLE-CLICK THE SEND KEY. ENJOY YOUR BANDING EXPERIENCE.

She shrugs. Then she presses the Send key. Nothing happens. She looks at the screen on her forearm, sees flashing orange words.

BANDING ACCESS IS DENIED. SIT OR RECLINE THEN PROCEED.

She lies back on the bed and presses the Send key again. The resulting jolt penetrates her system. And she's somewhere else entirely.

"Glacier" is shrouded in a thundering blizzard of suffocating white fury-beyond-cold against which the shirt and pants are no protection. She shrinks down into herself. Blinded by chaos she tries to shield her head with her arms. Huddled down, she turns, trying to get her back to a gale that is constant explosions of frozen rage coming at her from all directions. She can hardly keep her balance. Her temperature is plummeting. Numbness is taking over, numbness from which there's no return.

Get out of here!

She remembers that it's a location and she can leave. She finds the Send key and presses hard.

POP!

Now she's at the edge of a cliff. The sky is angry slate gray. Far below, heaving waves pound black slabs with deafening explosions of force. Wind and rain are cold and biting but not like before because this is indeed a different place. Same world, different place.

Her arms are wings folded against her chest. Teeth clattering, shivering violently she turns around and looks at what's behind her.

A vista.

Mossy rocks and boulders litter grass that angles down from where she's standing to a path below that stretches from right to left as far as she can see. On the far side of the path are hills and a few thick stands of trees then low roiling sky.

Everything is perfect but something is missing. One-Who-Wanders raises her left arm, bringing the navigator to her face. She lightly taps the control key with her thumb. Words happen.

DO YOU WANT TO ADJUST ASPECTS OF THIS SELECTION?

She taps Yes.

WOULD YOU LIKE TO START WITH WHAT YOU NOW HAVE OR WOULD YOU RATHER START FROM THE GRID?

Not knowing the difference, she pushes the button that points at the word GRID.

POP!

Instantly, everything goes neutral. Everything is interwoven strands of silvered gray. Dense networks of glowing threads crisscross from all directions and angles above, around and below, stretch out from her apparent center-point and vanish in the infinite distance. Between the strands is utter neutrality.

She reaches out to touch a strand. Her hand passes through. She moves her hand along the thread and feels nothing. She steps forward as though on hyper-sponge, bounces a few times and stops. She turns slowly, sees only innumerable silver strands threading utter neutrality. There is no sound here. Nothing to activate the senses but infinite crisscrossing silvery threads of utter neutrality.

Then her vision adjusts.

At first the scene appears mirage-like, diaphanous, wavering all around her as though about to melt. Then through the simmering strands she's able to distinguish the faintest outlines of what she understands to be this location, "Ocean Cliff." She checks the navigator on her forearm, sees the same image.

One-Who-Wanders presses down ever so lightly with her thumb. Slowly, the schematic becomes a sketch then a painting then the full-blown semblance of a world. She blinks at the navigator. The picture on the screen exactly matches the semblance.

She taps the key that controls placement within the location. Instantly she's atop a hill on the other side of the path, looking back at where she just was. She taps that key again and is immediately on the path itself, in the valley between cliff and hills.

Spinning from the rapid shifts in perspective, she taps that key again and stands disoriented at the bottom of the cliff as a huge wall of water is poised above her about to collapse on her. She slams that key down, pressing hard and is instantly back at her point of arrival. When the spinning stops and the location is stable again, she lightly touches the key that controls climate.

At first everything is balmy and dry. As she continues to press, the location cools and moistens. Then there's fog and bone-chill then snow then everything is ice. She eases that finger back up through climates until the air is warm and dry. Then she touches the key that controls light/dark.

It's the first hint of dawn on "Ocean Cliff." She can see it on her forearm and all around her in the semblance. The sea is calm, its backdrop sky slowly bleached by the rising sun as she presses. The air warms as a sun rises from the pressure of her finger, arcing up and over behind her to set beyond the hills. She presses that key all the way down.

Depths of night.

Rivers and shawls of stars crowd the sky, their light casting silver glow on sea and hills. She eases the pressure off that key until the sun is directly overhead. Then she lightly presses the last key, the one that controls obstacles.

Nothing happens.

She looks at the navigator and sees words flashing.

YOU MUST SELECT THE NATURE OF THE OBSTACLE.

She scans a list of options and chooses "Natural Phenomena." She presses the key lightly. There's a sub-list of options. She makes her selection and presses the key lightly.

At first she feels nothing. Then she's aware of the slightest trembling beneath her feet. She presses the key down farther. The trembling becomes rolling as the ground beneath her feet seems to be turning over in its grave. On the far side of the path, trees topple as though snapped off at their bases. A chunk of the cliff she's standing on breaks away. The slabs far below are heaving. She continues to press down.

Barely able to stand for the quaking, she stares down at the navigator on her arm, wanting to take it off and throw it over the cliff then run. But this is semblance. Fantasy. They'd get her back – she's got that figured out.

Still pressing down on her control button, she looks up to see a tidal wave, a wall of water coming from far out to sea. Even from here, she knows the wave will swallow the cliff, indeed, the entire location should it get this far. But she can't stop pressing the key down, wants that tidal wave to get here and swallow everything up, wants the earth around her to be washed away even though she knows there's a safety feature on the device because they will not let her die. The quaking and cracking and rolling and the wall of water coming on can do no real damage. All of this can only generate a safe and momentary surge of adrenalin.

She presses the key down all the way and raises her head to face the wall of water as it races faster than a galloping horse toward her, looming, shadowing everything in its path. She doesn't care. This is a dead world. She wants only not to be here anymore and if that's not possible then not to be at all.

The huge wave slams into the base of the cliff with unimaginable force but she feels only the suggestion of its power before she hears a thundering POP! and once again she's back on the bed in the pale, indefinite space waking from a dream exhausted. The navigator refers to this place as Home. Yet there's nowhere she'd less like to be. So she sits up, reprograms the navigator for another trip and is gone again while lying on her back on the bed, twitching ever so slightly – a dreamer trapped in someone else's fantasy.

***

Pack on his back and ready to go, Axl is standing at the bottom of Mist Canyon in front of a junction of trails with his headlamp on, projecting a cone of yellow light at his options. He's still hurt and angry, mostly at Skye One-Who-Wanders for coming and changing everything. But he's also really angry at Isham for not letting him go in with Curanda.

Time is passing and he knows elder Martin's plan won't work because there are too many contingencies. They'll be caught and instead of one person to get out there will be four – forget the newcomer who caused all this in the first place. The question is how to come up with a better plan.

He wipes his forehead with the back of a sleeve. He feels responsible for his part of the plan with elder Moss, Schiara and Wim. But elder Moss is a favorite who can do anything. Her team will be fine. Anyway, their task is of little conseqence. Curanda and Esa and Isham are doing the important work.

Mist swirls around the canyon walls, moistening his long blond hair and his face so like his da's only fuller. HeH shivers. He adjusts his pack, heavy and bulky with surface gear, knowing he can't stay here any longer. He studies his options.

The tunnel on the left is the way to Little Bitter Falls with elder Moss, Schiara and Wim. To the right is a main artery with offshoots that lead to very different parts of the wilderness. Through that tunnel he can branch off and go to elder Martin's group. Or he can branch off and go back to wilderness-people. Or he can branch off and enter a chain of trails and eventually arrive at canton Equa.

Axl closes his eyes. He tries to implore Source for help. But he doesn't believe in Source right now, not after what happened to his da.

Uncertain what to do, the lad adjusts his pack again. He starts off one way, toward Little Bitter Falls then turns around and heads into the tunnel that leads either to elder Martin's group or back to wilderness-people or on into canton Equa, depending on which cutoff he takes.

***

Still wearing her old stone-people clothes, One-Who-Wanders pops out of a location called "Pinnacles" on the Banding spectrum and returns to the indefinite space that has become leaden with impossible heaviness for her as she continues to go in and out of different locations. Lying on the bed, she unclasps the navigator and tosses it between her legs.

Needing the ground she scoots to the edge of the bed and slides down so she's sitting on the floor, feet crossed, leaning back, mouth open eyes closed, exhausted from the tower of red rock she just virtually climbed and descended in high-sun heat. Not that "there" was any better than "here." In this realm it seems that all possibilities are thin and lifeless, none desirable.

Trembling, she rests her forehead against raised knees, unable to support the weight that descends when she returns from exploring with the navigator and running, running blindly, recklessly toward a way out, a way back to something familiar, running away from the despair of not knowing who she is or why here or what this world is, only that it isn't real and she is. Or used to be, somehow – if there was, indeed, a place before here and a time not now.

So far she's found only semblance – a sort of imitation here/now. Thrills without skills. She's been through all the locations in the navigator, explored to exhaustion and not found a hole or a seam or an end or a way out. Only perfect, empty semblance.

She doesn't understand this place with its slippery realities. And spacious as its variety of locations might seem to be, when she comes back to the indefinite space with the bed in its center and sleep and attendants and food, she has an overwhelming sense of being on the verge of panic from which there is no return. So she runs again, stopping only when she can run no more.

Leaning, she drags a container of pink fluid out from under the bed, shakes it to a neon froth, uncaps it and sucks down deep swallows – not because it tastes good but because she knows she must if she is to get stronger. She recaps the bottle, puts it back under the bed and sits slumped, unable to raise her head. Then she freezes, suddenly aware of not being alone.

Someone is here.

Off to the side. Not far away.

Standing.

Not Katya. Not one of the attendants.

Someone as still as darkness between dreams.

How long?

One-Who-Wanders drags her awareness to two form-fitting

209

iridescent green boots then up oiled legs that are black, heavily muscled, long and smooth. Tight green briefs ride low on narrow hips. A green halter holds small breasts in place.

How tall the woman is! But it's the face beneath the gleaming dome of shaved head that commands attention. Black. Chiseled.

And the eyes. Black. Fierce. Penetrating.

"I didn't expect to approach you so easily."

The woman is glistening ebony, of indeterminate age and at her physical peak. Majestic and tall, she would be lean but for dense muscles wrapped in masses around her torso, and impossibly long limbs. A navigator is clasped to her right forearm.

"I am Rogue, champion of champions."

Blink.

One-Who-Wanders gets to her feet slowly and peers out through isolation at someone called Rogue. The champion moves closer, to less than a body-length away. Her breath is musty. Her gaze is penetrating black fire that burns through the heaviness between them.

Eyes lock.

Snap.

Something familiar happens.

One called Rogue is looking at her. Seeing her.

Until this moment all contact here has been clinical. But now she's being assessed. She's being explored, weighed by one who seems to be fully present.

"One-Who-Wanders. You may call me that," she whispers, cautiously.

Rogue's eyes flare with triumph and something shifts. It's as though she, One-Who-Wanders, is standing in a dimly lit clearing, coming awake because of being studied by someone called Rogue.

What's real here?

She wants to reach out, touch, trust. The need to trust is almost overwhelming. But not here. Nothing and no one here.

Rogue stands tall and dignified, eyes flaring. Then turning around slowly she speaks, as though making an announcement.

"United Cantons of SubTurra! I, Rogue, champion of champions, challenge Skye One-who-wanders, to a match!"

It's a pleasant enough sound.

"…Skye?"

"That's what you're called: Skye One-Who-Wanders."

The woman is easily a head and a half taller. Her skin,

210

gleaming obsidian, is tight over high cheekbones and a long nose. Her lips are carved and full. Her eyes are snapping black fire.

"Get your navigator."

"What's a match?"

"Something that may or may not happen between you and me somewhere down the line. For now, we complete the rite of challenge with a little game called Hunter/Quarry. Get your navigator."

One-Who-Wanders retrieves the device from the center of the bed and clasps it on.

"Clear it."

She presses with her thumb. The word "CLEAR" flashes on the screen. She looks at Rogue who is holding her arm out.

"My navigator is identical to yours. It's also cleared and programmed for Solo. That means we're navigating independently. We can be in different locations or we can be in the same location – either by accident or by skill. Hunter/Quarry is a game designed to test my worthiness to challenge you.

"Choose twelve locations and adjust them as you will – omitting obstacles. Then traverse them in whatever order and manner you wish. I must find you in each location within a five seconds or you hear a pleasant chime and announce to all that I am not a worthy opponent." Rogue smiles indulgently. "Since you haven't done this before, I'll even the odds. Not only will I track you to each location but wherever you go I'll already be there, waiting. First time I miss, the challenge is off. Understand?"

One-Who-Wanders shrugs indifferently.

"Program your navigator." It's not a request.

She scrolls through locations choosing twelve at random. "Tundra." "Outback." "Bayou." "Rice Paddy." "Parking Structure." "Climbing Wall." "Pyramid." "Labyrinth." "Jungle." "Shopping Mall." "Bamboo Forest." "Steppes."

She taps the other keys, indifferently adjusting illumination, climate and location, omitting obstacles. Then she looks back up.

Eyes lock.

Rogue snaps her fingers. Attendants wheel in two padded slant boards and lock them down, one behind Rogue and the other behind One-Who-Waits who watches the champion step back then lean back relaxed against the board.

"Ready when you are."

One-Who-Wanders shrugs. She looks at Rogue, steps back,

211

leans back and surrenders her weight to the slant board. Then she presses Send.

The tundra is bathed in twilight. Sky and earth stretch out and out around her. Spots of tiny wildflowers are whorled by unpredictable wind. Stratified clouds move in different directions at different speeds overhead.

Scanning, she turns a circle.

Rogue is off in the distance, striding toward her.

She presses Send.

The outback is programmed for high-sun and dryness. Even the spit in her mouth is gone. In front of her is a huge breast of red stone. Squinting, shading her eyes with both hands, she looks up.

Rogue is there, the sun directly behind her. She stands relaxed, arms at her sides, head and hip cocked.

"Come on," the champion taunts, "make it a challenge."

Skye presses Send.

Again and again.

Wherever she goes – "Bayou," "Rice Paddy," "Climbing Wall" – Rogue is already there, closer each time. The instant she sees Rogue she presses Send until they're shifting locations faster and faster and everything is spinning. When they snap into the last location, "Steppe," they're face-to-face and almost breathing into each other.

She has a moment's comprehension that Rogue is unfazed by the rapid shifts of perspective. Then she's drowning in the spins. Falling forward she feels herself caught and held.

Pop!

They're no longer here but somewhere else and everything is spinning as Rogue puts her down. The spinning subsides. They step back from each other.

They're where she hasn't been before. Yet she understands this location to be the one from which all others are possible. Vast neutrality stretches around and beyond them – a twilight of everything and nothing. There's no sound and all sound. The air is pure extract. Rogue speaks hurriedly, her words hollow, distorted and barely audible in the non-location.

"There's little time. Headmon knows we're in the meta-grid where he can't track us. He doesn't like that. To the point: do you want to get out of here?"

"Yes." She has to trust.

"Good. You're not alone."

"How?" She blinks, startled by the information.

"I don't know yet. What I do know is that you came from somewhere else with someone else and you're not like us. So there must be something beyond SubTurra and the hinterlands."

"...Someone else?"

"Yes. Your companion is also here."

"Companion?"

"You remember nothing?"

Bewildered, she shakes her head no.

Rogue blinks then nods. She programs her navigator and holds out her arm. Images appear.

A tall gaunt man, stunned and bleeding. Red hair. Dripping wet, he's trying to stand, screaming "Skye! Skye!" Then he's struggling with people in funny suits and helmets. Then he's lying on his back in a tube of transparent technology, unconscious and emaciated. She hears familiar hissing, beeping and pinging. Then his head is shaved and he's put in a different transparent container and plugged in. And she understands him to be stuck at the border between death and life, not allowed to pass on and unwilling to return.

The last image fades. Rogue drops her arm.

Blink.

Nothing happens.

Then, impalpable at first, pressure starts to build and One-Who-Wanders is blinking as the pressure intensifies, becomes unbearable then explodes and an avalanche of water is thundering around her, pulling her down. And she's leaping for and almost getting hold of then losing her grip as churning water sucks her down, tumbles her over and over. Then him behind. And neither of them letting go of the belt then hitting hard and hitting again, stunned with pain.

Then something else breaks open and pours through.

His stance. His hands. His grace. His voice. His eyes the color of blue flame. His cheek in her palm. His lips. His scent. His nature.

Then climbing. Climbing fast and hard for a reason.

Until the time of quiet.

She blinks.

"R'io?"

"If that's his name."

"In truth?"

"Yes. Real-him. He's here somewhere. Also available as Banding content, though not many select him now that he's inert."

Suddenly, more breaks open. Her head snaps back and she gags on chunks of memory.

R'io.

Curanda.

Esa.

Axl.

People just trying to live.

Stone and wicklight.

How she got her name.

Handsign.

Traveling.

Drills screaming through stone.

Then a different, earlier place and time. The old man, One-Who-Waits. The grotto. Solaris. Then back further to confusion, wandering from a place called Great City and the archives with their precious and grotesque finds and she's overtaken as by seizure and Rogue is holding her because she cannot hold herself. Rogue is holding and stroking and whispering to calm.

"Headmon must not know that you remember or that anything has transpired between us."

"He lives, R'io? In truth?"

"Yes. At first he was active and, though badly wounded, tried to fight them off, screaming for you."

"Skye..."

"That's what you're called."

"Where is he?"

"Only Headmon knows."

"Then let me be with him on Banding, whatever that is," she pleads, desperate.

"All things concerning you must be cleared through Headmon." Rogue grips her tighter. "He must not suspect that you know *anything*."

"What does he want from me?"

"More of the unexpected fortune he's made off of you so far on Banding. The match heats things up quite a bit. When the match is over, he'll find a way to make you take him where you came from because he undoubtedly has plans for that place and those people."

"No!"

"Yes. And before the match, we must find a way out."

Barely able to stand on her own, Skye steps back from Rogue.

"Not without R'io."

"If that's possible."

She grabs Rogue's arms.

"Not without R'io!"

Eyes lock.

"If there's a way, not without R'io. That's the best I can do. Now we must return."

With that, Rogue picks her up like a baby and, pop, they're gone, back on the slant boards and she's overcome by the past spinning through her. She steps forward, leans over and vomits neon froth then tumbles onto the bed.

"What took so long Rogue?"

"Aw look what happened."

An attendant emerges to clean up.

"What took so long?!" Headmon's voice seems to come from everywhere, evenly filling the indefinite space with suspicion. "WHAT TOOK SO LONG?!"

"Her navigator jammed!"

"She's that quick?"

"She's that stupid. I had to drag her into the meta-grid to clear it and bring her back."

"Take her navigator to the technicians. I want it checked out now."

"After I shower and change."

"NOW!"

Rogue leans down and unclasps Skye's navigator. Flashing a rude gesture, she strides off behind the bed leaving Skye on her back, writhing from confusion.

After a moment, Skye leans over the edge of the bed and vomits again and again, strings of pink neon. Finally the spinning slows. She sinks back, rolls onto her side in a ball and starts to rock.

Then something happens. She doesn't know what. Something just snaps.

She's not aware of getting off the bed then ripping the covers and sheets to shreds. All she knows is rage. She's not aware of attacking the mat-tress, tearing it open and flinging its contents as far as she can, then going after the bed frame. And when everything has been destroyed, she's not aware of standing in the wreckage with her mouth open, pounding her head with her fists because the headache is back and memories make it clear that she's in the wrong place and has endangered those she loves by running into the very heart of what they flee.

And him, R'io.

Not dead not alive.

Should not be here but *is* because of her.

Exhausted, she sinks to her knees then all the way down on her side curled up in a tight ball again. She rocks and keens.

The attendants arrive. They clear away the mess and return with an-other bed. They center and lock it down. Then they come for her.

Curled up on the floor, mouth open, rigid, she's still rocking back and forth. Three hold her down and one injects her with comative. Another picks her up – still rolled in a ball – and carries her to the new bed.

The comative quickly takes effect. She goes limp. They roll her onto her back and straighten her out then leave her to sleep it off.

In far-flung niches of space, three H-V cruisers similar to Mohawk prepare to thread their wormholes – Galileo out of S.S. Columbus, Athena from S.S. Ulysses, Dervish of S.S. Friendship. Each is handled by a crew of four and carries a team of six elite first responders. The Eagles. The Condors. The Hawks. Each also carries extra supplies and ordnance.

Manta-like and in stealth-mode, the cruisers move into position in front of their respective wormholes. At the right moment the velocity-gatherers are reeled in and ignited. From separate distant points all three ships are instantly in the vicinity of earth's solar system.

Meanwhile, Command Ship Phoenix has come into position near the wormhole in her vicinity of the universe. The plan is to remain at this location until the conflict with Great City is resolved, thus giving all ships easy access to and from the wormhole, which from here is just a little whirlwind of brilliant light in a nest of blackness ringed with distant stars.

Pirouetting slowly, Phoenix glows white-gold and ablaze with action on most levels because all hands are on deck preparing ships, sending them off, receiving them, unloading them, and re-loading them. Only some of the constantly arriving and departing H-V craft are focused on matters earth. Most are on journeys that have nothing directly to do with Great City or the archives of the ancients because other Space State activities of gathering and transmuting base material into usable gold must continue if they are to survive.

In the middle of all this and responsible for it, the Captain of the ship, Beryl Porter, is still waiting for word from Falcon One and growing more perturbed about it by the minute, especially right now because she's not on the bridge where she wants to be but on the path in her walking togs. Ordered here by the doctor, she was told to walk hard for an hour with no choice but to obey because he can override her on health matters. So she's trying to walk off her apprehension on the paths that crisscross up and down and around and around the tubular body of the ship like strands of DNA.

Space State tradition has it that those who are off-duty signal their degree of sociability to others in some way. Such signals are necessary in a closed environment, even one this large. Beryl Porter's cap is on backwards, indicating that she is to be left alone. And others

217

on the path respectfully ignore her.

Captain Porter stops at the very bottom of the ship to look out at faint pink clouds against blackness and stars, so many stars, so many, many points of light and not one for humans to live on. "We had our chance," she whispers, shaking her head. Then she peers up and out at the bellies of several H-V cruisers being readied to go to earth should they be ordered.

Tethered mechanics in bright orange space suits crawl all over the ships, making adjustments, replacing filters, checking fuel cells. Two more cruisers are being similarly prepped on the other side of Phoenix.

Captain Porter stands at the very bottom of the ship a moment longer, inhaling the deep fragrance of jasmine that lines this part of the path. Then she turns and starts the long way back up through gravity to the top of the ship.

At least it's Pilar Mezon out there trying to find out what's going on. At least it's a pro. Though Porter isn't all that comfortable having the son around. But then again Porter isn't much for youth any more and endures the cadets who have it so much softer than did she and M'Gree or any other officer over 50.

***

"Get up!" It's two voices in one – male, commanding.

She surfaces too fast, struggling to cohere. She lifts her head, heavy and throbbing with hangover from the comative, confused by dreams of being chased by a giant creature with too many hairy legs. Dizzied by the impact of here/now, she blinks at where the sound came from.

Three tall blurs come slowly into focus. They're standing near the foot of the bed. Rogue, dressed as before in halter, briefs and boots, gazes straight ahead, manifest indifference. She's flanked by two males.

Identical.

Twins.

Reminiscent of ancient Aztec warriors, they are the color of sunlight on sandstone and hairless but for a long braid of glistening black that falls from the very top of each otherwise shaved head.

218

Shorter than Rogue, the twins are thick and square with dense, sharply defined muscles. They're wearing turquoise briefs and boots. Like Rogue, they are of indeterminate age and at physical peak.

The three of them are wearing navigators. But these navigators are different. A bit thicker perhaps, larger, with extra control buttons.

"Get up." It's two voices in one, commanding again.

They wait for her to respond. She remembers that Headmon must not know. Rogue says "Do as they say" as though nothing ever passed between them.

Very well. Sullen, she sits up.

Four attendants appear from behind the bed dragging and pushing a big mobile pod of some kind, a silvery lozenge-shaped thing of sufficient size to serve as a comfortable dwelling for one or two. They position the pod and lock it in place then depart. The twins approach the foot of the bed.

"Come."

Headmon must not suspect. She shakes her head once. No.

"Do as you're told," Rogue advises.

Skye One-Who-Wanders lies back down on the bed and rolls into a ball remembering that there was a before and another place and people. She remembers, first and foremost that she must not betray those people. She remembers even though remembering has transformed her and that mustn't show but how can it not?

"Very well," Rogue whispers.

The twins approach. They pluck her from the bed like a weightless thing rolled in a tight ball and position her between them – upright, back to one twin, head and knees to the other. They step together and fold her into herself in such a way that she can't move and breathing is difficult.

They lock arms and move closer together. She can't breathe. They squeeze harder. The pain is excruciating. She groans. When she's turning purple, they step apart and gently put her back on the bed where she writhes, trying to gasp, unable to unfold.

"Though reluctantly," Rogue's words are spoken without pity, "they can cause more pain than you can bear without leaving a mark or doing permanent damage. I guarantee that however long it takes, eventually you'll go with them. Your choice when."

Grimacing, gasping, she slowly unfolds until she's lying panting on her back. Then she crawls to the edge of the bed and labors to stand.

"Come." It's two voices in one.

The twins turn and move toward the pod. Barely able to walk, she follows them into a sparkling clean environment and sits on the low stool they point at. She looks around. Everything is spun aluminum. Rounded surfaces gleam.

The twins are at a sink, navigators off, washing their hands and arms with something pungent. A gurney with a white sheet over it is off to one side. Through an open door she can see a bathroom with a shower.

Finished, the twins approach carrying a tray of tools and a large transparent bag. They unzip the bag and hold it open.

"Your garments, please."

"No."

"They'll be waiting at your destination as they are now, untouched by anyone but you."

"Not the belt."

"Agreed."

She stands, takes off the belt and drops it on the stool. She removes the doublet, the shirt and knee-pants and drops them into the bag. The twins seal the bag and set it on a counter. She puts the belt back on over her head. The twins point to the bathroom.

"Shower."

She nods and goes into the bathroom. They close the door.

***

Having been impeccably barbered by a woman from a different band of wilderness-people, Isham One-Who-Waits is now naked but for leather undershorts. He's sitting on a portable stool so the woman can rub stone-dust on his face and body. When she's satisfied he looks sufficiently gray, she steps back and, nodding, wipes her hands clean.

"You've memorized the documents?"

"Yes." He points to his head. "It's in here."

"Then I'm off. Source be with you."

"And also with you," he stands and returns her blessing then helps her put on the pack with his surface gear and traveling clothes. She's agreed to deliver it to elder Martin on her way back to her people.

The woman hands him the leather packet of carefully forged documents. He takes the packet and, eyes closed, holds it out in front of him not quite at arm's length. She smiles sadly.

"It's important to somehow transcend your revulsion at the feel of these things. Everything in SubTurra is made of stone, metal, glass or re-cycled human. You will be touching a lot of it. It will be touching you. That is the hardest part of those forays in and out for my research, getting used to the feel of my body clothed in human flesh."

Eyes closed, he nods. His face is drawn and determined. Then he looks at her and smiles. She hugs him again, "blessings," and is off.

Gritting his teeth, Isham puts on a gray dress shirt, an old but beautifully tailored black suit, ankle boots and a black tie, all made of human flesh. Looking up, forcing himself to take deep breaths, he eases his arms into a long brown trench coat and adjusts the black bowler so it sits straight on his head. He puts the packet of papers in a special inside pocket near his breast. Then he leans down for the old valise, raises it to his chest and embraces it.

Isham One-Who-Waits can't move. He stands frozen, eyes closed, face drawn back almost as though by Gs as he struggles to accept the fact that to achieve his purpose he must be disguised in someone else's flesh. He stands like that for a long time, feeling the clothes on his body and accepting what he knows about them. Then he expels a long breath and, without opening his eyes, sinks through to a deeper level and touches Curanda who is with Esa, heading for a different way into canton Equa.

Blessings, love. I'm going in. Source be with us all.

Without waiting for a response, he moves silently through a long, confusing maze of passages. Then, inhaling truly foul air, he steps out of shadow to join a stream of migrants, their faces almost black with stone-dust, crowding the concrete tunnel that leads to the processing center at this entry-point to canton Equa.

For a moment, Isham One-Who-Waits can't breathe. Can't see. Can't hear. Can't feel anything but the impact of total disconnection from anything not made by humans – except for the clothes he wears, which are a patchwork of other people. He reels and falters a step or two. Then he's swept up by the crowd, lifted along by the density of those here for a better life.

The crowd is eerily quiet for so many people. The dominant sound is from the commercial screens along both sides of the tunnel, high up so they can be seen, loud in competition with each other as they hawk their particular Banding features or propaganda called news.

"...IN AN UNPRECEDENTED MOVE ROGUE, CHAMPION OF CHAMPIONS, HAS SUCCESSFULLY CHALLENGED SKYE ONE-WHO-WANDERS TO A MATCH!"

A ripple of interest rolls through the crowd, causing dropped heads to rise. People stop and listen.

"HAS THE SLUMP IN HER RATINGS SINCE THE ARRIVAL OF OUR CAVE-GIRL FRIGHTENED THE CHAMPION OF CHAMPIONS INTO DOING SOMETHING NEVER DONE BEFORE AND, WELL, FRANKLY, DEGRADING?"

The message and blare of one sign blends in with the next and he can make little sense of any of it so overwhelmed for the moment is his system by the sterility of the place and the gray dullness of the people around him.

"CAVEMAN REMAINS IN A COMA! CONDITION STABLE! HEADMON IS SPARING NO MEASURES TO TRY AND REVIVE HIM..."

Bowler straight on his head, valise held tight to his chest, Isham towers above most around him and even to his forgiving nose, the stench of humans dressed in flesh of their own kind and needing to bathe is almost overwhelming. Moving slowly, locked in the docile crowd, he notices a sign on the left. Nearing the sign he can make out a picture.

Skye's face. Life-size. Words arc across the sign and shout at him with triumphal music in the background.

"CAVE-GIRL AVAILABLE ON BANDING FULL-TIME! DON'T MISS ANY OF THIS STUPENDOUS DRAMA! BEST QUALITY AVAILABLE! WE EXTEND CREDIT!"

Now in the center of the stream of people, unable to stop and approach the sign, Isham stares at the advertisement as he passes it. As though alive, Skye's head turns and her expressionless eyes follow him. He can see little Skye's wearing stone-people clothes, running circles and zigzags and leaping over what seems to be a bed, going from side to side of the sign, back and forth. Then the sign is behind him and another of her is coming up on the right, similar and even more garish.

He notices the crowd around him. Their necks are craned to the advertisements as though mesmerized by Skye. He hears murmuring and realizes it's about her. Then, up ahead, he can see the opening into the hall where the bulk of those seeking entry to canton Equa are processed, and he focuses on his reason for being here.

Skye emerges from the bathroom naked, clean and dry, holding the belt in one hand. The twins examine her. Satisfied, they spritz her all over with something cold that smells sharply medicinal. They move away.

"That'll take a moment to dry."

She stands shivering. The twins point to the gurney and move to their trays of instruments. She hefts herself up and sits perched on the edge of the gurney. They approach, help her lie down and check her from head to toe, front and back – making certain that all incisions are healing, all bruises are yellowing, carefully checking her foot and her elbow, nodding, satisfied that the fast-healing techniques are effective. Finished with that, they tend her teeth and ears, trim her toe and fingernails.

"On your stomach," they murmur in unison and massage her, working through the pain they caused as she dips in and out of awareness.

***

While Lt. Pilar Mezon rested, the shape-changers were busy on the super-lead hatch that separates the fore section of the Emerson from its own cargo hold then the transfer station. Redirecting elementary particles, the shape-changers opened a hole in the hatch big enough for Pilar to pass through. But she wants one more check.

Falcon One turns and peers through the hole, scanning the cargo hold. Readings say it's empty. It looks empty. But five mysteriously dead people are reason to check again. And again. And again. Especially given that she's out here all alone in com-silence.

Pilar shivers. Using the keypad on the back of a glove, she calls the currently active shape-changers to her, reduces them back to cartridge size and puts them back in their holders to recharge from energy stored by the windrider. Then she takes three fresh shape-changer cartridges from her bandolier, programs them and releases them into the cargo hold for a final assessment before she enters.

***

Moving quickly, Curanda and Esa darken their faces with stone-dust then drop the long black leather garments down over their heads. They were told that SubTurran females indicate sexual unavailability – either because of age or blood flow – by wearing a veil or a burka. Curanda's face is completely obscured but for a patch of lattice-work cut into the leather. Esa's eyes are exposed. Other than that they are completely covered. Beneath the burkas they are wearing plain leather garments of simple cut and very high quality.

Ready to go, they stop and take a moment to adjust to the feel of being covered with layers of human flesh that once belonged to someone else. Then they sling on packs full of herbs and potions. Curanda nods.

Now.

Unnoticed, the old woman and the girl step from shadow into the noise and glare of a dense herd of people in a big open square. For a moment, neither of them can move. Or breathe. Or see. Or hear. So great is the din and the glare and the stench and the sense of disconnection. Then the crowd jostles them and they are swept up, Esa clinging tightly to Curanda's sleeve.

There's scaffolding around the edges of the space. Stone-cutters with jackhammers are up high, expanding the ceiling. Dust falls like rain.

Though not the largest, Equa is one of the main cantons of SubTurra, sort of the unofficial cultural capital. Most migrants avoid this particular point of entry because there's little chance of getting in – the way through a point of entry being employment, which is difficult to get when the skill level is set so high. The advantage for Curanda and Esa is that the lines are shorter. It's been a long trip and time is not to be wasted.

Construction noise doesn't drown out the constant blare of screaming signs that hang out over the heads of the dense crowd. Carried along with the smelly flow, Esa looks around for their first destination. Then her attention is snagged by a newsflash that comes on all the screens in the square at the same time. A stiff man is sitting behind a big desk, shouting.

"ATTENTION! ATTENTION! *THE INSIDER* HAS A

224

DEFINITE CONFIRM! ROGUE CHAMPION OF CHAMPIONS IS GOING UP AGAINST SKYE ONE-WHO-WANDERS! IT'S THE BANDING EVENT OF THE CENTURY! GET YOUR BANDING SLOT NOW FOR THIS EVENT OF EVENTS!"

All movement and other sound stops as heads crane to catch images of Skye and a tall black athlete of a woman. A swell of energy passes through the crowd.

"FROM THE TIME CAVE-GIRL GOES TO THE STADIUM TO BE TRAINED UNTIL THE MATCH, OUR NEWCOMER WILL NOT BE LIVE ON THE BANDING SPECTRUM! REPEAT. WHILE SHE'S BEING TRAINED BY THE CHAMPIONS, SKYE ONE-WHO-WANDERS WILL NOT BE AVAILABLE REAL-TIME ON BANDING.

"YES, FOLKS, HEADMON WAS WORN DOWN BY THE CHAMPIONS WHO INSISTED THAT IF THEY AGREE TO TRAIN HER, THEY'RE GOING TO DO IT RIGHT. SEEMS TO ME THE CHAMPIONS HAVE A BIT TOO MUCH CLOUT HERE. WHADDAYA THINK?!"

As if the announcement of Skye's unavailability is a pin pricking a balloon, the energy escapes from the crowd. A numbing silence fills the big square. People stare dumbly at blank screens. Then someone is screaming.

"BACK TO WORK, MAGGOTS!" The announcement seems to come from everywhere.

Immediately, the jackhammers resume their pounding. Stone-dust falls. The screens belch to life again, each advertising a different part of the Banding spectrum in clever ways to capture attention, hawking various shows at bargain prices with no credit check.

But some people can't seem to recover from the announcement. A few of them panic and are left where they fall, curled up, rocking back and forth. A few others begin to wail but the sound is drowned out by jackhammers on stone and screaming announcers.

Eyes wide, blinking, Esa finally sees their destination, diagonally across the square. She squeezes Curanda's hand. Worming her way through the dense crowd, the girl leads her grandam to a different immigration center than the one used by Isham One-Who-Waits.

According to shape-changers, the cargo hold of H-V Shuttle/Barge Emerson is empty and harmless. It's safe to go on in and try to find out what happened.

Falcon One activates her optics, braces herself and peers through the thick hole at green darkness on the other side. It's a closed space, that much farther away from openness. First responders are trained for this.

Okay.

Taking slow deep breaths, Pilar pulls herself on through, looks around, flicks on the light in her forehead and broadens the beam – for comfort more than anything else because something is getting to her in here, the bodies, the closed-in part and she doesn't like to use tranks on a mission, nothing to dull her laser focus. So she has to live with what she feels because closed-in windowless places aren't pleasant for any Space Stater, even one trained for them.

Pilar turns her headlamp back off because all she sees with it is bare metal walls and bracings. The cargo hold glows green and empty again. Shivering but not from cold, she takes a slow tour of the hold, recording as she goes. It has been stripped of everything, even the fire extinguishers.

She checks the barrier separating Emerson from the interior of the transfer station. The big hatch is locked and sealed. It's also much thicker than the barrier she just broke through.

Falcon One calls the shape-changers back and programs them to examine the hatch for the best and fastest way through it. Almost immediately the different little sounding and analyzing instruments agree on a method. She releases them to their work and because it will take a while goes back out of the cargo hold into the fore section of Emerson and out through the hatch into the blessed openness of space.

"Off the table."

The twins go to another part of the pod and open a closet from which they take several items. She puts the belt back on and rubs a hand across her skull, amazed that she's getting hair. It's fingertip short but hair nonetheless. The twins return.

"Put these on."

A twin offers her light blue briefs that are like water in her hands. She steps into them and pulls them up. They fit like skin and ride low around her hips. She's handed a matching halter.

"It goes over your head. You'll need to remove the belt."

Holding the belt between her knees, she finds the front of the halter, which isn't easy because the garment is so liquid. She pulls the halter down over her head and shoulders and tugs it into place. It feels good. She slings the belt back on. The stool is rolled over.

"Take a seat."

She does. Boots are tossed, same fabric and color as the briefs and halter. She catches. They're soft, slipper-like, made of spun-metal but of a heavier gauge. She pulls them on. Very comfortable.

"Back up on the table."

Skye One-Who-Wanders hops up. A tray of food is rolled across her lap. Flooded with the indifference that invariably accompanies eating here, she forces herself to take a bite. Then another. And she finds this food different. It tastes like food. She eats until it's gone. She finishes her drink then releases a long satisfied belch.

The tray is rolled away.

"One last thing. Stand up."

She does.

A navigator is clasped onto her left forearm. This one is like theirs, a bit more substantial than the one she's been using though still sleek and smooth. One of the twins grabs the bag with her soiled clothes.

"Outside." It's two voices in one.

The bed is gone. Rogue is standing as before, looking off into the distance, her focus elsewhere.

"Stop," two voices instruct.

She does.

The twins leave her side to bracket Rogue and stand facing Skye. Attendants arrive and guide the big pod off into vagueness behind the bed. Then, orator-like, the bald and black champion of champions turns around in a circle, arms spread, to make an announcement.

"All of SubTurra and the hinterlands! From now, Skye One-

Who-Wanders is under the authority of the champions! She will be tested at the Stadium! If she fails the tests she will be brought back to you immediately! If by some bizarre quirk of fate she passes the tests, the champions will train her for the match. Either way, while in our custody she will not be available live on real-time Banding! Take your last look for a while! Who knows? Perhaps when you see Skye One-Who-Wanders again she will be an opponent worthy of a match with the champion of champions!" Rogue drops her arms and looks at the twins. "Ready?"

They nod. Rogue touches her navigator and, with a quick shiver to the atmosphere, vanishes, leaving Skye and the twins behind.

"Press your Send key." It's two voices in one.

She does, wondering at the same time why they aren't using slant boards. Then they're someplace else and she's blinking against bright sunlight shining down on the ground of what resembles an ancient arena – large and after the classical fashion in that concentric ascending rings of seats surround a circular playing field. She and the twins are down on the center of the field looking up.

Squinting against the glare, Skye One-Who-Wanders gazes around, sees dirt surrounded by a high wall beyond which are tiers of bleachers then bright banners flapping against a fat disk of cloudless blue sky. She sees Rogue sitting high up in the stands, one leg over the other, arms stretched out and resting on the back of what she's leaning against. Several sections below Rogue, a dozen or so others, male and female enter the stands and find seats. They're similarly dressed in briefs, halters and boots, wearing navigators.

Turning around in place she sees shadowed archways evenly spaced around the wall that separates the field from the stands. The twins clear their throats, drawing her attention.

"This is the Stadium. Real. All but the sky, of course."

She nods, not quite sure what "real" means anymore.

"The Stadium is isolated from the rest of SubTurra. Technologically shielded and accessed only by champions. No one, not even Headmon, is allowed here, otherwise we go on strike. You are a one-time exception."

She has no way of understanding the magnitude of that statement.

"Now to the business at hand. Before you can be trained for a match we must ascertain two things. First, do you have the capacity to be Banding content? Second, do you have the spirit of a champion? That's the deal. We won't train an unworthy candidate for a match with the champion of champions."

"How did we get here?" She's squinting at them, trying to follow what doesn't make sense because she has no frame of reference for it. "Am I really here standing up or somewhere else on a slant board?"

"That is to remain a mystery unless you become a champion. Which brings us to your first test. Stream-viability. Banding content is delivered to consumers via the Stream, meaning that all Banding content must be Stream-viable. The only way to determine Stream-viability is to go into the Stream. To do that you must have champion-level navigating equipment, which you are now wearing. We call it Streaming gear."

"I have questions?" she interrupts.

"Ask."

"What's a match?"

"Briefly put: a match is a contest between a champion and a hacker. Hackers are from the public. Champion-level gear is very expensive to train on. Only a small percentage of the most promising are able to obtain the necessary sponsorship. Those who become good enough…"

"Hackers."

"Correct. Are allowed to challenge a champion."

"But if I'm not a hacker, how can I be in a match? And Rogue challenged me."

"Yes. In your case, tradition has been broken. Champions don't challenge. They accept challenges from worthy hackers. The only way to become a champion is to defeat one. Rogue has done something never done before. Headmon is, of course, delighted because it's a brilliant idea that blasts open another chute for the money to flow through."

Skye One-Who-Wanders looks at Rogue up in the stands. Champion of champions. What does that mean? She looks back at the twins who don't seem impatient with her confusion.

"I still don't understand what a match is."

"It's a test of endurance, skill and determination between a champion and a hacker. Most matches don't last very long because only the rare hacker can defeat a champion or even play longer than a few minutes. We haven't had any turnover in a long time."

229

"What happens in a match?"

"Typically, a match involves two players getting from A to Z through an agreed upon series of locations. Whoever gets to the end-point first, wins. Play is a twofold endeavor. Your first objective is to get to the end-point. Your second objective is to prevent your opponent from getting there first or from interfering with your progress."

"Is contact involved?"

"Sometimes."

"Death?"

"Occasionally. When you're playing at that level and that speed, the unexpected happens. Sometimes death. Though that's never the desire of a champion."

"What's different about this equipment?" she looks down at the device on her arm.

"The possibilities. The navigator itself is similar to the one you've been using in that the control principles are the same. There are differences, however. Many more locations, for instance." They grin at her. "And with this navigator we can create new locations, places beyond imagination."

Her attention is drawn by movement in one of the shadowy archways. A tall thin woman wearing a yellow halter and briefs emerges loping toward them. Her gait is graceful and unhurried though she seems to cover the considerable distance from the archway to the center of the field in no time at all and now stands straight and tall, intensely still, studying the new arrival.

"I am Hurricane, oldest champion. Here with the twins to take you into the Stream. If you can tolerate the Stream, we go to the next level. If you can't, the deal is off and you'll be returned to Central Control."

"No!" Not there. She knows that much. Not back there.

The oldest champion raises an eyebrow. Tall and stringy, the woman is diaphanous and not nearly as young as she seemed from farther away. Her skin is leathery and brown, like weak tea. Yellowish white hair is tied in a knot on top of her head. Her eyes are penetrating midnight blue.

"Those are the stakes, Skye One-Who-Wanders. If you can tolerate the Stream *and* pass the test of mettle, you may stay here for training. If not, you go back."

"What's the Stream?"

"A technological field composed of all locations on the

230

Banding spectrum. A din of chaos not friendly to everyone."

Skye's face is blank because she has no way to make sense of Hurricane's explanation.

"Don't worry about it," the oldest champion smiles, her teeth long and straight. "I'll take you in. The twins will be with us. At the first sign of distress we'll bring you out. Test over. Ready?"

"Wait a minute. Shouldn't there be a bed or a chair or a slant board, something to recline on or something?"

"Not for Banding *content,*" Hurricane smiles.

"But then where will I really be while all this is going on?"

"You'll be where you are," the oldest champion's murmurs through an enigmatic smile. "Ready, or would you rather not go on, quit right now, go back?"

"No!"

"Very well, then. Gentlemen?"

The twins move in place on either side, facing Skye, as Hurricane comes up close behind her.

"Hold on to my arms and lean back."

The older woman wraps her arms around Skye. Standing, they spoon, Skye's back to Hurricane's front.

"Activate the Stream."

The words resonate as they are spoken right into her ear. The twins do something to their navigators. An enormous thud explodes the atmosphere.

Skye's feet are knocked out from under her and she's sucked into a raging river of something like screaming electricity. The Stream cascades up and down and in and out and through like a sudden flashflood of unchanneled juice. They are enveloped by raw energy and it's getting more and more dense. Blinding. Saturating. And she senses herself merely at the shore, being taken in, dragged backward into what is deeper and faster.

So fast.

Fierce neon sparking.

Searing.

Thrumming her. And the sound, the roar of all open channels flooding her at once is reminiscent of the archives but much more turbulent. Denser and faster and deeper and faster and denser until it can't possibly get any more so but it does as she's dragged backward.

Then she's no longer being dragged but drifting, held more loosely. She looks down and sees herself shimmering, ignited. She looks at the twins, studying her, shimmering, too. Ignited. They grin.

"We're in. Breathe."

It's two distorted voices in one, very close. She clings to the familiarity.

Holding Hurricane's wrapped-around arms as tight as she can, blinking, turning her head this way and that, she knows the Stream as billowing veils of light and sound, glittering, sparking, churned directionless waves and currents. She sees the Stream and the twins and, behind them, the stadium with Rogue and the others up in the stands. She raises her face and presses her head back against Hurricane's shoulder as with a lover. She closes her eyes and is intensely aware of vibrant buzzing around and through her entire being. And the current is very strong.

"Let's move a bit." It's Hurricane, not so close to her ear this time.

She feels the older woman about to release her and clings.

"We're right here." It's two voices in one, a bit farther away.

After a moment, trying to relax, turning, she let's go of everything but Hurricane's fingertips and the two are floating like sky-divers, looking at each other, one face serene, the other locked in an astonished "O" and she's floating, a newborn in water that isn't wet.

"Let the Stream take you where it will," Hurricane whispers, releasing her with a slight flourish.

For a moment the four of them float in place like blissful astronauts outside the ship. Then, suddenly, she's sucked away from them. They fade from awareness. The Stadium disappears.

Conflicting storms of raw energy scream through her. She's caught by gusts of chaos then hurled by the heels, flung by the arms, spun. She's plunged backward down an endless falls then swooped up again.

She resists at first, struggles against the Stream. Then she remembers journeying into the archives, how it sometimes felt like this in data-storms and there was nothing to do but surrender.

Let the Stream take you where it will.

Forcing herself to breathe, she begins to relax. And as she relaxes, she understands the Stream's energy as something neutral, like a tool one learns to use. The key is to relax, surrender, learn to use.

Tumbling, head back, she lets the Stream take her where it will. She catches her breath for the surprises. She screams gleefully on the plummets and radical orbits.

Then she tries to work with the Stream. Awkward at first, she tries to swim with then against the current. But there is no current as such, just colliding and intersecting rivulets of energy.

Like a competitive diver, she opens her arms and points her toes and arches her back and raises her head and plummets endlessly. Not laughing now but working hard, she moves her arms and legs as though swimming. Then she tries to run and just looks like someone falling through space but she's not falling.

She looks around for the twins and Hurricane. She finds three dots in the distance. She waves. They wave back. Looping around crazily, trying to swim with the Stream, she works her way back toward them.

Exhilarated, she walks as through a tingling stiff breeze of energy and sound, toward the shore of the Stream. Hurricane and the twins are already there, waiting, mouths open, eyes wide. Surprised, perhaps.

The twins do something to their navigators.

Thuup.

With a huge hiss of decompression, the Stream collapses back into itself and is gone. Hurricane looks at Skye who is panting and dazed. The oldest champion nods, smiling.

"I'd say that was conclusive."

The twins nod. They smile at Skye. Then they turn and trot to adjacent archways. They disappear inside and return almost immediately, trot-ting back toward the center of the field. One is carrying a bottle of something and the other is carrying a small bag.

Her attention is drawn up to the stands. Rogue hasn't moved. She's still sitting, leaning back, legs crossed, inscrutable but for a faint tinge of arrogance. Below her, the dozen or so others are standing, hands on hips, the brilliant colors of their Streaming gear flaring veritable rainbows.

Trembling, still catching her breath and shaking off the effects of the Stream, Skye turns back to Hurricane and the twins. One holds out the bottle. The other holds out the bag.

"Food and drink." It's two voices in one. "It'll help you come back."

She takes the bottle and slugs down a few swallows of something cold with a slight taste of citrus. Then she reaches into the bag and pulls out dried fruit. As she munches and sips, the effects of the Stream begin to dissipate. She turns to Hurricane.

"What's next?"

The oldest champion smiles enigmatically.

"What's coming next will happen when you've rested from the Stream."

The interior of the transfer station is a series of eight concentric rings, like a shooting target. A schematic of the structure resembles an ancient circular walking-maze. Space Staters are allowed on the two outer rings. The six inner rings are off limits to everyone but stewards and citizen-units.

Shape-changers deployed earlier are spread out through the rings, examining, recording, sending back data to a transceiver strapped on Lt. Pilar Mezon's upper arm. Two of them have gotten all the way into the center or bull's eye and are sending back readings that don't make sense. That means she has to go there and find out what's generating the readings.

Before going in she sent two more shape-changers to find the quickest way to the center and give her a map so she can get there and back as quickly as possible. They've sent a clear and surprisingly direct route. It's time to go.

Heart pounding, Falcon One pulls herself headfirst through the hole in the barrier between the Emerson's cargo hold and the transfer station's first rim – the initial automated receiving area that is now dark and dead. Sterile and empty.

She drifts on into the first ring. The metal wall in front of her is 40 yards away. There are no walls to the sides so she can see the curve of the ring as it arcs on around darkly in each direction.

Pilar orients to the map sent by the shape-changers. She shivers. Recording everything and fighting claustrophobia, she taps the jets in her elbows and heels and floats toward the wall in front of her and an open hatch.

Falcon One coaches herself to breathe. She tries to stay focused but fear is starting to take over. She reaches down, presses a protected button on the outside of one calf. A jigger of lime-flavored liquid spurts into her mouth. She holds it under her tongue and instantly finds breathing easier as her heart rate slows and the perspiring stops.

Focus on the map. Just that. Follow the route in then back out.

***

235

Isham One-Who-Waits is standing in one of many long lines waiting for an immigration clerk. There's one more person in front of him – a man pleading for work and being told this isn't his kind of canton but the man won't stop arguing. Finally the clerk signals for enforcers and the man is led away, struggling.

Trench coat and bowler hat off because of the heat and closeness, Isham stands tall and dignified, his white hair cut almost military short, his face smooth and brushed with stone-dust. Occasionally, inconspicuously, he pats a hidden pocket. The forged documents are still where they belong. He's been camped out here in the smell and the din of the incessant screens blaring overhead, making no contact with others, never releasing his valise and holding his place in line by sitting in it, sleeping on it, scooting forward bit by bit having taken care to fast completely before starting this part of the journey as per elder Martin's warning that should he leave to go to the bathroom he would lose his place. And from the smell around him it's clear that others are not leaving their places for that purpose, either.

"Next!"

He steps forward, extracts his documents and hands them over.

"Name?"

"Edwin Reynolds, sir."

"Purpose here?"

The clerk is a small bald man with sooty gray skin. His voice is high and hoarse from trying to be heard over the constant noise from people and the overhead media. His eyes bulge and glisten from medication, their pupils extraordinarily large and dark, as are the eyes of most SubTrranns he has so far encountered.

"I seek employment, sir."

"Who doesn't?" The clerk rifles through the papers, stamping some of them, snorting at others. "As? You seek employment as?"

"A butler, sir. I have served high ranking…"

"Why here? Why now?"

"As you can see from the documents, sir, I'm qualified to serve at a higher level."

The clerk looks up. Eyes lock. The man now called Edwin Reynolds smiles. For an instant – and an instant is all it takes – the man is caught unawares. Isham seizes the opening and slams an *Approved* message into the clerk's awareness.

The clerk blinks and looks away. He checks the papers again.

236

He looks back up, blinking, confused.

Eyes lock.

The opening again. Isham seizes it.

Approve.

"Go in there," the clerk jerks his head at a closed door behind him. "They'll test you. Pass the test and they'll tell you what to do. Fail and you can try another canton."

"Thank you, sir."

Isham bows ever so slightly. Then valise in one hand, bowler hat in the other, coat over an arm, he walks to the door indicated and knocks.

"Yeah, yeah!"

A woman in a gray leather lab coat opens the door. He enters. The door is closed behind him.

***

Elder Moss, Schiara and Wim have arrived at Little Bitter Falls. Their normally inquisitive spirits are subdued by the gravity of their purpose and because Axl has so far chosen not to join them or respond to their attempts at contact. Here for an indefinite stay, they've stopped in a spacious cavern that is complicated with shiny black stalagmites and stalactites.

A comfortable camp has been pitched off to one side of a sweet spring. They've nibbled and napped and are presently gathered around a small fire over which hangs a pot of maturing vegetable stew. Until it's ready, they're leaning back against packs fat with surface gear popping seeds into their mouths and sipping icy water from re-filled flasks.

"I think it's time for something normal," elder Moss nods vigorously. "Like a lesson. We haven't had one in a long time. And if memory serves, we were last talking about story."

Schiara and Wim nod, eager for something that feels normal. Elder Moss leans back against her pack and studies the two youngsters.

"Story." She crosses her arms and looks up at stone sky. "It didn't always exist. Ponder that. There was a time before the first story. How might that be significant?"

For a moment, Schiara's dark eyes grow wide with interest.

237

Then they go dull with worry again. Wim is trying to answer elder Moss's question but can't seem to figure out where to start.

"What is story?" elder Moss muses. "Why does story exist? Why is it that sometimes even a bad story is comforting and makes us feel better?"

"Like when we found out more about what happened to R'io and Skye?" Schiara hugs her knees. "It helps to know."

"Helps to know what?"

"It helps to know what happened. It helps to have an explanation."

"Ah," elder Moss nods.

She looks at Schiara and Wim, sees fatigue and concern and decides to keep the lesson easy. Smiling mischievously, she settles back against her pack, hands clasped behind her head and drifts away on a slow stream of thought.

"Story and pre-story. Notions of pre-story are difficult to grasp for those raised on story, for whom pre-story is something vague like white noise or fog or mist or formlessness of one kind or another. Unformed cosmos and unformed awareness go together and may be said to characterize the time of pre-story, the time before imagination, which is the generator of story.

"Then something happened. The moment arrived. Distinctions were made. Names were needed. Mist and fog took form as did hide and horn, fang and claw, heat and cold, wet and dry, plenty and want, dark and light, this and that, you and me, and sometimes awful ugliness or wrenching beauty. A line had been drawn in the sand marking the arrival of humans and our stories."

"Weren't we human before?" Wim looks confused.

"We were creatures ripe to be human. But Imagination had not wakened and there was no story yet. Contrary to what the ancients thought, humans are not those who know but, rather, those who imagine. *That* is our distinctive trait.

"For humans, story is indispensable because it is experience captured. Captured experience can be studied, learned from, passed on to others. But there's a problem, a paradox. Once story appears, it is indispensable and as such it tends to harden when, by nature, it wants to be fluid and dynamic."

Elder Moss looks at her two young students. She sees them tired and worried and tries to distract them.

"Either of you want to try and explore the difference between fluid story and rigid story?"

She waits for one of them to try. They both sit with their mouths open, struggling with slippery questions. Then they look at her, blank. She smiles, amazed at how perfect they are.

"The difference between fluid story and rigid story can be summed up in that one word: experience. Fluid story is continually reshaped by what happens, by what's learned along the way. Where fluid story prevails, there's constant change and adjustment, sometimes even total transformation, birth after birth after birth.

"By way of contrast, rigid story excludes experience. Story that can't be affected by experience is called Dogma and is an inflexible version of human existence that would impose its will on everything it touches. In addition, experience stops when it no longer affects story. And when experience stops, so does life even for the living."

Sniffing, elder Moss determines that the stew has matured. The big woman gets to her feet and stretches. She looks down at the top of Wim's head, at the cascade of blond kinks barely contained by the cord at the nape of his neck. She smiles down at Schiara's long silky braid, falling over one shoulder. The girl looks up, her eyes dark and serious. Tears have formed but not fallen.

"Maybe that's why Axl can't be with us yet, elder Moss. Maybe he just can't agree on the story the rest of us share about how to go in and get R'io and Skye."

"Maybe," the elder smiles sadly, stooping for their three bowls. "Clashing stories have ruined many a good relationship. But we can't know anything about Axl unless he tells us, right? And he can't tell us anything if he won't either come here or meet us in common-awareness." Elder Moss uncovers the stew and stirs the pot. "Wash your hands."

***

The immigration supervisor sitting across the desk from Curanda and Esa wears a long dark leather gown and a veil indicating that she is sexually unavailable. The reason for this is clear. Her belly is distended by a well-advanced pregnancy.

Above the veil, the woman's eyes are extraordinarily dark and large, glittering with medications designed to combat pain and anxiety.

After looking at the two candidates for a moment, she shuffles through their documents, trying to get comfortable in her chair. Occasionally, she pauses and perfunctorily studies something about one or another of the papers. Then she brushes the stack aside with the back of a hand and looks at the pair sitting in front of her, seeking entry to canton Equa. Upon entry they were instructed to remove their burkas and now sit in ordinary SubTurran leather gowns of high quality.

"What do you have to offer this canton?" The woman is indifferent, distracted by her pain.

"I am a healer of some renown in cantons Carlisle and Lay," the old woman inclines her head modestly and smiles. "As you can see from my letters of recommendation."

"Using what methods?"

"Herbs, potions, hands."

"What brings you here now?"

"My skills merit placement in a higher class."

The woman's eyes widen over her veil.

"Cocky."

"Truthful."

"And the girl?"

"My assistant. My apprentice. When necessary, my eyes."

"Why should I believe you?" The woman can't get comfortable in her chair and winces trying.

"I'll give you a demonstration. You're in pain. I can help."

Surprised, the woman tilts her head and squints at Curanda. She stirs in her chair and rubs her distended belly all the while studying the old woman sitting in front of her. Fearless and calm. As is the girl.

"You're blind. How do you know I'm in pain?"

"An old woman can smell such things." Curanda taps the side of her nose with a fingertip.

"So? Who isn't in pain?"

"I'm not," Curanda smiles. "May I stand?"

"Why?" the woman blinks.

"If you would permit me to approach, I might be able to offer some immediate relief. You could then determine for yourself whether I should be advanced."

The supervisor thinks this over for a moment, during which Curanda whispers, *yes*, to her awareness.

"May I approach?"

After a long moment, scrutinizing, the woman nods then holds up a finger in warning.

"If you cause me more pain, I'll have you recycled immediately. Make no mistake about it."

Though it's not necessary, Esa leads her grandam around the desk until she's standing directly behind the immigration supervisor.

"May I touch?"

"You risk your life if you hurt me."

Curanda reaches out and places her hands on the woman's shoulders ever so lightly, resting them there for a moment so the woman can get used to her touch. Then she moves her hands up to the woman's neck. She reaches under the veil from behind and presses strong forefingers along the woman's jaw and strong thumbs up behind her ears. She begins to lift and knead.

The woman's eyes flutter closed as relaxation almost overwhelms her. When Curanda speaks it's a soothing murmur, though her speech is just for those who might be monitoring this exchange. Beneath what is apparent, Curanda is addressing the woman in a very different way.

"You have had many pregnancies. This one is particularly difficult because your spine is damaged. The disks. Holding on makes it worse. Re-member to breathe." *If we are forwarded to Headmon, he will take us on and thank the one who found us for him.*

The woman sighs deeply as though Curanda's hands are releasing her from something unbearable.

"How do you know this? About…other pregnancies, about my back?"

"It's just something a blind old woman understands," Curanda shrugs.

The supervisor relaxes even more as Curanda works on her neck until pain that seems to have been with her always eases and she is free. Astonishing. Then something like fog seems to eclipse her awareness. She hears words that aren't spoken, words she won't remember.

What you are feeling now is why you must send us on to Headmon who will reward you handsomely for it.

Then the fog is gone and the woman is aware only of being pain-free for the first time since she can remember. Curanda removes her hands and is led back around the desk to the single hard chair in front of it. The woman opens her eyes and looks around dazed.

"…What about…when you're gone, when the pain returns?"

241

Curanda chuckles. She reaches into her pack, extracts a vial of brilliant blue glass and hands it to Esa. The girl takes the vial to the supervisor who opens it and pours out nuggets of crystallized herb.

"The damage to your spine is structural and can only be fixed with surgery. The herb on your desk is for pain. Not addictive. It won't interfere with your duties and will help you through the birth. Just put one of those nuggets under your tongue as needed. There's enough to last until after the child is born. You will know that I am with Mr. Headmon. If you can get word to me, I'll send more."

The woman looks at Esa who nods encouragement. Then she picks up a nugget of herb and, lifting her veil, puts it under her tongue. Sucking, she frowns at the salty-sweet taste then looks up at Esa again and studies the girl.

"I had daughter. A little girl. Once. I got to hold her for a moment before they took her away. She would have been about your age by now. All the rest were boys, they said. I never saw them."

"What do you mean, she would have been about my age?" Esa draws the woman all the way into and through her eyes.

"No doubt she was used as meat and finest fabric. She would have been tender."

"And the babe you carry now?" Esa asks.

"They said this one goes to full term," the woman shrugs. "I've begged to be sterilized. They said…maybe," the woman closes her eyes, sucking on the herb.

"Perhaps we should go on now," Esa whispers, "leave you to rest."

The woman nods. Humming an old stone-people lullaby for the babe the woman carries, Esa returns to Curanda and picks up their packs. Curanda stands.

"We go now," the Esa coos softly. "Open the way."

Sitting as though lost in herself, the immigration supervisor nods ever so slightly at the wall behind Curanda and Esa.

"Through there," she whispers absently, pressing a button under her desk. "They'll test you."

Esa turns to a whitewashed concrete wall. A large metal door is sliding open with a grinding squeal. She takes her grandam's elbow.

"Thank you for your assistance."

"Yes…yes," the woman swats absently as at an insect near her face. "Go on."

The door is closing behind them. Wide-eyed, Curanda and Esa both exhale and look around, blinking in bright glare that smells of disinfectant.

***

Rested from the Stream, at Hurricane's suggestion Skye One-Who-Wanders is now walking around the field to loosen up and have a moment to anchor her focus. Hands on hips, head down, she remembers R'io and Curanda and Esa and Isham One-Who-Waits and all the others but mostly R'io and the promised time of quiet. And the prospect of a time of quiet with him sets her purpose square in front of her so that, ready, she turns back to Hurricane and the twins and approaching them sees someone else emerge from an archway and trot toward the center of the field where they are.

He's a great bear of a man, the color of coffee and cream, with long steel gray hair and streaming gear that gleams bronze in the sunlight. He has a barrel chest and thick, heavily muscled arms and legs. His eyes twinkle light blue. He stops and stands with his feet apart and his arms crossed, looking down at her like a big genii. Amused. Studying. Then he sticks out a paw and steps forward.

"I am champion Yan, here to determine if you have the proper qualities." The voice is as big as he is.

She involuntarily steps back then forward and takes the paw. It's huge, warm and calloused. She smiles and squeezes granite. His eyes are full of mischief and surprise. Grinning, he releases her hand.

"A champion must have two qualities. Courage and determination." He claps his great paws together. "I'm here to test you for those."

"Oh."

She tries to swallow and finds her mouth dry. One of the twins hands her a bottle of something. She takes long slugs of water and hands the bottle back.

"I'm going to test you with one of the most important toolsets used in a match. Illusion. That's what these controls up here are for." He points at the keys near his elbow. "Every match involves an agreed on number of locations and illusions. Now listen carefully. The illusions I'm going to cast are threatening and aggressive. Your job is to stand your ground when everything in you is screaming RUN!"

Yan laughs. The sound comes from his belly. Eyebrows raised, he grins. And for some reason, she's reassured.

"There's no need to activate the Stream for now. Illusions can be cast independent of the Stream. But champions know how to put Streaming and illusion together and sometimes it's a beautiful thing. Ready?"

Seems like the path only goes in one direction and that's onward and there's nothing to do but take the next step.

She nods. Yan backs away from the four of them. Hurricane moves close to Skye. The twins flank the two women. The older champion explains as Yan grins, waves then turns and trots toward his archway.

"For now the important thing is not to move – except for your head," Hurricane's voice is soft and clear coming from close behind her. "As Yan said, the illusions he's going to cast are competitive and aggressive. If you move, you'll be attacked. That's why we're here. If you don't move they won't feel challenged and there's nothing to fear."

In the archway, Yan touches his navigator up by the elbow. The atmosphere implodes and he isn't here anymore.

All the fine new baby hairs on her body stand on end and current is running up and down her spine. A confusing dark mass is standing head down, shoulders hunched, in the archway used by Yan. She can hear it breathing. Smell it, feel its heat all the way out here in the center of the field at least 60 yards away.

What *is* that thing?

Mammal. Quadruped.

The creature raises its head and bellows. Then it walks out onto the field and begins to trot around, staying close to the wall. Four hooves like slow thunder. A massive beast.

Squinting, she shuffles through data from the archives. After a moment, she identifies Bull – as in the breed used by ancients for manly and elegant tests of courage. Turning her head as far as it will go first one way then the other, she watches the bull round the field and arrive back where he started from. He stands still again, facing her, head lowered, panting, a mass of slick black muscle studying her carefully from iridescent red/green eyes under long, deadly horns.

The bull lowers his head and paws the earth. He snorts. Clots of white foam dangle from his open mouth. He glares, horns gleaming in the brilliant daylight. Then he seems to decide. Snorting he trots forward a few steps, pauses, trots forward again.

The instant before it happens she knows he's going to do something but not what. Then he does it. He charges. She doesn't move though it takes everything she has to remain where she is. And when he's halfway to her there's a deafening thud to the atmosphere.

Bull is gone.

Trembling, she's aware of her own heart beating too fast. Hurricane and the twins don't move. They seem relaxed while she, like a tuning fork, is vibrating with adrenalin. She waits.

Nothing happens.

Silence.

Adrenalin surges.

Then she senses it. Something has arrived. But what? Where?

Finally she can hear it through her thrumming heartbeat. Overhead. Flapping.

Then silence.

As she looks up, she hears a high-pitched, sustained cry or call. She follows the sound to its source.

Hawk.

On the hunt.

Wings wide, it glides a circle around the top of the Stadium, up by the banners. It screams again and, tightening its orbit, descends somewhat. And again, the instant before it acts, she knows something's going to happen and she's right.

The hawk screams a third time and is plummeting straight down toward her head faster than she can see and it takes everything not to move. But she doesn't.

As the hawk is closing in on her head, its heels snap down and its wings are flung open. For a heartbeat, the bird hangs an arms-length above her face – red eyes glaring into hers, yellow talons razor sharp and ready to grab. Then with a piercing scream it veers off and is ascending a great arc up toward the top of the Stadium when there's another thud to the atmosphere and hawk on the hunt is gone.

Everything is silent but for the banners flapping overhead. She can't stop trembling but hasn't otherwise moved. Then something's here again. Behind them now. Hurricane and the twins step away from her.

"No!" she rasps. They keep going.

She knows it's not alive, whatever has arrived. No. It's a thing.

A big thing. She can tell by the strange deep hollow hum-ming sounds it makes circling slowly around the field near the wall. She turns her head that way as far as it will go and the thing floats onto her peripheral vision.

Hurricane and twins move farther away. She doesn't want them to do that. Then she forgets about them because she's looking at a large globe with a diameter of perhaps six feet. As the globe drifts around, it changes trajectory and arcs out toward the center of the field, where she is now standing alone.

The globe stops several body-lengths away, directly in front of her. Rusty and stained, the thing is featureless but for many small holes that puncture its surface. Rotating slowly, humming louder now, the globe seems to be studying her. And she's almost mesmerized by the sound it makes as it floats out in front of her, humming many different discordant wavering tones, rotating slowly and smelling of rust.

Then the globe advances.

She begins to tremble. Perspiration rolls down into her eye and stings. Forgetting, she raises a hand to wipe that eye.

The globe lurches out of range then arcs around in front of her again. And just before it happens she knows it's going to but not what. Then a hale of something like electric bullets is coming out of the holes on the globe, silhouetting her, grazing her. Cold! And to move would be to die.

The atmosphere implodes again.

She blinks out salt tears and opens her eyes. When she can see again, she's looking at a long thin needle that's not a hand's breadth from the bridge of her nose. A heavy drop of something she knows to be poison is hanging from its tip.

An instant before it happens she knows something is going to happen but not what. Without awareness or forethought, knowing only to do it, she flicks a hand up, grabs the needle – hot! – and flings it away. She hears some-one gasp.

The atmosphere implodes. For a moment, there is only silence. Then Yan is leaning against his archway, laughing. The twins chuckle to each other as Yan trots back to the center of the field to clap a heavy paw on her shoulder.

"I underestimated you, girl. That won't happen again."

"Would that have won the match?"

"No. That was a Throw. Takes three throws to win a match."

"Without anyone getting killed or hurt?"

"Sometimes. You gotta be very, very good not to hurt a flailer."

"Am I a flailer?"

"Only because you don't know enough yet. So far, you're doing fine, though. Right, Hurricane?"

The elegant older woman nods then turns and looks up at Rogue who is still seated several rows above the dozen or so other champions, legs crossed, leaning back, apparently bored. Rogue nods ever so slightly. Hurricane turns to Skye, smiling.

"The testing is to continue."

With that and nothing further, Hurricane and the twins move toward the stands, handily leap the tall fence and join the other champions seated in front of Rogue. Yan remains on the field with Skye One-Who-Wanders. He stands looking down at her, his expression grave though with Yan, even his gravity twinkles.

"This is the last part of the test." He clears his throat. "Do you know what determination is?"

"Yes," Skye nods, understanding that word. "I do."

"Okay, let's check. Supposing I said, 'see that archway over there? Race you to it. Let's see who gets there first.' What would you say?"

"Why does it matter who gets there first?"

"It's a race." Her question surprises him. "From here to there. Who gets there first. Takes determination. I'm challenging you. Get there first."

"Why?"she nods, trying to care. "What's so important about getting there first?"

"To win the game." Explaining things is not one of Yan's strengths.

"What game?"

"Getting there first. Who gets there first wins the game. You never played a game before?"

She thinks of Great City. No games there. She remembers the Refuge but not playing though there was joy. She remembers learning handsign from Esa and laughing. Was that playing? Was that a game? She shrugs.

"I don't think so."

"Not a competitive bone in your body, huh?" he laughs and pats her on the shoulder. "We'll see about that. Beat me to the archway."

"That's my task?"

247

"That's all you have to do." He grins.

She shrugs, measuring his massiveness against her own lithe frame. Even with the tender ankle, it's no contest. She decides to set a pace that will allow him to keep up with her.

"Okay."

He squints at her mischievously for a moment then takes a starting position and counts.

"One. Two. Three. GO!"

And she's off, reining her deer-swift self in so he can catch up with her but he already has and is moving out in front and they're not halfway there yet so she pours on a little steam and passes him then adjusts so he's next to her but he's out front again though not by much so she cranks and reaches the archway just as he does and pulls up short.

She's winded. He's not. Smiling, he stands with his hands on his hips, looking down at her while she catches her breath. Then she straightens up. She studies him, surprised. He chuckles, grins and raises a forefinger.

"First rule of play. Never underestimate your challenger."

She nods. He points.

"See that archway directly across from us, on the other side of the field?"

"Yes."

"Beat me there."

"Sure," she shrugs, "nothing to it."

"Ready?"

They take their positions. Then he stands up straight again, shaking his head no.

"All right, all right, you're indulging me and I don't like that. So we're going to bypass this step and leap ahead. Program your navigator for an illusion. This key here," he points up by his inner elbow. "Press it and you'll get a menu."

She does.

"Stay close to your genetic home-form first time out. Go to Mam-mals."

She does and shows him her navigator. He nods.

"Choose your form."

She scrolls down a long list of mammals and chooses one in particular that interested her back in the archives. There are sub-selections. She doesn't know that much about different kinds of horses so she makes an arbitrary selection and looks back up at him.

"What'd you choose?"

"Thoroughbred Mare Running to Win," she reads from her screen.

"This could be interesting," he laughs then programs his navigator. "Now we're in sync. But wait." Yan pulls a small rectangular device from the back of his briefs. It's smooth and silvery in his callused palm. He holds it up between thumb and forefinger. "This is a neutralizer. In case you have trouble wielding the illusion. It's a very unusual sensation at first. Not for everyone because not only do you cast the illusion, you *are* the illusion. Or at least the technology makes it seem so. If you get in trouble, I'll know and this gadget here will neutralize your navigator and pop you out of the illusion. Now, when you're ready, press the Send key and see if you can beat me to that archway."

Skye One-Who-Wanders thinks of R'io and presses Send. The jolt is instantaneous and bone shattering, a rearrangement of her system so sudden and complete that she pops out of being for an instant or so it seems. Then she's re-congealed with equal force, aware that she is one and she is two. Equally and fully. Simultaneously. Each completely itself. She is Skye One-Who-Wanders *and* Thoroughbred Mare Running to Win.

Stumbling, lurching forward, she feels her spine realigned. Her relation to gravity shifts radically as she now has four legs (in addition to the two in her other body). Her field of vision is radically different. And how fragrant the dirt is as she trots around stirring it up, snorting, bewildered only for a moment then she is loping back and forth in front of a big stallion the color of coffee with cream she recognizes as Yan.

He whinnies. He rears, challenging her. She trots back and forth in front of him, exploring the nature of her own new strength.

Then she spots it. Over there. A goal. And she must get there first.

Circling back toward the stallion, she stops. She rears and paws the air, screaming a challenge. He answers. Then she's down on all fours, running for the spot. And the stallion is right beside her.

When they're halfway to their target, running flat out, there's a massive thud to the atmosphere as the Stream is activated. The Stadium is filled with churned Stream and she's running into the heart of it, running through the incredibly loud drumming of hooves.

Pounding.

Out in front by herself, the stallion falling behind.

She knows the rhythm and the sound and the feel of the pounding. It's never *not* been familiar. It's never *not* been her.

Running. Fast. She's running so fast because her body is stretched out horizontally and there are four legs now, fueled with power from big flank and rump muscles. She moves easily through a blur of Stream-flurry and knows she can stay in front of the stallion.

Running.

Where?

The Stream is featureless, a non-location. There is no *where* there, only Stream.

Running. Rhythmic pounding. The sound is played by her muscles and bones.

Then she's rippled by a series of deep thuds in the Stream behind her. Through ears laid back, she hears pounding coming up behind. And now she's not alone.

It's Rogue.

Right beside her. A black mare.

And the other champions are there, too, fanned out in a line not far behind. A small herd led by Skye and Rogue, running flat out to the same finish line.

Where?

Thundering upstream they veer off into a sudden vein toward partic-ularity. Running faster now, they pass through a thinning veil of energy and emerge onto a vastness of prairie sunlight and thick smells of dirt and grass. She checks her navigator and reads "High Plains."

Rogue is right beside her. They're nose to nose with the others fanned out behind. Running. Stretched out.

Then she sees it. A feature. A goal in the distance.

There.

A young tree on a slight rise.

She must get to that tree and she must get there first.

Rogue edges ahead. Skye wants the tree. Stretching out even farther, she reaches down, still not finding the bottom of her power or her pleasure in

the movement. She pulls up more speed. Pounding, gasping, breathing fire and spurting clots of foam, she runs faster and faster.

Then, about a hundred yards from the tree Rogue seems to shift into another gear. Skye can see the back of the black mare's head. Then her shoulders. Then her rump. Then Rogue is around the tree heading back where they came from – purple mountains in the distance.

Skye rounds the tree. Turning to follow Rogue, she sees and hears the other champions behind her, running full out. They, too, round the tree and make the turn and all are now running back toward the mountains with Rogue even farther in the lead.

Then the champions behind Skye put on a burst of speed and pass her with Yan in their midst. Flicking their long tails they race ahead to catch up with their leader.

As Skye One-Who-Wanders struggles to hold speed, the location begins to thin out. Details fade and become fewer and farther between. And they're back in the fullness of the Stream, thundering back. Then the Stream is thinning, evaporating like mist. And there's a numbing thud to the atmosphere.

Skye stumbles out of the ebbing Stream. Panting, desperate for air, she bends over. Unable to catch her breath, her eyes roll back up into her head and the rug of awareness is yanked out from under her. The twins break her fall.

On the ground, heaving in air, fluttering in and out of awareness, Skye knows that Yan is bending over her. He's holding her wrist, studying her intently. He raises an eyelid. Then he rests the back of his hand on her forehead.

"Not bad, girl." He looks up at the others. "She's fine. Let her sleep. Recharge."

"Let's take her in." Rogue is obviously relieved. "Keep watch one at a time."

Yan picks her up gently and carries her like a baby toward an archway. Hurricane and Rogue are on either side. She vaguely hears the older woman from off to the left.

"Now we must teach her all things."

Then Rogue, softly on the other side. "Taking it slowly, of course. We want to drag this out as long as possible and avoid a match Headmon will make certain I lose."

***

Waiting to be tested, Isham is sitting on a rickety chair near the entrance to an unadorned stone room that is long and narrow with a door at each end. Lining both long walls are identical cubicles. Each contains an occupied chair in front of a screen and keyboard. When it's his turn, the woman in the grimy lab coat points to a just-vacated

251

folding chair in front of a screen and accompanies him to it.

"It's a literacy test."

"Shhhhh!" a man hisses, bent over his keyboard.

The woman raises her hand as though to give the back of the man's head a furious whack. But instead of following through she stays right behind him, bellowing.

"It's a literacy test! Timed! One hundred questions that tell us what you know in terms of a possible position you might apply for here! It's all self-explanatory! Follow the directions! How much time you have left is indicated at the bottom of the screen! Test starts as soon as you touch the keyboard!"

"Thank you for your assistance."

Something in his voice causes her to turn and look at him.

Eyes lock. Hers are large dark SubTurran eyes that glisten with drugs. It only takes an instant for Isham to go deep and plant his message.

I like you.

He smiles. Then he sits down and touches the keyboard.

Behind him, the woman blinks, confused. Then she clears her throat, spits and looks around, shaking her head. Her attention is drawn to the man who tried to shush her. She didn't like him the instant he walked in the door.

"Time's up. You're out of here."

"But…"

"Now! Or I call the enforcers!"

"My time isn't up!"

"ENFORCERS!"

Coattail flying, the man rushes out of the testing room, banging the door closed behind him as two burly enforcers appear. The woman points. The enforcers are out the door and the others taking tests try to focus again.

So easy is the literacy test that Isham has to slow himself down and miss a few to make it look challenging. When he has zero time left, the woman comes back. Leaning across him, flooding him with smells of leather, sweat and rotten teeth, she pulls up his score. She frowns then looks at him.

Eyes lock.

It only takes an instant. He sends.

Someone for Mr. Headmon and bonus Banding time…

"Ninety-eight percent. Very rare." She smiles as though she

just thought of something naughty. Usual high is around 85%. Go through that door," she points to the closed door at the far end of the numbingly institutional space. "Wait with the others. You'll be told what to do."

He stands. He puts on his bowler hat, places the neatly folded trench coat across one forearm and picks up his valise.

"Thank you again for your assistance."

She nods, bewildered for some reason. She stares after him as he moves to the indicated door. He turns and smiles. Then he opens the door, goes through it and is gone.

Sixth Gate – Power

The deep interior of the transfer station is a maze of corridors, low ceilings and pipes – all of it metal, all of it dark and silent, all of it turned aqueous green by the optics in Lt. Pilar Mezon's helmet. Using little jets on her heels and elbows, she follows the map in toward the core where the shape-changers are still getting weird readings. She's making good time, recording all the way and fighting panic. In that regard, even in zero-Gs there's a sense of urgency to her movements.

Pilar tunes out the sounds of her heartbeat and breathing because they're too fast, spooking her even more. She filters in sounds from ancient nature – rain, wind through leaves, crickets, loons, waterfalls, all blended in a symphony meant to sooth. She presses the protected button on the outside of her calf for another dose of lime-flavored trank.

One good thing is that since entering the transfer station proper there have been no obstacles of significance to slow her down, only a few locked doors quickly opened. She's beyond grateful for the map because it would be easy to get lost zigzagging inward through the structure's concentric rings – through the guest quarters section, empty receiving and sorting bays, control and maintenance rooms, a galley, a gym, the infirmary and a hall of private quarters for the stewards. That leaves the large bull's eye right in the center.

Following the map, attentive to the weird signals from the shape-changers, Lt. Pilar Mezon floats over to a big metal door, opens it and pulls herself into another wide curving corridor with a low ceiling and pipes running in all directions everywhere but on the floor. The corridor is lined with unevenly spaced metal doors. She approaches the first door and reaches for the handle.

At that moment something gently nudges her from behind, hitting the back of her helmet. Gasping, she turns and stifles a scream because she's face to face with someone who is bright orange, drifting upside down and clearly dead. Panting, crouched as though to attack, she retreats an arm's length and turns upside down to study what was once some kind of person though it's all she can do to make herself look.

Male but she can barely tell. Gaunt. Covered in skintight orange fabric of some kind, eyes open, also bright orange. Expression-less.

Breathing hard, forcing herself to approach and reach out, Pilar turns herself and him over so they're both upright in the corridor. She moves him to the wall and secures him with a couple of straps from her pouch. Then she turns her attention back to the door.

It opens onto a large plain room full of transparent capsules most with their lids closed. Maybe three dozen of them. She moves into the room, latches the door open and holds herself in place with her back to the wall. Then she scans the circular room through green optics while her audio is a thunderstorm in the distance, moving across ancient desert.

The capsules with open lids are empty. The closed capsules are occupied by orange people and brown people and maroon people and red people and green people, maybe two dozen. Another handful – different colors – are drifting here and there. Three oranges ones are bobbing up by the ceiling like dead goldfish.

Falcon One forces herself to take deep breaths and think clearly. First, there aren't enough bodybags in the shuttle. That means more will have to be brought from Mohawk. These people can't just be left here.

Suddenly Pilar Mezon is shivering violently, flooded with an irresistible urge to be somewhere else. Moving as fast as she can in zero-Gs, she backs out of the room, commands the shape-changers to lead her out of here now, fast, away from this impossible confinement and death back to H-V shuttle/barge Emerson and the blessed outside.

***

Skye One-Who-Wanders is asleep then suddenly aware of pounding in her head, as if someone is knocking insistently on her awareness. Confused, holding her head she sits bolt upright to everything new and still the same.

What is this place? Where?

Blinking and disoriented she looks around, sees a dim space lit by several paraffin candles. It's a stone room. Rectangular. Small but ample in size for one.

Her heart slows down. The pressure that woke her subsides. She takes several deep breaths.

Something feels safe here, not part of SubTurra, not part of the desperate desolation she remembers from back at the indefinite space

256

with the bed. She tosses the blanket aside and sits on the edge of a narrow bed, still wearing the Streaming gear and R'io's belt. Remembering the Stream throws her into a kind of vertigo that takes a moment to subside. Then she looks around at where she is.

The space is unadorned, about twelve by twenty feet with a ceiling high enough to be comfortable for a tall person. The bed is against one long wall. At the foot of the bed, also against the wall, is a large metal wardrobe or cabinet. Those two things pretty much take up that wall.

Across from the bed is an open door through which, she can see a bathroom illumined by a flickering candle. Also on the wall across from her is a galley with a sink, counter space and cabinets. There are two doors, one at either end of the room.

She sniffs, smells wax and dry stone. She touches the wall next to her. Roughly tooled solid rock. Then she remembers why she's here and what must be done.

R'io.

Get him out of here – wherever this is.

Closing her eyes she sees him. Close. On the other side of the wick he carried. She feels his face in her hand – until the time of quiet. She sees him on Rogue's navigator, not dead, not alive. Then her bladder is suddenly full to bursting and she moves quickly to the bathroom, closing the door behind her.

***

Great City's head of Security enters Dav Baxter's suite and stops in shadow at the door for a moment to look around. It's one of their institutional hospitality suites – a sitting room with kitchen, bedroom, bath and closet. Furniture is functional. As per Reed's instructions, everything is gray.

One of the two guards she has stationed here is sitting on the couch working away at his tech-pad when she walks in. He stands quickly, almost at attention. The other guard is in the bedroom with Dr. Baxter.

"Get Edwards and take a break. Stay just outside the door."

"Yes, mam," the guard nods, goes into the bedroom and returns with Edwards who looks confused.

257

She dips her head to the door. They step out of the suite, quietly closing the door behind them. Not caring what the guards may or may not think because they can be silenced easily enough, she moves to the other door and looks into the bedroom, finds it dark but for the single light shining down on Dav Baxter.

The ambassador is spread-eagle on his back on the messy bed, snoring softly and wearing only undershorts. The other ambassadors and stewards think he's sick. That's what they've been told. In fact, he's sedated until she gets a few things figured out.

Lassiter enters the bedroom and sits on the edge of the bed. She stares. She places a hand on Baxter's naked chest. She strokes his long, cool arm. Then she pulls a syringe out of her tunic pocket, uncaps it and injects him in a vein on his forearm with another low dose of benign narcotic.

After capping and pocketing the syringe, Lassiter leans down so her face is in his neck and she's inhaling the slightly sour scent of him. She reaches a hand down to feel his runner's thigh but nothing else because of an uncharacteristic sense of propriety. She gets onto the bed and moves close, cuddles, purrs, strokes. Then she scoots up so her face is over his, closer, and she's whispering into his lips.

"I know what you saw." She kisses him tenderly on the lips as though to forgive him for all the trouble he's causing her. "They will kill you for it and I'm not going to let that happen. Only a while longer then we can be together forever. Just us."

She kisses him again and stands abruptly. Without looking back she leaves the bedroom and exits the ambassador's guest suite. After a moment the guards reenter and Edwards returns to his chair by the door.

Elsewhere in Great City a power-chair squeaks ever so slightly as the Presider leans back to regard his head of Technology.

"Just as you said, Shen."

"Yes, Edwards is a comer."

***

Isham One-Who-Waits, now called Edwin Reynolds, was escorted into the residence and stripped. Clothes and documents were taken away. He was sprayed with disinfectant and told to shower then given a complete examination. When he got out of the shower, he was given cloth clothes – a white shirt, dark four-in-hand tie and suit plus appropriate socks, shoes and underwear.

Dressed, clean and dignified, he was escorted into the residence through the Specials entrance. Thus, what he has seen of the place so far has been concrete hallways with the occasional door here and there. Then his silent escort took him through a door and left him with the girl who was waiting in a small room down by the kitchen.

"Come," she said softly.

He followed. It being clear she was not interested in conversation, he remained silent. Now they're in a service lift, ascending on what feels like a serpentine path.

She's a lovely young girl, very fragrant, not much older than Esa. But her innocence was lost long ago. Something about her is cynical and passive. Her full lips are rouged and glossy. Long curled blond hair bounces around her face and on her shoulders even though she's not moving but to tremble. She's wearing tight flamingo-pink shorts and a halter. Her creamy breasts are no longer budding but in full bloom.

Isham looks up at the ceiling, sees a gray metal grate. He looks down at the floor and sees black and white squares a foot to a side. He inhales and smells cleaning solvents and the girl's perfume. He hears the constant soft grinding sound of the lift as it sometimes angles, sometimes curves, sometimes travels in a straight line. Always ascending.

Then the lift stops. The door slides open and they step out into a space that is bunker-like and filled with screens, banks and banks of screens. Music is blaring, something ancient and enraged coming out from between blazing screens that are the only light. So many screens. All displaying different shots of one subject.

R'io.

On every screen.

Holy Source be with my son.

Without betraying his purpose though his knees jelly for an instant, Isham One-Who-Waits quickly takes in some of the images. R'io and Skye being pulled out of a water spewing hole by a work crew wearing miner's gear. R'io wounded, fighting them off, screaming "Skye, Skye!" R'io in surgery. R'io recovering, naked, beginning to function then frustrated and enraged then despairing. R'io collapsing, alive though barely, held in something like an ancient iron lung. All that in less than an instant because Edwin Reynolds must tend to his reason for being here.

Focus only on that.

So far Headmon hasn't turned around or acknowledged their arrival but remains seated in a large high-back chair at a messy old wooden desk studying the images directly in front of him. Because of the chair and the viewing angle from behind it's difficult to determine what he looks like. Bald but for a long fringe of dark hair that hangs to his shoulders. He turns off the music.

After a long, awkward moment, the girl softly clears her throat.

"Yes, Ruelle, I'm aware that you have arrived and that standing by while I am interested in something else is not one of your favorite things."

"Mr. Headmon, you asked to see Edwin Reynolds, a candidate for the butler's position."

"Ah yes, that." Headmon turns and looks at the girl.

In profile, he's darkish and a bit jowly. His nose has a hump and his chin is weak. He smiles at Ruelle, takes her hand and kisses her palm.

"Wait for me in the penthouse," he squeezes a breast.

Her smile is radiant. She leans down and licks his lips. Then she returns to the lift and is gone.

Ignoring the latest applicant to serve as his butler, Headmon returns to his screens and in the ensuing silence One-Who-Waits demonstrates the art of non-intrusion.

After several moments of study Headmon is apparently sated with R'io. He extinguishes all of those images and replaces them with a single image of Skye One-Who-Wanders, wearing the navigator and her old stone-people clothes. Wet with rain, she's somewhere in a jungle, turning around, looking for something.

"You shall be called Reynolds," Headmon whispers.

Isham bows ever so slightly and remains where he is, standing tall and dignified with his hands behind his back, ready to respond. Headmon turns in his chair. Behind him is an image of Skye One-Who-Wanders, asleep, talking with her hands, calling for R'io then Solaris and One-Who-Waits.

Headmon remains seated, studying Isham/Reynolds. His eyes are dark. What hair he has falls to his shoulders and is also dark, though with gray coming in at the temples.

"I want you in service for this evening's meal. I'm going in for a few medical procedures tomorrow. You'll have a day to get oriented before joining me. Lead footman will give you the rules. Go to wardrobe for proper attire."

"Yes, sir." Again, Isham bows ever so slightly. "Thank you sir."

He turns to the lift and presses the call button. The lift arrives immediately and opens. He gets in. The door closes behind him. The lift descends. The first half of his purpose is achieved but he does not express relief because there is surveillance everywhere.

***

The faintest flicker of ego remains for George Biggs Boltin, Great City's former head of Security. That flicker of ego tells him he's completely confined in something, under the control of someone not here, not knowable. It tells him that all horizons are now tilted. It tells him that he is no longer human in some fundamental way. Enough of him remains to find that terrifying. He tries as though in a dream to cry for help and all his efforts produce nothing.

KEEP WALKING!

It's the voice again. He'd stopped and stood wavering. It tells him to go on.

Where?

Through blizzards of everything and nothing.

Obedient to the deafening voice that seems to be his voice but isn't, he steps forward. Unable not to, he keeps going, moving as best he can through the dune valleys around point B.

***

Solaris is sitting in the opalescent chamber, legs curled under her, trying to contact One-Who-Wanders when something most unpleasant dis-turbs the big spider. It's something new. From beyond the sound up above – the digging and explosions.

She opens an eye and lumbers to her feet. Her severed foreleg has now almost completely grown back but is still a bit short, causing her to limp. Head cocked, she stands listening to a perversion of the calling-dream.

Spiky jaws open, Solaris hears pain. Someone is up on the surface. But this signal is not like the others that have come in the hundred plus years she's been keeper of the Refuge. This is different, someone screaming in agony, pleading for relief from torture.

What does this mean?

Solaris raises her rear end. A translucent drop forms and falls to the ground below. A tear. Another and another. They begin to form a growing puddle, a message calling One-Who-Waits who isn't here to help.

***

Freshly showered and naked, streaming gear neatly folded against her chest, Skye One-Who-Wanders emerges from the bathroom, moves to the metal wardrobe at the foot of the bed and opens the double doors. Several full-length garments are hanging on one side, boots on the floor. The other side is stacked on the bottom with big pillows. Above that are shelves stacked with sheets, towels and blankets. The top shelf is empty.

Skye tosses R'io's belt on the foot of the bed, slides the Streaming gear onto the top shelf and takes a plain, finely woven gown off of its hanger – pale dusty blue by candlelight. She lifts the gown up over her head and lets it fall like a long sigh to her wrists and ankles. She puts R'io's belt on over her head, letting it hang from shoulder to waist then pulls on the boots, finds them soft and warm.

Her stomach growls. She crosses to the galley and looks around. She finds a metal box standing on end. The box is as tall as she is and wider than her shoulders. It has a door. She opens it. Bright light pours out. The inside is cold.

Finding shelves of food and drink, she pulls out a bottle of something white, removes the cap and takes a sniff. She sips then sucks down long draughts of what is cold and perfect. Satisfied for now, she recaps the bottle, returns it to its place and closes the door.

The transparent bag with her stone-people clothes is on the counter. She pats it, checks that everything is there then turns and studies the doors at each end of the room. Shrugging because, from here at least, the doors are identical and she doesn't know what's beyond either of them, she moves to the one on her right, releases the latch, opens the door inward and gasps because someone is there, brought up short, too, not an arm's-length away as they almost collide.

"Ho, give me a start!" the other yells out.

The two of them step back, hands to hearts. Skye is in the open doorway. The other is short, squat, robed, hooded and sexually indeterminate, standing in a stone tunnel big enough for two abreast and illumined by infrequent candles.

"I'm Champion Jael." The voice is low and husky.

They squint at each other, unable to see more than shadows.

"Was just to come for tendin' the candles and freshen your food."

Skye cocks her head, listening hard, trying to catch champion Jael's words because the accent is heavy.

"As the one on watch when you waked, I have special duties toward you now. Until the match."

"I am Skye One-Who-Wanders, just wanting to find out where I am."

"We go inside. Maybe eat. I brought food." A cloth-covered basket is raised front and center. "Okay?"

Jolted out of a frozen moment, Skye nods, gestures toward the open door and steps aside.

***

The dim conference room up in The Heights is warm, stuffy and large enough for the newly formed task force given the assignment of defending Great City. The Presider is at the head of the oval table. To his right is Karin Lassiter Kohl, head of Security. Also present is Malcolm Pierce Whitaker of Engineering, Magrit Abram Shen of Technology and Virginia Kahn Baker of Human Resources. At issue is the possible creation of a defensive force, a citizen-army.

"Fifteen thousand?!" Baker is on her feet, face flushed, looking aghast at Shen who threw out the number. "Fifteen thousand?! That number is way out of line!"

"It's a renewable resource," Shen smiles politely at the outburst.

263

"Infants can't instantly be turned into adult workers!" The ball of spit bounces between Baker's lips. "Fifteen thousand is beyond what we can produce or siphon off of the workforce at this time," she looks to Reed for help. "Plus, we don't even know the size of the group down there. We know almost nothing about what we're facing. Maybe they're a little isolated group. Certainly not enough to justify the loss of fifteen thousand citizen-units."

"Are you assuming we would lose those units?" The Presider turns an icy stare on his head of Human Resources. "Or are you saying that Great City should not defend itself whatever the cost?"

"I'm talking about the functioning of Great City. The sudden loss of that many citizen-units will make it impossible to function. And we're on half-measures now. Incubating replacements was cut from my budget as non-critical at this time."

"I'm with Technology on this," Reed nods to Shen who is fragile and thoughtful in her chair. "Besides, it solves another problem, which is that we need to thin out the herd to cut down on use of resources. We'll keep the heartiest and put the others to good use defending us."

Baker's mouth falls open. Reed's smile is chilling. He looks thinner, worn by the strain but no less competent and focused.

"Sit down, Virginia. You'll work with Shen on this. She's got it figured out." He smiles at Whitaker. "That brings us to the shape-changers."

"Yes, sir. Our shape-changer options are exhausted. There is an abundant supply up at the transfer station, however. In the shuttle/barge on lockdown."

"How do you know?" Lassiter leans forward, smelling a possible escape route.

"It's standard equipment." Whitaker turns to Reed. "We need those shape-changers ASAP. The shuttle that brought the ambassadors here is up in the port. It can be prepped for a quick trip to and from, bringing back everything that fits in the cargo hold. Twenty-four hours in and out."

Reed closes his eyes to think. Then he looks at those present and announces a bit of news.

"The transfer station is empty but for several dozen citizen-units who are now dead who were left behind on the last trip when the ambassadors were brought here. We've been bringing goods down since the trouble started. Are the shape-changers that necessary?"

264

"Yes," Whitaker and Shen nod passionately.

"Very well. Which brings me to another issue." Reed looks at Lassiter the way an eagle regards a mouse. "It has come to my attention, Lassiter, that through your incompetence ambassador Davenport Baxter was exposed to citizen-units. It has also become apparent of late that you have got the Space States contaigion and are besotted with the ambassador. Therefore you are relieved of your duties."

Karin Lassiter Kohl sits frozen in her chair, staring dumbly at Reed.

"You understand we can't be bothered with you now. I will decide your future when there is time. Guards!"

The door behind Lassiter opens and two burly Security guards march into the room and go right to her. Morton Edwards Hale, the assistant who informed on her is standing in the hallway, smiling.

"Come!" The guards stand on either side, gesturing to the door. Lassiter stands. When the guards reach for her, she jerks away, repulsed by their touch and walks out of the room on her own, head high.

"Come in Edwards, take your seat," the Presider beckons. "A memo is going out at this moment notifying stewards of Great City that our new head of Security is Morton Edwards Hale."

Confident in his ability to swim with sharks, Edwards enters the conference room and takes the seat vacated by Karin Lassiter Kohl who is already long gone and forgotten.

**

Using a cover and cushions from the wardrobe, Skye One-Who-Wanders helped champion Jael turn the bed into a sofa. She was then given a tour of the room, called a cell – though nothing was said about the other door, the one she hasn't opened yet. They started in the bathroom with cabinets over and under the sink. Champion Jael pointed.

"Soap and lotions. Ointments. There's sponges for yer female hygiene needs."

Short, square and solid, champion Jael is now in the galley noisily sharpening a knife with brisk hot strokes prior to slicing fruit into a bowl. Skye is standing off to the side behind the little champion, studying her.

From this angle, the side of Jael's face glows bronze in the candlelight and a long dark braid slithers down her back to the waist of her wine-colored gown. Done slicing, Jael pours hot tea into mugs, wipes her hands then puts the bowl of fruit and the mugs on a tray she picks up and hands to Skye.

"On the table. Have a seat. Boots off."

Skye carries the tray to a low table in front of the sofa and sits. She slides off her boots, plumps up a cushion and scoots into the corner. She tucks her feet up under her gown and leans back.

From here, champion Jael is of indeterminate age, standing with her feet apart, arms at her sides, stolid as a pillar. Her smooth skin glows golden brown. Her eyes are lidless slits. And under each eye is something else.

Skye leans forward, peering at champion Jael's face. She sees little blue circles with tails. Four falling from one eye, five from the other. Falling from each eye down across each plump cheek.

"Yer noticing my tattoos," Jael hasn't moved a muscle. "These are gang-flags. My family. The Tears. That's where I started. In the gutter of an alley run by The Tears. We show no pity, no mercy, no joy." Champion Jael moves to the other corner of the sofa and sits. She takes off her boots, drops them on the floor and leans back against the side of the wardrobe. "You got questions?"

"Where are we?"

"Directly under the Stadium where the champions live."

"In SubTurra?"

"Technically speaking yes but not really," the little champion reaches for a piece of fruit. "We're kind of independent and answer to Rogue, not Headmon."

"Why are you doing this?" she reaches for her mug, brings it to her nose, sniffs cinnamon and likes the warmth between her hands.

"Rogue said whoever's there when you woke has special duties until the match."

"No, why are the champions training me for a match with Rogue?" she sips.

"Two reasons," Jael holds up stubby fingers. "Ratings and ratings. As long as our ratings stay high, we got some leverage with Headmon. If they go down, so do we."

266

"What makes you think I can hold my own against the champion of champions?"

"You can't," Jael sucks down a piece of fruit. "You could learn to be good. Quick, too. You tolerated the Stream and took to illusion like I never saw before. But Rogue is the best ever. No one can beat her."

Skye sips her tea and studies champion Jael.

"What if I don't want to do this?"

"You got no choice," Jael snorts. "Premium Banding-content don't belong to itself, it belongs to Headmon. The public is willing to pay whatever Headmon charges for access to you. That's why he agreed to let us bring you here for trainin'. We could have trained you any number of other places. But Rogue reminded him that a shortage of supply drives up demand.

"In yer absence, Headmon is teasing the public with reruns and speculations about what he's calling 'The Match of Perfections!' It's on. It's off. You're injured. Rogue is being temperamental. He's yanking everybody around."

"What happens to whoever loses the match?"

"Rogue will lose the match. Headmon will see to that. He's been wanting to get rid of her for a long time."

"Why?"

"Because she's got too much power with us and the public. Because she's smarter than he is."

"What will happen to her?"

"Who knows. Probably recycled like everybody else in SubTurra."

Digesting the information, Skye looks around at the cell then studies Jael for a moment, curious.

"What's it like here?"

"The Stadium?"

"No, SubTurra."

The little champion blinks then looks straight ahead. Her profile is almost flat. Forehead, nose, eyes, lips, chin all flow together in one expressionless lump.

"Ordinary folk is worked to death until they're someone else's dinner and another person's shoes and that guy's new shirt and whatever else can be squoze out of 'em." Jael squints hard at nothing on the wall in front of her.

"Someone else's dinner?" Skye remembers eating lots of meat.

267

"Oh yeah," Jael nods. "We've all et human. That's all there is: meat, mushrooms and mold. Except for Headmon. He has anything he wants from his gardens and farms. And us. Champions don't eat human. We have our own food."

"SubTurrans eat human flesh?"

"Yep. We eat the young and wear the old. All SubTurran females have a quota of pregnancies. You lose Banding-time if you don't make quota. Since I started bleeding I had a pregnancy every two years until I made champion. A few went all the way to term but I never saw the babes." Jael leans down for her boots. "Not talk no more. Train now."

"Am I free to explore?" Skye scoots forward and reaches down for her boots then stands, takes the tray of food to the cold-box and puts it inside.

"You can use that door anytime," Jael points to the door Skye went through for their encounter. "It leads up to the arena, which you can use whenever you want but you are not to go into the Stream without a spotter. Even old pros always use a spotter. It's a rule." She points at the other door. "That leads somewhere else. You'll know if and when to use it." Jael moves to the door that leads up to the arena and opens it. "I'll go change. Get your Streaming gear on and meet me for a workout."

***

Undergoing an examination process identical to Isham's, Curanda and Esa are now lying on adjacent gurneys in a softly illumined metal chamber. They're both naked, covered by a sheet and sedated to a twilight sleep. Electrodes on their bodies are connected to technology monitored by a doctor in a fine leather lab coat. The electrodes are measuring deep autonomic responses, looking for concealed tension, which is an unmistakable sign of duplicity in a person.

The doctor is re-checking his data, running the test a second time. He's never seen such calm readings except earlier when a man went through with similar ones. Must be the food. Whatever.

He turns to their gurneys and looks down at two peaceful faces, one young, one old, not otherwise special. He checks the old woman's

268

chart.

"Curanda," he murmurs. "Odd name."

He looks at her, fascinated by so peaceful a face. He wonders what it must be like not to be afraid. He looks at the girl and sees the same peace – remarkable in one so young. He stands between the two gurneys lost in thought.

A soft chime signals the end of the exam. The doctor glances at the two screens then extinguishes them. He looks at assistants who are standing in a glass control booth.

"Wake'em up and take'em to wardrobe."

***

"The butler's quarters are separated from the other staff and Specials. At present you are alone on this corridor, though Mr. Headmon occasionally houses a favored special here, too."

Isham One-Who-Waits known as Edwin Reynolds follows the lead footman down a long neon-lit concrete corridor that is featureless but for the occasional intersection. His new clothes are being altered so he's wearing a white bathrobe and slippers that make a shushing sound on the tile floor.

"In here," the lead footman stops in front of a door and opens it onto an unadorned concrete studio apartment. He enters followed by Headmon's new butler who stops and looks around, sees a toilet and stall shower on one side and a small closet covered with a sheet of human skins on the other side.

The apartment is furnished with a single bed and gray skin blanket. Next to the bed is a metal folding chair and a lit floor lamp. Directly across from the entrance is another door, closed and bolted with elaborate locks.

"This room is adjacent to Mr. Headmon's penthouse. That door," the footman points, "connects you directly. It is opened from the other side. You will be paged. The door will unlock. Go immediately where you are called." The lead footman moves back to the front door and stands looking bored. "As soon as your clothes arrive you will be on duty. I will prep you for evening meal."

"Thank you."

"Butler's basics. You are to be clean and odorless at all times,

269

especially your fingernails and hair. No cologne. Do not speak unless you are spoken to and then only to address the issue at hand as parsimoniously as possible. Never touch Mr. Headmon or look him in the eye."

Isham nods warmly to the lead footman – a man of military bearing, short, dark, lean and tightly wound.

"When paged, how will I know where to go?"

"A tech-map on the door will tell you where the page is originating and provide directions for the quickest way there. In essence, you are to be either in here alone or with Mr. Headmon. More questions?"

"Yes," Isham/Reynolds smiles. "Do you have a name?"

"I'm lead footman." The man seems offended. "That is all you need to know. That is all you need to know about anyone here. We are not at the residence for our own pleasure, Reynolds, but to serve Mr. Headmon. Those who do that well survive longer than those who do not." He steps out of the room, closes the door and is gone.

Isham moves to the metal folding chair and sits down in the lamp's weak light. Taking advantage of the break, he sends to Curanda without waiting for a response.

Positioned.

Then he concentrates on the most important test of all. So far there's not been time because all his energy as been focused on getting here. Now, sitting straight, eyes closed, hands on thighs, he sinks down and opens to common-awareness.

Elder Martin?

***

The crown of Great City rolls back to expose the port where, until recently, shuttles from the transfer station arrived and departed with goods and occasional passengers. Inside, a lone shuttle like an ugly cigar stub is erect in a bed of roiling steam, about to take off on an urgent mission. The steam changes colors, from gray to yellow-white.

Slowly, thundering, the shuttle lifts up, up, straight up. As it clears the structure and disappears in the constant haze the dome slides

270

closed. Six re-programmed Security guards are on their way to the transfer station for the supply of shape-changers believed to be aboard H-V shuttle/barge Ralph Waldo Emerson out of S.S. Hope.

***

In position and asleep at Narrow Gorge, elder Martin stirs and wakes abruptly.

Isham, blessed be Source!

Yes. Positioned. Source willing, Curanda and Esa will arrive shortly. What's the status on your end?

Elder Moss and her team, absent Axl, are in place and waiting for the signal. We're in position here and ready. Source willing, we'll get you all out of the vicinity before they even realize you're gone.

Axl?

Nothing. He does not respond.

I am going to take advantage of this moment to try and contact R'io and Skye.

Blessings, friend. Stay with Source.

Aye, and you.

Then Isham is gone.

Enormously relieved, elder Martin sits up. Eyes closed, he relays the news to Jabaz and elder Moss.

Lt. Pilar Mezon's trip from the core of the transfer station back through the Emerson to the beautiful outside took much less time than going in. Rushing, batting away images of floating dead people she set course for Mohawk and entered half-sleep. Now, feet together, knees bent, arms folded across her chest, she's traveling fast in stealth-mode with no sense of speed and halfway to her destination.

The hairtrigger alarm sounds.

Pilar is instantly awake and turning it off. Only a bit blurry from tranks and memories of the transfer station's core, she checks to see what activated the alarm. Then, surprised, she furls her wings, comes to a sudden stop and turns to face earth – the source of the stimulus according to her technology.

"Alert." The auto-voice is female and pleasantly soft. "A shuttle has lifted off from the port of Great City and is headed to the transfer station."

"That's all we know?"

"For now."

Needing to get the information from this mission back to Mohawk so it can be forwarded and now also needing to protect the bodies back at Emerson, Pilar makes a decision to go just far enough behind the moon to send her report then – barring contrary orders from command on Phoenix – return to the transfer station with the rest of team Falcon.

***

After a quick outline of match rules up on the field, champion Jael led Skye One-Who-Wanders through a series of warm-ups. Then they practiced casting and parrying illusions. Without having seen any of the other champions, Skye returned to the cell, showered, put on her gown and laid down to sleep. But the feeling came back – not a headache exactly, more like a buzzing sensation, like a call that wants to be answered but she doesn't know how.

Unable to rest, she sits up, gets up, seeks distraction and so puts on her robe and moves to the door that hasn't been opened yet. It's

272

made of wood. Very old. Smooth like wax.

She lifts the latch, pushes and hears the low scrape of wood on stone. She steps forward blinking at darkness. Then her eyes adjust.

It's a stone tunnel, roughly carved, squarish, just big enough for one and dimly illumined by a candle at the far end. Leaving the door open behind her, stooping, she approaches the candle and almost there discovers on her left several steps that lead down to darkness. Hands touching the wall on either side, feeling with her feet, she takes the steps down to a small landing and a heavy wooden door with a metal ring in its center. She grasps and pulls the ring.

Perfectly balanced and oiled, the door swings toward her with a soft scraping sound. Then she hears water dripping slowly, smells water and fire.

Skye One-Who-Wanders steps into a big domed space that is illumined by several large candles on stands. A cavern. Untooled. Raw stone. Smooth as flesh. And the hollowness of the place is deafening.

The ground is water-smoothed and ever so slightly concave so that the whole space is shaped rather like an egg. At its center directly under the highest reach of the dome is a pool, round and dark and deep as mystery. The water is quiet and liv-ing. It smells sweet and clean.

She stands looking around for a moment, breathing it in, blinking, amazed. Then she notices cushions, widely and evenly spaced around the pool. She moves to the cushion in front of her, lowers her hood, takes off the robe, folds it and sets it on the ground next to the cushion. She walks to the pool and stands at its edge, head lowered, looking into black water-mirror.

Tears form and fall. Sinking to her knees, she lowers her forehead to the pool's stone rim. After a moment she begins to keen a long wordless prayer that starts softly as grief and ends with a whisper of gratitude. Then she cups her hands and dips them in the water to bring something real and holy and alive to her lips.

Skye One-Who-Wanders sips then drinks and finally goes back to the cushion to sit. Candlelight licks the black surface of the quiet water, flaring it with rainbows. She sinks into a silence that is deep and perfect, a stillness that has no bottom.

SNAP!

It's as though she's suddenly ripped out of herself and sucked from this location, tumbled through a firestorm of sparkling seed and she knows this is not the Stream, which is a mere trickle in comparison.

What then?

The sense of plummeting abruptly stops.

She's someplace she's never been before, another realm perhaps, standing on air before an abyss of twilight. The air is warm and dry. Behind her is what feels like desert though she can't turn to look. And she's vibrating like a hammer-struck bell announcing the approach of solemnity.

Gradually, a presence becomes evident without assuming form or image. She is embraced, absorbed by what cannot be described because it is the source of description and there is no name, sentence or story long enough, encompassing enough to begin the task. Then words happen without being spoken. Meaning arrives without a carrier.

You have only to step forward. I will part time and space for you.

That's what she hears – not hears but *knows*.

Clearly.

Then it's gone and she's falling off the precipice into the abyss.

SNAP!

Gasping, Skye One-Who-Wanders finds herself flung on her back looking up at the shadow-licked stone dome, dislodged from her sense of self and terrified by that. She scrambles to her feet and runs out through the door not bothering to close it behind her. She takes the steps two at a time, turns right at the top, bounces off the walls of the narrow tunnel and re-enters the cell, closing the door and leaning back against it, trying to catch her breath.

What was that?

She rushes into the bathroom and looks in the mirror over the sink. Illumined only by a single candle off to one side, she sees animal-Skye staring back – eyes large, dark, ablaze, jaw clenched to keep it from hammering. She remembers words.

You have only to step forward. I will part time and space for you.

Mute and bewildered, mouth open, she looks at herself then abruptly flings off R'io's belt, moves to the bed and the wardrobe pulling off the gown and boots, tossing them in the vicinity of the bed. She reaches into the wardrobe for the bag with her stone-people clothes, unzips it and pulls on the pants and shirt.

Ignoring muscles that are already sore, she runs up the stairs into the empty Stadium. The sky is deep cobalt blue washed on one side with ma-genta. The air is cool and smells of dirt.

Someone steps out of a nearby archway and is walking toward

274

her. Short and square. Robe on, hood up. Champion Jael.

"What you doin?"

"I...I need to move."

"After the workout we just had?"

"Yes."

"Hummm," Jael's chin is jutting out. "Like I say, as the one on watch when you woke it's my duty to keep an eye out. What happened?"

Skye shivers. Her teeth clatter.

Jael steps closer. Head back she squints up, clucks her tongue and shakes her head.

"Like I said, what happened?"

"I woke up. My head...I can't describe it, can't respond."

"What are you talkin about?"

"I don't know. I don't know. But I went through the door, the other door into that place. I don't know what happened. But I'm not back yet. I, I can't get back."

"Oh," Jael nods. "Yeah. Sometimes that place can have a slammin effect on a person." The little champion grinds a fist into the palm of her other hand. "Then again sometimes it's real gentle. But what's certain is that each time you come back you gotta re-ground, do normal things – clean your cell, tend your gear. Eat. Wine is good for it."

"Stay with me," Skye whispers fiercely.

"What?"

"Stay with me for a while. I could try to cook a meal. Maybe we could just...talk?"

"Ahhhhh, I hate talkin. But I am hungry. You a good cook?"

"I don't know."

"Well I guess we're gonna find out."

***

Headmon is in his control room surrounded by lit screens. Ancient jazz is floating from the speakers, a woman sighing about strange fruit. The screens behind and around Headmon flare with different views of SubTurra. Those in front of him are filled with scenes of R'io and Skye. But the screen he's paying particular attention

275

to shows the new butler, what's his name, Reynolds, from several different angles.

The dignified old man is in his apartment, sitting straight in the chair, hands on thighs, eyes closed, motionless, waiting for his new clothes. He hasn't moved for a while and looks like someone resting peacefully.

Headmon presses a button on his console. The page sounds in the butler's quarters. Instantly, Reynolds is on his feet, at the panel, pressing the Reply button.

"You called, sir?"

"An error. Go back to what you were doing."

"Very well, sir."

On the screens, Headmon watches as Reynolds relieves himself, washes then dries his hands and takes a sip of water from the glass on the sink. Then he returns to the chair and once again sits, eyes closed, apparently resting again.

***

Champion Jael hasn't moved from a comfortable perch on the sofa. Stretched out, feet crossed at the ankles, hands clasped behind her head, she's watching Skye One-Who-Wanders through narrowed eyes, weighing, taking stock, measuring unseen qualities.

Following detailed instructions, Skye changed from stone-people clothes back into the light blue gown. She cleaned up the mess she left. She started food that takes a while to cook.

Through all of that Skye occasionally stopped for a few seconds to stand pressing the heels of her hands into her forehead, grimacing – a gesture interpreted by Jael as natural given the circumstances, the spook-out and all. Each time, the sensation passed and Skye continued with her tasks. Now, slowly beginning to cohere, she is arranging the little folding table next to the sofa. Jael crosses her arms.

"I noticed yer robe ain't in the closet. Noticed that when I hung mine up. Where's yer robe?"

Blink. She can't remember, then does.

"I left it in that place." She points at the door.

276

"Oops," Jael is suddenly very serious. "You gotta go get it."

"I...I..."

"That's property of the champions. And you can't leave yer stuff lyin around for others to trip on."

"I...I..."

"You gotta go get it."

"Will you come with me?"

"I beg yer little royal pardon," Jael's look is one of total astonishment.

"Will you stay here then, not leave?"

"Do I look discomfortable?"

Skye One-Who-Wanders remains where she is for a moment then turns to go. Jael clucks.

"And close the door on yer way back."

Then Skye is running out of the cell into the tunnel, down the steps. The door at the bottom is closed again. She opens it and stops because the egg-shaped chamber isn't empty.

Two people are here, robed and hooded sitting across from each other on cushions. They don't seem to notice her arrival – or if they do, it's given no energy. She sees the robe where she left it, neatly folded next to the cushion directly in front of her. Bowing, she skitters to the cushion, plucks up the robe and, bowing again, retraces her steps almost running now, back up to the cell where, panting, she slams the door closed and leans against it, folded robe clutched to her breast.

"That was quick," Jael snorts a sharp laugh.

Skye nods and when she's caught her breath moves to the wardrobe to hang the robe inside. Then she returns to the galley, "wash yer hands," and picks up where she left off. She puts two goblets of wine, a lit candle and bowl of sliced fruit on the tray and carries it to the table in front of the sofa.

Jael pulls in her feet to make room. Skye sits and leans back, knees up. They reach for their wine goblets and sip in silence. The smell of wild grains on the boil fills the air. The wine is light and layered, very good.

"Can I ask a question?" Skye seems hesitant.

"Can I stop ya?" Jael snorts.

"Where are you from?"

"I was born way out in a toilet of SubTurra." Jael takes a sip of wine, stares at nothing in front of her. "Canton Squat, we called it. Two people did it in a sewer and there was me. I never found out who

277

they were. Didn't care. Anyhow, it's forbidden. Anyhow, I was working as soon as I could walk."

The words are spoken without inflection. Jael takes another sip of wine, swallows. Her face remains expressionless.

"Once when I was real little a supervisor on my crew took a shine to me. Looked after me. Named me. Jael. Snuck me special treats. It was our secret. Oh, she never touched me or anything – not allowed. But I could tell she wanted to hold me and couldn't let herself. And I wanted her to and couldn't. Forbidden. Talky-talk, not allowed. Havin' a friend, not allowed. Just work. But I like her and her me, too. I could tell."

Jael seems oddly disconnected from the story she's telling, as though it's about someone else.

"Anyhow, one day Headmon hit our sector with a Banding blackout. There's different kind of blackouts. Just hope you never get near one. We were down in the mine, working double shifts. He claimed production was off and hit us with one.

"We could feel coming. Blasting our eardrums, coming toward us like the very breath of evil. BLACKOUT! We started screaming. Then it came, a rolling wave, a wall of panic and blood."

The little champion swats at her face once, as though shooing an insect away.

"The supervisors wouldn't turn on the gas to knock us out. Non. They wanted to teach us a lesson. They waited. We stampeded. Then the raging started. Blood everywhere. Screaming and squealing like devils drug into the light.

"That woman, she grabbed me and thrown me down and fell on me all curled up mother-like. Probably why I'm still alive. Next thing I know I'm in another mine, working again. Her? Who knows? Probly dead. A mercy."

Jael raises her chin then looks over at Skye. The newcomer is hugging her knees. Her eyes are enormous and dark. Her mouth has fallen open.

"You ready to be alone yet?" the little champion inquires as if they've been talking about how to make a bed.

"No."

"Then ask a question or something. I don't know how to make it up without a question."

Skye leans for her wine, takes a long sip then gets comfortable again.

"What is the champion of champions?"

"Rogue?"

"What does it mean?"

"That's two questions. Slow down, okay?" Jael clears her throat. "The champion of champions is the best champion at any given time. Since Rogue became a champion she's had that slot. Does what no one has ever done before on Banding.

"As champion of champions she has a lot of duties." Jael ticks them off on her stubby fingers. "First she has to take on all worthy comers. Two she has to keep the rest of the champions working hard to make sure our ratings stay up. Three, she's our rep with Headmon, makes sure he sticks to his end of the contract, meaning she's sometimes away from here out in SubTurra on business, like coming to get you because she got it right away that Headmon is addicted to you along with everyone else."

"Addicted?"

"Yeah."

"Why?"

"Yer not like us. You came from somewhere else and you've been dominating the Banding spectrum since you got here."

"I don't understand."

"Ain't you aware that every instant you've been in SubTurra – until you passed through the Stadium shield – you've been on the Banding spectrum, available to anyone who can pay? You've been available non-stop to the fat folk while Headmon has constantly teased ordinary blokers with snippets. That's great for you but for all other Banding content it's a huge threat. Rogue understood that. She got it that to survive we had to co-opt you – whatever the cost and it might be her life."

"No!"

"Yeah. Rogue gave Headmon the idea. A dream match. Rogue, greatest champion of all time versus Skye One-Who-Wanders, primate-girl. He loved it, was so determined to make the match happen he gave in to most of our demands."

"What does it mean that I've been accessible on Banding since I got here?" Skye's eyes are big and her mouth has fallen open.

"Every move you've made, every sound, has been accessed by anyone who could pay for it."

"How could that be without my knowing?"

"Only an experienced champion or hacker can tell when the

279

public is present. There's no way you could have known." The little champion reaches for her glass. "Food smells done. Let's eat. You got another trainin' session coming up all too soon."

***

Suspended in the seam between the light and dark sides of the moon, Lt. Pilar Mezon stops, furls the windrider wings and blends right in while she transceives. First, she sends her reconnaissance report to H-V cruiser Mohawk so it can be forwarded to Command Ship Phoenix where decisions are made. She includes the latest data on the shuttle now on its way from Great City to the transfer station. She is told to hold position while her report is reviewed. In no time at all Commander Ingrid Steele forwards a response.

"FROM: Captain Beryl Porter, Command Ship Phoenix. TO: Falcon One. MESSAGE: Deploy team Falcon and return immediately to vicinity of transfer station in stealth-mode. Observe only. END MESSAGE."

Pilar orders Falcon Two, Quester Bates, to deploy the team in stealth-mode ASAP with Bates in the ambulance, McCloud and Salonnen on sleds, Rogers and Kim on scooters. She also requests three-dozen bodybags plus extra cutting gear to free the Emerson.

After synching destination-coordinates with Falcon Two, Pilar signs off and eases into the light. She snaps into a T-formation, transparent wings open wide to catch the wind. Moving very fast, she heads back to monitor the shuttle and the transfer station while awaiting the arrival of the other falcons.

***

After the meal with Jael, Skye One-Who-Wanders washed the pots, bowls, mugs and utensils then dried and put them away. She pulled the gown off over her head, dropped R'io's belt back in place, got under the cover and fell sound asleep. Immediately she began to dream, as she is now. Vividly.

280

...Cooing reassures her to the marrow and she is rocked in mother's arms. What is mother? Cradled against abundant breasts, wrapped in the smell of sweet strong milk and warm flesh. Rocked back and forth, back and forth and hummed to.

Nothing.

Black void.

...Veils. She's surrounded by diaphanous veils, translucent curtains the color of amber. Veils. Layers of them. Hung from a ceiling she can't see to a floor that isn't there. Lit from beyond. Wafting against her. Nudging from behind, opening up what is not quite a path.

She's walking through veils, moving slowly, weightlessly, easing each overlapping membrane of fabric aside with the back of a hand. Then she arrives at the last veil. She stops and stands peering through at someone lying on a bed.

A man.

He's in a clearing defined by veils, illumined by a shaft of bronze-colored light that shines directly down from beyond. He's lying on a bed, on his back, naked but for a cloth across his hips. Sleeping or dead, she can't tell. But his hair is long and red, neatly combed on the pillow, ignited by the light shining down.

R'io.

She moves the last veil aside and steps into the shaft-lit space. She walks to the bed and looks down. He seems inaccessible, beyond reach, on the other side of a dark divide, resting in the time of quiet.

Or dead.

She sits on the side of the bed.

He's pale and stringy. Reaching out, she lowers a hand to the center of his chest, touches the fine gold hairs, strokes cool flesh. She rests her hand on his chest and leans closer, nestles her face in his neck. Then she finds his cheek with hers, smells him, finds his mouth, slightly open. Kissing, she tastes. He's cold and dry. She whispers his name into his mouth.

"R'io..."

She says it again.

"R'io."

From a great distance he seems to draw in a long draught of her breath.

Heat rises under her hand. Pulsing. He warms, moistens, stirs.

She pulls back and looks down.

His eyes open.

So blue.

He recognizes instantly. His hand finds hers on his chest and draws it down to where he wraps her fingers around a budding erection and shows her what to do. He hardens to the density of hot stone, slides an arm beneath her and lifts her up so she's on top, straddling him, wincing at first then relaxing and slowly sinking down onto him. From then on she needs no instruction.

Suddenly, because she must, she rears back and they lock hands, squeezing and bucking and heaving. They both cry out and she is injected with fire all the way up to her belly, to her throat, and they are both silent but for their breathing.

Then someone is standing beside her, next to the bed. Water-woman, speaking.

We act and we are acted upon.

A vial is pressed into her hand.

This is for his seed. Collect all of it. Keep it safe. You will know when to use it.

And she is holding a babe, nursing the child. His and hers. Theirs. Lost in the feel of the warm babe melded to her body, sucking her breast for sustenance.

A girl.

Born under the caul. Curly red hair.

One amber-colored eye. One eye the blue of hottest flame.

Each eye regarding its own horizon from a different dimension.

Mother of a new world.

Call her Shadow.

Shadow?

Yes. And know that the time of quiet is a pool of sunlit silence you will seek all of your life and find only in the longing for it.

Then water-woman and the babe are gone and the dreamer is holding the vial in her hand and he is softening, growing cold.

Squatting, she reaches down carefully. As he slips out she places the vial on her opening and feels the seed slide down into it. She squeezes hard with her muscles, expelling all the seed into the bottle. Then she stoppers the vial, drapes the cord around her neck and is leaning down to embrace him when she realizes he's gone.

So is the bed. So are the veils. So is dream.

Only sleep remains.

282

"These are specials garments. They indicate to anyone in the resi-dence that you are on Mr. Headmon's personal staff and answer only to him or the butler – *if* Mr. Headmon accepts you into service, that is."

Esa and Curanda are in Wardrobe, a large concrete room with racks of clothes neatly arranged from floor to ceiling. They're standing in front of a broad full-length mirror. The light is harsh neon. The place smells of chemical preservatives.

The girl helping them dress for the interview is wearing a jewel-green silk jumpsuit that hides nothing of her full young body. Only slightly older than Esa, possibly just into her menses, her long blond hair falls loose to her shoulders around an oval of face. Her features are carved and delicate. Her skin is pale porcelain blushed with pink. Her lips are full, glossy and rouged. When her eyes meet Esa's in the mirror, they're blue clouded by melancholy.

"What's your name?" Esa asks shyly.

"They call me Ruelle." The girl moves quickly and efficiently, ad-justing their long black slips. "It means sad one. In addition to my other duties I tend Mr. Headmon when he wants to be around what he calls beautiful sorrow."

"Tend in what way?" Curanda inquires as a rust-colored gown is eased over her head and zipped up the back.

Ruelle doesn't answer. Instead, she holds up a similar gown for Esa and helps the girl put it on. Then she produces soft black slippers and kneels to put them on strangers' feet.

"And last of all…"

The girl rises, moves to a wardrobe, opens a drawer and pulls out two soft white caps with ribbon ties for under the chin. Returning to Esa and Curanda she hands each a cap, helps put them on and tie the ties.

"There. You're ready."

"Tend Headmon in what way?" Curanda asks again.

Ruelle looks at the old woman and experiences a flash of being seen for an instant even though Curanda is obviously blind. Her lip trembles. She looks down at her hands then back up defiantly.

"I tend Mr. Headmon in whatever way he desires," the girl

whispers fiercely. "And I enjoy it." With that, Ruelle moves to and opens a door onto a concrete corridor.

The new butler is standing just outside in the hall – tall and dignified in his formal attire. He smiles professionally and Ruelle is unaware of the conversation going on around her.

"This is Reynolds, Mr. Headmon's butler. He'll take you to the interview."

Expect the unexpected, Isham bows ever so slightly –

Si, Curanda and Esa both nod.

"Right this way, please," he gestures.

Curanda takes Esa's arm and squeezes ever so slightly. The girl squeezes back. They approach the open door. Curanda stops and smiles up at Ruelle. Then she reaches out and cups the girl's cheek in her hand.

It's as though Ruelle is struck dumb by something she doesn't recognize because she's never felt or seen it before. But it instantly calms her. Then she doesn't so much hear words as receive a stiff shot of meaning.

The one who uses force to control another is to be blamed, not the one on whom force is used.

Curanda smiles sadly and lowers her hand. Then she and Esa move out into the corridor and follow Headmon's new butler to an interview they must pass to be in position to achieve their purpose in being here, Source willing.

***

Skye One-Who-Wanders wakes abruptly sitting up in bed with an undeniable urge to return to the chamber that so frightened her, where she left the robe. Tossing the blanket aside and moving quickly she pulls her gown out of the wardrobe and puts it on then the robe and boots. Lifting her hood she strides to the door and opens it.

With an inexplicable sense of urgency she rushes toward the candle at the end of the tunnel, quicksteps down the stone stairs to the door with the ring in its center, opens it, steps into the big domed chamber and stops because someone is here. Someone very still is seated directly across from her on the other side of the black pool.

"Sit."

It's Rogue.

Skye One-Who-Wanders moves to the nearest cushion and sits.

"There's been a change of plans. The champions have been in here since the middle of last night, conferring. Now you must be informed what has been decided." Rogue stirs slightly, tucks her hands in her sleeves.

"Headmon has insistently inquired after you and been informed of your progress though warned that your training has just begun and you are barely a novice. Yesterday evening I was summoned. We met virtually and I was ordered to bring real-you to the residence immediately."

Skye One-Who-Wanders feels a drop of ice sink through her core. Rogue continues.

"This is most unusual but he wants to meet you and make an announcement of some kind. I negotiated the finer points of such a possible visit and told him I'd have to confer with the champions. We've spent the intervening time in here, deciding. They left. I waited. You were called. You arrived. That's how I know our decision is the right one."

"And it is?"

"You and I will go immediately to the residence. The other champions will remain here. For their safety."

Skye shudders remembering what Jael told her about SubTurra and the man in charge. She remembers what it felt like to be kept prisoner in a suffocated world.

"And if I refuse to go?"

"Why would you?" Rogue shrugs. "More important, why would we allow it? But for your edification let me tell you what would happen should you refuse to go and we agree. First, you will be returned to central control."

"The place with the bed?"

"Yes."

"Why?"

"To distance the champions from you and Headmon and the unavoidable perception by the public that the champions had anything to do with what's going to happen when Headmon starts initiating random Banding blackouts beginning in areas of least profitability. You will be exposed to what this means in ways you can't now imagine. The longer you hold out the more workers will go mad with panic. It will be a very public thing. And you will be exposed to all of it, forced to witness the consequences of your willfulness. Eventually you'll go with us. Why be the cause of so much suf-fering first?"

Skye lowers her chin to her chest and exhales. Then she looks at Rogue.

"Very well."

"Return to your cell." Rogue stands. "Jael will help you dress. Then go to the Stadium." The champion of champions touches fingertips to her heart. "I've come to like you, Novice. May we both survive."

"You and Me and R'io." Skye stands. "Three of us. Or I don't leave."

They stare at each other across the perfect pool of black water. Then both women turn away and rush from the chamber the same way they arrived.

***

Wearing elegant plum-colored silk pajamas, Great City's head of Technology is in her private office leaning over her ignited desktop screen. She was about to take a shower an hour ago but got snagged by a hunch and has been in here following it since. It just paid off.

Magrit Abram Shen pumps the air with glee. She claps her hands. Long dark hair hanging loose, little girl face sweet and faery-like, she has found the ace she always likes to keep up her sleeve.

Ancient classified maps indicate the presence of engineered locations beneath the surface of the earth on all continents. Lots of them. But the place of particular interest at the moment is not all that far from Great City.

North and east of here several sprawling multi-layer underground installations are connected by tunnels large enough for six-lanes of traffic. Legends on the maps identify most of those locations as military or corporate installations though religious organizations also went below taking with them the wealth that provides such privilege.

Large numbers of people could have gone down like the Founders but not re-surfaced thus vanishing from anyone's radar. They could still be down there, planning a return to the surface, using Great

City's resources to show them how.

Shen extinguishes the desktop screen and straightens up. For a long time she stands squinting at nothing, trying to figure out how to prepare for what's coming. Finally, she runs her hands through her hair then pads cat-like down the corridor of her private quarters, which are all feminine and mauve, the last stop on her way up to where she really wants to be, which is in the Presider's seat.

***

Skye One-Who-Wanders and Rogue champion of champions pop into the center of the indefinite space where she was once confined. As statements of sexual unavailability they wear dark burkas made of cloth. Everything is covered but fingertips and eyes.

The bed is gone. They're not alone but looking around, Skye can't see anyone because of the lights focused on the two of them.

Given what she now understands about SubTurra and given that Rogue said they'd be on Banding again and accessible to all of SubTurra, she knew it would be difficult to come back to this dead place. But the swell of panic and nausea she's trying to swallow is unexpected and powerful.

Abruptly, the light is elevated to a blinding level. She raises her hands to shield her eyes. After a moment, heart pounding, she sees the place, its shape and nature, for the first time.

"One condition of our agreeing to this little journey," Rogue leans down to whisper, "is that you be allowed to see your cage first. I want you to know what you will come back to should you decide to be foolish."

It's an enormous place, like a huge concrete hanger. Complicated technology covers the walls and hangs from what ceiling she can see – her vision being interrupted by a great transparent donut sort of thing, like a command center, suspended directly overhead. Inside, severely foreshortened by her vantage from below, small groups of people are standing, looking down at her through the floor. Many others, technicians at all kinds of consoles, manipulate away. She tries to swallow and can't.

"Steady," Rogue grips her arm.

287

She drops her hands from her eyes.

"Real?"

"Yes, this is Central Control." Rogue nods out at the scene around them and chuckles sarcastically. "One of Headmon's conditions is the troops. For our protection from the masses."

Skye follows Rogue's gaze. Surrounding them is at least a company of troops head-to-toe in armor made of rust-colored leather scales. They wear backpacks and helmets with shiny faceplates, and they're holding weapons at the ready.

She closes her eyes. She remembers that her purpose is to get R'io out of here. Nothing matters now but reparation of her horrible error in judgment that got him here.

"We're going to the residence on foot." Rogue is squinting up at the control center, looking for someone. "Headmon's condition. Don't know what that's about. No telling how far it is or where."

"Attention to those en route to the residence!" It's the crisp voice of a female who could be anywhere but is probably directly above them. "You will now follow the lead vehicle!"

A large rust-colored van, bristling with technology and full of armed troops, arcs slowly out in front of them. Skye exhales and looks at Rogue. The champion nods. Accompanied by troops on either side, in front and behind, Skye and Rogue follow the lead vehicle out of the big hanger into a bright, white tiled avenue that has been swept clean for their passage.

Elsewhere, in his bunker, Headmon is sitting at his screens with the butler standing silently behind him and the silky sounds of a tenor sax whispering from the shadows. A pressure bandage is tight and flesh-colored on his head and face, with little eye, nose and mouth holes. Some of the fat has been sucked out of his body and he's quite sore in his wheelchair, cranky with discomfort, impatient because he won't know if his idea worked until the pressure bandage has been removed.

"What a magnificent creature to be hidden by that rag," he murmurs watching Skye, irritated with Rogue for choosing such a costume but at least he's in charge again and his prize is back on his turf as the parade exits Central Control for a journey he will manage, a journey that will last until he's ready for her.

"Turn it off!"

Without disturbing the air Isham/Reynolds moves around from behind the wheelchair to the control panel and extinguishes the screens.

288

"Take me back to the medical center. And get one of those lame doctors to come up with something more effective for this pain. And I want that new special, I call her my gypsy, what's her name? Kolander!"

"Curanda, sir?"

"That's right. Her. I want her."

"I'll take care of it, sir."

Reynolds maneuvers the wheelchair into Headmon's private lift that is lined with wine-colored leather, shiny brass rails and mirrors.

"Yes, I want her. Kolanda. Doctors don't know what they're doing and some blind peasant from the hinterlands is the only thing that makes me feel better. What's on the schedule?"

"We go from here to physical therapy then lunch."

"When do I see my face?"

"The doctor says very soon, a matter of hours perhaps."

"Then what, after the bandages?"

"Water-therapy. Snack. Then a session with Curanda."

"Move her closer to me. Across the hall from you."

"I'll see to it, sir."

The lift door opens and Isham/Reynolds wheels Headmon out into a long, carpeted hallway hung with chandeliers and lined with paintings and small sculptures on pedestals carefully lit from above. Two footmen are stationed across from each other in the middle of the hallway. They wear long black coats, vests, white ruffled shirts and royal blue knickers with hose and patent leather pumps. They snap to attention. Reynolds pauses long enough to instruct one of them to take charge of moving Curanda and her assistant to quarters directly across from the butler. Then he wheels Headmon on down the hallway to his comfortable recovery suite.

***

In stealth-mode, wings furled, resting on her feet like a translucent exclamation point between earth and the moon, Lt. Pilar Mezon returns from diffuse awareness as an alarm wakes her to the approach of the other Falcons. She blinks, instantly focused and scanning for visual but they're still too far away and in stealth mode so they won't be apparent until they're almost on her.

289

Rested and reasonably fresh, Pilar completes her isometric pump and feels a slight click in the new knee, probably from being immobile for so long. She sucks down water and nutrition then activates her optics to fine-focus on her team and is just able to make out the ambulance in front, piloted by Sergeant Quester Bates who is flanked by Sh'rai McCloud and Salonnen on sleds, trailed by Jika Rogers and Kim on scooters – all hauling pallets of bodybags and equipment.

They'll be able to talk amongst themselves soon. Until then, Pilar works with her knee, stretching, bending, twisting, trying to get rid of that click.

* * *

The lift opens onto the butler's corridor. Isham leads Esa to a door across from his and opens it.

"Mr. Headmon wants Miss Curanda to be closer to him. These are your new quarters."

He turns to Esa and signs, the movements of his hands barely perceptible in the dim corridor.

~ Surveillance everywhere. ~

~ Comprehende. ~

Esa steps into a concrete studio apartment similar to Isham's and also lit by a single dim floor lamp. The room contains a metal stall shower, a toilet, and two neatly made narrow beds, both with blankets made of human skin. There's also an old overstuffed chair, a desk with a swivel stool and a refrigerator.

"We've created a small laboratory for Miss Curanda to mix her healing potions." Isham points to the refrigerator and desk, on top of which are a magnifying lamp, tools, instruments, scales and measuring devices. "The ingredients you requested are in the refrigerator. If something else is needed, please inform me."

Nodding, Esa moves to the refrigerator and opens it. Inside are bags of herbs and jars of chemicals and vials of different colored liquids. The girl nods.

"This looks sufficient." She turns to her grand da who is standing in the open doorway and signs almost imperceptibly.

~ Still nothing from Axl? ~

290

~ Correct. ~

He crosses the room and pulls back a sheet of grayish stitched-together hides behind which is a closet with hanging silk gowns and robes, similar in fabric, cut and color to the garments Esa is wearing only much finer.

"Ah, good, they've arrived. These are garments for you and Miss Curanda. Specials are often invited to Mr. Headmon's occasions and are expected to dress accordingly. When you're summoned, you'll be instructed what to wear. There are also shoes, towels, bath supplies and so forth." Isham smiles professionally. "I'm just across the hall." He signs.

~ Try again to warn Skye that we are here lest her reaction undo our purpose. ~

~ Comprehende. ~

"Do you remember the way back to the terrace?"

"Yes."

"Good. Return to your mistress while I fetch Mr. Headmon's lunch." With that, leaving the door open, he is gone.

Burka long ago discarded because of the heat, Skye One-Who-Wanders is wearing remnant-people clothes and Rogue is wearing forest green warm-up pants and a tank top. They are surrounded by SubTurran troops marching on foot or riding in conveyances. Those walking are in perfect synch. The avenue is bright and wide. The rhythm is hypnotic.

For Skye the surrounding troops have faded to unimpor-tance, as has the destination. Walking thus, she is reminded of another kind of synchronization. From before. With R'io and Curanda and Esa and the big spider back at the Refuge. They called it something.

Common-something. Mind, perhaps.

…No.

Something else.

Then her head hurts again. Rather, there's a sort of desperate knocking on her door and she can't find the key and suddenly Skye is catapulted into that state but it's not crisp and clear like before. It's laced with static and difficult to read. But she knows.

She knows someone is trying to make contact in a peculiar way. Someone familiar. From before. Someone from back there/then has found her in common-awareness.

That's what wilderness-people called it. And she's in it now – slid, slipped, was drawn, called, whatever. And she's not alone. Someone else is here – not in this literal space but here with her nonetheless.

From wilderness-people?

………Aye………we…..ee…

Who? Where?

…Not…far…

Why?

…Do…not…reveal…

And as though unable to sustain penetration of dense stone and the unknown, common-awareness is gone.

"HALT!"

Weapons aimed and cocked, the troops have snapped into a threatening formation because Skye stumbled, fell out of step and Rogue lurched to break her fall.

"STEP BACK!"

Rogue helps Skye to her feet.

"STEP BACK *NOW*!"

"Okay, okay." Holding her hands up and out, all innocence, Rogue retreats slowly to her place. "I was just…"

"No talking!" It's a not-so-gentle command from the female who could be anywhere.

Trembling, mouth open, Skye looks around like one returned from a mild seizure. She moves next to Rogue and tries to catch her breath. When everyone is settled down, the troops are signaled back to their places.

"Continue!"

Skye and Rogue look at each other then step out again. It takes awhile to find the rhythm because Skye is strangely distracted and lacking in her usual grace.

Do not reveal.

Do not reveal *what*?

***

Isham/Reynolds leads Curanda and Esa into a large medical examination room with a padded table and a bank of bright overhead lights. Headmon is lying on the table, flesh-colored pressure bandage still on his face and head, wearing a black and red antique silk kimono of breathtaking beauty. Behind him, a doctor and nurse in scrubs are quietly busy at a tray of instruments on a rolling cart.

"Ah, good, you're here," Headmon murmurs to Curanda.

The three new arrivals move to one side and stay near the wall. Headmon, looks at the doctor.

"Proceed."

The doctor and nurse move into position, obscuring the patient as they snip off the pressure bandage then deftly remove the micro-sutures. When they're finished, Headmon shoos them away and sits up full of anticipation. He gets off of the table and walks with only residual discomfort from the work on his body to a full-length mirror on the wall across from Curanda, Esa and Reynolds.

The surgical changes on his face are actually not all that significant – a nip here, a tuck there, a bit of scraping, a bit of injected fatty tissue. The finishing work will be done by the aestheticians with their wigs and powders and tattoos.

Headmon turns from the mirror to look expectantly at Reynolds, Curanda and Esa. They stare at him, taken aback.

"This is the new me," his smile is chilling for an instant before the charm returns. "Do you like it?"

The hair confuses Esa. Headmon is bald but for a ring of muddy brown strands falling to his shoulders. Then, looking closer, it dawns on her. Her mouth opens and a whispered word escapes.

"...Da?"

Esa takes Curanda's hand and looks up then remembers that as far as Headmon is concerned grand dam is blind so she looks at Isham but remembers that he's a stranger so she looks back at Headmon who has been looking at her.

"Do you like it?"

"Sir, to overpraise what is, is to reduce what was by comparison." Curanda clears her throat and steps forward humbly, her tone meant to distract him from what just happened to Esa who recovered quickly but not quickly enough. "You ask for the impossible – that I fall out of love with one man to make room in my heart for another and, there," she snaps her fingers elaborately, "it is done and my heart has a new master."

"Except that you're blind, sly devil," he smiles, amused. "And I asked the girl."

"Yes, sir," Curanda steps back. "I can feel the change, however. It is palpable. Such transformation is not merely of one's exterior. It is total. And to answer your question, yes, sir, I like the new man. I find him honorable."

"Honorable..." Pleased with himself, Headmon turns back to the mirror and studies the changes for a long time, turning his head this way and that, scrutinizing his slightly thinner nose, chiseled jaw, granite chin.

Headmon takes off the kimono and tosses it to Reynolds who folds it over his arm. Wearing only silk undershorts he turns back to the mirror and stands studying his new figure, flexing his muscles, checking out his chest and stomach. He turns to one side then the other. He turns around and looks over his shoulder at his backside. Pleased indeed, he looks at the doctor and nurse.

"Well done. Take a rest. Collect 10 bonus hours of premium Banding time each."

Relieved, the doctor and nurse depart quickly and quietly.

294

"Reynolds!"

"Sir."

"Approach."

Isham crosses the room to Headmon who is still standing at the full-length mirror.

"No, no. Come closer."

"Yes, sir."

"Look at me."

Isham regards Headmon politely and professionally.

"No, no, Reynolds, *examine!*"

"Ah. Yes, sir." Hands clasped behind his back, Reynolds leans for-ward and regards Headmon's face as if it were an unusual artifact of some kind.

"Well? What do you think?"

"*Very* handsome, sir," the butler nods approvingly.

"Yes, but is it like? Is it very like?"

"Sir?"

Headmon studies his new butler.

"Answer the question."

"Sir, I don't understand your reference."

"I'm asking you if something's missing. Is something missing?"

"Nothing of which I am aware, sir."

Exasperated, Headmon turns back to the mirror.

"Is it very like the man who fell into SubTurra with my Skye?!"

Reynolds blinks then gets it.

"Ah. Oh, yes, indeed, sir. From the adverts it is very like indeed, sir. Your new self."

"Call my aestheticians," Headmon is delighted. "I'll have them now."

He moves back toward the examination table, brushing by Esa on the way and smiling mischievously down at the girl. Reynolds opens the door to the hall and beckons. The aestheticians enter the examination room and silently position their equipment. Headmon sits on the table.

"Leave me, all three of you, with my artists. But keep my secret for the official unveiling, which will happen soon."

Esa, wide-eyed and trembling, follows Isham/Reynolds and leads Curanda out of the room to a service lift. As the lift door closes, the three of them look at each other.

We must try to warn Skye.

***

The situation room directly beneath the bridge of Command Ship Phoenix is lit only from outside – different-colored beams cast by vessels of all kinds, arriving, being serviced, departing for the wormhole. Occupying the shifting shadows are Captain Beryl Porter and her cadet-aide, Ero Mezon. Otherwise the room is empty.

Defined by a circular floor-to-ceiling nu-glass outer wall, a featureless ceiling and dark blue carpeting, the room is furnished with a big round table and chairs, one for each staff-level officer. Captain Porter is standing on one side of the room close to the wall, looking up and out. Cadet First Class Ero Mezon is standing at attention on the other side of the room.

Upstairs, the bridge is busy with all hands on deck, tending the myriad details that accompany new orders from the four Space States. Well-informed commoners have voted their response to the crisis with Great City. Though not unanimous, the decision is a clear majority call for action.

So Captain Beryl Porter has excused herself from the deck for a moment and asked Cadet Mezon to accompany her here because something is on her mind and it won't wait any longer. Without turning she speaks and he's not certain it's to him.

"I've never sent people out to kill or possibly die, only to bring others back from peril."

"Yes, mam." He clears his throat softly.

"Let's get to it, cadet." She doesn't turn around.

He snaps to attention. She sighs.

"Stand at ease."

"Yes, mam." He tries.

Beryl Porter turns from the window, her face grave with responsibility.

"I don't have mental space to accommodate the fact that two of the people out there in harm's way are your mother and father. It's a distraction I don't need so here are your choices. You can return to S.S. Hope for some R&R until this crisis is resolved with no penalty in terms of your schooling. Or you can go on exercise with a team of trainers and cadets out by S.S. Ulysses.

"A shuttle leaves for Hope in two hours. The team of trainers and cadets is being held up for your decision. H-V cruiser Everest. A shuttle is waiting to take you there if that's your choice. Go get your kit and be on one or the other of those two ships."

Ero Mezon stands at rigid attention. Captain Porter looks outside again then turns to go up to the bridge. She stops near his shoulder and stands looking behind him, her face granite.

"I never flew with a better sailor than Ingrid Steele. Two of the Falcons have served with me. And your mother saved my life." She softens, looks at Ero. "I hear your father is a good man, much respected by Pilar. I take this personal, cadet."

"Yes, mam."

Beryl Porter steps back so she can see the boy's face. He's looking straight ahead, stoic, braced, trying not to blink. She knows her decision is the right one.

"What do you intend to do?"

"Mam, if I could have a few minutes."

"Of course. Go get your kit. Avoid the bridge – no sense feeling even more conspicuous. Make your decision and inform your proctor." She pats his shoulder. "Blessings."

"Thank you, mam." Braced, he blinks back tears.

Captain Beryl Porter salutes crisply. The salute is returned in kind. She takes the spiral stairs up to the bridge. Cadet First Class Ero Mezon stands for a moment looking at nothing, examining his options.

***

Unlike her predecessor, Karin Lassiter Kohl has always been too disciplined to overuse mood-swingers. Thus she was deposited in the dirty white cell quite sober and so she struggles to remain – in the very same cell once occupied by George Biggs Boltin. With a hole in the floor and a faucet that no longer works because of half-measures. And tight surveillance.

Lassiter has switched into a new gear. Love will do that, open one to all human possibilities. Captive, she's energized. Focused and full of purpose: to get them out alive and go…

297

Where?

One thing at a time. That question can be dealt with after she's come up with a plan to get out. Meanwhile, there's no surrendering to negative possibilities even though the cell hasn't been cleaned since Boltin was taken out and even though she was stripped of her steward's clothes, but not her underwear, and given his old stinking robe, which was tossed in a corner.

Dav Baxter is in the cell next to her. She saw them put him in, awake and struggling. She can hear him occasionally screaming, desperate with panic. Pounding on the door. Rebelling against his absent captors. When he's quiet, she talks to him, calls, tries to sooth.

The cell is hot. The water supply is insufficient though she pounds on the door demanding more. Despite this, Lassiter never stops moving, pacing, doing pushups and stretches, aerobics. That's how she thinks.

***

Aestheticians finished with him, Kimono flying, Headmon rushes out of the lift into his penthouse loft, which is done after the ancient southwestern style. The butler is right behind him, carrying a large hand mirror. Headmon strides to one wall and flips back a small framed masterpiece to reveal a control panel.

"Turn away, Reynolds," he says playfully. "You're not to see the code. You're not to understand the lock that opens the door to my treasure."

"Yes, sir."

Isham/Reynolds turns away and looks out the window that is one wall of the penthouse. Forty-seven floors below is a great rectangle of park in the middle of an endless city. It's winter outside despite the season everywhere else in the residence at this particular moment. Outside from here, everything is holiday white in the glare of high day.

When Headmon has finished punching in a lengthy code, pop, the window goes dark and opaque. With a loud hissing sound, the wall is hydraulically raised and slides back across the ceiling out off the way. Bright steam billows out of the newly opened space, eclipsing what's inside.

"Come."

Headmon strides into the steam followed by the butler with the mirror. When the steam clears, what remains is a space rather like an oversized bank vault in the center of which is a large transparent capsule with complicated and noisy medical technology.

"Shhhhh, this is my secret," Headmon whispers. "No one knows where he is or how to find him. Only me. And now you."

They approach the capsule and look down at its occupant – emaciated and barely alive. Kept alive when it seems he would rather not be. Isham opens as quickly as he can and sends a message meant to pierce.

R'io, Skye lives! We've come for you!

There's no response and Isham doesn't know if the hot message got through and has no time to try again because duty calls. Headmon's hand is out for the mirror, fingers snapping impatiently. Reynolds holds the mirror up and positions himself so that Headmon can see his own reflection as well as his model. Turning this way and that, Headmon looks at R'io, inert in the capsule, then at himself in the mirror.

"Oh, very like," he whispers delighted, comparing.

Reynolds nods appreciatively but does not speak because he has not been spoken to.

"She won't know the difference."

Admiring himself, Headmon turns one way then the other. He studies R'io. He studies his own image in the mirror.

"She won't know the difference will she, Reynolds?"

"No sir."

"But how am I to know what he was *like*, Reynolds? How am I to assume his air, his attitude? How am I to go beyond the merely physical? Answer me."

"Perhaps Mr. Headmon migh consider consulting Miss Curanda. She did mention how honorable you are now and how such transformation occurs in more than one's flesh."

"Oh, very good. Bring her to me now."

"Yes, sir." Isham bows slightly, turns and exits the penthouse to fetch Curanda, betraying nothing about what he just saw, what he now knows.

***

Dull earth small below them, Lt. Pilar Mezon and the other five Falcons are in stationary V-formation about 100 nautical miles from the transfer station, which cannot be seen from here nor can the moon though its glow is powerful. In stealth-mode, the Falcons blend in with their environ-ment, eerily becoming evident when they move to make an adjustment or check something.

Nobody's talking. Usually they chatter and joke around, mocking the danger. Now they're quiet, serious, using whatever grounds them at such moments though there has never been a moment such as this before, a time to possibly use their skills for the killing others.

Sgt. Quester Bates is in the ambulance on point and murmuring over her prayer beads. She's visible in the roomy cockpit of what resembles an ancient van with windrider technology in the form of a big fin along its spine. Since she's inside she wears only an abbreviated pressure suit and helmet that could keep her alive for several hours should something happen to her craft.

Rogers and Kim are steady on the scooters, positioned high above the ambulance at a considerable distance apart. The scooters look like what they are named for except that they're bigger and sleeker and loaded with technology – spigots and nozzles and such on the fenders and handlebars.

McCloud and Salonnen are on the sleds way down below from this perspective and spread out even farther. The sleds are multi-purpose vehicles almost like flatbed trucks but instead of a cab they have what looks like the body of a high performance motorcycle with a fin of windrider technology on the tail. All wear space gear that is similar to Pilar's but theirs is more substantial and includes pads and shielding.

The shuttle from earth has docked. According to the shape-changers Pilar left behind, four humans who give off funny readings left their shuttle, entered the transfer station then went into the Emerson, which they are now tearing apart for some reason. Pilar holds the team back, resisting the urge to approach and rattle some bones.

Can't do. That would tip their hand and they've been ordered to stay in stealth-mode until otherwise informed. So, energized and focused, the Falcons wait.

***

Skye and Rogue follow the lead vehicle and half of the troops through a rolling metal door into another enormous hanger where another company of troops is standing at attention, armed and ready, on the left and on the right. In front of them, at the far end of the hanger, is a line of uniformed brass. The lead vehicle peels away and they're approaching an officer who has stepped forward.

"Halt!"

They do.

The officer is wearing crisp leather fatigues. Behind him and his staff is a wide mote of seriously disturbed water that smells like acid. On the far side of the moat is a rusty iron wall, ground to ceiling, side to side. In the cen-ter of the wall, indicated only by its dark seam, is what appears to be a huge closed gate.

The officer raises a hand and signals. A soft explosion of electricity inside the iron wall is followed by sounds of heavy bolts retracting from impressive slots then hydraulic hissing. The gate opens slowly, a drawbridge, lowering. And the threshold exposed is filled with a rippling veil of blue-white light so dense and bright that what's beyond it is obscured.

At another signal, a squad from the company of new troops moves out across the drawbridge. As they pass through the gate and the rippling veil of blue-white light, their skeletons are visible for an instant inside the armor. Those guards disappear on the other side of the veil. After two more squads move through, the officer signals Skye and Rogue to go next.

Skye reaches for Rogue's hand.

"No contact." It's the female who could be everywhere so intimately god-like is the sound.

Skye releases Rogue's hand and they walk side by side across the drawbridge. As they step into the blinding veil of blue light they freeze for an instant, looking at each other – blink – skeleton-Skye and skeleton-Rogue then they're on the other side, still blinking.

Eyes adjust.

They look around. The troops are nowhere in evidence and forgotten because Skye One-Who-Wanders and Rogue champion of champions have stepped into a vast landscape of willow-dotted hills beyond which are snowcapped crags and bluest of skies busy with white cloud-traffic. Ahead, at the end of a long curved road lined with palms and bright bougainvillea, is an enormous, complicated structure. The residence.

Sprawling and wide rather than tall, the residence is an elegant arrangement of glass and metal planes nested on a breast of hill. The structure gives the illusion of something about to take flight. Floors and wings hang suspended over bubbling streams, carefully positioned boulders and exotic plants.

"It is said that no one leaves here alive." Rogue leans and whispers then waits a moment and leans closer. "I was testing the surveillance. That no one interrupted once we got inside means it's subtle here. Take care."

"Welcome to the residence." It's a new voice in the air, female and friendly. "Please proceed up the drive."

Skye and Rogue glance at one another and start walking unaccompanied toward the perfectly balanced structure. As they round a curve they are able to see waiting for them at the end of the drive a line of footmen who are wearing long butter-yellow satin coats and silver vests with white ruffles at their wrists and throats and knickers and gray silk hose and patent shoes with fancy buckles. Swords in scabbards attached to ornate sashes hang angled at their thighs.

Lining both sides of the road are ceremonial guards with bright red trousers and black military tunics and tall brown fur hats held in place by gold chains that run from ear to ear under their noses. The guards hold identical banners of black satin with a gold eagle emerging from flame and the words "NEVER YIELD!" blazoned crimson across the whole.

***

When the groups were formed back at Mist Canyon and Axl was given his assignment he learned everything he needed to know about what elder Moss's group was supposed to do and how and why but he was not privy to information given the group going into canton Equa. Consequently, he knows very little about survival in SubTurra.

Shortly after entering the outskirts of Equa and joining a stream of immigrants, Axl understood that he was the center of no little attention. The immigrants, all wearing leather, came close – pressed against him reeking of sweat and rotten teeth, wanting to touch his clothes. Frightened but undeterred then finally understanding, the boy slipped into a bathhouse, stole a set of black leathers sizes too big for him, found a shadow, and put them on over his wilderness-people clothes.

Now, Axl is standing in line, one person away from an immigration window. He's overwhelmed by the smells of unwashed people all wearing human skin. He's numbed by their desperation and fear. He's stunned by the blare and images on the overhead screens, images of his da and her, Skye, the reason his da is here. And in addition to everything else he needs desperately to relieve himself and has not because he didn't want to lose his place in line.

The middle-aged man in front of Axl is pleading with the same clerk who admitted Isham. The man is insisting that he's a skilled jester and comedian. He's trying to convince the clerk that he should be on the Banding spectrum because he makes people laugh in this dismal world. The clerk is tired of the man's aggressive insistence.

"Enforcement!"

Two burly guards arrive immediately to take the man away. He doesn't want to go. He wriggles and tap dances and sings, trying to make everyone around them laugh. To no effect. He's ignored. To laugh now would be to draw the wrong kind of attention. So the guards use force and take the man away.

"Next."

Axl stands dumbstruck, looking after the man.

"NEXT!"

He leaps to the window and stands tall and straight. He clears his throat. The clerk looks down through eyes that are large and dark and glit-tering with medication. Impatient, he holds out a hand.

"Documents!"

Axl's mouth drops open.

"...I..."

"Gimme your documents, kid."

"...I..." Axl pats the pockets of the strange clothes, looking for documents. He finally finds and pulls out a battered leather ID card. Relieved, without looking at it, he hands the card to the clerk who squints at it then at the boy.

"What are you doing here? Where are you from? What do you want?"

"...I...I..."

"Why so nervous, kid? You need some Banding time? Meds?"

303

The clerk squints at the ID card again then at the boy. "What's your name?"

"…I…"

"You got a name, right?"

"Yes."

"What is it?

"Axl."

"Axl?"

"…Yes."

"Hummm. Says here your name is Mikkos. That don't sound much like 'Axl' to me."

Sometimes, Source is utterly clear even to the most obtuse. And sometimes when that happens, it's like getting hit by a falling grand piano.

In one flash, the boy understands that he should not be here trying to do this. He understands that his grand da was right to exclude him from the group going inside canton Equa. He understands that he has made a terrible mistake in judgment. He understands that he has let his da and his team and their purpose down, perhaps irretrievably.

The clerk looks at the boy and makes a quick decision.

"ENFORCEMENT!"

Axl turns around wildly. Then he's bolting across the immigration hall, pushing his way through clumps and lines of people.

"HALT!"

Metal whistles shriek. Axl can hear steps pounding behind him, getting closer as people move out of the way for the guards but not for Axl. Someone catches his long blond braid. Hands grip his shoulders and lift him up then slam him down on the ground. Then he's yanked to his feet, soiling himself in both ways.

"You ain't goin nowhere, kid, except with us."

Two big enforcers wearing leather uniforms and helmets, with grit-stained faces turn him around roughly and, snap, clasp his hands behind his back, too tight. That done, his feet are kicked out from under him. He lands on his face and chips a tooth. He kicks and struggles as each guard picks up a foot. Then he's dragged on his belly to a holding cell.

***

Wide stone steps lead up to a deeply shaded porch that spans the width of the front of the residence. Skye's head is throbbing, pounded on from inside, almost blinding her. She looks around.

"Real?"

"Apparently," Rogue whispers back.

A tall dignified gentleman steps forward from shadow. He's formally dressed in charcoal gray and stops to stand in front of the massive door waiting to receive them in place of Headmon who is maintaining his sense of control at the moment by observing others without their knowledge.

The gentleman clears his throat. Skye looks. The pounding in her head is fierce.

Blinking, she sees an older man who is tall and thin, clean-shaven, with bright white hair too short to comb. Blink. He's wearing shiny black pumps, gray-striped trousers, a swallowtail coat, a dove-gray vest, a crisp white shirt with a spread collar and a pewter-colored four-in-hand tie, per-fectly knotted. After bowing ever so slightly, he speaks and she hears a voice more familiar than her own.

"Mr. Headmon is temporarily indisposed. I am the butler, Reynolds, at your service. On Mr. Headmon's behalf, welcome to the residence."

Skye can't breathe. Can't move. Rogue looks puzzled then concerned by her traveling companion's dumb-struck reaction to being here. The butler clears his throat, handsigning most subtly.

~ Do Not Reveal. ~

"Mr. Headmon has asked me to take care that you are satisfied with the arrangements." He repeats the handsign.

~ Do not reveal. ~

Trembling, she nods.

"A private suite has been prepared for each of you," he nods to Rogue.

"That won't do." The champion of champions is imperi-ous.

Skye can't breathe. Her heart is beating too fast and too hard. She can't control the trembling and something is welling up in her that will not be contained. She looks at the man who introduced himself as Headmon's butler. How can this be? She raises her face, grimacing, unable to hold what wants to pour out.

"The agreement is that the challenger and I are not to be separated." Rogue is firm.

"Mr. Headmon instructed flexibility should minor differences arise." Isham/Reynolds nods patiently then smiles.

"Good." Rogue glances at Skye and sees her jaw clenched, face raised, eyes closed tight. A tear has leaked and is running down or maybe it's perspiration. "Can you not see that she's exhausted and needs to rest?"

"Indeed. Please, follow me."

Without warning even to her, Skye seems to stumble forward. The butler manages to break the fall just as Rogue appears in front of him crouched with the heel of her rigid hand but a hair's breath from the end of his nose and ready to kill. The two of them look at each other, for a moment then, hands out in a gesture of retreat, Isham straightens up and steps back.

Rogue relaxes somewhat. She stands and bows formally.

"You have my apology. Such a response is instinctive for me."

"I take no offense, mam."

Rogue leans down and picks Skye up like a baby.

"...I'm...okay..." Skye's protestations are feeble.

Rogue looks at Reynolds, "Let's go."

He steps aside and sweeps an arm out to indicate the door then leads them into a cool foyer with a skylight and a glass lift. Held by Rogue, Skye One-Who-Wanders slides in and out of awareness during the ride as the lift ascends vertically, horizontally and diagonally, turning slowly on its axis to reveal vistas exquisitely framed by exterior planes and angles of the resi-dence. Isham One-Who-Waits, now Reynolds, stands near a control panel, hands clasped behind his back, chin up, looking straight ahead.

The lift stops and opens onto a suite of rooms that hang out over emerald lawn sloping down to a large mirroring lake and a dock with several small sailboats. On the far side of the lake is a cliff with wide waterfalls and above, sky taking on the first brassy glow of sunset. None of the rest of the residence is visible from here.

Rogue, with Skye, is led across deep carpet and gleaming wood through a spacious lounge area with comfortable furniture, potted plants and elegant arrangements of fresh and fragrant flowers. They're led past a kitchen/dining area to a hall at each end of which is an open bedroom door.

She's carried into a bedroom and lowered onto a canopied bed whose sides can be closed with heavy drapes now artfully pulled back. The drapes and bedding are blood red. She places a forearm over her

306

eyes and turns her head away, swallowing nausea.

"There's a full bath in here." Ever formal and professional, the man now called Reynolds gestures to an open doorway then moves to indicate a wall that is actually a broad expanse of sliding doors. "A closet with clothing to fit Miss Skye." He turns to Rogue. "An attendant will bring garments in your size to the other bedroom."

"Don't bother. We have our own clothes."

"Very well," he nods. "If there's nothing more I'll leave you for now to rest and freshen up." He turns to go then stops. "Oh, Mr. Headmon instructed me to inform you that while you are guests of the residence you are not live on the Banding spectrum."

"Thank you," Skye whispers, looking at him, trying not to reveal.

Rogue glances at Skye then at the butler. Then she moves off to inspect the suite. At the doorway, One-who-waits pauses and sends clearly to Skye's awareness.

Surveillance everywhere. Do not reveal. Elixir in bathroom cabinet, red bottle. Use it.

"After you've rested and bathed I'll return to fetch you both for the welcoming." And the butler is gone.

Skye One-Who-Wanders sits up to remove her doublet, shoes and socks. Nauseated, she sinks back on the bed and can hear Rogue in the bathroom, opening and closing cabinet doors. The champion emerges and goes to the closet.

Rogue slides the doors open, exposing a large room that smells of cedar. Inside are racks of clothes for all occasions and rows of shoes. A waist-high square island occupies the center of the room. The drawers are filled with accessories, silk underwear, stockings, sex and sleep-wear. Racks of shoes swivel out of the way and are replaced by full-length mirrors with adjustable lighting. After quickly examining the racks and each drawer Rogue emerges and slides the doors closed.

"Would you rather be alone or have me stay?" Her tone is without preference.

"Alone, please." Skye is about to gag.

"Call if you need me." She turns to leave the room. "Door open or closed?"

"Closed, thank you."

And Rogue is gone.

On her back, Skye struggles out of her trousers then flings off her shirt. She rushes from bed to bathroom where she vomits until there's nothing left. She sits and relieves herself of great toxic quantities even though she hasn't eaten all that much lately. When she's done, after figuring out how to use the spritzer to wash and the blower to dry, she stands, gropes for the sink, rinses her mouth then washes her face with icy, living water.

Trembling, she dries her hands and face on a towel that feels like vel-vet. In front of her, above the sink with gleaming fixtures, are three mirrors, cabinet doors. She's naked but for her undershirt and green in all three until she opens them and disappears.

Inside one cabinet are feminine hygiene products and perfumes. She closes that door because the blend of sweet fragrances makes her feel like throwing up again. Inside the middle cabinet are tools of oral hygiene, deodorants, lotions, deodorizers, and things she has no idea what to do with. The last cabinet contains creams and lotions in beautifully shaped, brilliantly colored bottles and jars. One of them in particular draws her attention.

It's a small garnet-colored vial of spun glass with a black silk cord attached so it can be worn around the neck. She picks up the vial, uncaps it, sniffs and is carried back to wilderness-people when they were making the difficult part of a long ascent. This smells similar.

Sip only.

She puts the cord around her neck. She uncaps the vial, raises it for a sip and holds the syrupy liquid in her mouth as long as possible. She recaps the vial and drops it to settle between her breasts.

Swallowing, she returns to the bedroom, picks up her garments and takes them to the back of a long sofa that's positioned for a perfect view out the glass wall. The vista is bathed with sunset. The light is just turning green, yellow and salmon against deepening blue.

How did Isham One-who-waits get in here?

She arranges the garments neatly across the back of the sofa and drapes R'io's belt the way she likes it. Naked but for the belt and the vial on its cord around her neck, she returns to the bed where she releases the heavy drapes and crawls into a cocoon of darkness. She moves to the center and sits legs crossed.

She sips again. Her stomach begins settle but not her thoughts.

Eyes closed, she opens to common-awareness and tries to reach One-who-waits. But she can't settle down. There's only static. Her own static. Like a wall. And though everything is different, she's still the same Skye One-Who-Wanders, infused with yet another purpose.

Do not reveal.

"Aw, man, this kid reeks."

The two enforcers shove Axl into a plain concrete holding cell with a drain in the middle of the floor. They slam the door closed and yank the boy to his feet. He stands head down, numb.

"What a freak, took a dump in his pants and watered all over himself."

"Get these clothes off. Hose him down."

One of the men pulls down the leather pants Axl is wearing.

"What's this...?"

The enforcer pulls the jacket down as far as it will go with Axl's hands bound behind him. Grimacing at the stench, the other enforcer, himself reeking of leather, sweat and rotten teeth, approaches the boy. He reaches out, feels the fabric of Axl's shirt.

"Well lookee here. Fancy pants."

Humiliated, blood on his lips and chin from falling on his face, Axl struggles to hold himself together. The enforcer touches the boy's shirt and looks down into frightened eyes and a face that is clean by SubTurran standards.

"These clothes ain't from this level of SubTurra, boy. We don't have no cloth down here."

"Who are you, boy? Where you from?"

The guards look at each other and suddenly smell bonus Banding time in addition to Axl's stench.

"These clothes has gotta go up the food chain."

"Yeah, who knows? Maybe all the way to the top."

Tears fall as the curious enforcers release his hands and remove the leather jacket then the cloth shirt and doublet. They fasten his hands behind him again. Complaining of the smell, one of them kneels and removes the boy's boots. They jerk both pairs of pants down and off and separate them. The two enforcers step back and look at their prize, now naked with blood on his mouth, tears on his cheeks and waste on his legs.

"Who are you? Where are you from? How come yer wearing cloth?"

Axl doesn't know how to respond.

One of the enforcers puts the leathers Axl stole in an evidence bag and seals it. Then he delicately plucks the soiled stone-people clothes up, drops them into another evidence bag and seals it.

"Swab his wank and sphincter for pathology then hose him down. I'm taking these to the captain."

309

The enforcer in charge departs the holding cell, evidence bags in tow. The remaining enforcer pulls an evidence kit out of a pocket, selects a swab and a vial and turns to Axl.

"Fancy pants."

He runs the swab between Axl's legs and drops it in the vial. He swabs Axl's nose, ears and mouth, drops each specimen similarly. He seals the evidence kit and drops it back in an inside pocket.

The enforcer picks up the business end of a hose that is coiled on the floor. He turns on the wall faucet and starts spraying Axl down with cold water. The boy stands shivering like a frightened animal.

"Bend over."

Axl can't move.

"I said bend over. Turn around."

Axl tries.

When the enforcer is satisfied the boy is relatively clean he turns off the water and drops the hose to the floor with a wet smack. Then he moves to Axl, towering over the boy, and shoves him against the wall. "Who are you? Where you from? How come yer wearing cloth?"

Axl is unable to answer. He's whacked across the face by a fist the size of a baby's head.

"I asked you a question, cheese-brain. Stop that bawlin and answer. How come yer wearing cloth clothes?!"

The door opens and the other enforcer leans in.

"Captain wants to see him right now," he winks at is partner. "This looks good for us, Bud."

Naked and wet, shivering, weeping almost uncontrollably, Axl is taken roughly by the upper arm and led to the next station up the food chain.

***

In Great City, one by one, selected citizen-units of lesser value are culled from the herd and, unbeknownst to them, directed to a cordoned off area in the bottom of NorthEast Quadrant. In the mood and cooperative, those selected find their ways to the appointed place and join a proto-group of one hundred. Experimentation on this group is intended to determine the feasibil-ity of a citizen army.

First, the units are taken off-line, meaning they no longer do what they used to do in workbays. The impact of the loss of the proto-group to the functioning of Great City is evaluated. Adjustments are made. The next step is taken.

The personalized MED regimen for each member of the proto-group is gradually altered. No one knows what will happen when they start trying to change the mood. Thus, the Medical Primes have been instructed to proceed slowly and avoid unnecessary loss of resources.

A large majority of the citizen-units in the proto-group become increasingly energized and agitated. They require more calories and close monitoring. They are no longer cooperative. Their doses are adjusted. A small number of citizen-units in the proto-group become dysfunctional, as though locked in static. Unable to tolerate the mood change, they are removed from the proto-group and attempts are made to normalize them so they can be returned to their former duties.

When the transformation is complete, the proto-group is tested. They're found to be borderline aggressive and difficult to control. The experiment is deemed inconclusive. Based on what was learned with the proto-group, however, it's decided to process a second group of one hundred to see if they can do better.

***

Isham/Reynolds is in attendance as Curanda and Esa work on the now nearly invisible scars on Headmon's face and body. The music is ancient windchimes and gongs and fluttery flutes, nauseatingly serene. Standing in the doorway, Isham withdraws his attention from that scene, opens, and calls.

Elder Martin?

It takes a moment.

Si, here, Isham.

All is in place. Relay to elder Moss. Tell her to begin and follow the trajectory mapped out. Tell her to be most careful the farther east she goes as drones may be on the way. Source-willing...

"Reynolds!" Headmon is snapping his fingers.

Must go.

Source be...

"Yes, sir."

"Is there anything sweet on my new diet?"

"Fresh fruit, sir."

"Bring me a bowl. Sliced. With yogurt. A big bowl."

"Yes, sir."

Reynolds bows politely and leaves Headmon in the capable hands of Curanda and Esa. It's all about timing now. That and clear guidance from Source.

***

The task force for the defense of Great City is meeting in one of the larger conference rooms with rounded walls that are also screens. It's warm and close. The ceiling is low. Individual beams shine anemically down on the Presider and his staff now consisting of Virginia Kahn Baker of Human Resources, Malcolm Pierce Whitaker of Engineering, Magrit Abram Shen of Technology, and Doug Smythe Hews of Medicine.

The one piece of good news is that the arrival of the shape-changers from the transfer station is imminent. Otherwise, the situation is increasingly grim.

"Which brings us to you, HR." The Presider looks pointedly at his head of Human Resources. How are you doing with the citizen army?"

"A second group of 100 has been selected to be withdrawn from the general population. The first group has completed the transformation process. We have some…learning to do."

"Explain."

"It's difficult to get the proper blend of obedience and ferocity. Alphas tend to want it their way and as of now managing that first group is taking a lot of our energy. Medicine is working on adjustments. Pending success with the second group we've begun selecting a larger group of 500."

"Accelerate the transformation process." Reed stands and throws up his hands. "Whatever you do, Virginia, we need an army and we also need to trim the citizen-unit population by a third. Figure out how not to waste that third!"

"Sir," Engineering raises a finger and is recognized again. "I've met with Efficiency. We're already noticing the effect on production

312

of the loss of even this small number of workers…"

"Do you not understand," Reed brings a hand down on the table, "that Great City can no longer support its current population of citizen-units, even cutting back yet again on their rations?!"

"For the sake of productivity may I change the topic?" Doug Smythe Hews of Medicine raises a tentative finger.

Reed looks at Smythe, startled by the man's sudden brass. He nods curtly.

"What is it?"

"Boltin has been down there a while. Our real Prime Researcher was snatched up almost immediately. What do you make of that?"

"What do I make of that?" Reed ruminates. "They're smart. They want to see our hand. But they're not going to see our hand until we're ready to play it."

Eyes closed, smile beatific, Shen decides that this is the moment to bring that beautiful ace out of her sleeve.

"Maybe whoever helped our Prime Researcher isn't there anywhere near point B anymore. Maybe they've gone farther east. Or north."

Reed raises an eyebrow. The others turn and look at Shen, see her porcelain face illumined from directly above by a thin beam of smoky light.

"What makes you say that?" The Presider is curious.

"Maps. I've been studying classified maps from the time of the great collapse. Very interesting." She stands, ignites the tabletop screen and pulls up her file. "By the time of the great collapse there were already many large underground installations," she points to several. "They were built for ancient military, corporate or religious groups. A few of them were located north and east of here several hundred miles."

"Meaning?"

"Meaning it's possible that at least one sizeable population went down around the time the Founders did and stayed down there and is still down there and might have an outpost near Great City. If any of the above is true, they might know a lot about us while we still obviously know nothing about them. It might be time to reconsider the nature of the enemy."

Silence hangs heavy in the room. Nobody breathes. No-body moves. Shen breaks the silence at exactly the right moment.

"In that light, I've taken the liberty of sending several long-range listening drones east and north, way beyond our previous perimeter."

"WHAT?!" It's Whitaker of Engineering, unaware of what his former student has been doing. "That could be why they haven't surfaced to get the bait!"

"The drones were sent a roundabout stealth route."

Shen taps code into her tech-pad and pulls up maps of underground installations, one deep location after another carved out leagues beneath the surface, where threat to Great City could be lurking. And it dawns with cold suddenness on those in the conference room that they must indeed rethink the nature of the enemy.

***

Headmon is alone in his control center. All screens are illumined but he is focused on two images. One is of Reynolds during his physical. He's stripped to shorts and Headmon brings the image closer, to focus on his head and shoulders. Headmon leans to the screen. He magnifies the image, studying two little marks at the base of Reynolds' throat.

Another image is of Skye during her initial treatment. He zooms in from directly overhead to her neck and chest. He brackets the two little scars on her throat and matches them to the marks on Reynolds throat. He checks images of Curanda and Esa. No marks. The man who arrived with Skye One-Who-Wanders doesn't have them, either.

"I'm sending you two images, different people," Headmon leans into a small mic. "They have similar markings in the throat area. Scars, maybe. I want to know what those marks are. Soonest."

***

Skye One-Who-Wanders wakes almost herself again. She parts the heavy drapes around the bed and emerges to darkness, night, aware

314

that she must not reveal. Rounding the foot of the bed she's stopped in her tracks by a fat buttermilk almost-full moon. She's seen them before, of course, moons, back with the navigator. But this one is different. It's perfect, not like semblance at all. Nothing here at the residence is like semblance.

Skirting the sofa she moves to the window and stands looking out for a long time, drinking the night and the stars and the moon and the cliff and the wide glistening waterfalls and the mirroring lake and the dock with three little sailboats tethered bobbing and the lawn rolling up toward her, disappearing somewhere beneath her toes.

This can't be real. Even though it seems to be. It can't be real. But how convincing!

After a moment Skye One-Who-Wanders moves away from the glass wall into the bathroom. She turns on the light, dialing it down to a pleasing softness. She takes off R'io's belt and hangs it on the back of the door. Then she puts the empty vial back where she found it in the cabinet and turns on the water for a shower.

* * *

Surprised by the sudden departure of the earth-shuttle, Lt. Pilar Mezon and the other Falcons pull up to the transfer station and, using magnetics, lock their vehicles against the Emerson's exposed fuselage. According to shape-changers left behind, the transfer station is empty but for the dead Space Staters and the other bodies in the core.

Cautious nonetheless, the Falcons alight their vehicles and one by one float into the Emerson through the still-open hatch, Pilar leading the way without medication to prove to herself that she can at least go far enough back inside to help with the bodies.

Everything is disarrayed, overturned, opened, emptied and floating nonsensically here and there up and down in the zero Gs. But the only thing taken was the supply of shape-changers.

Staying close together, the team follows Pilar to the cabin that contains the bodies. They open the door and look in at the secured bags.

"Let's hurry it up," Pilar points. "Get our people outta here in one trip and go on with the rest of the mission. Deal with the earthlings later."

315

The Falcons work as quickly as they can in weightlessness. They unfasten the five bodies from the wall of the cabin and tether them in a long chain. They guide the train of bodies out of the cabin down the corridor to the open hatch. It takes a bit of doing to get all of them outside and then into pressurized slots in the aft section of the ambulance. Then they're done.

"Alright, we got no orders on Great City's dead so we're leaving them here for now." Pilar heaves in deep breaths, relieved to be outside again. "Bates and Rogers, take the bodies back to Mohawk then meet up with us for phase-two."

"Copy-clear."

The Falcons board their vehicles, release their magnetics and separate from the body of the Emerson. Bates and Rogers head back toward the moon and on around to Mohawk. Pilar, McCloud, Kim and Salonnen veer off in the other direction toward earth.

***

Wearing surface gear, elder Moss, Schiara and Wim quickly exit a portal into cold night. Running, they fan out and climb separate dunes. At the top, each raises a baton-like beacon that is ignited for several seconds, de-activated and stowed. Then the three run back toward the portal.

At least that's the plan.

But it didn't work with Wim. It was ill advised to send him out onto the surface in Axl's place but the boy pleaded and elder Moss acquiesced. Blind but with the radar of a bat down in stone-realm, Wim is helpless on the surface because he can't hear. Ash swallows sound.

Meanwhile, far overhead a satellite now programmed to deep-scan everything in its path picks up an anomalous signal. Then another. And another. Three of them. Each of the same duration. Then nothing again.

The raw data is forwarded to the Security Primes. A chime goes off in the new head of Security's office but he's in a meeting with the Presider and the taskforce. The Security Primes find him there. A little red light starts flashing and an alarm throbbing on his tech-pad.

"Excuse me."

Morton Edwards Hale turns away from the others and mutes

316

his tech-pad. He's a bit young for the post but he was second on HR's shortlist of candidates to replace George Bigg's Bolton way back when and he was the one guarding ambassador Baxter and is the one who turned in Lassiter. Shen's solid endorsement sealed the decision.

Mouth open, Edwards is staring down at his tech-pad screen. It's a hardball, coming his way.

Back on the surface, Wim is frantic, running hard toward where he thinks the portal should be. Inside, elder Moss knows not to wait for him any longer because something is wrong.

"Stay here," she instructs Schiara.

Elder Moss bolts outside and looks around. She spots Wim, zigzagging off in the wrong direction. She starts running toward him, sending a sharp pulse through his awareness.

STOP!

Bewildered, he spins around, orienting to elder Moss who is scrambling up the side of a dune toward him. Lurching, she grabs his cloak and drags him back toward the portal.

When they're finally inside, Schiara slams the portal closed. Elder Moss and Wim stand bent over, hands on knees until they can move again then they're following Schiara, hurrying down, down to where they can take off the surface gear, don their big packs and go on to the next point of egress.

"What happened, Wim?" Facemask off, elder Moss takes him by the shoulders.

"I don't know." He looks up at her, his face ashen. "I just...couldn't figure out how to know where I was."

"That's it for you on the surface."

"But..."

"No!" She raises a hand, palm out to him, a stone-people sign meaning this discussion is over and which he has no trouble reading or, rather, hearing, now that they're back inside.

"But we need another person," he insists.

"We will adjust," she whispers. "Let's go."

Staying on schedule, the three of them scramble through veins in stone, heading farther east and slightly north. And the elder can feel her old knee injury starting to complain a bit. No problem. She'll brace it and rest it when she can.

At the same time Great City's third head of Security since the crisis began looks up from his tech-pad.

"We have sightings confirmed by satellites. Three of them.

Repeated several times."

Members of the task force stir and glance quickly at Reed, at one another then at the new head of Security. Young, fleshy and pale with baby-fine colorless hair, Edwards seems as adept as anyone at scrambling up a steep greased learning curve.

"Just now. Three beacons were ignited northeast of here by three bio-forms."

Suddenly inspired, Edwards activates the desktop screen. He looks for and finds a spot on one of the maps.

"Here and," he pulls up one of Shen's underground installation maps, places the two maps side by side then superimposes them. "And here. It's a match. Those signals came from directly above an underground installation that was and mabe is as big as a sizeable city. It could be the location of our concern."

***

Showered and edgy, Skye One-Who-Wanders moves from the bath-room into the bedroom where she puts on her old stone-people clothes and eases R'io's belt over her head. Then she takes a big breath and goes off in search of Rogue.

The other bedroom door is open but the champion of champions is not in there. She's not in the kitchen though there's evidence of tea having been made because a clean cup is in the drainer. Ah.

Rogue is in the lounge area hanging suspended from a beam in the ceiling, using a few straps for handles and working out every muscle in her body. Wearing a black T-shirt and briefs, the champion of champions is illumined by full-moonlight. She glistens like blue silk and when she's finished, still hanging by one wrist, she unfastens the other straps and lets them fall to the floor. Then she drops down without making a sound or causing the nearby leafy plant to tremble. She stands hip cocked, long arms at her waist, relaxed and alert.

"You have recovered?"

"Yes."

"What happened?"

"Fear maybe," Skye shrugs.

"Hum. Are you ready to be welcomed?" Rogue's tone is

318

sarcastic.

Skye shrugs, makes no other reply.

"Then let's find out what Headmon has in mind and how to survive it. I'll shower and dress." And the champion of champions is gone.

Skye wanders into the kitchen, opens the fridge, finds juice and pours a glass. Between slugs she hears the shower in Rogue's bedroom. She finishes the juice, washes the glass and puts it in the drainer. As she's going back to the lounge area there's a polite knock on the door and the shower is turned off.

"Come," she murmurs, squinting out the window/mirror at moonlit waterfalls across the lake.

The door opens. Isham One-Who-Waits now Reynolds steps inside. She can see his reflection in the glass. Dressed as before, standing in the entryway, door open behind him. She turns and smiles as at a stranger. She flicks a finger to her head, signing ever so subtly.

~ Comprehende. ~

~ Expect the unexpected. ~ To mask the sign, he pats a pocket and smiles at himself as though he's found what he was looking for.

Rogue enters the lounge area wearing comfortable trousers and a soft sweater both of dark green. She turns to Reynolds. He bows politely.

"If you will please follow me? Mr. Headmon thought you might like to walk through the residence rather than take the lift. That way you'll see more and begin to learn your way around."

"Lead." Rogue shrugs.

Elsewhere in the residence, Headmon is alone in his bunker. The staccato first movement of a Bach piano concerto is bouncing in the shadows. But his attention is elsewhere, on Skye. He is examining her on several screens from all angles as she's being delivered to the proper floor with Rogue by the new butler, what's his name.

Oops.

Frowning slightly, Headmon leans forward and reverses the images on one of the screens, going back to the moment the butler arrived to fetch his prize.

The knock.

"Come."

The butler enters the suite and remains at the door. Professional and impersonal – Reynolds, that's his name. Or is it? Skye turns from the window and looks at the butler as at a stranger.

319

She flicks at something on her temple then rubs that place. The butler pats his vest as though looking for something then smiles, having found it.

What?

What was he looking for? What could he possibly be looking for here where everything is provided?

Headmon pulls up two images, one of Reynolds and one of Skye, naked heads and shoulders. He zooms in on the puncture wounds. According to the researchers, those are insect bites – his old, hers fresh – from something very big. He leans back and smiles at how enjoyable it is to be interested in something. Then he returns to real-time images of Skye and Rogue and the butler stepping out of the lift onto the proper floor.

Captivated again, Headmon pours a glass of very old wine and sips as, elsewhere in the residence Skye and the other two meander across an arched bridge over a koi pond and enter a series of dark rooms lined with big aquariums that are filled with brilliantly colored fish of all sizes. They're led through aviaries filled with different kinds of birds that are as brightly colored as the fish and quite noisy. They move through a greenhouses filled with flowers not to be outdone by fish or fowl – orchids, roses, fragrant herbs, exotic cacti in full bloom then ferns.

"Real?" Skye asks Rogue who shrugs, equally impressed.

"Oh yes," Reynolds stops and turns back. "The residence is called The Ark because everything here is real."

"The Ark?"

"A term from the distant past. Mr. Headmon is the caretaker of all that remains of the previous dispensation. Each Headmon lives out a sacred trust to save what must not be allowed to perish, sheltering it, sequestering it, keeping it safe. A noble enterprise, don't you think?"

Smiling enigmatically, Reynolds turns and continues the tour by leading them into a large room with a high ceiling and hollow quiet. The floor is dark marble. Their footsteps echo crisp and clear. Comfortable padded benches form a square in the center of the room so one can sit and study or ponder or drift.

"This is only one of Mr. Headmon's galleries."

Paintings.

Large and small, light and dark, blaring and subdued, perfectly framed and hung and lit, some of them familiar. Rapidly scanning data from the archives, Skye One-Who-Wanders pulls up files and identifies what she's seen before but only as technological reproductions that were nothing like what's around her now. The depth and luster of the actual colors is almost blinding.

Then she hears something. From overhead. Then from all around. A fullness that becomes sound. Soft at first. Then louder. Clear. She gasps. Her head snaps up.

Music.

Filling the space at a perfect volume, coming from everywhere.

She turns around, scanning, and sees no source for the sound. She stops, lowers her head and listens intently. After several more phrases she looks up at Isham and whispers.

"...Bach?"

"Yes," he nods, politely. "Concerto for Piano and orchestra."

"No. 3 in D major, second movement."

"How do you know this?" Rogue's mouth drops open.

Skye turns around again, slowly. Listening, she approaches a piece and studies it for a moment.

"Giotto," she whispers, not looking at the brass legend. "*Lamentation*. 1305 ancient era."

"Yes," Reynolds nods.

Rogue looks astonished as sometimes listening, sometimes looking, Skye moves slowly from piece to piece, able to identify some by memory from the archives.

Bosch. Caravaggio. Rembrandt. Goya.

Each one steals her breath in a different way. Curious, she turns to Reynolds.

"These are copies, of course."

"Oh, no. These are the paintings themselves. Remember, this is The Ark. They were saved, some at the last moment, and have been passed from Headmon to Headmon as caretaker of all that remains."

Skye nods thoughtfully, suddenly aware of Rogue's intense focus. Then she turns and scans the gallery. "Am I free to return here?"

"Mr. Headmon said that you are to be free in the residence."

"Then I've seen enough for now. I would like to meet him, please. Without delay."

"Very well," Reynolds gestures to the exit. "We are adjacent to the main hall."

He leads the two women out of the gallery into a large airy foyer. Reynolds crosses the space and knocks on the door.

***

The captain for enforcement at this entry-point to canton Equa is standing at his desk ignoring the stench as he looks down into the evidence bag and scrutinizes Axl's clothes. Wiry and rodent-like, his eyes are dark, intense and close together. His face is long and narrow. His skin has a yel-lowish tint beneath the film of stone-dust that covers everything in SubTurra. Dyed black hair and a pencil-thin mustache are waxed and shiny. Wearing a rust-colored uniform, he smells of leather and roses.

"Hummmm…"

He zips the bag closed and moves it to one side of his desk. He puts his feet up on the desk and sits tapping a thumbnail against two long front teeth as he studies the fine specimen standing naked in front of his desk.

"Interesting."

Not yet quite a man, the boy is tall and well built. His face and body hair are still downy golden fuzz. He looks terrified. Lost. Like he's done something horribly wrong. This is a guilty boy.

Guilty of what?

Handing over an ID card that belongs to somebody else? Running? Fighting with the guards? Such things are commonplace. Routine.

But not the clothes. The clothes are most unusual. The clothes are so unusual, in fact, that the captain has never seen or touched cloth before. Cloth is for the most privileged. Only they can afford it.

"Where you from?" The captain's voice is smooth, oily, like his hair.

Axl does not respond. He just stands there naked and shivering, bound hands covering his genitals. Wretched, ashamed and completely lost, he is clearly not SubTurran.

"Where'd you get those clothes?"

The boy is silent.

"You'd do best to answer me, Axl, is it? That's the name you used at immigration. The clothes, Axl, where'd you get them?"

The boy shrugs.

"You know why I ask?"

Axl shakes his lowered head no. The captain drops his feet to the floor. He stands and comes around to the front of the desk and stops an arm's length away with his hands behind his back. When he speaks this time, his voice is soft and full of intimacy Axl doesn't understand.

"Good looking boy like you. I can make it easier as we travel up the food chain, and travel up we must. Or I can make it difficult. Your choice. Now, back to the clothes. You know why I asked about them?"

Axl shakes his head no.

"I asked because most people in SubTurra don't wear cloth. Cloth is for rich folks. Most people wear skin. Human skin. Did you know that?"

Axl turns his head away and swallows nausea.

"Hummm, I guess you didn't." The captain tilts his head, raises a plucked eyebrow. "That leaves us with several options then, doesn't it. "Let's see," he ticks the options off on his fingers. "Either you're from rich folk. Or you stole the clothes like you stole the leathers. Or you're not SubTurran. Which is it?"

Shivering, Axl shrugs. The captain chuckles and strokes the boy's cheek.

"Nice clean skin."

Axl shudders. The captain runs a hand down the boy's chest.

"Good muscle tone. Better than most."

The captain comes closer. Axl steps back. The captain smiles.

"We have ways of getting information from people whether they want us to have it or not. If you cooperate, I'll make life easier for you as long as you're in my custody. Do you know what that means?"

Axl shakes his head no. There's a long silence. Then the captain steps closer and tilts Axl's chin up so he can see the boy's face.

"Open your eyes."

Axl looks somewhere in the vicinity of the captain's chest.

"Look at me."

Axl does. The captain studies the boy's eyes.

"Amazing eyes. Full of life. Vivid blue. Sad. Why are you sad? What have you done?"

Axl closes his eyes against tears.

"What have you done, Axl? That was the name you gave the clerk, right? Where are you from?"

323

The captain waits. Axl remains mute. The captain sighs and moves around behind the boy to lock the office door. Then he leads Axl to the desk, sweeps the bag of soiled clothes off onto the floor and bends the boy facedown over the desk.

"I'm going to have you now. I hope you like it so we can enjoy each other. Utultimately, however, it doesn't matter whether you like it or not. I take my pleasure where and how I want. And I like it when they're unwilling, when they're afraid."

The captain takes off his uniform jacket. He unlaces his trousers. He approaches the boy from behind, stroking and purring.

"…No…" Axl whispers, no longer fighting the tears. "…No, Please…"

"Yes, boy. I'm going to teach you a few things. Just relax. We'll start one way and finish another. And, Axl, you will please me whether you want to or not."

***

Isham/Reynolds opens the main hall's big double doors and steps through the threshold then to one side, leaving the two women exposed in the doorway as he raises his chin for the announcement.

"Mr. Headmon, this is Miss Skye One-Who-Wanders and Rogue, champion of champions!"

Skye gasps and struggles to keep her balance. So does Rogue.

A tall slender man is standing with his back to them in front of a wall that is both mirror and window. He's reflected in the glass along with everything behind him. He's wearing stone-people clothes. His hair is sun-bleached red, tied at the nape of his neck in a ponytail that hangs down between his shoulder blades.

The man is staring at Skye in the glass. She's studying his back then his front, reflected in the mirror. She stares at him framed by the reflection of the room, with Reynolds closing the door behind her and Rogue beside her and, through that image, moonlit sea – dizzying reflections on reflections on reflections.

After a moment Headmon turns around and steps forward, his movements elegant and graceful. He stands poised and relaxed, hip cocked, hands behind his back, head tilted to one side, looking at her, not staring but measuring, as though evaluating something very

324

expensive that he might buy. His eyes are the blue of hottest flame and she can't release the gasp that seems to be trapped in her chest with no way out.

"Headmon...you've outdone yourself," Rogue whispers, the slight tremor in her husky voice and the smell of her breath indicating that she, too, is taken aback by what she sees. "What's with the clothes and new look?"

Ignoring her, Headmon continues to examine Skye, measuring her response to him.

"...Who?" Skye whispers.

He smiles as though having decided to buy.

"...Who?"

Skye has no other word. It's all she can do not to turn and look to Isham for help. And she can feel static from his attempts to sooth her but she's too agitated to receive it.

This is R'io and not R'io.

Which?

She's at one and the same time powerfully drawn and equally re-pulsed.

"Please," Headmon graciously steps forward, "come in."

It's the same walk. But not the same. R'io's confidence is of a dif-ferent nature.

Skye looks for help from the window-mirror reflection of Isham. There is no help. He remains just inside the open doorway, hands clasped behind his back, gazing up, unobserving and unobserved.

Headmon/R'io approaches and stops, studying her. Then he steps forward and reaches for her hands with both of his. Something won't let her respond and take his hands. He waits. Then he nods and brings a hand to his heart.

"I couldn't want you to be more beautiful," he whispers with un-invited intimacy in R'io's voice and clipped accent.

She closes her eyes against his unwavering gaze and finds her purpose all confused. She forces herself to breathe, opens her eyes and looks at Rogue – who also wants to know what's going on. Skye abruptly turns away to look at something else, anything.

The main hall is a big space with skylights in the wood beamed ceiling. Three sides are dark wood. The fourth wall is mirror-glass through which can be seen moonlit sky and sea. Three females, dim in candlelight, are standing off to one side, near an arrangement of sofas, tables and plants. Somehow all three seem familiar. She turns back and regards Headmon intently, finds him still studying her, looking both pleased and challenged.

"You have stolen my manners," he smiles. "Let me introduce you to the others and beg them to forgive me for being…spellbound."

"Headmon, what are you doing?" Rogue hisses.

He smiles, looking at Rogue for the first time, eyes marble-hard blue.

"I'm presenting a more desirable option."

Eyes lock. His are deadly. Hers are narrowed with suspicion. Then he smiles and turns to the three females, indicating that they are to come forward.

"You have already met Katya, of course – my sister and heiress apparent because my offspring are, well, frankly unsuitable. Shame. She would be only the nineteenth female Headmon. Females are not particularly suited for the job."

Katya is tense, wearing a skintight sleeveless black jumpsuit, unzipped to her waist. A big chunk of emerald on a gold chain rests between her breasts. Dark hair cascades down across her shoulders. Her eyes are the color of petrified moss. They glitter with suspicion. She doesn't smile or offer a hand but merely nods.

"Skye."

"Katya," the nod is returned.

"This is Esa." Headmon has moved behind a young girl and is ruffling her blunt-cut cap of dark hair. "Lovely name, don't you think?"

"…Yes, lovely." Skye swallows a gasp and struggles not to reveal.

Esa seems already to be taller, no longer a child. Her eyes are huge and black, wide open with innocence. She wears a long rust-colored silk gown and a white cap.

"Esa?" Headmon prompts.

The girl steps forward shyly and curtsies, hand extended. Skye takes the hand, bows over it then releases it. Looking down, Esa steps back. Skye is trying to breathe. She glances at Rogue who has noticed something but seems unable to figure out what. Headmon is beaming.

"And this one here," he gestures to someone small and old who is stiller than stillness itself, "is my gypsy. Best one I've ever had. She calls herself Gurlanda. Odd name, don't you think? And don't let the blindness fool you. This old woman sees everything."

Curanda steps forward, hand extended in welcome. She, too,

is wearing a rust-colored gown and white cap. But it's the same nut-brown face and milky eyes. And Skye's heart is beating too fast again.

Blinking, full of questions Skye smiles as at a stranger and manages to reach out for the offered hand. The touch is electricity that catapults them into common-awareness for a quick exchange, inevident to the others.

He's not R'io. Don't forget that even for a heartbeat.

R'io lives?

Reveal nothing.

Her hand is released. The old woman rises from her curtsy and steps back with the others. Skye is trembling, finding it almost impossible to contain what wants to explode. Headmon clears his throat.

"Now to the purpose of the moment." He looks at Skye. "Your welcoming. There's been a sudden change of plans. When it became evident that you recognized the nature of the contents of the great gallery, I added music – what I happened to be listening to at the time – to see what you would do."

Headmon brings joined palms up to his chin and studies her intently. Smiling, he takes a step closer.

"Lo and behold," he whispers, fascinated. "Not only did you recog-nize the sound, you were able to identify the composer, the piece and even the movement. In addition, you knew some of the paintings without looking at the legends." He shakes his head slowly and chuckles to himself. "I am, to say the least, impressed."

Headmon takes a step closer. She smells alcohol and cologne, not R'io. R'io does not mask his unique scent.

"How do you know these things?" Headmon whispers.

Eyes lock. She meets his scrutiny with scrutiny of her own. He senses the shift. She does not respond. He's not R'io. Nothing like. Only semblance.

Her breathing steadies and deepens. He blinks and leans closer.

"How do you know these things?"

She does not respond. And her eyes are steel.

Unaccustomed to waiting for answers, when none comes, Headmon suddenly shifts mood.

"We'll get to it later. In private. This is a festive occasion and as I said, there's been a change of plans. I have something special to celebrate your arrival. A gift and a little test."

Her skin crawls.

"I have a master specialist who is going to play for you. She came here as a young woman already accomplished and through my tutelage has gotten steadily better. She's going to play one of my favorites. Let's see if you can name it."

Skye shrugs.

"Reynolds!"

It's a command. Servants appear and quickly, qietly begin to rearrange the space.

"Shall we sit?"

Headmon leads the women to a suddenly-arrived arrangement of overstuffed chairs separated by little tables on top of which are snifters filled with amber-colored liquid. As they take their seats the space is transformed into a small concert hall. A big cornucopia-shaped device is rolled in and locked in place with its open end pointed at the arrangement of chairs and people. Headmon leans over and whispers to Skye, on his left.

"That's a sound-cone. I chose to have the orchestra else-where because I want this to be an intimate affair. Just us and a few friends."

She shivers.

A long black shiny concert grand piano is wheeled in and locked down, positioned sideways across the opening of the sound-cone. The lid is raised all the way. Attendants waiting to address any need move into place behind the overstuffed chairs. Seeing that all is done, Reynolds moves to the back wall and stands with half a dozen footmen.

The lights are dimmed. A large woman wearing a rust-colored silk gown and white cap emerges from shadow, waddles to the piano and sits softly illumined from above. Of late middle age, she adjusts the bench to her satisfaction, lowers her head, and rests her hands in her lap, fully aware that her life is on the line each time she plays.

Headmon picks up his snifter, swirls it then holds it up.

"To us."

He waits for Skye to return the toast. When she doesn't, he sips and puts the snifter back on the table between them. It is instantly refilled.

"Begin," Headmon commands.

The woman at the piano nods and raises her head. There's a loud orchestral chord. Her hands meet the keys with swift, sure muscularity.

Sound.

In the air.

Actual sound.

Music from the instrument itself.

Skye immediately identifies the piece. She activated it many times back in the archives even though, there, she heard it in her head because of the monitor suit and that was nothing in comparison with the sound in the air around her now, full and loud, dizzying with its power. Then she's aware of Headmon studying her.

"Beethoven. Piano Concerto No. 5," she whispers, staying focused on the woman playing, who handles the opening arpeggios with perfect technique and authority.

"The Emperor," he leans to catch her eye.

Skye nods, unwilling to be further distracted by him.

Great City's head of Technology was awakened by an early morning page from the Presider's tech-secretary ordering her to brief him immediately on the latest signals from the surface. Magrit Abram Shen hopped out of bed, threw on a robe and ordered her citizen-housekeeper to bring a cup of steaming tea to her office where she is now seated at her desk, sipping, answering his questions.

The briefing is voice-only. She can hear him on his end. From the distorted words, it sounds like he's shaving the old fashioned way, with a blade.

"What about the bio-forms?"

"Definitely human. One male, two females."

"Our Prime Researcher and her accomplice moved northeast and met up with someone else?"

"Negative. These are three bio-forms we haven't seen before." She hears the sound of running water then the water is turned off and it sounds like he's walking into another room.

"What about the signals themselves?"

"So far we're unable to decipher them. But it's the same technology they used in the previous signals."

There's a pause on his end of the connection. She can hear him putting on his clothes. Hear him decisively zip his fly then his tunic. "What's this about, Magrit? What's your best guess?"

"Hummm," she puts her cup and saucer down then runs a hand through her long dark hair, still tangled from sleep. "There are several pos-sibilities. I don't have a preference yet."

"I suggest you get one."

"Very well." Unruffled, Shen drapes a leg over an arm of her executive chair and snuggles down. "One. They're trying to attract our attention."

"To what end?"

"Hear me out. We can go into depth in a minute." Shen can hear him walking down the hall to his office, sit in his chair, take a sip of something. "Two. They're just surfacing for some reason having nothing to do with us, talking to themselves unaware that we can pick up the signals. But that leaves a question. After generations of silence, why surface now? Just to chatter to each other? That's a possibility. But I don't buy it. Not in the light of recent events."

"Go on."

330

"Three," she picks up her cup and sips. "And this is quite chilling. If, as I suspect, there's a large population beneath the surface somewhere northeast of Great City and they have been helping our resources escape, they could know a lot about us while we remain in the dark. Everyone's agreed on that, right?"

"Correct."

"They could know that Great City is the last remaining jewel on the surface of the earth – a big fat jewel that trades with the Space States. They could be longing to return to the surface and there's no place to go but here. They could have been preparing for this for a long time and just now be ready. And there's one other possibility."

"Which is?"

"They could somehow be in league with the Space States. There's no other way to account for what's happening to Great City now from above and below. I don't believe in coincidences. Nope. Forces have been joined against us."

Paul Prescot Reed stands. He starts pacing slowly, thinking out loud.

"If I were them I'd try to flush us out. I'd want to know just what Great City can muster by way of defense. I'd try to get Great City to come to the battleground of my choosing."

"Yes, I agree. Those last sightings are a lure." Her voice is high and girlish.

"Do we have the capacity to capture one of those bio-forms and get it back here?"

Reed returns to his chair and sits. He can hear her rustling about in her office. Settled again, she exhales a soft humming sound. Then he hears her tapping code into her console.

"I've been working on something with Engineering. A pod I'm calling a retriever. Self-propelled. Human-sized. The plan is for it to go to a sight and pick up someone disabled by a drone. It's in prototype stage."

"Accelerate."

"Yes, sir, will do."

"Alive. I want that specimen alive."

"So do I."

***

331

After the captain was finished with him, Axl was hosed off again and taken to the chief's office. Naked and shivering but not from cold, the boy is standing in front of the chief's desk, numb and dumb, staring at nothing on the floor in front of him. The captain is standing off to one side in semi-shadow.

The chief is sitting at his desk. A single naked bulb hangs down glaring yellow light, igniting his baldhead with oily perspiration. Behind him on the wall is the room's only decoration – a black banner made of human hide with the words "Never Yield!" spelled out in Gothic red.

A big potato of a man, the chief is wearing a rumpled gray leather suit and shirt and a bolo tie with a clasp made of inlaid fingernails and teeth. His face and hands are permanently grimed with stone-dust. His eyes are small, dark and unreadable as he looks back and forth from Axl to the evidence bag with the soiled stone-people clothes. After a long time looking back and forth, the chief fixes a hard stare on Axl. When he speaks, his voice is soft and deep and it sounds like he needs to clear his throat.

"Where you from, boy?" the chief shifts the fat stub of a black roach from one corner of his mouth to the other.

Axl knows very little right now but he does understand not to tell them anything about who he is and how he stupidly happens to be here endangering everything.

"I asked you a question, boy. When I ask, you answer."

The chief nods at the captain who moves around behind Axl. The boy begins to shiver violently. The chief takes the stub out of his mouth and stares at Axl through little raisin-eyes.

"Where you from, boy?"

"...Uhhhh...hinterlands."

"Hinterlands of what canton?"

The boy shrugs. Best to play stupid, like he really is, like he's not very bright, like he's all confused and needs to sob because he's dumb and doesn't understand what's going on. He stands mute, shivering.

The chief looks at the captain quizzically. The captain shrugs, bemused. The chief squints at Axl. Then he stands and comes out in front of his desk and leans back on it with his hands clasped under his sagging belly.

"Where you from, boy?"

Axl's eyes glaze over. The chief nods to the captain who pulls a short thick wand out of his hip pocket and aims a sharp jab at Axl's left kidney. Mouth open, startled, unable to breathe, the boy sinks to his knees. The chief looks at the captain.

"Take him back to the cell. Soften him up. Don't leave marks. Don't break nothin. We got to take him forward. Up to where they got different ways of making him talk."

"Get up." The captain moves away from Axl.

The boy struggles to his feet and stands bent over, gasping for breath. The captain opens the door onto the hallway.

"Come."

***

After the Beethoven was finished they shared an elegant sit-down dinner served by footmen. Skye ate none of the meat though Headmon repeatedly assured her that this meat was beef from the ranch. The pianist, having performed flawlessly, was invited to join them. Relieved to have survived the ordeal, she's the only one still eating. Headmon, seated next to Skye, stands and taps his glass with a fork.

"Now we adjourn to the parlor for games."

"I won't be joining you," Skye stands. "I wish to be alone and remember the music."

"I can have it played for you whenever you like!"

"No," she looks at the tired pianist. "I want to hear it in my head."

"That's not an option," he blinks, stunned to be refused.

"Headmon…" it's Rogue.

"It's what I choose to do now," Skye turns to leave.

"No!" he grabs for her.

Skye jerks away. Eyes lock. She's not afraid. She doesn't want to be with him. He spoils the wine of the music and her memory of R'io.

"You can't and won't stop me," she says to his utter astonishment.

"Really? And why is that?"

"Because force won't get you what you want from me."

333

"You have no idea of the persuasion I can employ."

"That's correct. But whatever its nature, the force at your command cannot make me love you."

Headmon steps back. His blue-flame eyes narrow to slits. Then sud-denly, abruptly, he shifts. He laughs. He yawns elaborately, stretching.

"I'm tired of this. And tomorrow's duties are fast approaching. Reynolds!"

"Sir?"

"Take them back to their suite." He turns and offers his arm to Katya. "Bed with me, sister."

Katya is startled. Then she smiles catlike and takes the offered arm.

"You," he shakes a playful finger at Skye. "We'll start over in the morning." Headmon turns to Katya. "Shall we?"

"Lead on," she murmurs into his lips.

"Ladies, if you will follow me?" It's the butler, at the door.

"By the quickest way," Skye murmurs.

"That's my intent. I must return immediately and tend to my master's needs." He leads them into a concealed lift that deposits them in little more than a wink at the door to their suite.

Skye turns to nod as the lift door is closing on Isham/Reynolds then follows the champion of champions on into the suite and closes the door. Rogue stops in the kitchen for a glass of water and Skye moves toward the hall to the bedroom, pausing only long enough to make eye contact with Rogue who is staring at her, full of questions.

"What's going on?" the champion of champions sets her glass down on the countertop.

"I haven't a clue." Skye smiles at how easy it is to tell the truth and moves on down the hall to the dark womb of bed.

***

Great City's current Presider is asleep on his bed, bathed in perspir-ation and incidental light from hall. Because of the heat, instead of his usual gunmetal gray silk pajamas he's wearing only cotton briefs, black. He and the bed are drenched in perspiration because it's hot and because the medicine isn't working anymore, the little pills that are

334

supposed to keep the dreams away.

Asleep and alone, he hears soft women's voices, strange languages that have not been heard on earth for millennia. Women keening and wailing on and on. Something about the sound terrifies him but he can't wake up, can't cry out but instead grows more and more frightened of the voices, whisperings, murmurings, accusations, blame. Then he's falling forever, gasping and waking with a start.

Paul Prescot Reed tumbles off of the bed and rushes into the bathroom. Braced against the sink he stares wide-eyed into the mirror. Then, hurrying, he opens the shower and turns on cold water as a form of punishment for a crime he can't remember having committed.

***

The chief leans back in his chair and puts his feet up on the desk. He thinks for a moment, fleshy face furrowed in concentration. Then he lowers his feet, sits straight and adjusts his tie. Putting on a smile, he taps code into a rusty keyboard.

"Central Control." The voice is female.

"This is chief of enforcement for canton Equa. I need immediate connection to a Clearance supervisor."

"One moment."

During the wait, the chief bring his hands up out of his lap and folds them on the desk in front of him, near the bagged clothes taken from the boy.

"Yes, chief." It's an older man, reeking with authority.

"You want visual for this, sir. I have something here that might be of interest."

There's a slight pop and the chief knows he is seen without being able to see the observer.

"Go ahead."

"We picked up a boy earlier. Adolescent. Trying to get into canton Equa with no papers and a stolen ID card. We strip-searched him and found him wearing these under pilfered leathers," the chief indicates the evidence bag with Axl's soiled clothes.

"None of this is uncommon."

"The clothes is made of cloth, sir."

335

The chief hears a sharp intake of breath followed by a pause then the Clearance supervisor breaks the silence.

"What are you saying?"

"I don't think he's from SubTurra or the hinterlands." The chief rubs his face wearily. "I think he might be connected to our visitors. Skye One-who-wanders and the guy who arrived with her. Similar kind of clothes. I think you want to look at these things and decide whether or not to pass the information on up to the boss."

"Bring the boy and the clothes immediately."

"I'll take care of it personally."

"Transport is on the way. I'll be waiting."

There's a slight pop to the atmosphere and the chief knows they've been disconnected. He stands and reaches for his black leather trench coat and hat. He picks up the evidence bag with Axl's soiled clothes. Then he bellows.

"Enforcer!"

The door to his office is immediately opened and a burly enforcer leans in.

"Sir?"

The chief tosses the bag of Axl's soiled cloth clothes.

"That's not to leave your hands. Get the captain and the boy and a squad of enforcers. Find something for the boy to wear then bring him to me at the tracks. Be quick about it, we're going to Central Control."

***

Freshly showered, wearing her stone-people clothes, Skye One-Who-Wanders is standing at the kitchen sink finishing a bowl of fresh fruit. Ebony skull freshly shaved and gleaming, Rogue strides into the kitchen wearing her dark green slacks and sweater. Someone knocks politely on the front door.

"Come," Skye calls out, mouth full, chewing.

Rogue picks a piece of fruit and starts slicing and eating as the butler steps into the foyer, elegant in shades of gray. He bows slightly.

"Mr. Headmon would like to see both of you in the library, please."

Skye smiles politely. Then she turns to rinse out her bowl and sets it in the drying rack.

"I have plans for the morning. Maybe later today when I'm back from the lake."

"I would advise Miss Skye…"

"I said not *now!*"

Rogue is surprised. The butler clears his throat. He looks down at his shoes then up at the ceiling.

"I've been instructed to inform Miss Skye that Mr. Headmon's finger is poised to initiate a random Banding blackout should you not come immediately. The residence is of such a nature that wherever you are, whatever you're doing, you will be unable to avoid knowing the effect a Banding blackout has on its targeted population." He pauses and clasps his hands behind his back. "Mr. Headmon would like to see you in the library now."

Rogue stops chewing and watches Skye One-Who-Wanders who smiles slowly.

"Very well. I would not want to be responsible for one of those, a Banding blackout, whatever that is."

The champion of champions brings the bowl to her mouth and drains it in long swallows. She moves to the sink and starts to wash her bowl and spoon.

"Miss Rogue, I suspect that you do not want to be the cause of needless suffering. Mr. Headmon will not wait."

Nodding, Rogue wipes her mouth on a towel and leads Skye out of the kitchen past the butler. All three step into the lift and its door closes immediately.

***

The task force for the defense of Great City is meeting in its dim and airless room. Present are Paul Prescot Reed and his heads of Technology, Engineering, Human Resources and the new head of Security. They are hot and tired. Worse, they are stymied.

Taking the bull by the horns, Magrit Abram Shen of Technology stands and looks pointedly at each member of the committee.

"Something's been bothering me about those warheads, the one's left over from the ancient missile defense systems."

"Please no more bad news," Virginia Kahn Baker whispers to

herself.

"Do they still work?" Shen answers her own question. "The war-heads. Has one ever been tested?"

She looks at each member of the task force, sees lassitude, defeat. She, too, is tired of not getting any results.

"People, we have to try something. Do you want to survive or would you rather just die of thirst or thermonuclear meltdown? I need to know if those warheads work," she leans over the conference table. "We need to test one."

"What if we took a test shot in the vicinity of our target location north and east of here? As a warning." Now under the tutelage of Shen, the new head of Security is learning quickly.

"Hang on," Reed interrupts. "I'd like to see what they have by way of resources before blasting them to vapor."

"Agreed," Shen stands and begins to pace, thinking as she walks. "We can fix the warheads to do anything we want them to do. And what we want is a surface blast, not deep penetration. Think of it as sort of a big hello from overhead."

"No," Reed rejects the idea. "It tips our hand."

"It redefines the game." Shen is working on convincing the others as much as Reed. "We pick the battlefield and the moment. The time and place of our choosing. It allows us to go on the offensive and set new terms of engagement."

"When?"

"Sooner than later."

There's a long silence in the room. They can hear the infrastructure struggling with half-measures. Reed dips his head to tented fingers and closes his eyes. Then he stands and looks at the others.

"I'll ponder it. When will those shape-changers be here?"

"Shuttle should be landing about now," Whitaker pipes in.

***

Big bay doors in the belly of H-V cruiser Mohawk open to receive the ambulance and Rogers on the scooter. The doors close seamlessly under both vehicles, which are neatly docked by their pilots. Lt. Ethel Marin, the navigator and second in command of Mohawk is up in the control cabin holding the ship steady while Commander Steele, Big Wanda Mu and Cha-Hua are here to help with the living and the dead, and suited up for space to do so because the hold is a zero-atmosphere zone.

Sgt. Bates is out of the ambulance, helping the crew-members remove the bagged bodies from the aft-section. Rogers is checking both rescue vehicles for mission-readiness. Meantime, orders have come in and are being relayed by Commander Ingrid Steele, also helping with the bodies.

"From Captain Porter, just now for you and Rogers. Remaining in stealth-mode, you are to rejoin team Falcon ASAP and wait for orders concerning retrieval of the ambassadors from Great City. Three more responder-teams are on the way but will hold deployment until you call for them. Command wants S.S. Hope to have all opportunity to vindicate herself unaided if possible."

"Ah, Porter was always a class act." Bates and Rogers slap five. "Thank her for us if you would, commander."

The two first responders float over to Ingrid. They bump helmets with Steele and slap gloves with Big Wanda and Cha-Hua.

"Go!" Ingrid holds up two thumbs up and drifts into the airlock after the rest of her crew.

The airlock hatch closes, causing the hold to shudder. Sgt. Bates gets into the cab of the ambulance and completes a quick flight-check while beneath her the big bay doors open onto infinity. Then Rogers on the scooter is tumbling down and out followed by the ambulance – spinning and yawing away in slow motion, clearing the much larger ship and in a wink both vehicles are gone, leaving no trail in the starry darkness.

***

Reynolds the butler opens wide double doors and steps aside exposing a big room with an ancient Persian masterpiece on the floor.

"The library," he murmurs gesturing for them to enter.

Dazzled, Skye steps just inside. Tall windows with open maroon velvet drapes are on one wall. Outside, an orchard is in full bloom complete with a gardener on a ladder up in one of the trees.

Headmon/R'io, sun-bleached red locks hanging loose around

his face, softening his sharp features, is wearing perfectly tailored navy blue slacks with matching v-neck sweater and tobacco-colored loafers, no socks. He's sit-ting in a wingback chair at one end of the room in front of a roaring fireplace with his feet up on a footstool and his hands clasped under his chin, staring into the flames. Across from him and equally angled to the fire is an identical chair.

But Skye is not looking at that. She's mesmerized by row after row of books in floor-to-ceiling cases that line all available wall space.

"Real?" she asks wide-eyed.

Still sitting, gazing into the fire, Headmon responds.

"The originals turned to dust long ago. These are duplicates, exact in every way. Real in that sense."

She hears music from an adjacent room. A piano. Scales and arpeggios that traverse the entire keyboard in ever more intricate patterns.

"I like to hear her practicing," Headmon observes. "It soothes me. Do come in."

Skye takes a few steps into the room then stops and turns around, staring. Rogue strides in and goes straight to Headmon.

"You sit there," he points at a single overstuffed chair in front of its own smaller fireplace, facing away from the other two. "You should not be included at all. But I decided to honor our agreement. Do not forget, however, my dear champion of champions, that you are not a participant in the conversation about to take place."

Eyes narrowed, uncertain of the game, Rogue examines Headmon. Then she strides to the indicated chair and turns it so it's facing the other two. The butler approaches to explain that the chair is to be left where it was positioned.

"Let it go, Reynolds," Headmon laughs good-naturedly. "She's stubborn and will have her way in even the tiniest matter. Now leave us but stay within reach."

"Yes, Mr. Headmon," Reynolds bows politely, steps out of the room and closes the doors without making a sound.

Skye has moved to a breast-high pedestal on which, all by itself, is a large book, open near its beginning. She's staring down at actual words on the actual page – how small the words are! She brings a fingertip to the page and touches ever so lightly, carefully. The paper is tissue thin. Then Skye One-Who-Wanders lowers her finger and reads.

"If you make me an altar of stone, do not build it of dressed stones; for if you use a chisel on it, you will profane it." Her mouth falls open. "Exodus 20:25."

She is astonished to utter stillness.

"They're in random order."

She jumps.

Headmon is standing right behind her, too close. She moves away quickly, half a step, and turns. Staring at him Skye takes another step back and knows she can't lapse like that again. He's too quick and subtle, able to turn a chink into an open door. And he's too much like R'io without being like R'io at all.

"They're in random order. Do you know what that means?"

"Yes."

"It's a quirk of mine. I like being the only one who can find anything in here." He smiles, assuming too much. "Come. Sit. Let's begin again."

He tries to take her hand and it's not available. He tries to touch the small of her back and she's on the other side of the chair, pausing to regard the fire then the library from this new perspective. He gestures for her to sit. After a moment, she does.

The chairs are angled toward each other, each with its own ottoman. There's a small table between the chairs. The table is set with coffee service and glasses of water. A blood red rose is elegant in a standing tube of spun glass.

Headmon sits with his elbows on the arms of his chair, fingers tented at his lips, gazing at her from under his eyebrows. He leans back and crosses his feet on the footstool. Stretched out, hands clasped behind his head, he examines her. She stares back. Then he breaks the silence.

"I'm going to ask you a few questions. Then, depending on your answers – and you *will* answer – I'm going to offer you a better option than the one Rogue so brilliantly proposed."

In the nearby room, the pianist switches from scales to Bach two-part inventions.

"First, who are you and where are you from?"

She has questions of her own.

"Where is the man you are trying to imitate?"

He tents his fingertips and brings them to his lips, studying her.

"What will it take for you to understand who's in charge here?" Mocking inspiration, he raises a stiff forefinger. "I know!"

Rogue gasps as Headmon reaches into a trouser pocket and

341

pulls out a small silvery device. He unfolds the device. Then he presses a combination of keys.

Pop!

The library goes dark. Then – jolt – it's as though somewhere else has been sucked into the room.

"This is a Banding bar, lowest quality, out on the edge of the hinter-lands in canton Uni." His voice is slightly distorted, fuzzed.

Through the semblance she can see Headmon in his chair and, peripherally, Rogue sitting rigid. Another place entirely is now here, too, though. Two overlapping worlds are transparent and completely detailed, full to the senses.

"It's good enough for this lot who can only dig. The more skilled can pay a higher price for better quality."

She feels him looking at her.

"Quite a step down from the technology you've been using, eh? Nonetheless it suffices." He smiles. "As you can see, these people are all happily hooked up, enjoying their fantasies."

This Banding bar is a huge cylindrical space carved out of stone, the color of rust stained with mold. She counts at least five rings or levels with just enough space between them for an adult human to stand. Metal ladders and catwalks connect the levels.

Old, stained cots are everywhere, separated only enough for the occasional departure or arrival to squeeze through. Every cot is occupied. The people on the cots are wearing big helmets over their heads. Substantial tubes snake up and connect each helmet to the low ceiling.

She holds her breath against smells of urine, feces, vomit, sweat and leather on a background of molding rust. The slow throb and hiss of working technology is a constant. What illumination there is comes from the occasional lightbulb and from the filthy window of the Banding bar's entry kiosk.

"This is normal activity in a low-grade Banding bar. And this," his thumb drops casually on the device, "is what happens when I shut them down."

Immediately the energy is sucked out of the Banding bar. It's totally dark. And she can feel it slam in on them, panic that is contagious, that hits her too though Headmon seems impervious.

"We'll observe on another frequency."

He presses a combination of keys and everything glows a horrible red as people are flinging off their helmets, bolting off of their cots, trying to breathe, trying to get out or down or up or anyplace but where they are. Desperate howling increases in volume and intensity until, unable to stand it, Skye presses her palms over her ears – though she cannot seem to close her eyes.

Most head for the ladders and catwalks. Some people attack others, tearing and ripping for advantage. Some shiver and vomit and stain themselves. Some jump off of the scaffolding and land on the floor below. A few stay on their cots, rolled up tight, rocking back and forth. All howl, screech, scream for mercy from a god who has none.

She bolts out of the chair and confronts him.

"STOP!"

Headmon chuckles.

"STOP *NOW!*"

Pop!

The Banding is reactivated.

Pop!

The Banding bar vanishes and the library is itself again, quiet with books and fireplaces and the masterpiece on the floor and Exodus 20:25 on its pedestal and draped windows and a gardener up on a ladder in the middle-distance, different tree. She's standing with her back to the fireplace, heart pounding, shaking, eyes closed tight, focused on just trying to control her breathing and the pianist in the next room switches from Bach to Chopin.

"Why?!" She brings her hands to her head as though to squeeze the images out of it. "*WHY?*"

"Ahhh," Headmon smiles, putting the device back in his pocket. "I find a chink in you."

"A chink?" Glaring, she takes a step back, feels the fire's heat behind her. "Is that how you get your way, by finding weakness?"

"You can't tolerate the pain of others," Headmon chuckles, "an endearing trait but not fitting in one destined for power." He smiles at her like a kind teacher. "You'll need to work on that."

"Do no harm."

A laugh explodes then Headmon collects himself.

"Aw, do no harm. How quaint. And how impossible. To benefit one is always to harm another. That's the central fact of human life."

"I want no part of this," she whispers.

"You have no choice. There's no place you can go in the residence or on the grounds to escape the Banding blackouts I can

343

trigger. You have a weakness. That means I can make you do anything I want. I can turn off Banding in SubTurra anywhere, anytime – and you'll know all about it wherever you are, whatever you might be doing. What you just saw is nothing. One expects it from that sort. Wait until you see what happens in a high-end place."

Headmon stands again, suddenly all business. He points at her chair.

"SIT DOWN!"

After a moment, glaring hard, Skye moves around him and sits back in her chair.

"Now, who are you and where are you from?"

She reaches for a glass of water on the table but her hand is shaking too hard to lift it so she brings that hand to her lap and holds it tight with the other. She looks into the fire and nods, remembering. Then she whispers.

"I am a Prime Researcher from Great City."

"Great City?!" he blinks. "What's Great City? Where?"

"On the surface."

"There's nothing on the surface!"

"Incorrect."

"Where?"

"I'm not sure."

"You got here from there. How?"

"I walked."

"On the surface?"

"Yes."

"That's impossible."

"I was there. Now I'm here."

"All right, we'll leave that for later. Tell me about this Great City."

Remembering, Skye closes her eyes.

"Great City is human evil at its extreme."

"That tells me nothing. What does it look like?"

"The same."

"What does that mean?"

"Inside," she shrugs, "everything is the same. Outside, it's a smear on the surface. Huge."

"How big is it? How many people?"

"I don't know. Tens of Thousands maybe. Maybe less. Maybe more."

"Thousands?!"

"That's my guess," she shrugs indifferently.

"How does Great City support itself?"

"With product from the archives of the ancients." She stares at the fire without seeing it.

"Product?" He returns to his chair and sits on its edge, leaning forward. "What do you mean, product?"

"The archives are a measureless mass of disorganized data from the ancients. In all conceivable modes. Great City extracts product from the archives and readies it for trade."

"Trade?! Who's the customer?"

"Product is sent to the Space States in exchange for resources. There are no more resources on the surface…"

"Space States?! Resources?!" He doesn't bother to hide his Aston-ishment. "What resources?!"

"I was not privy to that."

Stunned, he gets out of his chair and stands in front of the fireplace again. Then he turns to face her. She doesn't look at but through him, unable to forget what a Banding blackout can cause with so little effort on the part of one person.

"What's a Prime Researcher?" he asks.

"Researchers mine the archives." Her voice is flat, toneless. "Prime is the highest rank. Only Prime Researchers are allowed to mine anti-Dogma, which is premium product. My area was Western ancients. Texts, primarily, also music and art."

"Hence your ability to identify the paintings and the Bach."

"Yes."

Headmon remains at the fireplace, squinting at her.

"What if I don't believe you?"

She shrugs.

"Don't believe me."

He nods and changes tack again.

"Does Great City know about SubTurra?"

"I don't know."

"You don't know?"

"I don't know if Great City knows anymore than the fact that it no longer has a resource it used to have. And this may not be a good thing for you because Great City guards its resources jealously and will go after them if it knows where to look."

"Is SubTurra in danger?"

"That's my guess."

He paces, trying to digest the information. Trying to believe it. Then trying not to believe it.

"Where is Great City?"

"My best estimate is…somewhere south and west of here."

"How far?"

"Don't know. Far."

"If you had maps could you find it?"

"Maybe. If it's on maps. But then if it was on the maps you'd already know about it."

"Where are the Space States now?"

"I don't know," she shrugs and waves a hand. "Out there. Far, I guess."

Headmon steps closer. Leans. Peers.

"Why are you here? Why did you leave Great City?"

"I found a way out."

"And the man who arrived with you? What's his name?"

"I don't know."

"You don't know? Isn't he one of you? From this Great City as you call it? Weren't you traveling together?"

She shrugs. He examines her long and hard. He pats his trousers pocket.

"Unless you answer, I'll provide more entertainment."

Eyes lock. Then she stares into the fire.

"He's a bounty hunter. Great City does not surrender resources gracefully, especially Prime Researchers." Her tone is flat. "I managed to stay just ahead of him on the surface. My guess is that we were being tech-trailed right into and down the ancient mineshaft I found."

"You asked to see him."

When? When did she ask that? In a dream? Or is this a trick?

Headmon is in front of her again, confronting even though she won't look at him.

"Why did you ask to see him?"

"To spit on him. His job is to take me back."

Eyes lock.

"Really," Headmon is amused. "His job is to take you back to the ultimate evil and all you want to do is *spit* on him? I find that hard to believe. In fact I find all of what you're saying hard to believe and I'm going to investigate."

"Go ahead," she shrugs.

Headmon stops in front of the fireplace. He stares at her, conflicted and suspicious. Then he bellows.

"REYNOLDS!"

The doors open immediately and the butler steps into the library.

"Yes, Mr. Headmon."

"Take them out of here. They're free to roam the residence or the grounds until I call for them."

"Yes, sir." Reynolds turns to Skye then to Rogue. "Ladies?"

Rogue is staring at Skye as though she's never seen that person before. She stands. Wavers. Then both of them follow the butler out of the library.

Seventh Gate – Purpose

Great City's retriever is skirting the contours of the dunes, flying only a few feet off the ground and illumined by dull morning sun. Shaped like a big aluminum tube rounded at both ends, the vehicle has a few bristly rods protruding from its back like snail's eyes but is otherwise plain and on its way to the last sighting of the three new bio-forms.

Inside, the retriever is hollow, big enough for an adult human. The nose carries a flock of disabling drones, each about the length of a finger. The drones are plugged into their motherboard and constantly updated as information from the last sighting is further digested and refined.

For a change everything seems to be going as planned, at least in terms of the machine. But, then, Shen is in charge now. And she loves the chase, the hide-and-seek and peek-a-boo qualities of her opponent.

Alone in her private office, she's wearing lavender workout togs and standing poised over her desk like a hawk on a thermal about to plunge because she's had an insight and now anticipates a pattern of behavior from the enemy because she's studied people carefully and they always repeat what worked before.

Shen instructs her Technology Primes to direct the retriever several miles beyond the point of the last sighting. They're going to surface again – she's certain. All she has to do is follow the trajectory. Position the retriever to have a head start on the next sighting. Release the flock of disabling drones and be ready to go in an instant.

Meanwhile, elder Moss, Schiara and Wim are ready for the second trip out on the surface. All three are geared-up but Wim will be staying inside to man the portal, not an insignificant post and the one he was originally assigned.

"Okay," elder Moss whispers. "Now!"

Wim opens the portal. Elder Moss and Schiara run out onto the surface. The portal closes behind them.

Staying low, hugging ash, the elder and the girl scramble up different dunes. Once at the top they ignite and hold beacons aloft for a few seconds. That done they run to other dunes and repeat the process. Finally, they head back toward the portal Wim understands to open only at the last possible moment.

Just then, the little satellite overhead and the flock of disabling drones now released from the nose of the retriever only a few hundred yards away, perk up their technological ears and start screaming.

"BIO-FORMS! TWO. FEMALE. MATCHES FROM THE PREVIOUS SIGHTING."

The satellite and the drones relay the data to the Technology Primes in Great City. The Technology Primes in their workbays ride the sudden wave of information from the ground and from space. As the data cascades down on them, the Primes alert Magrit Abram Shen who ignites all her screens and studies the data.

"Yes!" she claps her hands. "Give me status on the disabling drones?!"

"Now approaching targets at top speed."

"Get the retriever to that location. I want those bio-forms disabled and one of them brought back here. No mistakes!"

"Copy."

Back on the surface Schiara is running down a dune screaming to Wim inside the portal.

OPEN!

The flock of disabling drones is cresting a dune as the elder and the girl scramble through the portal that slams closed behind them. Poof! The bio-forms have vanished. The drones can find no trail. But at least this time they have an exit-point.

Inside, elder Moss and Schiara fling off their Breathers and stand bent over, heaving in air. Sensors pulse with high rapid tones that indicate the closeness outside of foreign technology. Staying quiet, Wim hands Schiara and elder Moss their water flasks.

Both nearly drain their flasks before handing them back. He sets the flasks aside and moves to help elder Moss take off her bulky surface gear. As the elder is turning to help Schiara, something pops inside her knee. The older woman gasps.

"Gaaaaaa…"

Elder Moss leans over and grabs her knee. The old climbing injury has flared up again.

"What is it," Schiara whispers, her eyes wide with alarm.

"Nothing." Elder Moss straightens up, releases a long breath, laughs at herself. "Cramp. Let's get going so I can move through it, work it off."

And in Great City, Shen does not hide her admiration for the skills of her enemy.

"What do you mean, disappeared?"

"The bio-forms have gone through a vanishing-point. They no

350

longer register on our technology."

Shen straightens up. She scans her screens. She closes her eyes to think.

"I need the shape-changers! I need them now!"

"The shuttle is just touching down."

"Get more drones in that area immediately."

"Copy."

"We're so close," she whispers to herself, "so close." She stands still for a moment, doll-eyes blinking at nothing. Then she calls up the Presider's tech-secretary and requests an immediate face to face.

***

"First, check historical records – from as far back as they go." Headmon is alone in his control center giving orders. "Search for references to something called Great City – plans for, designs of. Anything. Any com-bination or configuration of those words. It might be called something else.

"What I'm looking for is a structure on the surface big enough to hold thousands of people. Maybe south and west of here. Maybe not. I also want you to search the records for something called the Space States. And I want every map we have from the beginning to the end of the Great Collapse."

"Yes, sir."

As usual, all his screens are lit but the ones directly in front of him are most significant. Skye One-Who-Wanders and Reynolds the new butler. The bites on their throats. Must have been some spider.

"Second. I want two platoons of reconnaissance troops equipped for the surface immediately. They'll need transportation with long-range cap-ability. They'll need supplies for an indefinite deployment. They'll need extra ordnance. They're to be in constant contact with Central Control. I want to know how soon we can get those platoons up and out if we crank it to highest priority."

"Yes, sir."

"Third. I want to know exactly what the surface is like now. What would be needed to sustain an army up there? Then I want a complete in-ventory of our military capabilities and readiness. Most important, I want to know if we have technology that can protect us

351

from a missile or surface attack?"

"Yes, sir."

"I want a report on all of this by evening meal."

"You'll have it, sir."

Headmon disconnects from Central Control. He shifts to a real-time image of Skye in her suite with Rogue. Not talking much, they've both changed into swimwear and are heading out to the lake. He pages Esa, the young assistant to Kurinda, the new gypsy.

"Sir?"

"Put on swimwear. Get a basket of food and drink and meet Skye and Rogue at the dock. Stay with them. Get going."

"Yes, sir."

He disconnects from Esa and pulls up real-time images of the cantons, from places of privilege to places of wretchedness. It's all his. And now maybe there's this thing called Great City. And the Space States.

Fiction?

Fact?

Friend?

There are no friends.

Who's the fool here? How could all the Headmons before him have been so dumb and blind?

A pleasant chime indicates that a call is coming through from Central Control. Headmon activates the connection.

"Yes?"

"Possible point of interest. A boy recently tried to enter canton Equa using stolen clothes and an ID card he didn't bother to read before he handed it over to the immigration clerk. Enforcers took the boy in for questioning. They stripped him and found he was wearing cloth clothes under stolen leathers."

"So?"

"Sir, the cloth was rough-weave, crude by our standards. Like..."

"Like what?"

"Sir, I checked personally. The cloth and the cut are almost identical to what Skye One-Who-Wanders and the fellow with her were wearing when they got here."

Blink. Reality keeps shifting.

"Where's the boy?"

"In Central Control. A holding cell."

"Let me see."

The biggest of the screens in Headmon's surveillance center is fuzzy for an instant. Then crisp shots pop up – Axl from several angles.

The boy is in a small concrete enclosure with a narrow ledge for sitting or sleeping and a hole in the floor for elimination. He's sitting on the ledge wearing a black leather trench coat that is too big. His head is down. He is beyond despair.

Headmon leans forward and examines.

"Does he have a name?"

"Axl. At least that's what he called himself at the immigration desk. Hasn't said a word since then."

"Bring me the clothes."

"We need your permission to clean them, sir. The boy soiled himself when he was being interrogated. They smell…"

"Take samples then clean the clothes. I want to see them. And I want to see his face, this boy. Take off the trench coat."

Immediately, a technician enters the cell. The boy is instructed to stand and he obeys. The coat is removed and placed on the ledge. Axl stands naked as the technician takes him firmly by the chin and positions his head.

Headmon punches keys. The big screen is filled with Axl's face. Headmon catches his breath.

"How like my other specimen." He leans forward in his chair and squints at the boy's face. "How very like me."

Headmon checks the base of the boy's throat. He finds no bite marks, no scars. He ignites a close-up of R'io's face from when he first got here and was still healthy and active and puts the two images side by side, the boy and the man.

"Very like, indeed."

***

The sun is high and hot. There are no clouds. The breeze is taking a nap. It's seventy-eight degrees and dry with no annoying bugs by order of the man in charge. They call it summer.

Skye, Rogue and Esa are drifting in one of the small sailboats out near the center of the lake. All three are in swimwear but have yet to go into the water. The girl's basket of food and drink remains untouched between her feet. There's tension in the air and the three of them are spread out as far as possible in the little craft.

Still haunted by the Banding blackout, Skye is at the stern, trailing fingertips in water. Remote and distracted, she wants to be alone and isn't. So she's withdrawn her awareness from the others.

Rogue, apparently asleep, is lying on a bench that spans the waist of the boat. She's covered from head to toe by a microfilm of shawl she found in a closet back in the suite where she curtly answered a question no one asked. "In ancient times, as you call them, my people were black. But generations under the surface turned us gray. In their honor, I am tattooed. Sunlight bleaches me."

Esa is in the bow, facing backward, eyes closed and silent, apparently neither here nor there. Unable to penetrate the static that is Skye's awareness, the girl opens her eyes. She brings a hand to her brow to shade her eyes. She yawns and finally has Skye's attention. The girl handsigns, her movements no more than quick stretching and flexing of wrists and fingers.

~ R'io is here. We have a plan. Do not reveal. ~

Skye nods ever so slightly as she studies ripples on the water. Two other sailboats are filled with footmen carrying impressive weapons and staying a good distance away as Reynolds instructed.

A whisper of breeze kicks up. The boat bobs and lurches forward. Skye adjusts the sail and steers them toward the falls on the far side of the lake. When they get within easy swimming distance she drops a small anchor.

"Race you to the falls," it's Esa, playful.

Skye nods. They both stand, rocking the little boat. Rogue stirs, takes the microfilm of shawl off her head and looks around.

"Hey Rogue, race you to the falls," Esa calls and dives into the water with Skye.

Rogue is in the water catching up and all three are spread out, swimming toward the falls with long graceful strokes. They swim through the falls into a little lagoon and wade to a narrow span of beach bound by a waist-high ledge. At the back of the ledge is a grinning dark hole, big enough for one at a time.

"Come," Esa whispers.

Skye hoists Esa up onto the ledge then the girl turns to give her old friend a hand. Their offers of help are ignored by Rogue who doesn't look at either of them. Then all three stoop through the hole into a cave that is dark, large and cool.

Esa takes a tech-torch from inside the entrance. She turns it on and holds it high, moving the powerful beam around slowly.

Skye and Rogue both gasp. They're standing in a big blooming cavern with complicated surfaces. Across from them is a jagged hole that would seem to be a way deeper into the cave. But that's not why they gasped.

The walls are covered with images that are painted on the stone in colors of earth and air and water and fire. Some images are large and elegant, flowing with the stone. Some are simple stick figures and crosshatches and wavery lines and dots that could be depicting something no longer com-prehensible.

Bison. Antelope. Horse. Owl.

Pure numinosity made by human hands.

How long ago? What is their story?

Even though Esa has been here before, she's no less stunned than the other two as she leads them deeper into the cave, indicating subtle markings here and there. No one speaks. Even Rogue's mood seems to be shifted by where they are.

Stags.

Maps.

Hands.

Crude pictures of what might have been the landscape above.

"We are not all that far below the surface now," Esa says softly, her words bouncing around the irregular hollowness. "Evidently, some of the ancients used to come down here. Why remains a mystery."

Rogue stops suddenly. She studies Skye and Esa, no longer able to contain her anger.

"Enough," the champion whispers.

The other two look at her, innocent and puzzled.

~ Do not reveal what? ~ Rogue signs.

The other two do not respond.

~ Do not reveal what?! ~

It's ingrained. They do not reveal. Esa looks quizzically at Rogue. The girl smiles then focuses the beam of light on a particularly elegant arrangement of arrows. "Come, there's more."

But nobody moves. Then Rogue signs again.

~ Do not reveal what? ~

Skye and Esa look at each other then at Rogue. They shrug.

"...Rogue?"

355

The sign is repeated.

~ DO NOT REVEAL WHAT?! ~

"…Rogue, what are you doing?" Skye whispers as Rogue signs again.

~ Talk with hands is common to those who live below. But your dialect is different and it has taken me a while to catch on but one thing I've figured out is that you two and Reynolds and Curanda know each other. What's going on? ~

Skye and Esa look at her, their faces blank.

~ WE HAVE AN AGREEMENT! ~ Rogue signs to Skye.

Nothing is revealed.

"Come," Esa whispers after a long, painfully awkward silence. "Something is ruining a beautiful place. I'm going back to the residence."

The girl strides off toward the entrance followed by Skye and finally Rogue. At the mouth of the cave Esa impatiently turns off the torch and drops it on the ground. Then she runs across the ledge, hops down, runs into the water and swims through the falls. Stooping at the mouth of the cave, Rogue grabs Skye by the jaw and draws her close.

"We have an agreement!" she hisses.

Skye jerks her head back. Eyes lock.

"I haven't forgotten."

***

Once again wearing the stone-people clothes taken from the fellow who arrived with Skye One-Who-Wanders, Headmon is in a dressing room in Central Control near where the boy is being held. He looks in the mirror, steps closer and examines his handsome new face.

"Who are you?" he whispers. "Where do you come from? Why are you here?" He opens the door of the dressing room and steps out.

A technician in the corridor snaps to attention. Headmon takes the boy's clean and folded clothes from the technician then nods and follows the man down a featureless gray corridor to the cell where the boy is being held. Headmon nods again. The technician punches in code and the door slides open. Headmon steps in. The door slides closed.

Axl is lying on the ledge facing the wall, knees bent, rocking.

He hears the door and freezes. Someone's here. The boy turns slowly and looks over his shoulder. Then he sits up, dumbfounded.

"...Da?" He's off the ledge and in Headmon's arms.

Hiding surprise, Headmon embraces the boy.

"Oh, da..." Axl sobs, "I couldn't stay away."

"I'm glad you couldn't stay away," he whispers into the boy's ear.

Then Axl steps back abruptly. He looks bewildered. He's blinking. Something doesn't feel right but he doesn't know what it is.

Smiling, Headmon holds out the clothes. Axl doesn't move.

It's the connection. The bond. The bond between the boy and his da isn't there. The connection is missing.

Axl's mouth falls open.

"...Who?"

"I thought you might want these." Headmon steps forward, holding out the clothes. "You don't want to be wearing human skin, do you?"

The voice is a hollow version of da's voice. Axl stares, mouth open. Finally, he takes the clothes and sets them on the ledge. He flings off the trench coat and kicks off the stiff shoes he was given to wear. Naked, he steps into his trousers and fastens them. He lets the shirt fall down over his head then eases into the doublet. Sitting, he leans over to pull on his boots. While leaning, he closes his eyes and sends as hard as he can.

DA?

Nothing.

R'IO?!

Nothing.

Axl straightens up. He looks into Headmon's blue-flame eyes.

DA?!

Darkness.

Void.

Axl closes and leans over to fasten his boots, trembling from a sudden surge of adrenalin.

This isn't da. This isn't R'io. That's certain.

And if not da then who?

Reveal nothing.

Is it too late?

The man speaks.

"I've come to take you to more pleasant surroundings. Would

357

you like that?"

Axl shrugs then stands. The cell door opens. The man smiles and then gestures.

"Shall we?"

The boy takes a step then stops and looks at Headmon.

"What's your name?"

In the silence that follows the question the two look at each other, understanding that they are adversaries. Then Axl moves past the man trying to be R'io out into the corridor. The technician standing at rigid attention is obviously terrified. He steps aside and bows as Headmon joins the boy and leads him toward the residence.

***

The wind stiffened. The little sailboat carrying Skye, Rogue and Esa made good time coming back across the lake and is now approaching the dock.

They haven't spoken. They haven't looked at each other. Rogue's unexpressed fury made the trip back across the lake thick with tension.

A footman helps Skye tie off the boat. Other footmen are waiting for the escort boats. Esa stands. Rogue hops out and marches away, off to the side, ignoring everyone.

Reynolds exits the residence and strides down the long hill, hands clasped behind his back, face grave. Esa's basket is still heavy and full of food. Skye helps her lift it out of the boat.

"What's in here? We might as well eat something."

Esa looks at Skye, astonished that someone could think of food right now.

"Fruit, yogurt, dark bread, and water."

Reynolds approaches the dock and stops. He clears his throat. Then he addresses Skye One-Who-Wanders.

"Mr. Headmon would like to meet with you alone. Then he would like to meet with family and friends for a formal announcement. Please follow me to the residence so you can prepare for the meeting."

"That's not the agreement!" Rogue is striding toward the butler, her eyes spitting black fire.

"I'm afraid, Miss Rogue, that you have no choice in this

358

matter."

Rogue's mouth falls open. She steps closer to Reynolds.

"He's never broken an agreement with the champions before! He knows the cost!"

"I'm afraid it's decided, Miss Rogue." Reynolds is not remotely perturbed. "According to Mr. Headmon there's no discussing it."

Rogue takes a step back. She looks from Skye to Esa to Reynolds then back to Skye.

"We have an agreement," she hisses.

"We do." Skye nods.

Reynolds clears his throat and smiles politely.

"If Miss Skye will please come with me."

He turns and moves with long sure strides back up toward the arrangement of planes and angles and shapes and colors that compose the residence. Heart pounding, Skye follows.

On entering the residence, Isham hands Skye a robe and slippers. She puts the robe on and ties it closed. She twists her feet into the slippers. Then she turns to him and opens.

Rogue is picking up our handsign.

That's why we must make our move quickly. You have an agreement with her?

Si. She wants to leave with us.

His response is an impartial nod. Then he clears his throat.

"Follow me, please."

Grateful for the warmth of the robe, she pads behind him down a long, softly illuminated hall. After passing several closed doors, he stops at one and opens it onto a large dressing room done in dusty pastels. Through an open door across from her she can see a large bathroom.

"If you will, please." He holds out a hand, indicating that she is to enter.

The first thing she notices is the smell. Sweet and chemical.

On the wall to her right is a vanity table with a mirror and all kinds of make-up and perfumes plus a chair. The wall behind her is a full-length mirror. Off to the side, a big antique Chinese screen divides the room in half.

Isham One-Who-Waits remains in the open doorway, dignified and impersonal. Surely this remote person cannot be the same one who birthed her back at the Refuge. But it is. Him. Remarkably transformed yet the same. And they are no less connected.

Skye One-Who-Wanders moves to and looks behind the screen. She sees racks of clothes and rows of shoes, all black. Wigs of different styles but all black are perched on life-like Skye-heads and arranged in a row on a side table. She turns and looks at Isham. He signs.

~ Source-willing, we will honor your agreement with Rogue.

He clears his throat. His words are soft and precise.

"As per Mr. Headmon's instructions you are to bathe thoroughly. Then choose from the clothing provided. The garments you arrived in have been taken to storage for safekeeping."

She gasps, automatically reaching inside the bathrobe for R'io's belt. It's there. Hanging the way she likes it.

"From now, Mr. Headmon prefers you in something more indicative of the contours of your body. For this occasion he has chosen black. He instructed me to inform you that these are real garments, from the storerooms of the Ark. What you smell is their preservative – though it will fade as they remain in the air. Mr. Headmon thought you might like to wear the genuine article. Evidently fashion was considered an art form back then." He dips his head. "I'll wait outside."

Then he's gone and the door is closed.

***

Axl is in a furnished concrete studio apartment on the other side of the residence, facing the sea. He's trembling violently. His thoughts are hurricanes of colliding self-accusations and contradictions. His feelings swing in wide, wild arcs. Everything is confused and confusing.

Everything got even more confusing when he walked into the apartment and saw the vastness of sand and sea and sky for the first time through a wall of window. Stunned by vertigo, the boy had to shield his eyes and turn away trembling until the man who brought him here closed the drapes and flicked on a lamp then told him to wait, saying "there's food in the kitchen." As he was leaving, the man stopped and turned to Axl, his gaze withering. "Have you come to get your resource? Great City sends children for this?"

The man left. The door was noisily bolted from outside. Axl

checked. He's locked in, pacing, trying to work his way through confusion-beyond-confusion.

He sits down. He gets back up. He peeks out the drapes at sand and sea and sky and glare and is overwhelmed. He has no pieces of story to help him make sense of anything. He has only an awareness of approaching precipice that tells him to be cautious on this most dangerous of grounds. And dominating his awareness is a question.

Who is this man who strikes fear in everyone, who is so like his da and not like R'io at all?

***

Wearing a beautifully cut tuxedo, Headmon is alone in his control center listening to pensive jazz. Skye One-Who-Wanders is on one set of screens. She's several floors below, down in the dressing room shower. Lathered and rinsed and clean, she stands in water and steam, head back, eyes closed, taking her time, revealing nothing.

Axl is on another set of screens. The boy seems alternately disconsolate and awed, worried and fascinated, overwhelmed and comprehending, restless and lethargic, determined and tentative. Sometimes he's pacing around the apartment. Sometimes he's limp on the sofa. Sometimes he's standing at the drapes, shielding his eyes, peeking out. Then he closes the curtains and starts roving around the apartment again, touching and examining everything.

Skye proceeds meticulously. Intense and focused, she steps out of the shower, towels herself dry and brushes her teeth. Remembering to breathe, she runs fingers through hair that is not an inch long. Then, naked but for the belt, she returns to the dressing room and moves to the big Chinese screen. She stops, closes her eyes and remembers what this is all about.

R'io. Get him out. Get them all out.

She opens her eyes and steps around behind the screens. There are too many choices. Moving closer, she reaches out, touches.

The question of color has been settled for her. Everything is black. There's not a speck of anything else.

Racks of clothes are laden with gowns and dresses and skirts and suits and slacks and shirts and blouses in every style and fabric imaginable. On the floor under the racks are rows of different kinds of

361

shoes and boots. Stacks of neatly folded filmy black underwear and stockings are on a table off to one side where the wigs are lined up in a row on their Skye-heads.

Defiance would leave her naked so she works her way along the nearest rack. Occasionally she stops and regards something simple in the mix of lace and leather and feathers and frilly silks. Finally, dizzy from options, she selects the simplest things she can find – a tailored silk shirt with matching trousers and a pair of soft boots.

Dismissing underwear as unnecessary and probably uncomfortable, she dresses then puts R'io's brown belt back on, draping it from shoulder to hip, a slash of color. A shred of defiance.

The garments are cool, like water on her skin. Buttoning the shirt up as high as it will go, which is to her sternum, then the cuffs, she turns, catches her image in the mirror and is arrested.

Leaning forward, head cocked, she studies a tall, angular stranger. Two big intense eyes the color of night stare back at her from a face that is more animal than refined. She moves to and opens the door onto the hall.

Isham/Reynolds is standing a respectful distance away with his hands behind his back. He dips his head in appreciation.

"If I might be permitted, Miss Skye has chosen well. But might I sug-gest that you let me be responsible for the belt."

"No," she flushes.

"Very well. Then if you will, Mr. Headmon is waiting."

***

Spread out in a cloud of ancient space-debris, the first responders are using dead satellites of all shapes and sizes, like high-tech insects, to further mask their presence even though they're in stealth-mode and camouflaged anyway.

Quester Bates is in the ambulance. McCloud and Salonnen bracket her on the sleds then Rogers and Kim on the scooters. Pilar is above and behind the ambulance, windrider wings furled. A slice of old moon is visible behind them. Great City is only a few minutes from here, straight down.

Such close proximity to the corpse of Home affects each responder differently. But all are quiet and there's no turning away, no avoiding the con-sequence of unbridled greed and certainty. Then silence is broken by Ingrid Steele of H-V cruiser Mohawk who identifies herself and is recognized to proceed.

"FROM: Captain Beryl Porter, Command Ship Phoenix. TO: rescue team Falcon. MESSAGE: Space States still attempting negotiate for a peaceful release of ambassadors. Should attempts fail team Falcon is to enter Great City and retrieve ambassadors using force if necessary and to the degree necessary. Once ambassadors are on their way to H-V cruiser Mohawk remaining Falcons are to enter the transfer station and free H-V shuttle/barge Ralph Waldo Emerson so the ship can be returned to S.S. Hope. Do you copy?"

"Copy-clear," Pilar flutters her wings and adjusts her bandoliers.

"Message continues," Ingrid's voice is low and steady. "Three teams of elite first responders have arrived earth-side of the moon and are under your command. All three accompanying H-V cruisers are in formation at the far side of the moon and ready to assist should that be necessary. Do you copy?"

"Copy-clear," Pilar dips down to the ambulance and stands in space right over Bates' head.

"Message concludes. Team Falcon is to exit stealth-mode immediately. Prepare to go down loud and proud. Thank you for your service to the commons. END MESSAGE. Do you copy?"

"We copy-clear."

"Mohawk is standing at the ready to assist. God bless and return to com-silence."

No Space State officer has ever delivered such orders. With a little click Ingrid Steele, the Viking, is gone and, with her, some kind of elemental connection to what is familiar.

Suddenly they are alone out here, six elite first responders. Falcons. Fierce and fragile, facing possible combat with other humans where before battle has always been with elements and phenomena. Sensing a shift in mood, Pilar yanks them back to focus with a sharp command.

"All right Falcons let's pop down from this cloud of junk and exit stealth-mode."

Pilar turns on loud fast music with a heavy beat and sends it blasting through their helmets as, arcing down from the cloud of space-debris the six elite first responders bloom into contrast with their surroundings and, by virtue of ignited color, become distinct from each other and instantly identifiable.

Bates and the ambulance are glowing candy-apple red. McCloud and her sled are sunburst yellow. Salonnen on the other sled is flaming pink. Rogers and her scooter are fluorescent chartreuse. Kim on the other scooter is an explosion of lavender. Pilar and the windrider are the glistening dragonfly-blue. They light up each other and the cloud of space-debris above them, flaring it with multicolored dawn.

"All right, everybody, down your SpeedBalls then check equipment on the double!"

Each responder presses a separate and protected button down by her ankle causing a jigger's worth of black-cherry liquid to spurt into her mouth. The effect comes on sudden – laser focus and instant relaxed responsiveness.

***

Paul Prescot Reed can't sleep at all anymore, not even his usual few hours. When he tries, he drowns in dreams. Not picture-dreams but sounds. Sounds cause him to lurch awake, exhausted. No, he wakes frightened, sweating. Something new for him: fear – a horror to be avoided at all costs.

So late last night, roused before he even reclined, he came to his private office and is sitting at his desk trying to get something constructive done, trying to think a helpful thought. The light is a thin yellowish beam shining down on dust motes that surround him. It's hot because of half-measures but he refuses to unzip his tunic even though perspiration drips while he sits expressionless, blinking at a fact that won't go away.

Unless something radical happens to change the layout on the playingfield, he, Paul Prescot Reed, will be Great City's last Presider, the one responsible for an end to all futures.

What looms on the horizon cannot be allowed to happen. But how to stop it?

Reed sips from a half-empty glass of Peaceful at his elbow. It's his third. It doesn't help. Nothing helps. He rubs his face.

"Just a little sleep," he whispers to no one, "a little rest. Even an hour." He drains the glass, leans back in his chair and closes his eyes.

Still awake, he hears the dream-sounds, intimate and inescapable. He hears people trying to breathe, many people, and he's in the middle of them, compressed by millions of people struggling to breathe and those sounds turn into mourning and keening then raging stormwinds against which he has no defense because there is none.

Reed stands quickly, swaying for a moment from vertigo. He moves to the wetbar and pours a tumbler of Focus. He slugs it down and begins to pace around the office, once again re-visiting the task force meeting that ended well past midnight.

His head of Technology wants to play offense.

Magrit Abram Shen wants to take the initiative and set the terms of engagement. She insists that the three new sightings are conclusive proof of a sizeable and sophisticated population beneath the surface north and east of Great City. We have the technology, she insisted with Whitaker nodding in the background while she explained that the warheads in the bunkers sur-rounding Great City are still functional and now being prepped. They were maintained in case the Space States decide to come back and claim what isn't theirs anymore. She argued forcefully for re-aiming a large number of them and deploying several warheads immediately.

The meeting ended inconclusively with Reed saying he'd think about it. Unable to sleep, he's either been doing that or hearing people trying to breathe. It's time to come back to reality.

"Tech-secretary!"

"Yes, sir."

"Connect me to the head of Technology."

"Yes, sir," Magrit Abram Shen answers the page immediately, sounding fresh and alert, like she's already working and it isn't even the beginning of the day yet.

"Yes, sir."

"Come to my office."

***

Headmon is alone in the bunker wearing his tuxedo and sipping a glass of wine from a very good year. He's surrounded by images on screens – primarily of Skye and Reynolds in an opulent mirrored lift that is ascending slowly in several directions at once. He's kept them

365

closed in that small space for a long time to see if they might crack under the pressure. So far, no luck.

Curanda and her young assistant have their own screens and can be seen strolling around the lake with Rogue. There are also images of Axl and the man who could be his father from the looks of the two of them. Headmon scans the screens as he listens to the report coming in from Central Control.

"First, sir, there's nothing on the maps and no mention in the ancient histories of a Great City or anything planned for the surface that could conceivably enclose that many people. However, there was brief mention of something called the Space States, buried in a highly classified file."

"Send that to me."

"Yes, sir."

"Go on."

"Second. Reconnaissance. Two platoons of enforcers are now equipped and ready for deployment from the gate directly over canton Equa."

"Is that safe? Why not deploy them from Uni or Pax?"

"To maintain contact with us the reconnaissance team has to have a direct feed into Central Control. That means we have to leave the gate open."

"Start working on an option."

"Yes, sir."

"Continue."

"The reconnaissance team requests destination coordinates and distance estimates."

"South and west of here. Far. Can't be more specific yet. What's my surface attack capability?"

"An abundance of surplus ordnance remains from the old border skirmishes. And there are half a dozen missile silos stocked with warheads that have been maintained in case of threat from the surface. Located near cantons Equa and Uni."

"Point'em south and west and turn'em on."

"We're working on that now, sir. In anticipation…"

"All right. I'll tell you if and when." Suddenly Headmon sits up, having noticed something on one of his screens. "Stand-by."

"Yes, sir."

Muting Central Control, he leans back and studies Skye and Reynolds in the lift. They're not looking at each other. They're just

366

standing there, dis-tant and self-contained but connected somehow. Something impalpable passes between them, connecting. Then their eyes collide in the mirror again and linger an instant too long.

"I'm right," Headmon murmurs then leans forward, pulls that instant out of the scene and plays it back.

He slows it down and zooms in close. He plays it several times, checking both faces from several angles. Again and again, their eyes collide then flick away – like maybe they shouldn't look at each other but can't help it, like maybe the length of the lift ride has begun to unravel the discipline it takes to mask a connectione because they know each other from before. There's no doubt about it. The identical marks on each throat told him that long ago and now he can see it. A relationship. But of what nature?

Father/daughter?

Teacher/student?

Superior/subordinate?

From Great City. That much is certain.

Here to do what?

"I'm ready for you," he whispers then leans forward and reconnects to Central Control.

"Yes, Mr. Headmon?"

"Put Enforcement in all cantons on highest alert for some-thing from the surface, maybe from south and west of here. That includes my personal guard."

"Yes, sir."

Headmon disconnects from Central Control. He sits glaring at his screens. He takes a sip of wine and leans back, thinking.

Then, one by one, he pulls up images of the new butler and the new healer and her assistant. He flips through scenes, stops at certain ones and marks them for transfer. He selects one of the saved scenes and plays it in slow motion. Leaning forward, he squints as the butler greets Skye on the front steps. Headmon sees connection and movement of hands.

He pulls up images of the butler with Esa and sees connection, movement of hands. He brackets scenes of Skye asleep and sees movement of hands. Headmon drains his glass and connects to Central Control.

"Yes, sir."

"I'm sending some scenes. There's more handtalk on them. Find out what they're saying. I want that translation immediately. Page me when you have it."

"Yes, sir."

Headmon extinguishes all but a single screen filled with Skye's face. She's still in the lift, looking straight ahead, nervous and trying to hide it. He studies her. Then, deciding what music to use for this meeting, he punches code into his console and steps back, illumined only by the glow from Skye's pixel-face.

"Time to reel you in, sweetling."

The lift carrying Skye and Isham stops almost imperceptibly. The door slides open onto a small vestibule with laquered black walls and a floor-standing red vase that contains a single long-stemmed arcing blossom of utter white simplicity. Across from them the door is a rectangular seam in the wall.

Reynolds steps out of the lift. Skye follows. He walks to the door and knocks once softly. There's no response. He knocks again. After a moment, she hears a muffled sound, from inside.

"Come."

The door is opened. Isham steps aside for her to enter, which she does.

Headmon is standing in the middle of the loft wearing a perfectly tailored tuxedo but no tie. Loose red hair is soft around the sharp angles of his face. His eyes are hard blue flame.

"Is the belt necessary?"

Skye doesn't respond. After a moment's irritation Head-mon turns and brings a small device out of his pocket. He sticks the device in his nose and squirts. He squirts into the other nostril. He sniffs several times and puts the device away. Then he turns around and is transposed, smiling warmly, open and relaxed, calm from the deeps. It's as though all traces of Headmon have vanished and only R'io remains.

She doesn't move, can't take her eyes from him, so like real-R'io is he at this moment. Then forcing herself, she glances at the penthouse loft.

The far wall is a window beyond which are glittering lights. Off to one side of the room is an arrangement of sofas around a low table in front of a lit fireplace. Candles and potted trees soften the stark lines and create an effect of warmth and safety.

She hears ancient jazz, a muted horn, soft and slow. As though glamoured, Headmon steps forward and holds out a hand.

"One thing is missing."

Something is sparkling in his palm. Though curious, she steps back. He smiles.

"Perhaps you will allow Reynolds to help you with this."

After a moment, Skye nods. Reynolds moves quickly to Headmon who pours a trickle of liquid fire into his upturned palm. He walks back to Skye and shows her a substantial cube of topaz on a short gold chain. Behind her now, he brings the chain's open ends around to the nape of her neck and closes the clasp.

The stone hangs suspended in the bowl of her throat between the two little tear-shaped scars made by Solaris back at the Refuge.

"Yes. Perfect," transfixed, Headmon mocks a frown. "Except for the belt."

She does not respond. All she knows is that his hair and face are glazed and chiseled by firelight and that the clothes she's wearing are wet silk on her body. She glances at the window then looks the other way, sees paintings, a hallway, an ancient wooden rolltop desk, a wetbar.

"Reynolds, tell the others to dress for a formal announcement and bring them here to wait outside for my call."

"Yes, sir," the butler bows and steps out of the room, closing the door.

They are alone.

Headmon doesn't move, doesn't take his focus off of her and standing so grows more and more like R'io and it's all she can do to remember he's not. Then the moment can sustain no longer. He breaks into her confusion with a gentle smile.

"I'll mix drinks."

"Nothing for me."

He tilts his head, no? Then he moves to the wetbar. Clinging to what she knows – that this is not R'io but Headmon – Skye crosses the loft to the window at the far end of the room. She looks out. Her jaw drops.

The penthouse must be fifty stories high. Outside, it's night and what they call winter. The time/season difference from the rest of the residence confuses her for a moment. Then she remembers that everything here is sem-blance and under his control.

She hears him behind her and sees his reflection in the window that is also a mirror. He's pouring liquids into a silvery container. He puts a lid on the container and starts to shake it, making a pleasant sound. She turns her attention back to what's outside.

The sky is steel blue and star-dusted behind rows and rows of intersecting perpendicular streets and avenues lined with illumined tall, taller and tallest buildings, most of their windows lit. Directly below – stretching out in a grandeur that is in no way diminished by the surrounding massiveness but, rather, framed by it – is a big rectangle of park, covered with untracked snow. From this perspective the space behind her is perfectly proportioned to the rectangle below as well as the surrounding skyscrapers, enhancing a scale of visual elegance she'd not imagined possible from human hands. He stops shaking the beaker.

"Where are we?"

She turns to him.

"Where are we in what sense?"

He uncaps the beaker and carefully fills two exquisite triangles of glass with liquid diamond. He pops a skewered olive into each glass. Smiling, he brings the drinks to the table in front of the fireplace and sets the full glasses down without spilling a drop. Then he straightens and stands looking at her for a moment.

"Where are we in two senses then. Where are we geographically? And where are we historically?"

"Ah," she nods raising a finger then turns back to the window.

Skye One-Who-Wanders studies the park and the buildings that surround it. She looks into the mirror and examines the room and furnishings behind her. Closing her eyes, with the jazz in the background, she sifts through data from the archives. Then she looks out the window again, nodding.

"This is meant to be the place called New York City or Manhattan. Early 21st century, ancient time. I'd say we're on Central Park South."

"Very good," he nods appreciatively.

"And guessing by the shape of the glasses plus the olives I'd say you just made martinis."

"Mixed, not made. One mixes a martini."

"I'll remember that."

"Shall we sit?" He gestures to the arrangement of sofas, pleased by the ease with which things are going.

"Is that a suggestion or a command?"

He frowns then immediately smiles at the challenge she presents. Not answering her question, he eases down onto a sofa, leans back, crosses his legs and sits with his arms stretched out, resting on cushions. And she can't remember who he is.

"What a mystery you are," he smiles. "Have I told you, by the way, that your choice of attire is, as I'd hoped it would be, stunning? Simple. Elegant. Only, the belt…"

"No."

"Then come, sit." Undeterred, he pats the sofa next to him.

Skye One-Who-Wanders doesn't move for a moment. Then she

371

walks to one of the other sofas and sits as far away from him as possible. Smiling, he stands, picks up the drinks and moves to the other end of her sofa. He places the drinks on the table and sits.

She studies him intently, trying to loath what attracts. Then she looks away, at the drinks on the table, at the fire in the fireplace. He leans and whispers.

"I have so much to offer you."

Skye tries to swallow and can't. The chained topaz is too tight around her neck. Turning her head, she looks off to her left again, at the fire. She can feel heat through the melting silk of her clothes and doesn't want to feel silky heat, not now. She looks back at him and shrugs, trying to remember who he is. Then he smiles.

"I'm offering you something beyond your wildest dreams."

"You know nothing of my dreams."

"I know what everyone dreams." He scoots closer. "I know you're human. That means you're no different."

Eyes lock. She remembers who he is. She shrugs.

"And what does everyone dream?"

"Of this," he holds his arms out, indicating the residence, the grounds and beyond. "Sole custody of everything that is. That's what everyone dreams of."

"You assume."

"It's not what I assume," he snaps. "It's what I know. There's no one who doesn't want what I have. All of it!"

Headmon takes a deep breath as though to calm himself then picks up his glass and drains it. He stands, moves around the table to stand in front of the fireplace looking at her.

"I am the sole owner of everything there is and what I don't have I can take. I'm offering to share it with you. As equals. Everything."

"I don't want it."

"You answer too quickly."

"I'm not interested."

"How do you know? You haven't even seen the beginning of it yet. Let me show you."

"It's all semblance. Nothing here is real."

"The books, the art, the music, the food, the plants, the animals. This is the Ark! It's all real!"

"At what cost to everyone else?!"

"The poor and wretched will always be here."

"You seem determined to make certain of that."

"Come." He won't be deterred. "Live with me. As equals."

"I'm not interested."

"You lie! I can see by the way you look at me and by the way you are drawn to everything I am and have that you are more than interested!"

"You misread."

Eyes lock.

"If you don't want what everyone else wants," Headmon whispers fiercely, "then what *do* you want?!"

She examines him for a moment.

"I could never tell you that. We are not intimate."

"But I want to be!"

Skye doesn't respond. Headmon paces back and forth. Then he ap-proaches her end of the sofa. She rises and moves around to the other side of the table. He sighs.

"I want you to be my partner. The Lady Headmon. After the way of the ancients. I want a marriage."

"What?" She manages not to laugh and instead clears her throat. "Marriage?"

"Yes! Us. You, me. Man and wife." He steps closer. "It's what I've always wanted and never found. An equal. Then you arrived." He steps closer. "I must have you!"

She stands astonished by the sudden arrival of leverage.

"What kind of marriage would it be with an unwilling bride?"

"No, no. I want you willing! That's part of how it has to go!"

"If you want me willing then I must have time." She backs away to put distance between them.

"What would it take for you to be willing?"

"Who knows what it takes, or how long, for the heart to turn toward what it loathes?"

"You loathe me?" Headmon is genuinely surprised.

"I loathe how you got what you have and how you keep it and what you do with it. And I fear you."

"You have nothing to fear from me."

"As long as I cooperate. Should I not, there will be suffering."

"Then cooperate!"

"You remind me too much of the bounty hunter."

"You lie! Whoever that man in there is," Headmon points at the window/mirror then catches himself and quickly lowers his arm, "you love him. And I'm him now. We are identical!"

Do not reveal!

Skye One-Who-Wanders does not allow herself to look at the window/mirror, where Headmon pointed, only at a painting on the wall then at his face then back at the painting, studying it intently.

"Beautiful piece, don't you think, Headmon, this particular Cezanne? One can feel the summer sun on that fruit." She turns to him and smiles "Maybe I should see more of the Ark, let you persuade me. However," she raises a finger of caution, "before I could even consider your offer we would have to negotiate a contract after a tradition of the ancients. Call it a bride-price. And the price for one who brings what I would bring to such a marriage will be high. Agree to this now."

"Or?"

"Force the marriage and learn how unhappy one person can make another."

"What about the suffering little folk?"

"Try to convince me they don't matter."

Blinking rapidly, Headmon pulls the atomizer out of his pocket, raises it to his nose then decides against using it. Instead, he flings it aside, needing to remain alert for this conversation. The atomizer rolls around for a while before it comes to rest as he takes a step toward her.

"You are full of tricks," he whispers. "But you have met your master and my joy has been delayed long enough. Skye, One-who-wanders is mine now. And to celebrate, we marry immediately. REYNOLDS!"

"Yes, Mr. Headmon." The door opens and Isham enters the loft.

"Bring in the others."

"Yes, sir."

Skye One-Who-Wanders moves to the window and stands looking alternately at the view in front of her then at the reflected loft behind her then at her own ghosted image. Nowhere in between can she distinguish another reality. But she knows R'io is there. Somewhere beyond the glass.

***

374

The door to Karin Lassiter Kohl's dirty white cell is yanked open. Two burly Security guards in glistening black monitor suits stride in.

"Get up. Come." Their voices are hollow monotones.

Gaunt and hollow-eyed, Lassiter gets to her feet.

"Water. We need water."

She's ignored. She can hear guards in the adjacent cell, being resisted for a moment by Davenport Baxter. Then silence.

"Put this on."

A guard hands her an old brown jumpsuit. She steps into it, pulls it up and on then snaps the front closed. They toss her a pair of work boots.

"Put these on."

She does. Too big.

"Come."

"Water."

She's ignored.

One of the guards steps out of the cell. The other waits to follow her. Light-headed she goes into the hall as Dav Baxter is being dragged from his cell unconscious.

They're taken to a lift. Lassiter knows the lift goes down and ends near one of the southern deployment bays. She flips through options – assuming she can get away from the guards and haul an unconscious Dav Baxter with her. The door closes. They descend.

***

Everyone is present. The women are seated. Rogue is on one sofa across from Katya. Curanda and Esa are on the sofa in the middle. Reynolds, the butler, and a dozen armed footmen are standing in the background on either side of the front door.

The loft is lit for romance, as it was before. The mood is tense. The jazz is mellow until Headmon strides to a control panel on the wall and snaps it off.

"Reynolds, take a seat on the sofa." He turns to Skye. "My love, do as you wish."

She remains at the window, turned into the room, watching. Isham walks to the arrangement of sofas. Rogue makes room for him.

He sits and leans back but remains ready to respond.

"Enough of the homey atmosphere."

Headmon adjusts the lighting to a bright overhead glare then positions himself in front of the fireplace. He doesn't speak for a while. He just stands there with an odd smirk on his face, studying those on the sofas.

"I brought you here to witnesses a ceremony so momentous that all of SubTurra will come to a halt for its occurrence. And as a token of my joy, everyone will be given an hour of free Banding-time." His eyes are electric blue. "But before that, a few loose threads need to be taken care of." He turns to Skye. "Don't you think?"

"Does it matter?" She shrugs.

"Indifference does not become you, my love." His smile goes cold.

Skye turns to look for R'io through the window. Headmon continues his address to everyone else.

"First loose thread. It has become clear to me of late that some of you know each other from before." He pauses to let that sink in. "You three, for instance. Curanda, Esa, Reynolds. You're not SubTurrans or from the hinter-lands. You're from beyond here, aren't you. Like Skye. From Great City."

Headmon waits for a response. Nothing is revealed.

"You're with Skye, aren't you?! You've come for her!" He raises a finger. "Ah, clever people. You need to know I have proof before tipping your hand. Then proof you shall have."

He moves to Skye and stands fingering the stone on the chain around her lovely neck.

"You never told me what those are from, my love, those marks on your throat. Fairly fresh wounds."

He waits for her to respond. She doesn't.

"I know, let's ask someone else! Reynolds. Stand. Take off your tie, unbutton your shirt and let me see your throat."

Isham does as he's told. Headmon approaches and studies the old man's identical scars.

"What are these from?"

"The bite of a mutant arachnid."

"In Great City?"

"Nearby."

"Oops, I've forgotten something," Headmon snaps his fingers. "Something very important by way of proof. My latest recruit needs to be in-cluded in this conversation." He looks at the lead footman. "Bring in the boy."

The lead footman goes to the loft's front door and opens it. Two enforcers escort Axl into the room. He's wearing his stone-people clothes.

DO NOT REVEAL! Snow and Curanda pierce the boy's awareness, stopping him in his tracks.

The loft is silent and remains so for a moment. Everyone stares at Axl. Finally, Headmon beckons.

"Come, join us."

The lad moves cautiously into the loft. He sees his grand da, his grandam, his little sister. He sees Skye standing at the window, a knot of concern between her eyebrows. He feels the connection. Isham and Curanda and Esa and Skye are who they seem to be. But who is the man trying to pass himself off as R'io?

DO NOT REVEAL! It's Isham and Curanda again.

Axl looks like he's going to be sick. Headmon moves to the boy and drapes an arm around his shoulders.

"Quite handsome, huh? Calls himself Axl." He tips the boy's head up with a stiff forefinger and aims it at each person he names. "Axl, this is my love, Skye One-Who-Wanders. This is my new gypsy, Koranda and her assistant, Esa. This is my sister, Katya. That dark baldheaded creature there who is scowling so is Rogue, champion of champions. Those men back there at the door are my footmen. They do whatver I say. And this is my new butler, Reynolds."

Headmon releases Axl's chin and turns to the others. He smiles, de-lighted. Then his expression changes to one of amazement at a curious coincidence.

"I think Axl looks very like that fellow who arrived with you, Skye. The bounty hunter as you call him. Don't you think?"

She shrugs indifferently.

Headmon studies Skye, Isham, Curanda and Esa as they adjust to the new arrival. He makes them wait before going on. Predator and prey. Playing with them before he speaks again, softly.

"What's going on here?"

There's no response but from Katya whose head is turning this way and that as she tries to figure out the game.

"Go sit with your friends on the sofa, Axl. There's more to the show. I want my guests to be comfortable." Headmon gently shoves the boy toward a sofa. "That's right. Between Curanda and Esa."

They sit like three strangers. But the connection is evident. Headmon studies them for a moment. Then he turns to Skye.

"My love, are you telling me the truth about Great City?"

"Yes."

"Are they going to come and get you or have they already come to get you?"

"So far as I know they have not come yet. But they will."

"Then who are these people?"

She shrugs. He smiles.

"Oh, you are very clever, aren't you. Such a clever girl. So subtle." He raises a forefinger to his lips, pondering. "How am I to know the truth? What am I to do? Who am I to trust?"

Headmon slaps a splayed hand against his chest. He turns around dramatically, addressing everyone.

"I trust ME!" I trust what *I* know. And what *I* know is that the four of you and this boy here are not from SubTurra or the hinterlands. You know each other from before!"

He raises two fingers. He turns abruptly to Rogue.

"Second proof! My champion of champions?"

Her black-fire eyes are riveted on his.

"You're beginning to figure it out, aren't you? Something is going on between them. Right?"

Rogue looks irritated. He handsigns.

~ Do Not Reveal. ~

After a long moment, as though puzzled, Rogue shrugs and shakes her head. Headmon signs again.

~ Do Not Reveal what? ~

Suddenly, Esa chirps, all childlike innocence.

"Is this a game we're meant to learn, Mr. Headmon?"

He turns to Esa then quickly back to Rogue, hissing.

"And, by the way, Rogue, what's your agreement with Skye?"

Changing gears, Headmon turns back to Esa. He takes his time regarding the girl. Then, grinning, he approaches.

"I'm going to assume, Esa, that Ruelle – poor Ruelle is gone now, did you know that? I'm going to assume that she did not properly instruct you on Specials behavior with Headmon – a lapse for which she would have been dismissed anyway. So I will forgive your having spoken without invitation this time. On one condition." He signs.

~ Do Not Reveal WHAT? ~

The girl smiles sweetly, all innocent interest.

"STOP PLAYING WITH ME!" he bellows in her face.

Axl, lunges to his feet and is shoved back down.

"Here you do what you're told, boy! I said sit with the girls and that's where you stay!"

At a signal from Headmon, the footmen draw their weapons and release the safetys. Esa lowers her head and slumps back. Curanda reaches across her grandson for the girl's hand.

"ENOUGH!" Headmon bellows again. "Skye handtalked in her sleep almost from the moment she got here. I just didn't know what it was at first. Then Reynolds arrives with his identical scars. Then Curanda and Esa were next. And, what do you know? They all talk the same handsign.

"Then Axl stumbles in here with all the finesse of an idiot and I'll wager the entire Ark he knows this brand of handtalk, too!" Headmon shrugs elaborately. "So what? Lots of immigrants and hinterlanders have their own brand of handtalk. Right?"

Headmon stands as though transfixed, a finger in the air. Then he paces, pretending to be confused.

"Ah, but this particular handtalk is a dialect unknown in SubTurra or the hinterlands." He stands with his arms outspread, scanning their faces. "Coincidence? I think not. But in case you need further proof there's genetic evidence. You four on the sofas and the bounty hunter are genetically related to each other. Skye is not related to any of you. That, however is a mystery for another day. Right now I want to know something else." He signs.

~ Do not reveal what? ~ Headmon waits, very still, focused on them like a snake. "Do not reveal what?" he hisses. "What are you intending? What's the plan? What are you hatching?"

Nothing is revealed though Axl is having a hard time.

"Whatever your plan, I never yield and will not be deprived of my prize."

Headmon looks at Skye. She turns back to the window-mirror and searches for a different reality between the reflections but finds no seam in the seeming. Headmon brings a hand to his forehead, mocking himself.

"Oh silly me again. I've forgotten the reason for calling you all to-gether. The most important part. My announcement!"

Headmon turns to Skye. He smiles at her openly like a lover then turns back to the others.

"I have chosen Skye One-who-wanders to be my bride and the next Lady Headmon. The ceremony will take place immediately and there will be nothing else on the entire Banding spectrum. As soon as a last thread is tied off."

"What?!" Katya stands abruptly, enraged.

"SIT DOWN!"

She does. Headmon turns back to Skye.

"My love?"

She looks at him and shivers.

"Do you understand that your friends here will stay alive and well as long as you cooperate?"

Esa blanches. Curanda squeezes the girl's hand. Isham sits dignified and straight, his eyes closed.

Elder Martin?

There's no response.

Elder Martin?

Isham, thank Source!

No time now. Take your positions. Let's go.

We're in place. There's been...

Source be with us all.

"What about the match?!" Rogue is on her feet.

"For now the match is off. I can't risk my love being injured at this time. Other things are more important, like an heir and preparations to surface and conquer Great City."

"But the profits from the match..."

"Spit in the wind against what I smell coming this way."

"The people will not allow it!"

"THE PEOPLE HAVE NO VOICE IN THE MATTER!"

Rogue's eyes spit dangerous black fire. She starts to speak. He holds up a hand to stop her.

"Your presence at the ceremony is a necessary endorsement from the champions otherwise I wouldn't bother. Immediately after the ceremony you will be taken to Central Control. From there, you will return to the Stadium. You are being allowed to live because of your contribution to my wealth. But you will never be seen or heard of again outside the Stadium because as we speak the public is being told that you have been fatally injured in a training accident. Now sit down. I'm not finished."

Stalled, Rogue sits. Headmon turns and strolls to the control panel behind the small masterpiece.

"Last thread. Earlier this evening, when we were negotiating the terms of our marriage, my love mentioned a charming custom from our ancestors up above. She called it a bride price." He smiles innocently. "I have hit upon the perfect bride price." He presses code into the control panel. "Look out the window, my love."

Skye whirls around and faces the window/mirror, seeing him behind her at the control panel. He taps the keypad one final time with a flourish. And in a blinding flash everything changes.

What was light before is now dark. What was dark before is now light. At first the glare in front of her is so bright she has to shield her eyes. She hears a soft sustained grinding sound and knows the window/mirror is retracting. Bright cold steam roils out of the suddenly opened space, thinning as it dissipates through the loft. She smells chemicals and hears the unmistakable sounds of medical technology.

Gradually, through the thinning steam she begins to make out a large transparent capsule resting on a solid base. As the steam diffuses in the loft she can see him inside the capsule. Locked in. On his back. Suspended in some kind of clear ooze or gel. Naked. Real.

R'io.

She doesn't have to verify.

Tubes go into his arms, mouth, ears, and up his nose. He's cathet-erized though the bag hanging outside the capsule is almost empty.

"Your bounty hunter," Headmon coos into her ear, having come up behind her, too close.

The smell of his cologne is nauseating. He touches her, puts his hands on her shoulders and upper arms, squeezes.

"I've been keeping him alive for you."

Headmon steps around her on into what seems to be a large brightly illumined vault. The far side has a big door with a wheel in its center so it can be opened mechanically. The only thing in the vault is R'io in the capsule that hisses and pings and drips with artificial life.

"Come, love," Headmon beckons.

Skye takes and releases an unsatisfactory breath and steps into the vault. She walks to the capsule. Looking down, she stops directly across from Headmon who is on the other side, tapping code into a keypad.

With a soft explosion of steam, the lid of the capsule unclasps and rises to the ceiling. She can feel the cold pouring out. Headmon enters another combination. The capsule drains with a long, deep

381

sucking sound.

Skye One-Who-Wanders forces herself to look down, see R'io coated with glistening transparent membrane. His head is shaved, as is the rest of his body. He is grotesquely emaciated.

"My bride price," Headmon whispers. "You need never be afraid again. Not of him. Not of Great City. Not of anything. You're mine now. I take care of what is mine."

She looks up and sees Headmon so like R'io. She looks down and sees R'io so unlike himself.

"When I asked why you wanted to see him, you said, 'to spit on him,' or words to that effect. Correct?"

She sucks down then releases another ragged, inadequate breath.

"Now's your chance." He holds out his arms. "Go ahead."

"There's no point. He's incapacitated."

"Very well," Headmon smiles. "Then he can be disposed of." He puts a hand on the keypad and before tapping in more code, stops to explain. "The capsule will be filled with a substance that will reduce him to a harmless liquid. He'll eventually go down the drain. I don't want him recycled. I don't want his molecules in our world." Headmon starts tapping in code.

"NO!" It's a startling command from Skye.

Eyes lock. Mocking interest, Headmon lowers the keypad.

"Do not reveal what?" he whispers. "What's your agreement with Rogue?"

There's a pleasant chime-tone, a signal from Central Control.

"SPEAK!" Headmon calls out.

"Sir, you are needed immediately."

"On my way." Headmon looks at the lead footman who bows. "No one is to move."

"Yes, sir."

Headmon strides toward the front door. Instead of exiting, however, he turns left down a hallway to his bunker.

***

Colors blazing, Lt. Pilar Mezon and the Falcons enter earth's atmosphere and let gravity do the work. Skipping and bouncing like stones on water, they arc down, down into the gray glare of high noon. They start breaking only when they must and pull up 5,000 feet directly above Great City, heaving sparks from the heat of the journey while they activate their tools and ordnance. In V formation with Bates and the ambulance in the middle, they hang suspended to let their sudden arrival register while the Space States again plead for negotiations.

The council does not respond.

Pilar signals team Falcon. Bates in the ambulance peels off to one side and hovers for a better firing position should Great City get aggressive. The other Falcons plummet to 2,000 feet above the very top of the dome.

Tools ready, Pilar, Sh-rai McCloud, Jika Rogers, Salonnen and Kim are bright guerilla cherubs floating high above the rusty crown of Great City, ready to open the structure by force if necessary. Looking down, the first responders wait in silence for word from command. They try to ignore the desolation surrounding Great City. They try to focus only on the seam of the dome, willing it to open so that drastic measures can be avoided.

***

Elder Moss, Schiara and Wim have arrived at their third and final point of egress. Packs off, they're taking a moment to catch their breath after a hard and hurried journey. Schiara and Wim are in the portal-chamber. Elder Moss requested a moment's solo time and limped off to be alone. She's having trouble with the knee and can hardly walk and it's time to go out on the surface again.

...Luz, Luz...

She can't get through her own sweaty fear to find comfort from her beloved who last reported good news about a possible pregnancy. Sitting on a boulder, knee throbbing, leg straight out in front of her, elder Moss lifts the flask she's been sipping from since the pain started, drains it and stows it empty in her pack. Then she adjusts and tightens the binding on her knee. It was improvised from every belt and strap they could spare from their gear. After several deep breaths, she closes her eyes, sinks down and opens to Source.

Be with us holy one. Please take us out and bring us back one more time. As you would have it.

After a few moments, elder Moss opens her eyes – no less apprehensive than before and no less faithful.

"Time to go," she whispers to no one, stands with effort and lumbers through the wide passage back to the portal where the youngsters are waiting, both in surface gear, worried, standing next to each other with something important to say.

Schiara takes a step toward her mentor. She holds up a thick coil of climbing rope, actually several climbing ropes knotted together.

"We talked it over while you were gone. If Wim and I are tethered, I can guide him back to the portal..."

"No."

"Then let me go out alone. That'll have to be enough beacons."

"No. You and me, Schiara. That's how we do it. Trust in Source."

"Aye." The girl nods, unhappy with this response, as is Wim.

Elder Moss and Schiara put on their masks. They nod to Wim. He opens the portal.

"Let's go!"

And they're both outside again.

***

The elite first responders are still poised 2,000 feet above Great City, bobbing in place like corks on water while their technology surrenders no sign of how it functions. Corporal Sh'rai McCloud is handling surface scanners for the team – paying attention to what might come at them unexpectedly from below.

Frowning, she adjusts her tuner but can't clarify the signals that suddenly flare from the surface some distance northeast of here, way beyond the point where a few primitive machines are digging in the ash. The signals stop. McCloud adjusts her tuner but can't find them again. Then the signals are back.

Pilar and the others are preparing a brief display of firepower as incentive for Great City to peacefully resolve the situation. They plan to aim a few impressive volleys around structure without doing actual harm. McCloud interrupts.

"Falcon 3 here. I'm getting strange signals off the surface a hundred nauts northeast of here. Doesn't seem to be related to anything from Great City."

"Go check it out," Pilar turns to one of the other responders to ask a question and is interrupted by Commander Ingrid Steele from H-V cruiser Mohawk who authenticates and delivers orders as McCloud peels off from the others to find out what's beeping over yonder.

"FROM: Captain Beryl Porter, C.S. Phoenix. MESSAGE: Team Falcon: do not display firepower. Instead, enter Great City soonest and return with your objectives. Blessings. END MESSAGE. Do you copy?"

"Copy-clear and we are on our way."

The remaining four elite first responders plummet like climbers rappelling down, down to the crown of Great City and the seam that needs to be opened. Ordered not to use blasters, they ignite acid-fire torches and start burning their way in.

***

After spreading out to ignite as many beacons as possible, elder Moss and Schiara turn back toward the portal. Slowed by pain and the brace on her knee, elder Moss struggles in the ash, falling farther and farther behind. Near the portal, Schiara screams, "OPEN!" and turns to look back as two dozen small drones crest the very high horizon, lock in on faltering elder Moss but do not register Schiara who is poised, stunned, in the shadow of the open portal. The drones zip around elder Moss, still on her feet, firing her disabler.

"WIM, CLOSE THE PORTAL!"

Schiara whips out her disabler and runs back up the dune toward elder Moss, firing at the cloud of drones. She hits one. She hits another. She hits one of the drones headed for her but isn't fast enough for the second one.

The drones circling elder Moss close in and try to inject her. She swats at them with her cloak. Then one gets her from behind. Stunned, she drops the disabler, reaches for the drone lodged in her rump and crumbles to the ground, writhing as the knee goes completely out. Then she's still and the drones take up defensive positions around their prey.

Schiara plucks a drone out of the back of her gauntlet and disables it. Then she sinks to one knee as even that limited amount of drug begins to turn her wobbly. She wavers for a moment, trying to fire at the drones still guarding elder Moss. Then she falls forward into ash.

***

Back in the beginning of the troubles, Great City's Presider made a decision not to negotiate with the Space States about anything until they resumed delivering goods. Now trapped in his own stubbornness he refuses to talk even though the Space States have cause and means to breech the structure in order to retrieve the ambassadors.

But the Space States refuse to cooperate. They continue to demand negotiations, this time promising a harmless demonstration of force all around Great City by way of incentive to talk.

Reed wants to see. Hear. So he's made another decision and is now leading his head of Technology from his private office out of Founders' Hall and across the public square that is busy with stewards whose stares are none too friendly. They pass through a locked service door to a catwalk that takes them across to the outer skin of the dome, which is reinforced concrete and almost as thick as the wall of a dam at this level.

Maintenance units in orange monitor suits are working here and there. The light is dim. It's cooler than in The Heights.

They descend a long gradually spiraling metal staircase to a door with an elaborate set of locks. Reed uses several codes and two different kinds of keys to open the door. He steps aside for her to enter.

"It's called the Crow's Nest. Known only to Presiders."

Completely unprepared for this, Magrit Abram Shen stands frozen in the doorway, looking into the narrow slice of concrete room that is defined by a glaring wall of high daylight from outside. Mercifully, the window is tinted, muting the light to a dirty brown.

"Come. I want to see their display."

Reed steps around her and on into the room. Shen is too frightened to move so he grasps her elbow and pulls her on inside then locks the door. She clings to the wall. He crosses to a tall metal cabinet and opens the doors.

Among other things, the cabinet contains a control panel through which Reed can access any morsel of any function in Great

386

City. He activates the panel and pulls up Shen's function, Technology, main menu. He turns to say something, stops then squeezes out a grim smile. Shen is pressed against the back wall, fighting panic.

"Yes, it has that effect on one." He pours a glass of Numb and hands it to her then pours one for himself. "I still need this in here."

She drains it in one swallow and holds out the glass for more. He steadies her hand and pours. Again, she drains it in one swallow and is finally able to take a deep breath.

"Why did you bring me here if I'm not supposed to know about this place?"

"As a gesture of trust, Magrit. You're going to be the next Presider. Very soon. You know that. I know that. We all know that.

"Yes. I've got the votes."

"It would seem. Virginia told me earlier."

"We want a council meeting. Now." She refills her glass with Numb and takes a hefty swallow.

"By law, I'm Presider until the council meets again and the Presider schedules council meetings." He takes the bottle from her, tops off her glass and returns the bottle to the cabinet. "I'm not going to make this difficult, Magrit. I just want to clear a few last minute details. Between us. Presider to Presider. Then you shall have your council meeting."

"Go on." Arms crossed, Shen moves to the window side of the room, stands back a few feet and looks out, sipping Numb.

"Given that Great City is in a time of crisis, what's most desirable now, Magrit, is a smooth transfer of power. My preference is to go away from here quietly as soon as possible, to a humble location down on the lane where I can continue with my work for the good of Great City in a less conspicuous position."

Reed looks gray and tired. He's moving back to the cabinet for more Numb when a sudden belch of incoming data interrupts his reverie. Then Shen connects to her Primes.

"Report!"

"DRONES HAVE DISABLED TWO HUMAN SPECIMENS AND ARE STANDING GUARD. FIVE DRONES LOST IN THE MANEUVER."

"The retriever, the retriever!" Shen barks at control panel. "Get it there now!"

"Retriever is on approach-path and closing in."

Jubilant, she turns to the Presider. He's standing looking out.

His face is rage etched in stone.

"More drones gone," he whispers. "Great City has been attacked a second time. You attack my resources, you attack me." He looks at Shen. "Deploy the warheads."

She stares at him, stunned.

"I think perhaps it would be a good idea not to launch the warhead until the retriever with our coveted specimen is safely out of harm's way."

"No!" Tasting salvation, Paul Prescot reed moves to the window and stands looking out. "There are more where they came from. Launch the warhead now. Launch all you have pointed in that direction. Wipe it clean."

***

Through his terror, Wim understands that something has gone wrong outside. First he was told to open the portal. Then he was told to close it. Since then, nothing.

Already dressed for the surface, hurrying, he puts on his breather, finds the coil of climbing rope he and Schiara prepared, clips one end to a handle on a heavy bank of technology. Then, rope in hand, he opens the portal and runs out then stops, immediately disoriented, screaming.

"ELDER MOSS! SCHIARA!"

Then he's running straight ahead, uncoiling the rope behind him with one hand, other arm out in front, groping and unaware that elder Moss is akimbo halfway up the dune and knocked out by dart-juice, unaware that Shiara is in his path trying to get up, and also unaware that the drones guarding the two of them and the retriever coming to get one of them have been called back because Shen can't afford to waste resources.

Schiara sits up as Wim reaches her. He trips, goes flying. They scream at each other through the technology in their facemasks.

"WHO IS IT?!"

"ME SCHIARA! GO BACK INSIDE, I HAVE TO GET ELDER MOSS!"

Groggy and frightened the girl spins around looking for her mentor and sees the woman lying tumbled and inert halfway down the face of the dune.

"GO BACK TO THE PORTAL!" she screams at Wim. "I CAN'T TAKE CARE OF BOTH OF YOU!"

Awkwardly following the rope, the boy turns and tries and do as he was told. Schiara starts running toward elder Moss. Then she stops short, looking up, dumbstruck.

A big bright yellow machine of some kind is cresting the high dune ridge in front of her, lightly stirring the ash, gleaming and quiet but for a pleasant sustained musical tone. Staring up, Schiara sits down in the ash because her legs have given way as she has never seen or even imagined such a thing as this. Her mouth falls open as the machine lands gracefully and toboggans down the dune to stop just up-slope of elder Moss.

Matching the machine in color and gleam, the pilot dismounts and checks that elder Moss is alive then moves on down the slope toward the girl. Even with all the extra gear and straps and pouches and the backpack, the newcomer is clearly a woman. She holds up her hand, palm out.

"Peace."

Schiara automatically returns the gesture and reaches for the hand held out to help her up and they stand transfixed, looking at each other, astonished, recognizing each other as human. From the ancestors. Then the first responder steps back and salutes crisply.

"Corporal Sh'rai McCloud from S.S. Hope. I come in peace. Do you need help?" McCloud speaks slowly and carefully, signing with her hands at the same time.

Both youngsters hear McCloud clearly. The words sound familiar but the woman's accent is thick and strange. McCloud goes back up the dune, kneels and peers into elder Moss's facemask.

"What happened?"

Unable to absorb this strange new reality, Schiara nods stupidly and points with urgency at elder Moss then at the portal then at Wim who is standing frozen near the portal. McCloud nods.

"Okay. You get that one inside. I'll take this one."

Paying no attention to her sore shoulder and elbow, McCloud grabs elder Moss's hands and drags the heavier woman on her back down the dune-face into the portal, recording everything as she goes and impressed by what she sees inside before turning to the girl whose face is visible through the mask, whose eyes are dark and frightened, who doesn't know what to do and is more and more grateful for the

389

help.

"Come." McCloud gestures. "There's medicine in the sled."

The first responder and the girl run back out of the portal to the sled. McCloud opens one of the equipment bins and hauls out a white suitcase with a big red triangle on the sides. She hands it to Schiara and is pulling out a large backpack and slinging it on when the sled's alarm starts screaming. McCloud hops up onto the big machine, rushes to a complicated control panel between the handlebars and turns off the alarm to hear the message.

"Attention Falcons. This is a code red. Return to stealth-mode im-mediately then ascend and head south and east from wherever you are. Great City is preparing to launch nuclear warheads in your direction. Repeat, ascend and head south and east NOW. They are preparing to launch!

Working against time, McCloud punches buttons on her control panel, programming the sled for three passengers, guessing at their weights. The screen flashes red.

"OVER WEIGHT-LIMIT FOR EARTH-Gs! MAKE TWO TRIPS!"

But the sled can't tell her where to take them if there was sufficient time, which there may not be. All else forgotten, McCloud whirls around to Schiara and points at the portal then signs as she yells.

"Where does that go?!"

"Down!" the girl points.

"How far?!"

"Big far!"

"That's were we gotta go now, now, now, faster than you ever moved before! GO, GO, GO, GO, GO!"

***

On the surface directly above canton Equa, an impressive concrete and steel structure like a big freight elevator has risen up from below and cleared the ash. The structure's door slides aside with the sound of metal on metal to reveal a brightly lit space filled with troops, gear and equipment, all now pouring out into the dune valley to orient and deploy.

SubTurra's reconnaissance troops wear rusty brown protective suits. They are heavily armed and technologized. They are also momentarily paralyzed by the glare and exposure to vastness. Then the medicine takes over and they feel nothing again as they form up and head south and west in search of something that may or may not exist.

And in seeking, they are found.

Overhead, Great City's satellites picked up the sudden burst of sustained signals from the surface and are relaying the data down to the Technology Primes who have taken over for the exhausted Security Primes. In addition to sorting out these new signals, the Tech Primes are also tracking the five Space Staters who were trying to burn their way into the port of Great City then stopped and ascended to the southeast. They're also trying to locate the single unit that peeled off from the others to go north and east precisely to the spot of the last enemy sightings. That vehicle has landed and been stationary for several minutes, verifying Shen's hunch that the Space States are responsible for all the troubles on the surface. And to come full circle, the troops on their way south and west from Canton Equa have picked up signals coming from several thousand feet above the surface to the south. They adjusted their course, picked up speed while informing Central Control, and Headmon was called away from his announcement.

"We're picking up signals, sir. Faint. Originating from 100 miles southwest of here."

"She wasn't lying," Headmon whispers, leaning forward. "Alert forces guarding the mouth of Canton Equa then launch a cluster of warheads at the source of the signals. Cover the whole area. I'll be right back."

"Yes, sir."

"My love, you were right!" Headmon runs out of his control room. "Come! I want you to watch it disappear, this Great City!"

He turns the corner to go back into the loft and stops abruptly because no one's there. The loft is empty but for Katya and two footmen sprawled on the floor, slowly regaining consciousness. He spins around.

No muss, no fuss. The door is open. The lift is gone.

"GUARDS!"

Headmon runs all the way into the loft, into the big vault. His prize is gone. The capsule is empty.

"GUARDS! GUARDS!" When there's no response Headmon runs back to his control center. "WHERE ARE MY PRISONERS?!

391

WHERE ARE MY GUARDS?!!!"

He starts pounding buttons, changing images on screens, looking for those who are gone.

"They have to be somewhere in the residence."

Then he finds a long snake of people running through one of the kitchens and down into the cellars. He zooms in and brings them up on the big screen.

"GUARDS TO THE CELLARS! THE CELLARS! STOP THEM!"

"Sir, we're picking up very strong very fast invader signals originating from south and west of here. Recommend you go to safety now!"

"LAUNCH EVERYTHING!"

Headmon pulls a pistol from a drawer and bolts out of the surveillance center almost colliding with Katya who is groggy but on her feet, as are the guards behind her.

"COME!"

He takes her hand and yanks her with him along the corridor to the master bedroom where he opens the door connecting him to the apartment used by Reynolds.

"Hurry, hurry!"

With one guard on point and the other securing the rear, Headmon and Katya rush through and out of that apartment into the corridor to the service lift. Once in and descending, Headmon punches up Central Control on the wall panel to give instructions. There's no reply.

***

The Presider and his head of Technology are in the crow's nest being informed that their warhead is on target. Reed turns from the window to look at Shen. She's standing at the control panel directing her Primes.

So young. So lovely. So brilliant.

"Congratulations, Magrit. We are now free of enemies."

"I won't be satisfied until I know they're all gone, Paul." She turns to him and smiles sweetly, full of new power. "Meantime, I'll see that you have an inconspicuous position somewhere down on the lane, where you can live quietly away from power."

"I should be grateful," Reed murmurs.

He strides to the cabinet. Standing next to her, he reaches into a drawer and pulls out a small, old-fashioned pistol. Calmly, he turns to Shen who is once again attentive to her screens and her Primes.

"Magrit?"

She turns to look at him, sees the barrel of a revolver then feels it pressed between her eyes. He pulls the trigger.

The sound is thunder in the closed concrete and glass space. A little black hole appears in the center of Shen's perfect forehead. She looks surprised. The hole begins to leak and everything that holds her up drains away. Her knees buckle. Magrit Abram Shen sinks to the floor.

"You'll not be the last Presider of Great City," he whispers to the lifeless form on the floor at his feet. "If no other, then at least that distinction belongs to me."

Exiting the Crow's nest, Paul Prescot Reed locks the door and stops to think. What he just did was satisfying but only for the moment because now there's no going back. Hurrying, he sticks the firearm in his pants and wipes blood-spray off of his hand. Then he's trotting down metal stairs, circling around with the gradual inner curve of the structure. As he nears ground-level suddenly deafening alarms go off, ringing through the space between the dome skins.

Reed is moving faster now. Running down the steps. Then he's on a maintenance ladder, climbing straight down, taking the most direct way to safety from whatever additional danger is on the way because the first blast was impressive enough then another and another.

Three days later and in orbit close to earth, H-V cruiser Mohawk has exited stealth-mode and gleams light blue against the moon. At this particular moment, the ship's velocity-gatherer and delta wings are lowered out of the way and she has risen to nestle in the open delivery bay of H-V Hospital Ship Paracelsus, which is directly overhead and identifiable by large red triangles conspicuous on its white hull. Ruined earth occupies the bottom half of the visual field. Great City is miles below somewhere beneath the enormous cloud of ash that refuses to settle.

H.S. Paracelsus is shaped like a big transparent donut. Nu-glass passageways intersect at an island in the center. The assessment-station.

The hospital ship stopped at Mohawk first to pick up the bodies of the three ambassadors. It's also picking up six critically wounded patients from Great City. Commander Ingrid Steele, Big Wanda Mu and Cha-Hua are present in the full-atmosphere airlock for the exchange. They're wearing dress blues and standing at attention, paying respects to the ambassadors. Ethel Marin is piloting the ship. She took one look at the wounded from earth and begged Ingrid to let her take care of everyone else's duties so as not to have to see them again.

Four of the patients wear strange skintight suits that cover everything, even eyes. The other two are stewards. Barely alive, none of them woke or responded to stimuli. None are conscious now as, one at a time, the orderlies gently guide the six transparent and portable sterile environments into the open lift that carries them up into the hospital for assessment.

When the last patient is rising, Ingrid and crew shake hands with the orderlies and move back down the ladder into Mohawk, securing the hatch behind them. The airlock closes with a noisy clang and much hissing. Then the two ships uncouple.

H.S. Paracelsus heads off for another load of earth-patients from one of the other first responder teams – all having been called down to help when the detonations finally stopped. Mohawk's crew can now attend its primary duty of monitoring team Falcon. And each of them can deal with the shock of what has happened.

The ghost of Great City is barely visible through endless twilight caused by ash that has yet to settle. The northeast quadrant of the structure is gone as is the crown. Curled and twisted steel ribs stick out in all directions. Except for the extreme southwest section, the outer dome-skin is pocked with big holes, broken all the way through in many places.

The space between the dome skins is a shadowy tangle of dangling catwalks, fried technology and collapsing infrastructure. Weak afternoon light shines through holes, shafting the space with dim clouded beams. Inside, levels have collapsed, are still collapsing one onto the other. Everything is covered with thick layers of toxic ash and debris, shifted here and there by wind that is constant now, wailing eerie melodies on the broken instrument that is Great City.

When the blasts finally stopped, team Falcon called for help then sent out a fleet of shape-changers for assessment while Jika Rogers went to the last-point-of-contact and tried to get a rise out of McCloud.

Of necessity still in space-gear, once in The Heights Pilar and team followed the beacon-implants and found the ambassadors fairly quickly. Three of them. Dead. Private Ria Siloam. Tran McKenzy. Raf Kyrry. But no Dav Baxter.

Bates took the ambulance filled with wounded and bodies up to Mohawk and just got back. Rogers is still at McCloud's designated area looking for either a person or remains. The other three first responder teams are searching The Heights and combing the lane where it is stable enough, looking for anyone alive, finding charred and melted bodies, thousands of them, tens of thousands, a few survivors and no Dav Baxter dead or alive.

Windrider wings furled and out of the way, Lt. Pilar Mezon is with Kim and Salonnen down at the base of Great City. They walk into the structure through a blasted-open bay and work their way over rubble toward the interior dome-skin where they find a heavy door jarred off its hinges, open enough to squeeze through. Somewhere above them, the structure rumbles as another level collapses. Headlamps ignited, the three elite first responders move into what remains of the lane.

Pilar takes a perfectly normal ordinary step and the new knee pops, goes askew and she's on the ground on her side, writhing in pain.

"Bates!" Salonnen yells kneeling to try and help Pilar. "Bates, we got a down lieutenant. We need you now! There's also more bodies. We gotta regroup, contact Mohawk, figure out what to do!"

"Copy-clear, I'm on my way."

***

Karin Lassiter Kohl props Dav Baxter against a stone pillar and eases him down to the ground. She hears voices up ahead. That means food and water. Maybe other necessities.

"I'll be back," she whispers almost without sound directly into his ear.

Shivering, he nods.

Lassiter managed to take advantage of the chaos to drag Dav Baxter far into a vast wide space with a low ceiling that is supported by row after row of squat stone pillars. This was once the womb of Great City. She stands up, breathing hard from laboring to get them both this far with him almost comatose from claustrophobia.

The voices are coming from directly ahead, maybe a dozen pillars on. Yes. Squinting she can see the glow of light. Maybe they have food and medicine for Dav.

Shivering, he whimpers.

"Shhhhh," she whispers. "I'll be right back.

Making no sound, she advances pillar by pillar until she's only three away from a small group of people she recognizes from The Heights. Amazingly, Paul Prescott Reed seems still to be in charge. Virginia Kahn Baker. Whitaker. A few others from the council. They're seated in old office chairs around a lopsided desk. Candles light the space they've defined with other discarded junk from before Great City.

They must have food. Medicine. They must be developing a plan of survival.

Lassiter moves silently back to Dav. She sits beside him, cradles his head, rocking him while he shivers.

"This is the place," she whispers. "All you have to do is stay here and be very quiet."

He tries to nod. Unable to tolerate darkness or complete enclosure, devoured by terror of the walls closing in, Dav Baxter is barely aware of her presence, barely aware they've stopped so she can try to figure out how to keep them alive.

***

The gate to canton Equa is now a big squarish hole in the ground. Ash has been blown away, exposing the skeleton of the elevator shaft and its de-stroyed mechanisms all the way down, miles, twisted and melted from top to bottom along with anyone who happened to be in the vicinity.

Most of Equa's population is gone. Remaining enforcers were called away. Banding is, of course, unavailable throughout SubTurra, adding panic to the chaos. Water is scarce. Food is each other, raw. There's nothing to re-strain the unleashed frenzy of the trapped and desperate inhabitants of Canton Equa who are still somehow alive.

Remote from all that, way down and out near the hinterlands because those in charge always have an escape hatch, a light hanging from its cord flickers on and stays on, casting shadows in a dim space that resembles a long unused ancient subway station out near the end of the line. A tunnel runs from right to left along a raised concrete platform that smells of damp decay. The floor of the tunnel is laid with a single set of rusty rails. Puddles of toxic water are small lakes on the platform. The walls are rough-hewn stone.

This station has not been used for a long time. The only sounds are the buzzing of the light and dripping that forms the puddles. Then there are other sounds, approaching from the right.

Footsteps.

Boots. Troops trotting in synch then splashing through water then running. From the right a dozen enforcers in battle gear run crouching onto the tracks below the platform. Facing the platform they sweep the dim space with piercing red and white beams attached to assault rifles.

"FIRE!" one commands.

The enforcers spray the platform area with screaming electric blue bullets as though to kill even the germs.

397

"HALT!"

They stop firing. Smoke fills the space. Dust rains from the ceiling. While the atmosphere clears they continue to sweep the space with the beams on their weapons. Satisfied, the commander presses his throat-mike. "Okay." The enforcers move on and disappear trotting into the left arm of the tunnel.

Another dozen enforcers run into the station. They hop up onto the waist-high platform. Weapons at the ready they spread out and stand guard, facing away from the tracks.

Sounds that are indecipherable at first gradually become clear. Metal on metal. Sounds of a laboring, coal-burning engine that appears, pulling a line of old railcars and a long plume of smoke through the station almost in slow motion.

Armed enforcers occupy cars following the engine and coal bin. The next cars are filled with what was salvageable from the Ark. Then a long sleek customized car of spun aluminum appears, its opulent interior lit and clearly visible through the expanse of windows.

Headmon is standing in the middle of the car. He's wearing crisp fatigues and an impressive pistol. His forehead and chin are bandaged. He's holding a communication device to one ear and barking orders inaudible from here.

Katya is seated in a comfortable chaise against the far wall. She, too, is wearing fatigues and a sidearm. The hand that raises her glass of white wine is bandaged. Having served her, the interim butler returns to his position at the front of the car.

Headmon turns to look out a window at the platform and its surrounds. He moves quickly and yanks down the shade, yelling at the butler to get the rest of the shades. Then the spun metal car is out of the station and into the tunnel.

The next cars contain staff and specials, most of them wounded. Then several cars contain equipment and technology. The last two cars are filled with enforcers.

When the train is out of the station the enforcers on the platform hop down and trot, splashing after it. Then the parade is gone. Buzzing and popping, the light flickers a last time before it goes out. Then the only sound to be heard is of water dripping slowly in the dark.

***

398

After being dismissed by captain Porter, cadet Ero Mezon stole some overalls, went to the loading docks, did a little scouting about and slipped aboard the Yosemite, a troop carrier headed for earth's vicinity with reinforcements for the first responders already there. Thus, not only did he disobey an order from the commander of the fleet, he also committed several felonies and if caught could be a long time in the brig, squelching any plans he might have had for a career as a first responder.

That thought never crossed young Ero's mind as he stole identity chips, clothes and gear from people he knew were on leave. He didn't think about it when he slipped aboard the Yosemite without authorization and disappeared in the energized and distracted crowd. Hat low over his eyes, he passed himself off as a swabby cleaning floors and heads, getting to know the ins and outs of the ship.

Strictly utilitarian, the Yosemite is a long tube with the con-trol suite in the nose, loading bays in the stern and the velocity-gatherer trailing behind. Twenty-one first responders currently occupy the area in the middle, the part of the ship that is crowded with portholes after the Space State fashion.

Since leaving Command Ship Phoenix, Ero has been lucky and he has been skillful. Staying as inconspicuous as possible he has slept in the ventilation system. Each foray for bathroom use and food he's stolen a different identity chip but hasn't had to use it because of the off-hour and nobody paid him any attention. To avoid using identity chips, food and drink have come from recycling bins he emptied pretending to be a swabby. So far everything has gone in his favor.

Then he sees four MPs working their way through the ship from fore to aft, checking IDs of anyone remotely matching the holo they carry of Cadet First Class Ero Mezon who missed their arrival in his furtiveness. The boy turns the other way, sees four more MPs approaching from the other direction.

Cadet Ero Mezon strolls casually to the nearest head and finds it empty. He enters the head and closes the door but does not lock it. Moving quickly, Ero climbs onto the toilet, removes the cover from the air duct and pulls himself up into a crawlspace that is big enough for him on his hands and knees. He carefully replaces the cover then slithers quietly into the maze of ducts and chutes that make human life possible out here.

***

The Refuge is crumbled and crumbling but not destroyed. Having done all she can to restore the main chamber of the cave complex to its former order, Solaris the keeper returns to her nest, curls up, enters a state of hibernation and begins to generate her replacement while elsewhere, beneath the surface of the earth is darkness of such density that deep space is paled by it. Like blood, this darkness fills the veins and hollows of the stone. It is the element in which the forces play.

As elder Martin said, a way out of the residence into the hinterlands was dug long ago by hand, one person at a time through decades and centuries. It was really very simple, as most important things are. When Headmon left the room, Isham One-Who-Waits turned to all and spoke.

"If you want to live, come with me."

Only Katya and two of the footmen chose to remain. They were dealt with gently.

Isham's group grew as they rushed quietly down, down to the root cellar and the tunnel, picking up a few others on the way. When the first blast hit directly over Canton Equa they were already in the tunnel on the way to meet up with elder Martin and his group. They felt tremors, heard distant thunder. Loose rock was jostled. They went on, moving south through a big canyon with no name that meanders for miles. Shaped like a deep, jagged V, the canyon's usual inhabitants are insects, crustaceans and mold. Sounds are crisp here, hollow and immediate in the dark.

Drip.

A crab skitters across wet stone then stops.

Silence.

The sound is almost imperceptible at first. Creatures heading this way. Sounds of gear. Footsteps. Labored breathing. And finally a hint of yellow glow.

Crab freezes looking up as shadowy figures emerge and pass by, not far away – a ragged line of people advancing with a sense of urgency even though they're weary from hard travel without rest except to eat, sleep and tend those needing it. Some wear headlamps and for a few moments, there is light.

Those who are able carry their own packs plus supplies and packs for the wounded and the two out on watch who need mobility – Esa scouting in front, Schiara bringing up the rear.

Isham One-Who-Waits leads the train across uneven canyon floor. He's carrying two packs and looks stricken. He's followed by Rogue who is also carrying two packs, staying near the old man to watch and learn. Then several footmen move by carrying lots of packs and bags.

Next Jabaz and Axl haul are hauling R'io on a stretcher provided by one of the footmen. Bundled up, he's being kept unconscious until they can stop and tend him properly. Skye follows immediately, helping elder Martin who is suffering from shock.

Two footmen carry elder Moss on a stretcher. Her leg has been splinted and Curanda has gotten most of the pain under control. Another big footman carries an unconscious Wim on his back. Curanda follows with Sh'rai McCloud, helping the elite first res-ponder normalize in stone, giving her powerful herbs and staying mind-to-mind with her when they stop because that's when the claustrophobia is really bad. Schiara is way behind, sweeping the trail.

Then they're gone. Darkness prevails. And quiet. The crab scurries away.

Drip…

    Drip…

        Drip…

Readers of the Four Realms:

You have come to the end of the first portion of translated material. The scribes continue their work of deciphering the contents of the cylinder and hope to release the next section soon but make no promises.

I remain,
Eo, Master Scribe of the Four Realms

Acknowledgments

No creative work comes out of a vacuum and that is particularly true in this case. I was born to a family of Bible readers and took up the habit for fascination with the stories. Later it was my privilege to toddle around the ankles of the great playwrights, especially Sophocles and Shakespeare. Long and luscious were afternoons curled up with Ray Bradbury, Frank Herbert, John Fowles, and Carlos Castaneda. Then there's Plato and the cave. This piece is particularly indebted, however, to the writings of the depth psycho-logists and Bruce Chatwin's book, *The Songlines* contains the Exodus quote that seeded the soil.

Thanks beyond measure to the writer Richard Geldard, who prepared this book for publication and shepherded it forward. First readers are an indispensable part of the writing process and I am profoundly grateful to Katrina Eastlake, Maureen Mercury, Christina Preciado, Eileen Rabach, and Gregory Rainoff for their responses. Thanks to Katrina Eastlake for the cover design and to Christina Preciado and the kind folks at Lightening Source for invaluable production help. Thanks to Albert Dytch who caught *From the Legend of Biel* flying over the transom last century and to those who received that book so warmly, especially Stephen Kettlewell. Thanks to Lucia Valys for the place I call home. Finally, a big bowwow of gratitude to Bairn, furry four-legged trail-companion and best dog ever born.

Mary Staton lives and works in Los Angeles.